Praise for

THE

CROW
GARDEN

'Excellent . . . [Littlewood] creates a chilling atmosphere
of skulls, séances, secrets and hysteria'
The Times

'[An] enjoyable excursion . . . gripping'
The Sunday Times

'A great seasonal treat'
SciFiNow

'A sublime blend of the psychological and the supernatural'
Starburst

'Alison Littlewood is one of the brightest stars in the horror
genre at the moment'
This Is Horror

'Hypnotic and intelligent with buckets of atmosphere'
SFX

'An excellent, chilling, autumn read, all about the dangers of
power, obsession, and guilt'
Blue Book Balloon

'A real page-turner'
A Dream of Books

'A book which I know I will want to re-read
time and time again'
The Bookish Bundle

Also by Alison Littlewood

A Cold Season
Path of Needles
The Unquiet House
A Cold Silence
The Hidden People

THE
CROW
GARDEN

ALISON
LITTLEWOOD

Jo Fletcher

BOOKS

First published in Great Britain in 2017
This edition published in 2018 by

Jo Fletcher Books
an imprint of Quercus Editions Ltd
Carmelite House
50 Victoria Embankment
London EC4Y 0DZ

An Hachette UK company

A CIP catalogue record for this book is available
from the British Library

PB ISBN 978-1-84866-988-8
EBOOK ISBN 978-1-84866-989-5

This book is a work of fiction. Names, characters,
businesses, organisations, places and events are
either the product of the author's imagination
or are used fictitiously. Any resemblance to
actual persons, living or dead, events or
locales is entirely coincidental.

10 9 8 7 6 5 4 3 2 1

Typeset by CC Book Production

Printed and bound in Great Britain by Clays Ltd, Elcograf S.p.A.

For Fergus
Twenty-five times over . . .

PART ONE

1856
Crakethorne

There is only one illness and only one cure.

Franz Anton Mesmer

Chapter One

Among lonely homesteads and mile upon mile of damp heath, all closed in by a desolate sky, it was easy to forget that Yorkshire had much to offer the mad. It was a strange time to begin a new life, this death of the summer – though not so strange, perhaps, as the way I had chosen to do it. The road had been long in reality as well as inwardly. Much of it was marked by noise and smoke and machine, the train rattling past all the chimneys and pattern-book houses of London and into the midst of scalped fields and drab hamlets which resembled each other so exactly I could not have pointed to them on a map. As I grew nearer my destination, however, the landscape took on a wilder, hillier aspect, speaking rather of tumultuous struggle than the sanctuary I expected to find.

But outward appearances often betray our expectations of what lies within, and my hopes lifted at the thought of what was before me. I was bound for Crakethorne Manor, an asylum for those troubled in mind, and I was to become its under-physician, the first step upon a longer road still: that of becoming an alienist or, in less enlightened language, a mad-doctor.

I found no pony and trap at the small and ill-equipped station, but after enquiring at a nearby house, one was sent for. After a rather impatient wait – for who could be content with any delay when their destination was within reach? – the trap arrived, and at its reins a rather surly fellow smelling faintly of drink, who uttered plosive expressions in tones that were scarcely to be deciphered. The pony did not lift its head and the trap was unsprung and creaked interminably, but we made tolerable progress, the silence all about us masked by the rumble of wheels on unpaved roads. I had seldom seen such empty lanes and quiet houses. It was well that the fellow knew the way, for it wound onward without a sign to welcome visitors or warn the unwary.

I shivered within my greatcoat, for the season – if nothing else, my mind added uncharitably – was more advanced this far to the north. Filthy rags of cloud gathered about the lower edges of the sky as the day faded towards evening, and I saw nothing but drystone walls and grey-looking sheep and crows, which sent up their rancorous calls from the fields.

'Means crow.' The driver did not turn in his seat. He had made little effort in the way of conversation thus far, barely responding to my questions, but he switched the pony's back with his whip as if to underline his remarkable statement.

'I beg your pardon?'

'Crake,' he said in hoarse tones, and for a moment I thought him imitating the birds' cries. I wondered if he was as mad as the people I was going to live among, and then I realised.

'Crakethorne Manor,' I echoed. So that was what the name meant: crow thorn. It was rather dismal, and as if to sink everything further, I began to see more and more of them, rising into the air before settling again, like charred scraps thrown upward by a fire.

The driver gestured towards a forlorn-looking hill and I surmised we were nearing my destination. I could as yet see nothing. This was not in itself surprising, and I decided to take it as promising. A good sweep of drive could not only help shield the eyes of passers-by from the unfortunates within, but save the afflicted from bold and unfeeling stares; and it was *not* forlorn. I had hopes that, tucked away in this unprepossessing corner of the land, was a beacon of beneficent progress.

'Plenty goes in,' the driver said. 'Not so many comes out.' He waved his arm, his movements as dour as his demeanour, and indicated a stone gate, one of its pillars leaning perilously inward. He steered the pony wide to more easily pass between them. We turned about an ancient oak tree that spread its limbs as if to prevent us, and the asylum came into view.

Grey stone was unleavened by lightness or decoration. It was a large, stolid creation, built for permanence rather than enjoyment. I stepped down to see it more clearly through the large rusty gate that barred our progress.

The aspect was no less forbidding than anything I had thus far seen. The whole edifice looked damp and cold. A severely slanting roof of stained slate appeared designed to withstand gales or snow. The many windows reflected back the sky rather than admitting views of what lay within, presenting a blank appearance rather than otherwise. Iron bars were positioned over them – the manor could never have been intended for an asylum, since the panes were too large to prevent anyone climbing through – which must have been dispiriting to those both within and without. The impression was not brightened by flowers or neat walks; only a few morose shrubs clung to their beds about the periphery.

But such was only my first view. I had not yet seen all. No doubt its true nature could only be truly appreciated upon closer acquaintance. From where I stood, however, its surrounds were as disheartening as the manor itself. The structure was set into a hill of rough heath, dotted with hawthorns all grown aslant in the prevailing wind. Lower down, stands of damp trees failed to quite conceal the mouldering fence that divided the inhabitants from the outer world. I thought fleetingly of some of the fine modern examples of asylum design. Here, no dramatic elevation provided a soothing view; it did not appear to be amenable to division for male and female occupation; its grounds were not extensive enough to provide varied and calming perambulations for its occupants.

But that did not mean that wonders could not be wrought within. I should not focus on externals, but the realm of the mind; and I was here, and this was to be my home. My future was laid before me, and I could have no conception of what that might hold.

I told myself that at least the grey stone was not darkened with coal smuts from the innumerable fires of London; that its large chimney stacks spoke of comfortable warmth, and whilst its grounds were not extensive, at least it was thoroughly encircled by verdure. Pictured in sunlight, on a better day and at a better hour than this, the manor might even be considered a rather grand abode.

As if to emphasise the thought of home, a distant drift of sound reached my ears: a pianoforte was being played, albeit discordantly. I was just wondering if my mother was at that moment similarly playing, when a loud voice cut into my reverie with, ''elp you?'

I turned to see a rough-looking fellow standing by the gate, a large bunch of keys jutting from his fist. Behind him, almost masked by a clump of trees and cast into shadow, was a small lodge. Here was the porter, then, though a slovenly one. The neck protruding from his yellowed kerchief was ill-shaven, the lines creasing his visage too prominent, as if ingrained with dirt. His mud-coloured eyes, sunk deep into their sockets, glared.

I reminded myself that I would be his superior and forced myself to meet his savage look, though in a moment I was distracted by something nudging the pocket of my greatcoat.

I looked down to see a large brown dog peering back at me, its rheumy eyes doleful. It did not wag its tail or show any other sign of being aware of my presence; now it was at my side, it seemed content to simply stand there.

"elp you?' the porter said again, without a 'sir' or any other form of common politeness. I told him that I was Doctor Nathaniel Kerner and here to see Doctor Chettle and he glared more intensely before nodding and selecting a key from his ring. Laboriously and wordlessly, he unlocked the gate, and I was about to regain my place in the trap when I recalled that in the coming days, I might have need for regular dealings with the fellow.

'What's its name?' I asked, bending to pat the beast's head, thinking this the best way to ingratiate myself with its master. I had to resist the urge to wipe my oily fingers on my pocket kerchief. The thing smelled musky too and I stepped away, but it appeared that the creature was not indifferent to a little kindness and insisted on following, once more besmirching my coat with its nose.

'Brown,' said the porter, in a tone that said it was obvious; and perhaps it was.

'Brown,' I repeated, unable to keep the dismay from my tone, and left them to whatever it was that occupied them in the absence of visitors.

My driver flicked his whip, stirring the pony into motion. As we passed through the iron gates, it began, fitfully, to rain.

Chapter Two

The north, despite its bluff inhabitants, austere weather and desolate landscapes, has indeed rather favoured the mad. The Quakers' Retreat at York is one of the finest institutions of our age, having provided a model of treatment for more than fifty years. With its scheme of moral management, they treat lunatics as rational creatures, housing them as if in a domestic environment and bestowing kindness and dignity upon them. It was a pity that London's benighted Bedlam had not followed their example. Indeed, I told myself I should not miss the city at all; if I did so, it would surely be only because my calling had taken me so far from my mother's side. My father had died some years before and so I had left her quite alone.

The advertisements for Crakethorne Asylum were promising. They told of good accommodation, curative water gardens and healing springs, clean air and roses – probably the reason for the 'thorne' in its name. Its principal, Doctor Algernon Chettle, had his degree from Scotland, which must mean Edinburgh, an esteemed and practical institution, rather than one of the less reputable places. The situation, close to the border between the North and West Ridings, would have all the advantages that a healthful situation and fresh clean air could provide.

I had often pondered the methods of the York Retreat, although until I arrived at Crakethorne I had never wondered what the place looked like. Might it be anything like this? The very same rain may be falling on it at this very moment. By the time we rattled and creaked our way to the entrance, the sky was fully dark with the downpour and I heard nothing but raindrops pummelling every leaf and stone and pane of glass. I could barely make out the sound of the knocker against the door and so was relieved at the responding clang of substantial locks within.

At last the door opened upon a female in a dark blue dress and an apron with feathered straps. I stepped inside, my bags were deposited within and I paid the driver, who retreated into the rain as if with relief. The door closed upon the sight of him with an effect as if my ears had been stuffed full of cotton.

The hall was empty of furnishings, although the floor was enlivened with encaustic tiles of cream, brown and black, their geometric arrangement a trifle marred by footprints. No mahogany sideboard gleamed; no grandfather clock warmly ticked away the hours. There were three doorways. Those to my left and right were barred not by doors but iron gates, each secured with a large padlock; the other lay ahead of me, opposite a stairway. I could smell wet hair, boiled dinners and, faintly, chloride of lime.

The girl informed me, in an uncouth accent, that she would show me 'up t' stairs'.

I left my luggage where it stood and followed her to the first floor, from thence to the second, and, interminably, the third. Here must be the staff quarters, I surmised, for no locks were set upon the doors. She approached one and knocked, and without waiting for an answer or saying a word, left me standing in the passage.

I had spent much time considering what sort of person my new proprietor, guide and mentor would be: I had built him highly in my estimation and so was surprised, when the door opened, to find him shorter than I. It was difficult at first to make out his features, for they were much obscured by a prodigious beard, ample whiskers about his jaw and a moustache that was a triumph of preening and wax. His white cravat was rather loose about his neck. His eyes, though, were bright – bright and sharp.

'Welcome, sir!' was his hearty greeting, ringing out loudly in the empty space, and he ushered me into the room. It turned out to be a study with another doorway set into the back of it. A small desk, devoid of papers, fronted a wall lined with pigeon-holes, similarly empty. A tall bookcase held some familiar-looking journals and books; I glimpsed *Human Physiology* by Elliotson, *The Physiognomy of Mental Diseases* by Sir Alexander Morison and, promisingly, Pargeter's *Observations on Maniacal Disorders*. That and a faint whiff of formaldehyde suggested a more practical and active aspect to his work and I admired the means by which it had all been rendered so neat.

Doctor Chettle vigorously shook my hand. 'I am delighted you could come, good fellow,' he said, moving around the desk. 'Delighted! I am in much need of assistance. My pursuits, my studies – all have suffered. The demands of the mad are a trial, sir – a trial and a tribulation. But you appear to be a good man, with a good eye . . .'

He peered at me as if he could make out the contents of my skull, until I shifted my feet. He grinned broadly enough to reveal white and slightly crooked teeth. 'I can always tell, you know. All in good time! But I have the perfect patients on which to begin. Allow me to introduce you.'

I made towards the door, but he vanished behind his desk and reappeared bearing a pile of case notes.

'Adam Sykes,' he said, touching the uppermost. 'A pretty fair imbecile. Defective from birth. Food and lodging more imperative

than reports, since he is incurable, obviously. Walter Eastcott –
epileptic. Hopeless, hopeless. His family likes to lodge him as
far from home as is practicable. Jacob Thew – ah, the farmhand!
A good worker, prognosis grave . . . Samuel Brewer – well,
you'll meet him. Hmm, Della Martin. Prognosis: doubtful. Nellie
Briggs is a maid, but we get a fee from her parish. You will find
domestics a class very prone to madness; little to be done there,
little to be done . . . You will take their charge. Lovely examples
of lunacy all.' As if he had finished, he pulled from his pocket a
large set of keys, which he added to the pile and pushed it across
the desk towards me.

I knew not how to reply. I had expected some explanation of
the terms of my employment and the demands of my duties. But
perhaps I was expected to know? I felt suddenly rather green. I
was straight out of Oxford and this was my first position.

'Do not worry,' he said, as if reading my thoughts, 'I shall be
here to answer any questions that arise. There are thirty-nine
inmates in all. Nothing too perturbing, no danger to health or
life – yours, I mean! You need to set a guard upon your soul,
of course.'

I did not think I had betrayed my reaction, but he smiled and
waved a hand as if to ward away any care. 'Just think of it,' he
said. 'All physicians face the risk of succumbing to the diseases
they battle. Cholera, diphtheria, consumption – all the bodily
terrors. Few suspect the dangers faced by specialists in the cerebral
sciences. But there are inherent menaces in spending your days
surrounded by brain-sickness, and the censure of Society is all
the greater for those susceptible to its curse. If I would say one
thing at the outset, it is guard your mind – or you may discover
one day it is entirely lost, and you may not find it again!'

Once again he laughed, then fell to staring blankly at the
surface of his desk.

'Have I a room, sir?'

'A room?' He seemed perplexed by the notion. 'Ah – of course! I dare say Matron will have set something aside for you. Ask her, would you, dear fellow? And – wait!' He stooped again, emerging with another casebook and a few sheets of closely written paper. 'I was not certain of giving you this one. But you look a capable sort – you may as well take it. Peruse it with care. A challenge, no less.'

It was thus that I found myself the presiding physician over Mrs Victoria Adelina Harleston. I did not hesitate to peruse her documents; indeed, I balanced them upon the rest as I stood in the hall with not an idea as to where I should go next.

Notice of Patient Transfer

31ˢᵗ August 1856

Mrs Victoria Adelina Harleston

Admitted: *8ᵗʰ August 1856*
  Transferred from Hope Spa and Asylum, Royal Tunbridge Wells, by consent of the Commissioners in Lunacy.

Enclosed: *a copy of the Order and Medical Certificates upon which Mrs Harleston was admitted into Hope.*

Physician's Certificate

Date: *7ᵗʰ August 1856*

Name: *Mrs Victoria (Vita) Adelina Harleston*

Sex and age: *Female. 22.*

Condition of life and occupation: *Married.*

Religious persuasion: *Church of England. No excess of zeal, religious mania &c.*

Place of abode: *Milford Lodge, near St Albans, Hertfordshire.*

Relatives similarly affected: *A gentleman only distantly related was known to suffer from dementia. No other insanity in the family line has been discovered.*

Duration of current attack and supposed cause (if known): *Patient presented with hysteria, characterised by breathlessness and distress, accompanied by mental derangement. Prone to headaches and a preference for solitude. Has expressed a marked disinclination to live in accordance with her duties as a wife. A natural interest in household affairs is entirely lacking.*

Mrs Harleston was discovered on the 5th day of August, wandering and, in her husband's words, 'in leave of her senses'. She had been visiting a shopping arcade when she left his side, apparently in some confusion. Seemingly forgetting her position in life she boarded an omnibus bound for Shoreditch. Upon questioning, she could not tell of her purpose in doing so.

The 'bus was forced to set her down, after something of a struggle. Mrs Harleston had concealed herself within a secluded compartment and worked herself into a fit. The other passengers were alerted to her condition by a series of piercing shrieks, which startled them to the extent that they called the omnibus to a halt. Upon opening the compartment, the conductor was subjected to wild blows from its occupant. When she calmed sufficiently to speak, Mrs Harleston insisted she had not been alone in the compartment, despite it being of a style designed for a single modest lady to travel out of the sight of other passengers. On no account would it have admitted a second.

It was allowed that, although her malady was of sudden onset, she had in preceding months shown a tendency towards unmanageable fits of crying and temper, without sufficient reason. I witnessed the former myself upon interviewing the lady. Her husband testified to the latter.

There is no known supposed cause for her insanity.

Previous attacks, if any, and age of the patient (if known): *Mrs Harleston admitted that, as* *a girl, she was prone to absent states, which she called 'trances'. She was at the difficult stage of life, at the age of 13 or 14. Furthermore, she was subject to vivid dreams, and confessed to hearing voices in the head: a certain sign of lunacy. It is a pity that no further treatment was then sought, since her current difficulty might have been alleviated.*

Behaviours and aggravations: *The patient does not have intemperate habits. She is not dangerous to others and is not subject to epilepsy. She was briefly subject to angry outbursts in the years before leaving her father's home to be married, and for a time was given laudanum for its sedative properties.*

Parish or union to which the lunatic is chargeable: *Not applicable. Bills to be referred to her husband.*

Facts observed by: *Dr A. E. Mountney.*

Appended note: *Mr Harleston is most assiduous about the lady's treatment, being particularly anxious that she be restored to him in a state of perfect health, and relieved of her strange notions, as rapidly as may be managed. He is more than usually insistent about her restoration and remains keen to be appraised of every form of treatment offered, lending a greater sense of urgency and complexity to this interesting case.*

Chapter Three

What a dull case! Having been led to expect a curiosity, I could not help feeling a pang of disappointment to find it was no more than hysteria. Still, I perused the certificate at length, along with the lunacy order signed by the husband and the requisite second certificate, which was plainer, but offered no more information than the first. The second certificate was probably more correct – I suspected the first of much hearsay, for all the necessity for direct observation had been specifically ruled upon by the Lunacy Amendment Act of a few years ago. But the observing physicians must be of the first respectability, and could by law have no connection to either asylum, so could have had no interest in seeing Mrs Harleston incarcerated, unless it were entirely necessary.

Hysteria is often thought of as the domain of indolent and cosseted ladies spoiled by lack of air and useful occupation, who derive the fullest value from all the attention their strained nerves may provide. My tutor sometimes said the condition was most suited to those with no particular inclination to be cured. But I reminded myself that although illness could provide its own diversions, it was no small thing to be incarcerated; the stain of it must follow her always.

But such thoughts were unworthy. I had come here with a

desire to do my utmost to ease the suffering of those afflicted with madness in all and any of its protean forms – and I knew what it was to lose someone to the clutches of despair; I knew what it was to be robbed of a voice. And the mad had all too often been abandoned to such – to empty rooms furnished only with straw, chained to the walls, their every utterance made the subject of mockery and laughter. I must never allow myself to judge; not before I had listened, touched – treated the *person* before me rather than any preconceptions formed against them. I steeled myself anew to meet the Powers of Unreason with all the capabilities and inventiveness at my disposal and all that effort could attain.

Such a determination did not assist me at the present moment, however. I had been entrusted with the keys to the asylum, but I had been left to wander its corridors alone, not knowing whither or whence I should go.

Upon returning to the entrance, I was fortunate to meet with the same servant as before, who offered to show me to my rooms and brought a lamp, since it was growing steadily darker. It transpired that my new abode was only a few doors from Doctor Chettle's study and consisted of a bedchamber with an adjacent sitting room, the furniture plain and chipped but tolerably clean. I brought up my bags myself and it was only when I had recovered from my exertion that I felt how cold it was.

I went to the window, which overlooked the sloping ground in front of the manor. The wind had risen. I dimly made out the massy crowns of trees shifting below and I could hear the gale too, buffeting and bullying its way around the hillside.

I passed a rather disturbed night listening to its moans, watching the curtains stirring about my bed in some draught and devoutly wishing for a fire in the grate.

Chapter Four

The morrow came at last, a bright if watery-looking day, and I went down to the entrance hall to begin my new life in earnest. It remained empty and silent, however, and I looked around it with nothing especially to seize the eye, until I became sensible that I was not alone after all. Between the iron gates that divided the realm of the mad from the sane and rational world, a small face peered.

I could not help but stare. It was a small boy of no more than nine or ten, with rather pale features and brutally cropped hair. I had not at first noticed him because he was low to the floor, crouching on hands and knees, his face resting against the cold bars.

'Good morning,' I said.

His nose twitched as if sniffing, and his haunches wobbled in an odd side-to-side movement. Then he opened his lips and let out such a mournful whine as never came from a human throat.

'Peter Ambrose,' came a voice behind me and I whirled to see a straight-backed, straight-faced woman, perhaps in her fifth decade, in a snowy matron's cap and apron. 'Thinks he's a dog.'

'He thinks – ah, and him only a child!'

'He's nine. Old enough to shame his family and that's what matters.' She opened her mouth little as she spoke, as if she begrudged letting even her words go free. She had not smiled; her face did not seem formed for it. Her eyes were hard, with a cast of knowing intelligence.

'He came here all alone at seven,' she went on. 'None 'ud play with him. He can't speak. Never has said a word, that's why he's here. But he liked watching the porter's old dog from the windows – he took to it like nothing else.'

'So he thinks he is become a dog.' The thought struck me at once that here might be one of the evils of having such a creature about the premises. Perhaps I should speak to Doctor Chettle about it. I did not suppose the surly porter would appreciate such interference, but it was the patients I must think of.

'Aye, that, or he *wants* to be a dog.' Matron nodded, as if to indicate her uncertainty as to whether the child wasn't right in his wishes after all.

There was much I wanted to ask, but courtesy intervened and instead I introduced myself and shook her hand and said I was happy to make her acquaintance. She gave out that she was Mrs Langhurst, but that I could call her Matron, along with everybody else.

Then she said, 'You'll need to know your way about, then. I don't suppose he's showed you.' She rolled her eyes upwards, in the direction of Doctor Chettle's study, and I confirmed her surmise.

I nodded towards the boy – or rather, the space where he had been, for he had vanished as noiselessly as he had appeared. 'That, I suppose, is the male patients' section.'

She shook her head. 'It's the women's.'

'But the boy—'

'Is just a boy, and there's none in the men's who'll take notice of him,' she said. 'So we take him in ours, where he might find a little womanly comfort.'

Her expression warmed as she spoke and as she took her keys from her belt and led me onwards, I reflected that she was perhaps possessed of more kindness than had been apparent at first perusal. She did not return my smile, however. Perhaps I was becoming familiar with the place already, for I found I had not expected her to.

Matron showed me the first-floor treatment room and receiving room and an administrative office piled with ledgers and records; also the dispensary, where a surgeon-apothecary, Mr Percival, came twice a week to oversee the giving of medicines.

'Do many of the patients take physic?' I asked.

She answered stiffly that this was not a hospital and I nodded with satisfaction. I did not subscribe to the idea of quieting inmates with extravagant doses of opium until they barely knew where, let alone who they were.

From a window, she pointed out the 'airing grounds'. I saw only more rough grass, no smooth gravel walks or blooming flowerbeds. I looked for the roses spoken of in the advertisement but the place was barren. Stepping closer to the casement, I saw all the way down to a little flash of water. Almost concealed behind the band of trees was an arrangement of stones. Crows cawed faintly through the glass.

'They don't go out alone, of course,' she said. 'They're supervised.' I thought of the unsteady fence I had seen edging the grounds and wondered if that was from supportiveness or necessity. I was about to ask, but Matron called me to another window and pointed out several small cottages and outbuildings which had previously been hidden by the manor. One was a workshop, she said, to provide the patients with gainful purpose, but she added that it was 'not used now'.

Finally, we proceeded to the wards, to see where the patients slept and ate and spent their days. There were, she explained, a few private rooms for first-class patients, though most slept in dormitories with attendants on hand to monitor how they did and ensure no harm came to them.

I was pleased to find the day-rooms commodious, with views from their tall barred windows revealing the sloping lawn at the front of the property, from whence I glimpsed again that flash of water. Generous fireplaces were enclosed by iron cages, albeit without a trace of them lately being lit. The men's area had a smoking room and the ladies' a pianoforte, although I noted the sheet music was upside down, which was perhaps the cause of the cacophony I had heard yesterday. Framed engravings, journals, chess sets, potted ferns, embroidery frames and paints and brushes completed the impression of a domestic drawing room, but I could not help but feel beneath it all a pervading sense of melancholy – even of profound loneliness.

The patients, of course, were the most interesting discovery. Adam Sykes I found drooling in a corner and staring at nothing; he made no reply to my 'good day'. From him we went to Walter Eastcott, who did not appear hopeless but greeted me in a tremulous fashion. And then we turned to Jacob Thew, whose sturdy build confirmed him as the farm worker of whom Doctor Chettle had spoken. Everything about him was on a grand scale – his hands, his shoulders, his height; even his square chin and the cast of his skull – but his strength was not echoed in his expression. His eyes were pale and watery and he sent constant nervous looks towards the windows, flinching as I watched.

'It's the crows,' Matron said.

I turned to her in surprise, thinking of my driver's odd statement of the day before, but she merely nodded. 'Listen,' she said. I did, and realised I heard them still. Their throaty and dreadfully forlorn cries were all around us.

Jacob heard them too; he let out a whimper and covered his head with his hands.

'He thinks they're come to call him to his final rest,' Matron said.

'He is superstitious, then? He thinks them omens of ill luck – harbingers of death?'

She nodded, as if to say, 'I said so' but the man suddenly reached out and caught my hand. 'My soul,' Jacob said, grasping my fingers painfully in his meatier appendage. 'They's coming for it, sir! Please don't let 'em in.' Then he brightened, and it was like dawn shining in his face. ''appen you know t' words, sir – the ones to keep 'em off?'

There was something disconcerting about such pleading tones being spoken in so gruff a fashion.

'Enough, Jacob.' Matron pulled his damp hand from mine. She addressed me. 'There's an old Yorkshire rhyme to ward off the crows, but he can't remember it.' Then she returned to the farm worker and told him authoritatively, 'You are quite safe, Jacob. Doctor Kerner will take good care of you, as we all shall.'

However, the man would not be comforted. He retreated to a wing-back seat where he shrank, rolling his eyes at the relentless cawing.

'They catch such things from each other,' she said, 'and him worse than any of them. Some say the crows are restless spirits, unhappy with how their bones are buried. Some have it that they carry souls to the next world. Others say, "A crow on the thatch, death soon lifts the latch." They tell such lunatic tales.'

I reflected how unfortunate it was for him to be placed here in such a situation, where he could hear the birds calling night and day, and see their black shadows cast over the earth. It was a painful delusion and I resolved to try and relieve his terrors, but there was no more to be done at that moment, for it was time to see the women's ward.

Despite the prevailing view that the tender sex was more prone to sickness of the mind – something I rather doubted – their day-room was more sparsely occupied than the men's. A rather thin but sweet lady named Lillian Smith grasped my hand as Jacob had, but she squeezed it as if welcoming me into her home, as she might well have believed she was. Della Martin was there too, twisting and twitching in her chair, watched over by a square-faced attendant introduced as Miss Olive Scholes.

'She's wayward,' Scholes said, gripping the woman's shoulder and pulling her hard against the backrest, as if to demonstrate how she should be treated. I opened my mouth to remonstrate, but she relaxed her grip at Matron's look.

'Della does have rather an unfortunate temper,' Matron explained. 'She tears her clothes – and her skin too, sometimes. We are non-restrainers for the most part, but sometimes she needs the gloves.' Della's arms, where her sleeves were turned back, were indeed riven with scars.

A sharp bark drew our attention to the unfortunate child, Peter Ambrose, who crouched on all fours, waggling his behind. I was about to address him when Miss Scholes hurried over, saying, 'Sit, Peter. Sit! Good boy!' And she looked at Matron with a sly expression, as if to say, 'Look! I *am* helping.'

'Good day, Peter. Isn't it a nice morning?' I said, and he tilted his head towards me. 'You see,' I said gently, 'it may be helpful to speak to him like the child he is, rather than encouraging him in his delusion.'

The hard-faced girl gave me a wicked glare, while Matron drew herself taller. I wondered if I had said too much, but Peter was unconcerned. He stretched luxuriantly before shuffling off on hands and knees, his tongue lolling from his smiling lips, leaving us rather silent and stupid. But I have always believed the mad to be at times much happier than those who attend upon them, and so it ought to be.

It was only upon returning to the hall that I recollected I had not yet had the pleasure of meeting Mrs Harleston, but as I opened my mouth to ask after that lady, there came a sudden commotion and Matron said, 'Ah. She's here.'

We turned to face the door. The servant had scurried in and was beginning the process of unlocking, whilst we stared and listened. Horses, rattling their traces. The stamp of hooves. The indecipherable cry of a coachman. It sounded as if a black hearse had indeed come for Jacob Thew, with the crows as its heralds.

Uneasy thoughts could not hurry the door's unlocking. When it swung wide, I saw not gleaming black horses, but a pair of lathered chestnuts and a smartly caparisoned carriage. A disgusted-looking coachman was engaged in flicking foam from the mouth of one of the horses. A liveried footman, as if drawing back a curtain on a stage, opened the carriage door. Waiting there, bearing an expression of doom, stood a thickset and beetle-browed gentleman. He jumped down and turned his back on us to help the next occupant to alight.

We all waited. Slowly, gracefully, a form appeared in the gap: a woman of such solemn demeanour it reduced us to silence. She was undoubtedly beautiful, though that of course was not of any importance; her travelling cloak was thrown back, revealing lustrous, artfully arranged hair and the elegant curve of her neck. But it was her eyes that struck me the most – her eyes, those windows on to the soul, which fixed of a sudden upon mine.

She stared at me with a gaze so penetrating I could not look away from her, and I felt, in that moment, how unfortunate it was. I had read much of the first encounter between doctor and patient and thought suddenly of the theories of William Pargeter. He said the first glance was vitally important. The doctor must fix the subject with his eye, to assert his control and wrest it from the malady within. Now the reverse had taken place. I jumped violently as the carriage door slammed closed; Mrs Harleston, I noticed, did not. I recalled with mounting dismay that Pargeter also suggested the first encounter take place by surprise – though he had of course meant that the patient should be surprised, not their doctor.

It was not to be helped. And the moment passed, for Matron murmured sidelong, 'No female attendant, you see,' and she *tsked*. 'Hope Spa would have sent one, but her husband insisted on conducting her himself. Most irregular. *I* would not have permitted it.'

'Then your bills would not have been paid, madam.' Mr Harleston had heard everything, despite her lowered tone.

Matron did not reply, but her posture stiffened. I found myself thinking her formidable – I should not have wished to cross her, but the fellow was unabashed.

'Well? Help us inside, damn it. My wife is fatigued from the journey.'

She did not appear fatigued, or even to notice him. His look softened, however, as he turned and took her arm, placing it tenderly in the crook of his. I observed the way his hand lingered over her unresponsive touch before he walked her, quite slowly, as if supporting an invalid, into the manor.

Mrs Harleston did not look at her new surroundings. She showed no curiosity at all. She moved with a languid grace, keeping her gaze demurely on the floor, and I realised she was not at all what I had expected. A flighty lady, thrown into a violent fit? She showed no sign of it, but such an evil could indeed be wrought by hysteria. I had to trust that with my help, she would be rapidly restored.

I stepped forward, but Matron was quicker.

'If you are ready, I will take you to the receiving room,' she said, 'and then show you your accommodation.'

The lady did not reply, but still looking at the ground, she suffered herself to be led away. She did not once glance back at her husband, who stared after her – not even when he called her name, his tone quite different from what it had been. Only when she had passed from view did his expression gradually turn to thunder.

'You do have all the requisite treatments?' he snapped. 'Cold-water bathing, vomits, blisters, all of that? You will be sure to rid her of this – you will reduce the pressure in her blood, and the rest? You must try everything. You will try everything. Cure her, or—'

'Of course,' I said somewhat hesitantly, for it occurred to me that I had not yet taken inventory of the range of treatments at my disposal. I had not even seen the promised hydropathy facil-ities, the baths of different temperatures surrounded by relaxing couches, and so forth. 'All within our power shall be done—'

'It damned well shall be! It is most important to me. Look, man, I care not for what Society thinks. Society be damned! I just want her back, the way – I mean, without these confounded notions that have taken up residence in her skull. Give me that, and . . .' His eyes became unfocused.

Her *notions*. The lady's certificate had spoken of them too and I wondered what they were. I found it peculiar that so little detail had been given. I was about to ask him to enter so that we could discuss them further when his eyes blazed with sudden vehemence.

'Just mend her,' he said. 'I shall expect your report.' And he turned and walked out as abruptly as he had arrived.

I heard his unmannerly shout to the coachman, the slam of a carriage door and the clamour of hooves as the horses were whipped into motion. I frowned after him, wondering what part his forceful demeanour may have played in his wife's misfortune. But he desired her back, that was very clear, and to be sure, his demands were in her best interests. All our sufferers might be fortunate to have such a one watching over them.

And then I wondered if Doctor Chettle had met with the fellow already. If so, I was unsurprised to find him absent now. *A challenge*, he had called the case. I supposed it would be, though not for the reasons I had expected. If Doctor Chettle had any disinclination to deal with the wife, I suspected it might have something to do with the necessity of also dealing with the husband.

But I would face all that fell to my lot. I had much to learn and much to achieve, for the path into my future stretched out in front of me, and I would not turn from it. I could not. I had once before refused to undertake the service of helping my fellow man and it had ended in the darkest of ways. I resolved afresh, as I had then, in the aftermath, never to do so again, as I saw my father, in my mind's eye, tilting back his head, pouring white powder into his mouth and falling writhing to the floor as the cyanide salts burned inexorably through his stomach. I could see the accusatory look in his eyes, opened too wide and unblinking, before the indefinable light of his soul slowly left them for ever blank.

I shook the image away. I had not seen such things, and should not imagine them. My father had of course ensured his family were not at home before he took his own life. I should focus only on what he would have wanted me to do; that had sustained me throughout my studies. I had never indulged in rowdyism like the other students; I had neither drowned myself in gin and water nor depleted my funds on chancy hands of *vingt-et-un*. I applied myself to the classics and rhetoric and the dissection room alike, driven on by the shadow of my dead father, ever at my shoulder.

My father had wished to discover a means of relieving mankind from the governance of pain. If it had turned ill, if he had gone astray, it had not been his fault. And his death was accepted under the law as an accident, suffered in the course of his experiments. It was only after I had earned my degree that I became aware of my parent's standing in medical circles – indeed, within Society too.

I wrote letters to numerous superintendents of facilities for lunatics, starting first with St Luke's, an admirable institution committed to science; then I approached the newer public establishments at Hanwell, Colney Hatch and Iffley, thinking to meet there a wide range of madness to observe. I wrote to Brislington, followed by other private asylums declining a little each time in standing. Increasingly feeling myself spurned, finally I was driven to try Bedlam, or *Bethlem*, as I should call it. Their reluctance to permit students to observe their practices was well known; perhaps they were conscious that they might not withstand close scrutiny . . . I told myself their outmoded ways need not impair my progress, so long as I recognised them for what they were; I could at least show their patients some kindness. But the methods established by the dynasty of the Doctors Monro must continue unabated, for they would not have me; my letter was returned unanswered.

During this time, as my fellow newly graduated doctors found their places, the suspicion grew that the name of Kerner was not unknown to the profession. I had thought that some might call my father mad, after his self-murder; I had not expected to be shunned myself. Did they think his melancholy congenital? But I knew that it was *not*. I closed my eyes, imagining him standing behind me, driving me on, like a . . . like a demon.

Then I found Crakethorne, in the northerly part of the West Riding of Yorkshire. It was not a part of the world to which I had ever aspired, but that mattered not a jot. I must restore the name of Kerner, and therefore I must see Crakethorne as good, as provident, as the place I was meant to remain, because despite all my application and ambition, Doctor Chettle had been the only one who had deigned to reply.

Case notes: *Mrs Victoria (Vita) Adelina Harleston*

1ˢᵗ September 1856

At first examination the patient sat quite calmly, without fidgeting or tearing at her clothes or her hair. She responded to questions with the same quiet demeanour. Claims to be eating and sleeping normally, though her head aches occasionally. Tongue a little white. Pulse slightly elevated, perhaps because of some apprehension at my visit, or a possible constriction of the nerves.

There is an intensity about the lady which shows through her surface calmness, which may be symptomatic. A nervous ailment of this type is likely to be accompanied by some dysfunction of the stomach or intestines, though she professes herself perfectly well in this regard. She has some delicacy which may, I fear, prevent her from being entirely open and will impede her treatment.

Close observation recommended.

Doctor Nathaniel Kerner's Journal

1st September

I have decided to keep a detailed and candid record of events, even including professional cases in my personal journal, since this is to be my first position of particular interest and responsibility. It was that fine doctor Thomas Percival who recommended every physician keep his own regular notes, to assist in seeing all and missing nothing, since madness is slippery and elusive, and I fully intend to do exactly that. At the same time, I shall not be constrained by professional bounds in my private papers, but will set down whatever passes through my mind or thrills in my veins. This journal shall be the mirror of my innermost thoughts.

I have thought much upon Doctor William Pargeter after my first meeting with Mrs Harleston. He was wise, I think, even if he did write his book at the close of the last century. I rather wonder, however, if the idea of personal contact with a patient could be developed somehow, even systemised, hopefully in a way that does not depend upon the alienist's ability to become a basilisk. Perhaps quiet conversation − listening − might be most soothing to the troubled spirit? I rather wish I had some confidant myself − how much more necessary must it be to those confined here! But I have the distinct impression that Doctor Chettle would be appalled if I troubled him with the detailed particulars of my cases, and so my journal shall be my listener, my own ever-present confidant.

Pargeter stated that the management of lunatics was as much an art as a science, dependent upon minute observation, and that the practitioner must use coercion or gentleness as required by the individual. Mrs Harleston would certainly appear a suitable case study on whom to begin – indeed, possibly the only suitable case in the asylum.

My interest in my patient had certainly grown since seeing her and I made no delay in making my visit. When I entered her room – she is naturally one of our first-class inmates, with a chamber of her own – I found her sitting quietly in a chair, her back turned a little towards me, and very straight. From the gentle curve of her cheek I could see her countenance was pale and I made a mental note to recommend that she take regular walks out of doors.

Her eyes are very dark – dark almost like ebony – and finely set, with delicate arching brows and a clear forehead. She has a way of looking that is quiet and yet soulful, somehow, as if she sees beyond the surfaces of the world. How poetical I wax – and yet that was how it struck upon me, and I have said that I will be my own faithful recorder.

Her nose is straight and neat. Her face tends towards the slender, but any hint of severity is leavened by full lips. Her hair is thick, the colour of chestnuts and very lustrous, lending a healthy impression; it is indeed the model of a woman's crowning adornment.

She was subdued, giving an impression of great stillness and withdrawal from the world about her, and it was not hard to intuit that, given the choice, she would much prefer isolation to the madding crowd. Indeed, I found it hard to imagine her at the centre of any circle of acquaintances that a man such as Mr Harleston must draw to himself.

I recollected everything that had been my intention when I entered the room, for all that upon first seeing her, I had almost forgot. Doctor Pargeter would have expected to establish, at once and irrefutably, an influence over the patient by his look. He was accustomed to tell them with his eye all that they required to know about how things would be.

I bent towards her as she turned, adopting what I hoped to be an authoritative yet kindly and approachable expression. She looked up and a momentary alarm flickered across her features. I endeavoured to soften my gaze, but she had already taken to staring at her hands. She plucked at her fingernails, that being perhaps the only outward sign of her malady.

I realised with growing discomfort that we were closeted together in her room and that neither of us had yet spoken, so I made haste to bid her good morning and introduced myself before proceeding to ask questions of the type required for her case notes. She assured me that she had breakfasted and that all was to her comfort.

When requested, she put out her little tongue, with some delicate hesitancy, despite having already passed a few weeks at Hope. Like her cheeks it was slightly pale, especially in contrast with the rosy hue of her lips.

I could not help but wonder why she had been transferred from such a grand-sounding place to come to Crakethorne, an institution so far distant from her home. I asked how she did there and she replied, in a voice that was deeper and more musical than anticipated, that she had not liked it at all.

I pressed my fingers to her wrist, marking the slight elevation of her pulse, and asked what she had so disliked. She stirred at that, her slender arm moving under my hands as she shifted. She murmured, 'I did not like that I could not reside where I chose, do as I chose or go whither I chose. I did not like wearing the things they gave me. I did not like being subject to their constant watching.'

I had not expected so full a disclosure, or to detect within her so decided an aversion to Hope. It was dismaying, for in those particulars Crakethorne was much as any other asylum. Mrs Harleston, of course, would be provided for here as well as she might expect *anywhere. Her room was comfortable, if plain: it held a pair of upright chairs, a washstand with bowls of carved wood rather than breakable porcelain, and a mirror firmly affixed to the wall – ensuring one's appearance to be both seemly and attractive is well known to being integral to the female life and supportive of her sanity. A small wardrobe, a table and a bed completed the arrangement. There could be no separate bedchamber and sitting room since the peephole at the door must permit all to be taken in at a glance. The walls were whitewashed, perhaps not so recently as might be desired, but the pale sun spilling between the bars at the window lent the room cheer, if not warmth. To be sure, the patient's brown linsey dress was somewhat drab; I had seen her finely cut travelling cloak, of rich material and adorned about the collar, and it was a shame that she must wear this, but it was necessary, for a time at least.*

'It will all be worthwhile,' I said, 'to be restored to the world once again, quite happy, and to know that you have been cured of what ails you.'

Her lips opened and she clasped the lower between small white teeth. She looked up into my face. My fingers were still pressed to her wrist – I had hoped that light conversation would settle her pulse, but it was throbbing under my fingers. Her eyes were now uncomfortably close to mine and I remembered the need to meet her gaze; I did not flinch from it; indeed, I could not have torn my eyes from her wide, eloquent eyes had I wished. They were darker than I had thought at first glance.

'What is it that ails me?' she asked.

'It is rather too early to tell. It is reported that you are subject to hysterical fits, that you had a violent attack on an omnibus, and of course you have been residing for some days in Hope Asylum already—'

She drew in air through her teeth and her gaze become anxious as if pained at the remembrance, as if she thought her time in the asylum was what truly ailed her. She looked so alone — and I realised she was, for here was a woman of delicate sensibility, of deep feeling, parted from her home, husband and friends, and with none among our patients who could likely supply the deficiency.

I wished to comfort her. 'I will help you,' I said, in a low tone. It was important to establish trust between us.

'Will you?'

She spoke in such a flat, dead, hopeless voice that at first I could not answer — then I said firmly that most certainly I would; that I would do all that was in my power.

She nodded only, and I pressed on with the requisite questions. She claimed to sleep well, although she did not look at me as she said it and I wondered if that was true. She continued in that same dull tone.

I am beginning to think that the power of conversation, on subjects other than her illness, could in her case have a remarkable effect. It would be such a pleasure to see an innocent distraction restore the lightness to her eyes. I would dearly love to see her smile, not in the wistful way that she had, but to cast off all care — even, perhaps, to laugh.

In short, Mrs Harleston was not at all as I expected to find her. She is no flouncing lady filling listless hours with sighs and vapours. She appears to possess no great vanity, despite her obvious beauty, or to demand constant primping attention. She does not strike me as one to enjoy a malade imaginaire, which is in its way unfortunate, since it means her illness must have some deeper, true cause.

I find myself impatient to uncover the nature of her 'strange notions', but I did not believe that was the moment to discuss them. Quiet and rest, and all the comfort and peace that untroubled sanctuary can provide will, I think, work upon her best. It is true that I have little experience, but it did strike me most strongly that that was indeed the case — and what doctor of the mind does not rely on his intuition?

Before I left the lady, I impressed upon her the importance of eating good plain food without brown meats, and the benefit of taking the air each day. She nodded, staring down at her hands as if she only wished for me to be gone. I lingered still, feeling something indefinable remained unspoken, until an attendant bustled in and broke the moment. I could not help but notice as I took my leave that Mrs Harleston pressed her eyes closed at this new intrusion upon her privacy.

I have made a recommendation that she should be closely observed. It is against all her inclinations and I felt a pang as I did it, something a little like guilt, but it cannot be helped. After all, I wish only for everything her husband desires: for her to be well and herself again, and to return to her proper home as soon as is practicable.

Chapter Five

At last the patients retired for the evening. I left the attendants to watch over them and let myself out of the wards to return to my own rooms, although I knew I would not soon relax. My mind was unsettled with so much that was new and I decided to heed my own advice and take a restorative stroll about the grounds.

It felt a little odd letting myself out at the front door with no one near, each clank of the bolts echoing too loudly in my ears. Once I closed and locked it again behind me, all was strangely quiet. I was unused to such silence in the city; there, iron wheels rumbled constantly in the streets, costermongers shouted their wares and men, women and children thronged about their business, unceasing, even after nightfall. Here, there was no one in my vicinity. The old grey building loomed over me and the moon rode high above it all, swollen and somnolent. There was still a little light in the gloaming to see by, however, and I walked down the slope towards the darker shapes of the trees.

As I went, Mrs Harleston's words echoed in my mind.

I did not like that I could not reside where I chose, do as I chose or go whither I chose. I did not like wearing the things they gave me. I did not like being subject to their constant watching.

Alone as I was, they chimed unpleasantly within me and I felt very conscious of the massy edifice at my back; I wondered who might be watching now, peering from its many windows. I focused instead upon the uneven ground, each dip and hollow outlined by ink-black shadows. I looked about for brighter colours, the roses the advertisement had spoken of, but all that emerged were the dark and tortured shapes of hawthorn briars. I had left it a little late to wander about the hillside, but I did not wish to face the cacophony of locks again quite yet, so I progressed as far as the first copse of oak and ash. Ahead was the dark gleam of water, but before that the earth changed in character, almost appearing to fold upon itself, forming a row of mounds all laid in a line. I blinked. Rough shapes at the head of each almost suggested—

'It's for the patients who aren't claimed,' a voice said, and I whirled to see Matron, her white-banded cap and apron standing out against the darkness.

'Those who die here aren't always worth the burying to their families. And so they stay.'

'So these are—'

'Graves. There are no inscriptions, of course. They cannot expect such.'

I supposed I should not have been surprised by it, but it was a melancholy sight and my heart sank within me at finding myself in such a place, especially as the light faded from the world. The idea of the poor souls entombed here, with not even their name to be remembered by—

A sudden harsh cry made me jump and I turned to see a crow sitting on a low branch, its gloss-dark feathers agleam, watching me with black, intelligent eyes.

'Some call it the Crow Garden,' Matron said. 'The patients, anyway. They pass it down among themselves, I suppose. We try not to bring them too close to it on our excursions – unless it's necessary, of course.'

I was wondering why on earth it should be 'necessary' when she said, 'Well, night is drawing in. Do you return to the manor?'

I allowed that I would, and we walked together in a silence that felt at one with the gloom that had fallen over the place, or perhaps had been there all the time, waiting to be noticed. It was difficult not to feel as if, rather than falling in with a new acquaintance, I was being herded inside; as if the guiding hands of Crakethorne Manor would prefer it if I did not go whither I chose either.

I would that the idea had never occurred to me, for it followed me that night into my sleep. I fell into bed and must have slumbered almost at once, my head as heavy as my limbs, and I found in my dream that I was unable to move an inch. I could not go where I would. I could not do what I would. My arms and legs were like iron and besides, my head spun and ached and I felt sick. I was lying on something hard and uncomfortable and could barely lift an eyelid. When I did, I found that someone was leaning over me.

Their appearance was a shock and yet the realisation that it was my father came as no surprise, for all I had never expected to see him again with such clarity. The lines etched around his eyes and across his brow deepened with concern. He reached out, his hand spread before my face, and it was only when he moved to touch my skin that I became aware of the cold, inflexible mask pressed against my features.

I remembered everything: my father, placing the thing he had made over my cheeks and nose and lips; the unpleasant, skin-like softness of the wadding sealing its edges. And I heard again his words, that I should *want* to help, I should be *grateful* to help.

But I did not want to help, and I had tried to say so, but my words had drifted into the air and dissipated and he did not hear me, or would not; he only turned and dropped clear liquid on to a sponge. Next to him, laid out in a case, were shining silver pins of various lengths and widths.

I shuddered. I was eight years old, and I was certain I would die.

The mask he had fashioned forced me to inhale the reeking vapours as the chloroform evaporated. The smell, sweet and horribly cloying, crept up and enveloped me; my father's outline wavered and solidified once more. His short grey beard, whiter at the chin, suddenly became sharply focused and his eyes shone. I realised his lips were opening and closing but his words were meaningless to me, and anyway my hearing had grown faint, as if I were submerged in deep water.

Then his fingers were in front of my eyes, too large and too close. It was all suddenly very funny, although I could not laugh because my face had become stiff and inflexible. He pulled one of my eyelids upwards and leaned over me. Individual features were horribly clear: the stubbly flecks where he had trimmed his moustache, the pale notch on his jaw where an old scar prevented the hair from growing. Mist gathered before my face like breath on a winter's day. I wanted more than anything to close my eyes, but the sweetish smell was giving way to something else; there was a rottenness beneath it that turned my stomach.

'You are drowsy,' a voice said. 'You are going deeper.'

I did not wish to go deeper. I did not wish to fall asleep. I wanted only to be free of it all: my father, the foul stench, the mask. I could not so much as raise a hand to tear it from me, and as the lights began to dance before my eyes, as I went deeper in spite of myself, I felt it sinking into my skin.

I awoke what felt in my dream like a moment later. My father, dead for fifteen years, was leaning over me, shaking me, snapping his fingers, calling my name. I had a strange notion that he had not done that for days and wondered if I should now be glad of it.

'Nathaniel? Are you all right?' He pulled me into a sitting

position and a wave of nausea rolled over me. My arms were sore, as was my chest. I could not think what he had done to me; I only felt as if my body had been rendered strange, at once numb and bruised all over. The first thing I saw with any clarity was the open tray of pins.

'Well?' His breath was warm against my cheek. I knew he did not ask how I was; he only wanted to *know*.

'I felt it.' If he wished only for his answer, he would have it. I tried not to let my feelings show in my voice. 'I felt it all; I could feel it every moment. It hurt and I wanted you to stop, but I could not speak.'

A change came across him as I said the words. He half turned from me, closing his eyes; then his hands curled into fists. Without looking at me again, he began to put away his things: the mask he had made, his ampoules, his horrible pins. He moved with quiet efficiency and sagging shoulders.

I swung my legs from the table and dropped to the floor. I had to grip the table to keep from falling, but he did not help me. He showed no sign that he was aware of me at all, and I walked from the room. I had expected to feel triumph, but there was only shame. I went into my bedroom and buried my face in my pillow.

It was the first time I could remember telling a deliberate untruth. I had not known, then, that it would kill my father.

I awoke in the unfamiliar room at Crakethorne with the wind singing some mournful dirge and rattling the windows and I tasted the falsehood on my tongue.

My father had been a good man. He was a fine doctor. And his experiment *had* worked; I had been insensible on his table and he could have stuck me with a dozen pins without me feeling a thing. He could have done anything to me at all.

My father had been the first to discover the efficacy of chloroform in saving patients from the pain of surgery, and because of my selfish inclinations, the world would never know it. He went to his grave, taking his own life, without the faintest inkling that his trial had been a success. He left others experimenting with chloroform and ether, discovering what he already knew, carving new paths into the future while he remained forever in the past.

In 1847, Doctor James Young Simpson discovered that chloroform could reduce a man to insensibility. Doctor Imlach found its usefulness in rendering a dental procedure painless. In 1850, Simpson was rewarded not only with renown, but with the presidency of the Royal College of Physicians of Edinburgh.

And I became an Oedipus, for I had destroyed my own father. In later years I strove to make up for it, and I would continue to do so. I must make new discoveries. I must become the doctor he always wished to be.

Chapter Six

I made a particular point, when next about my rounds, to greet Peter Ambrose like a human being. He was in the ladies' day-room and did not reply; he sat on a cushion on the floor and raised his head with a breathy huff. It was so like the sound a dog might make that I had to admire the ingenuity in his delusion – but at that moment it occurred to me I had not yet seen Mrs Harleston.

Perhaps she had not liked the company. There was Nellie Briggs, once a housemaid, busily staring at nothing; I had been somewhat shocked to discover she had been confined for smothering her baby at the breast – a terrible thing, though not as uncommon in our country's asylums as might be wished. Lillian Smith snoozed in her chair. Della Martin twitched with some irritable impulse. All the others must have been helping in the laundry, since busying oneself in useful occupation was considered beneficial to recovery. Mrs Harleston was naturally exempt from such menial tasks, and in any case, there was no one here with whom I could imagine her conversing.

I proceeded to her chamber, but found it empty. A book upturned on the bed spoke of recent occupation and I decided I must ask her what she was reading. Unsuitable indulgence of the imagination might inflame her condition, but that was of little matter beside that of her absence.

I found Matron by an open storeroom, directing an attendant in the correct folding of sheets. I enquired after my patient.

'She's outside,' she said, as if I should have known.

Sweet relief! The lady had not only a purpose in her absence, but must have resolved to follow my direction in taking the air. I thought of the patch of ground I had recently discovered and hoped that she, at least, had found the fabled roses.

Matron added, 'With Doctor Chettle.'

'Oh?' I was somewhat surprised. Since my arrival I had seen my medical superintendent emerge from his study on only a single occasion, and that was to reprimand the cook for burning his roast. I had supposed him too much taken up with his own avocations.

'Taking the cure,' Matron prompted. In response to my blank look she added, 'By the pool.'

I thanked her and, pausing only to ask of her where on earth said pool might be, went to find them both.

I let myself out of the asylum and hurried over the rough grass. I could not make out the way I had taken the previous evening – indeed, I was not certain there was a clear path at all. Only the hawthorns stood there, their twisted limbs reminiscent of watchers standing silently about the hillside.

As I reached the little patch of ground our patients called the Crow Garden, I heard the birds' hoarse and ragged cawing. I did not spy them, however, nor any living creature. But I could not pause there, and had no wish to. I could see the little flash of water that lay beyond the burial ground with greater clarity than before. The churned banking gave way to an opaque grey surface that looked bone-cold. Autumn had gained ascendancy over summer: the sun gave no heat and the air too felt chill, and I shivered.

Then I saw them; indeed, I could not think how I had failed to do so before. Doctor Chettle stood to one side of the water, his back turned towards me. A female attendant was nearby, holding a towel.

Then I saw Mrs Harleston.

She had been half hidden by a tree growing by the pool; as she took a tentative step forward, I realised she was immersed in the water to her knees. Another attendant walked with her, although he wore long boots to save him from the cold. In his hands was a large ewer.

Doctor Chettle gestured to Mrs Harleston, bidding her to go deeper.

She turned and stepped further into the water. Though she had wrapped her arms about her body, they surely afforded her no warmth, for I could see the way she shuddered. Her hair hung loose like a girl's, thick and massy to her waist. I wished I could scoop it up, to save it from the water, to arrange it more appropriately for such a lady. This was not to be borne!

At first my rage was nameless, and then I told myself it suited neither her station nor her delicacy; it was an outrage against her – her *loveliness* – that was the word that sprang to mind, though I told myself that was not it, not really.

Surely Hope would never have treated her so? What cure could be found in a place such as this, beneath the dying leaves, in such a pool? What could lie beneath icy water so short a distance from the abandoned bones of the unwanted dead? I could not imagine what Doctor Chettle might be thinking – this was no spa or watering place, no healthful spring. The pool was filthy and cold, the sky pale and sunless, the only sound, in that moment, the mocking call of a crow.

I bestirred myself and made my way precipitously towards them, and as I did, the attendant in the water lowered his jug and scooped the grey water over Mrs Harleston's head. She recoiled but made no other protest; it was I who cried out, but she who was so assaulted uttered not a word. Her white nightgown offered no protection as it clung to her, wrapping itself tightly about each curve, making her look as slender and helpless as a girl. It did not even fit her correctly, for it had slipped down to reveal her finely moulded white shoulder.

Mrs Harleston closed her eyes as if in denial of it all.

I opened my mouth to protest, but Doctor Chettle forestalled me, saying, quite mildly, 'Ah, Kerner. Are you come to observe?'

He stood with his hands clasped at his back: a man examining a curious exhibit. His insouciance stopped my words, but his tone was that of my superior, a man of far greater experience than my own and, furthermore, one who could turn me off at any time he chose.

That mattered not to me at that moment. '*Observe*, sir?' I could scarcely keep the anger from my voice.

'Our cold-water treatment is quite the attraction, you know. You must have seen mention of it in our advertisements.' He waved a hand as if to show how wonderful it was. 'This pool is a natural spring, you see.'

An image flashed before me of Continental watering places, of fine ladies taking themselves off to bathe and drink the sparkling healing draughts. I imagined the patients of Hope Spa and Asylum relaxing around a heated pool. I found I could not speak. Was this why I had travelled to Yorkshire? Was this his 'curative water garden'? This *treatment* should surely have been done indoors; I would have applied a little cool water to the lady's forehead and her temples, perhaps even bathed her arms. Such harsh treatment could never be fit for one of her temperament. It was . . . well, it was madness!

'So very refreshing,' Doctor Chettle went on, oblivious to my feelings. 'Applied to the cranium, the seat of the disease with which we join battle, the cold water induces a shock which helps to jolt the mind from its disturbed condition and recover its equanimity. Afterwards, when the subject is once more warm, the lasting effect is to soothe the raging spirit.' He sounded pleased to be able to impart such information to one so new.

'And yet,' I said, 'Mrs Harleston's condition is characterised by subdued rather than excited spirits.'

'Of course, of course!' He gave me a sharp look. 'That is a disturbance in its own right.'

'I think perhaps she has been disturbed enough. Do you not agree?'

For a moment, there was silence. I found myself wanting to look at her, but I could not bring myself to meet her eyes. I focused on Doctor Chettle, all the while remaining intensely aware of her fragile white form in the corner of my eye, like an undine risen from the water.

Then he raised a hand to the attendant and proclaimed his treatment complete. He bade the man help her from the water, and he did so. Still I could not look at her, but I followed every movement: the uncertain reach of her hand, the slowness of her steps, the sudden flash of a robe thrown over her shoulders.

As we made our way back to the manor, no one spoke. Outwardly all was calm, but inwardly I was shocked at the depth of my anger. I was here to learn, but had *I* not been entrusted with the lady's care? And yet she had been taken out of my hands after so short a time.

I remembered an infamous case from my studies and fumed over it. In 1725, Patrick Blair gave 'water treatment' to a female who refused to be a dutiful wife. He blindfolded and stripped her and strapped her to a bathing chair, and he caused freezing water to be sprayed unceasingly into her face until she broke and promised to return to her marriage bed. Thus did he claim to have cured her dislike for her husband!

Doctor Chettle spoke as we entered the hall. 'Come to my room as soon as you are able.' He left us, without looking back at Mrs Harleston, who stood shivering on the tiled floor. Her lovely hair was clumped into snake-like tendrils; she appeared to see nothing before her. An attendant threw a fresh towel over her – I did not know if it was for her benefit or to save the tiles from the murky water – and began to lead her away.

'Ensure that she is warm,' I called after them. 'A set of clean clothes. An extra blanket. And a fire.'

Mrs Harleston paused and slowly raised her head towards me. Her eyes were as dark as they had always been, but horribly blank.

'Who were the ones who watched?' she whispered, as if her words were intended only for me. 'Who were they who stood all about – who watched, yet had no faces?'

She reached out towards me, but the attendant chose that moment to move; she laid uncouth hands on Mrs Harleston and guided her away, shooting me a poisonous glare as I stared after them.

Doctor Chettle was still ascending the stairs; I could hear his steady step, all unconcern, and resolved to follow at once. I caught up with him in the passage, though he did not turn, and entered the room after him. He closed the door behind me.

'I apologise,' he said. 'I should have mentioned to you my intention to work the water cure on Mrs Harleston. I am unused, you know, to working with any other physician.'

'I . . .' was all my startled response.

'You will forgive me of course, if I interest myself in her case.'

'Well – I realise it is a most pressing one. But I would be grateful if—'

'I shall inform you in the future, yes, yes.' He gestured towards his desk, then walked over to it, picked up a sheet of paper and held it out. 'I am in receipt of a letter,' he said. 'Go on, read it.'

Doctor Chettle,

I trust I do not have to write to remind you of the urgency of the matter of my wife, since I am certain you will not forget it. It is not meet that we should be parted in this fashion, and for such a reason. She must be returned, in her senses, as soon as the thing may be done.

You are in the business of cures, so cure her. I removed her from the watering place in Royal Tunbridge since they made so little progress. They withheld treatments I am convinced could have quickly worked to her good. I remind you that yours is not the only institution providing such services.

I am willing to meet the expenses of all additional treatments that may be of efficacy in my wife's case. Do not spare them. All that science and invention can provide must and will be laid at our disposal to see her restored to me.

It is often said that you mad-doctors are happier to contain, not to cure, since to relieve the patient is to lose the terms of their board. Let me assure you that if you have her home within the month, in her senses and ready to do her duty as a wife, a substantial gratuity shall be yours. Fail and we try elsewhere.

I shall expect your report with all haste.

Peregrine R. Harleston

The letter was signed with such rapid, even angry flourishes that I could scarce make out the brute's name. What an astonishing communication. What treatments did he expect? Electricity? The tranquillising chair? Should we bleed her to death? Perhaps he would prefer Doctor Blair's water jets even to the icy pool at Crakethorne?

Doctor Chettle waved his hand in a resigned fashion. 'It is not long enough, of course,' he said. 'The lady requires peace and time to recover, but it appears that we must do without such things. If we delay she will be whirled about the country in his carriage until she is as deranged as he can contrive to make her.'

'Do you think him desirous of her incarceration?' But his face rose before me – the beetling brows, the temper – and I remembered the way his voice had softened when he spoke her name.

'No. No, I do not.' Doctor Chettle sighed. 'I believe he wants her back most ardently, as you can see.'

'But we must not let him influence her treatment—' Even as I spoke, I realised he already had. Did Mr Harleston know of the roughness of our 'water cure'? Had he placed her here in spite of it, or because of it? Patrick Blair rose to my mind once more and I could not help but wonder if her husband thought us so benighted that we would make her miserable enough to flee back to him? With growing horror, I remembered the other things he had called for when he left her at the gate. *Purgatives* . . . *Blisters* . . .

Doctor Chettle opened his mouth to speak, but I interjected, 'It cannot be so! We cannot do it to her. I will not see her blistered and scarred. She could not bear it.'

'I mentioned no such thing.' He stroked his ample whiskers as if in contemplation. 'Whatever we do shall be our decision – made jointly, of course. But do something we must, and I fear we cannot wait too long between treatments to properly assess their efficacy. Harleston waited barely a day before sending this letter, after all. We cannot have her made subject to his whim; she must have all that decency and knowledge can give her, moderated by our sense and experience. To move her again could be disastrous. Disastrous!'

His eyes flashed and he glanced away. He did not mention the payment that would be lost if she left us, nor the boon offered should we be the ones to set her on her right course, but I thought I could make out the glimmer of it in his eyes.

'I should prefer to let her rest,' I said, 'to – to *speak* to her. To engage her in conversation, to delve more deeply into her mind.'

I could see the husband's disdain as if he were standing before me. He would have no belief in time and understanding; he would rather see his wife spinning about the room in a revolving chair until blood gushed from her eyes than have her speak to me.

Doctor Chettle did not respond to my words either; he was staring at his books as if he longed only to bury himself in their contents. No doubt he would as soon as I left.

I parted from him, promising to assess the patient's progress that very afternoon. Indeed, I longed to do so, but first, I knew I must allow her to rest.

I busied myself around the men's wards for the remainder of the forenoon and ate in the patients' dining hall to observe their conduct. I was glad to see that no one placed young Peter's bowl on the floor, although he disdained the use of silver. The farmhand, Thew, showed himself a 'good worker', helping to pass the plates around. All the while he cast fearful looks at the window, though I heard no crows. All passed peaceably enough until Samuel Brewer, the man about whom Doctor Chettle had been somewhat enigmatic, overturned his bowl and swept the contents to the floor. He declared that he was a rich man and should eat from a golden platter; that if he could only visit the

Exchequer he would show us all, and that we could read of it in his journal, in which, one of the attendants told me, he scribbled without cease.

It felt like an age before a decent interval had passed and I could return to the ladies' wards, where no doubt Mrs Harleston had taken some refreshment in her room. I found her there, sitting much as I had first seen her, and very still. She held her book on her lap but it was closed and her gaze was fixed upon the window. Her hair was restored to neatness and she looked at me calmly, though with wariness, as if in fear I was come to freeze her to the marrow.

An apology for her rough treatment rose to my lips, but I forced myself to swallow it. Any trace of division amongst her physicians could not help her. Instead, I smiled and asked about her novel.

'It is not a novel,' she replied. 'It is poetry.' She turned the cover to reveal a little volume of Byron.

But this was bad! Poetry, and *such* poetry, was entirely unsuitable. For a sufferer of hysteria to wallow in sentiment, to excite the emotions without cause, could never run to the good. And Byron was surely worst of all, with his profligacy and unregulated passions, attachments indiscriminately and carelessly made.

'I cannot recommend it,' I said. 'I must advise you to moderate your reading whilst you are here. Your Bible or a book of sermons or hymns would be better, or even a morally instructive novel – Samuel Richardson, perhaps? After all, "The lunatic, the lover and the poet are of imagination all compact."'

I realised it was indelicate at once. To battle poetry by quoting the Bard, and in such circumstance – to call her a lunatic to her face – it was badly done. But I had wished to conceal the depths of my reaction to Byron, who was, after all, 'mad, bad and dangerous to know'. His own wife had thought him in leave of his senses.

'You do not altogether dislike poetry, then?' The flash in her eye indicated that the irony had not passed unnoticed.

'I do not. A little Browning could be edifying, perhaps. The intellectual musings of an unimpeachable character, probing the nature of creative endeavour and such.' But I did not wish to discuss my own preferences. I returned to asking more straightforward questions, and she made her responses in a low, well-regulated tone. She presented herself with steadiness, as if her torments were all forgotten: as one who would have no difficulty in managing their person or their affairs. I decided it would be an appropriate moment to enquire after the circumstances of her fit.

'Could you tell me,' I asked, 'what induced you to board an omnibus on the fifth of August? Can you tell me how it all began?'

She glanced at me in sudden alarm. Then her expression resolved into what it had been when she had stood to her knees in a freezing pond: she looked helpless. She looked humiliated.

I cursed myself and spoke more gently. 'It is quite all right. I am your physician, and am here to help you all I can. You may speak to me of anything you wish.'

She glanced at me with her lovely eyes, so dark and yet lucent. What a pity their light must be wasted in such a place! I found myself longing to see her expression enlivened – it would be reward indeed. However could I have thought her case dull? I was fortunate to have such a patient.

She did not speak and so I went on. 'In a case such as yours, uncovering the cause of the attack, increasing our understanding of its premonitory signs and tendencies, could be of the utmost service in dispelling its power over you.'

'Its power?'

'If you can tell me what happened – you do not seem disposed towards passions of that kind. None such ever seized you at Hope, I believe. Is there some evil at the root of it, something troubling you? If you can bring yourself to converse on the matter, perhaps I can help rid you of it, for – for ever.'

She let out a sudden high-pitched laugh. Her hand shot to her mouth, as if it had startled her as much as I. That laugh – it was like breaking through the surface of a frozen lake and glimpsing blackness beneath. It was a sign, at last, of the tempest that had shaken her soul.

'Pray, tell me.' I leaned forward, restraining myself from taking her hand.

'I will tell you something else,' she said, 'anything else! Do not ask me, I beg you. That day is inexpressibly painful to me.'

I gazed into her eyes. I *must* help her – I would! But a gentleman could not see her fear and press her further, particularly after the way she had already been strained, and so I let it pass. Yet here seemed to be an opportunity to explore her in another direction, and so I changed the subject. 'I understand that as a child, you were prone to auditory hallucinations.'

She shook her head in pained confusion.

'You heard voices, I think.'

I waited, thinking that way to encourage her to speak. Sometimes words were needed, sometimes forcefulness, sometimes gentleness and sometimes silence. Such was Pargeter's way, the art of managing madness in all its multitudinous forms, and I had to employ it to the best of my abilities.

At last she said, 'Very well. I said that I would speak of it and I shall, but it is not as you imagine. I will tell you of when I was a child, with my mother, in the days before I was made to feel a burden on the family.

'My mother was a sensible woman. Everybody said so. There was nothing whimsical or fanciful about her, no tales of fairies or goblins to mar my sleep when I was small. All was practical domesticity, with not a hint of the fantastical. My grandmama, however, thought differently. She *was* different. Oh, to outward appearance she was all that the world and his neighbour could require, but she had what my mother called "odd ideas"; no doubt that is what interests you.'

I tilted my head. If she was inclined to talk, I would be her faithful listener. I could unravel what it meant afterwards.

'It was she who heard voices,' said Mrs Harleston, 'but not *empty* voices, not just in her head. She said that real people spoke to her, only no one that anybody could see, because they had already gone beyond the bounds of this world. And she thought I had inherited her gift. She seemed eager for it, as if she thought it a special thing that I could share with her. I rather wanted that, I confess.'

She raised her hands and let them fall. 'She thought my grand-papa visited her and gave her advice. It was not so very wrong, was it? I have heard others speak so. Why, in America, there are sisters who communicate regularly with those who have passed beyond the veil. It is quite the stir. They ask questions and hear rappings in answer from all corners of the room. The most learned men believe in it.'

I frowned. I had heard tell of the Fox sisters and their conver-sations with their furniture some few years ago, and it had seemed preposterous. Perhaps it was only a question of time before they found themselves in a similar position to Mrs Harleston.

'My grandmama told me to listen hard for them,' she went on. 'I was a child, and I did all that I could do. I listened as intently as I was able. My imagination, I think, supplied the rest.'

'What did you think you heard?'

She looked at me questioningly – or perhaps its opposite; almost, I could have thought, as if she had expected me to know.

'What might I not have heard? I was impressionable. It was the duty of my life to be formed by her, to listen to my elders and my superiors – in years and in sense, as they should have been. My mother objected, but naturally she afforded her own mother the respect due to her – and what could she do? Cast her from the house? I sometimes thought she would have done it, had there been no risk of a scandal.' Her tone bore the tinge of bitterness. 'Where can widows go, when they no longer have the protection of their husband and their family will not take pity? Where can any woman?'

She looked into my face again, and again her expression was unreadable. Was she gauging the effect of her words upon me, or had she merely recalled herself to the present?

'My mother insisted on having the first place in my care, of course. She told my grandmama to say nothing of phantasms and ghouls. She even accused her of madness, though she never brought her to a place such as this.'

'Do go on.'

'There was nothing more. She refused to speak of it again, even when . . . I mean—'

'Even when you heard things? Is that it?'

'It all stopped,' she said, her voice a little too insistent. 'With no one to listen, who would speak?' Her laughter rang falsely upon my ear. 'And so it ended and that was all. There is nothing to tell. My grandmama did not speak of voices to me again, not until . . . But that was . . .'

This was bad. She had the sense to cover it at least, but she had plainly suffered some kind of auricular delirium, perhaps occasioned by the strain placed upon her nerves by familial conflict. Such a thing was a true symptom of lunacy; it could not be denied.

She reached out and grasped my arm with her pale fingers. 'But you know, do you not? For you have been there, among them – you have been in that place – with the dead!'

I was astonished.

She looked at me, something like despair growing upon her. 'You were with them, for a time. And you returned, but different.' Her voice faltered.

I reached down and touched her hand, feeling her cool skin, removing her fingers from mine – and yet it took a moment to relinquish them. An image flashed before me and although I knew I should not, although I knew I *could* not engage with delusion, I said, 'Do you mean that I have visited the Crow Garden?'

She froze, then looked away. 'I know of no such place,' she said. 'I am sorry.'

'Do not be. I said that you may say anything to me, and I meant it. You have no idea how helpful it may be simply to be able to talk, to unburden yourself. An unseen weed cannot be uprooted. Even something you feel to be unimportant may prove the key to all.'

A flicker in her expression revealed her doubt. She inhaled deeply. Thankfully, the wildness – the 'strange notions', perhaps – had left her for now. I was grateful for it, for her words had struck upon me rather more strangely than I had anticipated. And her eyes – they held such curious depths.

'I continued happily enough until my twenty-first year,' she went on. 'I had been out some time by then of course, and we went to balls and such, and – well, I caught the eye of Mr Peregrine Russell Harleston.

'I saw him looking at me, and I saw his expression when he did so. His preference was quite marked. He wished to dance with me, to the exclusion of all others. We even stayed at his house, attending parties where he had me play duets with him at the piano while his wife watched. My mother agreed to it – encouraged it, in fact. I imagine she thought I might catch the eye of one of his eligible friends.

'Then his wife died, and my mother began to speak to me of my father's business, how it had not prospered in the preceding years as they had hoped. It was quite obvious what she intended.'

I noted her tremulous speech, but felt it to be a sign of female delicacy rather than mental derangement. I found myself focusing on the corner of her lip. It was marked by a little line like a parenthesis, so tiny, as if etched by an exquisite quill.

She gave a sigh. 'I did not wish it, but what could I say? On his side were all his advantages of status and wealth and manner and connections, and on mine – that I did not like him. What of that? And he could be attentive – kind, even. I hardly knew what I wanted, only that there was *something* – a feeling. And now you will think me a silly woman who does not know her own mind, let alone reside in it.'

I wished to reassure her, although I could not quite form the words.

'I would have kept up my refusal despite all their persuasions, but for one thing. My grandmama came to me and said that she had a message for me – one that had the character of utmost importance. She said that if I married Peregrine Harleston, I was certain to find deep and genuine love.

'I did not feel it in my heart to be so, but I trusted her, and I had been taught by then to doubt myself. My fond mother often told me what it was to have such an undutiful daughter, pointing out that I had received no other offers. It became so difficult and—'

'You accepted him.'

She nodded.

'And *did* you?' I could not resist the question, though it was not relevant, not really.

'Did I . . . ?'

'Find love? Your husband must care for you a great deal. He misses you.'

'Do you think so? You met him, did you not? Did you think him a man of tender feeling?'

I made no reply.

'Ours was nothing but a counterfeit of marriage. My grandmama was mistaken. I refuse to believe she cared so little for me that her message was a thing of invention, but I do not know. I was unable to ask her, for she died before the wedding took place. The voices, the thing she thought she heard . . . At any rate, I know it all to be false. I have learned that better, I think, than anyone.'

That was a relief, at least. It was discomfiting to think that within that clear forehead, disembodied voices were whispering. And yet what had she meant about being in that place – being with the dead?

Whatever she may have intended, the fact that she had ever heard voices was not a promising admission, and her grandmother's hallucinations, which had not formed part of her record, would have to be noted. I did not hold faith with the outmoded notion that madness was hereditary, but this was unfortunately in its favour.

'And so you changed your mind?' I asked. 'Is that why you left your husband and boarded the omnibus, not even knowing where it was going?'

'No!' She gathered herself. 'What, do you think me so flighty and inconstant that I make a promise one moment and repudiate it the next? Of course I have a sense of duty. Why, it was for duty that I married him. That, and – nothing else.'

I spoke gently. 'Why, then, did you do it?'

'I . . . I cannot,' she declared. 'I won't! And you shall not make me. It is all so . . . Oh, I don't know.' The fire went out of her and she buried her face in her hands.

I cursed myself. In my inexperience, I had probed her too deeply. It was unfortunate; I must learn not to be so precipitate. And yet she could not know how pressing her case was. I soothed her, saying that all would be well and we need not speak of it now. I called an attendant to bring her a cooling tonic, and some vinegar and water to bathe her temples.

Mrs Harleston became meek as a lamb and said she would lie down and try to sleep. It was only afterwards I realised that, despite all her sweet complaisance, when she retreated to her rest, she had taken her little volume of poetry with her.

Dear Doctor Kerner,

Forgive the blunt manner of my writing to you. We have not been
introduced; indeed, I believe you were at Oxford just a year after
I left it. We may have met at that institution but for the reason
that I did not complete my studies, not for want of application,
but because I discovered a therapeutic method so astonishing
— so marvellous — that I gave up all else to devote myself to its
perfection.

You will have heard of Franz Anton Mesmer and will no doubt
scoff at the mention of his name, as do many other esteemed
members of your — almost, I should say, our — profession. I do not
pretend to share such disdain for his ideas, though I will share
a smile at the recollection of his methods. I assure you, however,
that within his grandiloquent and often misplaced actions, there
was a seed worth germinating — nay, worth tending with the
utmost care.

But allow me to explain before I try your patience beyond the
length of my letter. Mesmer did indeed stumble upon something
wonderful. His ability to place subjects in a magnetic trance,
inducing a crisis to affect a cure for all kinds of conditions, ought
to be commonly acknowledged as a triumph.

I will allow that some of his more outré methods — the use of
magnetised waters, of eating from magnetised plates or wearing
magnetised clothes, even of magnetising a tree and having men

cling to its branches — have all quite rightly been consigned to the dust heap of the past, and yet something remains. I venture to add that, if its efficacy had not been proved time and again, it would have long since perished along with its discoverer.

In short, I am a mesmerist, though one of a different dye. I do not believe in parlour tricks or devices, such as having the somnambule describe the contents of a letter the mesmerist has read or the taste of foods he eats; I would not have them travel by astral means to the moon and tell of the strange beings they find there. I do not believe in driving subjects into fits. I simply employ the patient's own faculties, the depths of their own mind, with gentleness and care, to assist them in finding peace and harmony of being. I have found particular success in placing those with brain disruptions or mind maladies into a magnetic sleep from which they emerge entirely restored. You may marvel — but then, it is marvellous!

Such is the tendency of my letter, and now to its purpose. I intend to pen a monograph, or perhaps even a series of monographs, showing the application of certain new theories about mesmerism (or monoideism, if you prefer, or hypnosis, as Baird would have it — both being more recently applied terms for what some believe to be a quite ancient art), giving certain facts and making studies of particular subjects. There is in certain quarters a degree of distrust, even accusations that some practitioners have carried out a dreadful imposture upon the public, and so I wish to try a new experiment, one that can leave its audience in no doubt. In its service, I wish to leave the selection of the subject to another party.

And so I come to my point, albeit by a somewhat circuitous route, which I beg you will forgive. There are certain requirements. I seek a patient whose spirits are in turmoil. An hysteric or a melancholic would do very well; someone in the grip of a delusion would adequately meet my need, though a certain calmness is required to enter a state of mesmeric somnambulism, so a raving maniac would not do, nor would an incurable. It would help also if the subject were not of the lowest classes, but one whose character and station would leave them above any accusation of play-acting for personal gain or satisfaction.

You will be aware of Doctor John Elliotson's exemplary experiments at University College Hospital, and his subsequent forced resignation. If he had not chosen subjects of an inferior type – two charity girls, whose actions were dismissed as tomfoolery – the cause of mesmerism would be far advanced in this country, nay, proclaimed from the rooftops as one of the Heralds of the Progress of our Age.

Finally, let me assure you that nothing untoward would arise from this experiment. It would be discreet – there would not be any need to publicly announce the name of the subject nor their whereabouts, so long as certain scientific men were able to verify my results. There would be no dramatics, no charlatanry. All would be calm and proper and decent, and carried out in the spirit of therapeutics, not theatrics. The subject will not be stuck with pins or injured in any way. Instead, we shall provide the relief of discussing their troubles in an entirely relaxed fashion, whilst partaking of my healing energies. Furthermore, it can all be executed under your very eye.

Naturally, since I am to benefit almost as much as would any patient you may offer, there would be no charge for my services at this time.

I write to you as an honoured professional with an enquiring mind and heart; one who is open to the idea of Progress and stimulated by the notion of Discovery; one who, in later days, would be able to say, 'I was there.'

Respectfully yours &cetera,

Professor Thaddeus Lumner

Case notes: *Mrs Victoria (Vita) Adelina Harleston*

Progress report: *4ᵗʰ September*

Mrs Harleston continues in indifferent health, characterised by listlessness, picking at her food and with a propensity towards solitude. I have removed her book, it being entirely unsuitable (poetry). Small doses of tincture of opium prescribed to settle the nerves. Cold-water bathing had little effect beyond a derangement of her senses shortly after, followed by episodes of crying for no reason, staring into space with an absent expression and disordered and irritable replies to an attendant's questions, entirely without provocation.

Doctor Nathaniel Kerner's Journal

4th September

What an infuriating place! Doctor Chettle has, without consultation or even mentioning it to me, decided to give opium to my patient, without a thought for her or how he undermines my position. I made the discovery only because I happened to require Mrs Harleston's case notes and found them missing from my rooms. At first I was all concern, thinking I had misplaced them or, worse still, left them with her, and I went to find Doctor Chettle with the notion that I should confess my error at once, only to find his study empty and the case notes open upon his desk. Furthermore, a new entry had been written therein.

What meddling! I was forced to remind myself of our respective positions to prevent myself at once going in search of him. I read the words again and decided he could not even have seen her. I was sure he could not, and yet here was a twisted account of my visit with her – derangement of her senses? It was hardly that, and if any man had the right to proclaim such a thing, it was I, not he.

But then, he must have had some report upon which to base such information. I suppose it must have been the attendant, Miss Scholes. Olive, I think she is called – an ill-grown, whey-faced creature, with hair so cropped she might be a pauper inmate rather than one of their keepers. A nasty, unsmiling sort of a body she is, and reading Doctor Chettle's comments, I am confirmed in my impression. She had not just been on hand, she had been ferreting away all that she could; she had been snooping. And the line about how the attendant had been spoken to, unprovoked − I could not doubt that Mrs Harleston had good reason and that it was the little chit who was at fault, though I suppose I should not write of it.

I was chastened when I took in the fact of Mrs Harleston's poetry book being removed. She would think I had reported on it − she would think I had ordered it myself. Possibly, I should have.

I went to Doctor Chettle's shelf, and there, out of place amid his own weighty tomes, was the little octavo volume. It was remarkably handsome, bound as it was in crimson morocco, with gilt-rolled pages and raised bands to the spine. I wished Doctor Chettle had not examined it before me and opened it at the flyleaf to see who had first given it to her, but the marbled endpapers were innocent of sentimental ink. I opened it further in, where the following lines caught my eye:

> Oh! then let us drain, while we may, draughts of pleasure,
> Which from passion like ours may unceasingly flow;
> Let us pass round the cup of love's bliss in full measure,
> And quaff the contents as our nectar below.

I fear such sentiments demonstrated that Doctor Chettle had indeed been right. My annoyance was not abated in the slightest by knowing it was precisely what I ought to have done. I would have preferred her to concur in my decision and hand the book to me herself; it would have retained the respect between us − perhaps, the trust. On some impulse I could not name, I brought the book with me to my rooms; it is before me as I make this record.

That was not all, however, for when I glanced at Doctor Chettle's desk again, I saw the book that had been half covered by Mrs Harleston's case notes. Electricity Made Plain and Useful was the title, the author John Wesley. My dismay has not abated since my first sight of it. I have no doubt that the proposed subject for any such *experimentation would be my patient. It was as foolish as the letter that had arrived for me that very morning; had the absurdity of it somehow clung to me?*

No doubt Doctor Chettle will say that electricity will dilate her capillaries and free the conduction about her nerves, but I consider it a novelty more fit for the fairground, where mountebanks shock unwary labourers for sixpence. The thought of Victoria Adelina Harleston, so elegant as she is, reduced to a twitching arrangement of limbs, out of the control of her own mind — of Doctor Chettle rubbing sparks all over her — I cannot countenance it. I know what it is, after all, to be reduced to an insensible shell laid out upon a table.

Respect, and conversation, and understanding: those, I am certain, are the keys to unlock whatever ails her. Pargeter's system of mildness, the sympathetic listening of Benjamin Rush — the power of gentle affection — these could surely achieve for my patient all that Doctor Chettle's tricks could not.

But my record is not yet complete, for I must confess that I was reduced to snooping myself. My blood being up, and with temptation before me, I did not stop at Doctor Chettle's desk. The door at the back of his study was ajar and I found myself wondering what lay within. It was but a short matter to walk to it and look inside.

I know now why his study desk is so neat. For there, in the inner sanctum, was business: papers strewn across a table, implements lying about, books left open. There were charts and lists and diagrams of the cranium from different angles, all minutely labelled. On the shelves, gleaming in the half-light coming from the door, were callipers of various sizes, well polished and shining, along with tapes and other measuring instruments. The walls were covered in lithographs, the portraits of men and women all looking down at me as if frowning on my intrusion. And here was the source of the chemical scents I had noticed previously: large glass jars full of murky liquid, half-obscured forms floating inside them.

I had not suspected Doctor Chettle of being one of those doctors. He had not spoken of this. It was not mentioned in any of his advertisements. For this was the room of a phrenologist, and a fanatical one at that. I had thought to find here a progressive institution, not one governed by a man who still believes that the contents of the mind, the character of man, can be read by close examination of the skull. It is a doctrine I had thought long exploded.

There were cupboards set beneath the shelves, but I did not try the doors to see if they were locked; that would have been too much. I did, however, examine the lithographs more minutely, identifying great men — Haydn, Robert Burns and Vice-Admiral Horatio Nelson — interspersed with images of the mad, with bulging eyes and misshapen heads. No doubt Chettle has tried to make out the shapes of their skulls to discover the root of their genius, or its opposite.

I decided to retreat and think on it afterwards. Indeed, I thought that setting it down in my journal might cast it in some more rational hue, though it has yet to do so. And now I must remember not to leave this record in plain sight, since Chettle has already entered my room to retrieve case notes; perhaps I should not have written so openly of thoughts that would better remain private.

At least the good doctor keeps his interests to himself. He has not attempted to push them upon me; he hides them away in a room the patients never enter. And if it were not for his phrenology, he would not keep to his own pursuits so often. He might not even need me here.

It still occurs to me to wonder, however, if the soothing and progressive name of 'asylum' would be better replaced by the older name of 'madhouse'.

Chapter Seven

Mrs Harleston sat in her chamber with her head hanging limply down, her chin almost touching her chest. Her face was almost covered by her disarrayed hair hanging loose and I could make out only her swollen, empurpled lips. The impression was disconcerting. This was not progress; it was not a cure. She must still be affected by Doctor Chettle's tincture of laudanum; she looked awful, even corpse-like.

She stirred and broke the effect. Slowly, she raised her eyes to mine. If they had been dark before, now they were black. They did not recognise me, and her pupils were slow to adjust. She did not smile.

I forced myself to greet her in what I hoped to be a reassuring manner.

'What dreams!' she murmured, not seeming to hear me. 'You were there, among the dead men. You could not move. You could not speak or lift a limb, and your *face* . . .'

A chill passed through me. I told myself she knew not what she was saying. How could she?

I cursed the foolishness that had brought her to such incoherent and unsuitable treatments, and I wondered if, after inducing such strange dreams with his medicines, Doctor Chettle would insist that she had become subject to visions and should be purged and bled forthwith.

I made to reassure Mrs Harleston, but a noise drew my attention and something knocked against my legs: young Peter Ambrose must have crawled in while I was in my reverie. Now he shuffled and sat at Mrs Harleston's feet, gazing at her with such loyal affection I could not doubt that she had shown him some kindness.

'Hey – brute!' His attendant hurried in after the boy and cuffed him about the ear until he yelped.

'Miss Scholes!' I reprimanded her, 'for shame!'

She turned her stolid face upon me.

'Please, do not refer to him as a brute. He is a child and he has a name. Pray, remember to use it.'

She dropped a clumsy, almost mocking curtsey before she withdrew.

I turned back to them both. Mrs Harleston had not moved; she appeared now to be peacefully sleeping. Peter turned his mournful visage towards me and I wondered at his situation. He was bereft of friends, occupations and family, without even his mother, and a wave of pity took me. I am rather ashamed that when I left the room, I reached out and patted the child on the head.

Chapter Eight

A new morning dawned pale and cold yet clear, and I began by taking a review of all the patients. Nellie Briggs inclined her head in agreement at my every utterance. Della Martin hissed. Lillian Smith remains sadly wasted in appearance and I ordered plentiful good food for her from the kitchens. Samuel Brewer told me he had been visited by the Prince Consort, who was to help reclaim the extensive estates due to him. He had recorded it all in extravagant detail in his journal, and obliged me to read his labyrinthine proclamations. I hoped that my own journal, upon later perusal, would not seem so wild.

I entered the dread word *Unchanged* in their case notes and then set about that task which weighed so heavily upon me. I made my way up the stairs and knocked on Doctor Chettle's door.

I found him within, staring into an open parcel with rags and crumpled paper emerging from the top. At first he did not appear to be aware of my presence, and then, without looking up, he said, 'Ah, Kerner. What do you make of this?'

I went closer. Almost lost within the rags was a cracked and yellowed dome; I had not at first glance recognised it as a skull. I forced myself to meet his eyes with a carefully blank expression.

Why did he show this to me now? Did he know I had intruded upon his secret room?

He bent to the parcel again, utterly rapt, and I tried to will my pulse steady.

'It has an almost rectangular hole in the lower part of the parietal bone, you see,' he said. 'Observe, if you will, the flattened and sloping features, the short nose. It is quite primitive. It has been trepanned – this hole was cut to let the spirits out. The wound is quite clean and deliberate, you see? No healing has taken place, so the procedure must have killed him. Isn't it splendid?'

Almost without a pause he looked up and said, 'I know on what business you have come. But the lady is much calmer and more docile now. A little mercury, I think, will increase the beneficial effect.'

More docile? I thought of Mrs Harleston's quiet dignity and again had to swallow my anger. 'Sir, I do not believe that her ailment is rooted in the physical,' I said. 'Spending time with her, engaging with her, would be a surer way to—'

'Electricity,' he said. 'It will realign her nerves, the source of her affliction. She will soon be quite cured and happy to leave us and be reunited with her husband. I have sent him a favourable report.' He raised his capacious eyebrows as if expecting my appreciation – as if it was something I should have thought of.

'But I am progressing with my method,' I said. 'I am winning her trust. To converse with her, I am sure, will uncover any evil that stands between her and sanity.'

'Evil? What, do you think her madness a demon, to be cast out?' He laughed. 'We are not in the Dark Ages.'

'That is not what I meant. I intend to listen to her problems, to reason with her—'

'Come, now! You would engage with madness? Have a discussion with it? Perhaps attempt to argue with it? You cannot reason with the irrational, with something that *has* no reason. That is why they call us alienists, because the mad are alienated from their own minds.'

'But something troubles her, and that, I believe, is the root of it. I am not sure that a diagnosis of hysteria—'

'They do not all present in just the same way. You should know that. Madness turns multifarious faces upon the world, and some of them are sly, but all must be dealt with – some more harshly than others.'

'Mrs Harleston is a refined creature.'

'I am fully aware of that. Have you not observed the care with which I am supervising her case?' His lips, half concealed behind his whiskers, had thinned.

'Of course. I simply do not believe—'

'In what, sir?' His voice turned cold.

Your diagnosis was my answer, but of course I could not say such a thing. I felt the full weight of the institution around me – its high gates, its barred doors, the solidity of its walls – and for a moment I sensed perhaps the merest hint of what she must feel: helpless. If I said the words, I would be ejected from this place. She would be alone, with only Peter Ambrose to show her any kindness at all.

'Forgive me. As you rightly say, we have had no real opportunity to let your asylum do its work. But with my sole attention, she might respond enough to show her husband that he should let it continue – even to have her reside here a little longer.'

Chettle caught his breath. 'And her treatment?'

'I shall attempt to reach her by examining her past, her behaviour, her future – in a calm and *docile* fashion. Reason shall battle against madness. Perhaps I may have the opportunity to try?'

'You have every opportunity. You are her physician.'

'But I should like to set aside all physical remedies for the duration, lest they jolt her from the process. Unless we agree together that such a course would be best, of course. It would naturally be for her physicians to decide.'

He narrowed his eyes and once again I pictured myself turned out of my new home. Perhaps I should soon find myself upon my mother's threshold, bag in hand. How disappointed she would be – and I – and my father!

Doctor Chettle leaned over his desk, across from that ages-dead and empty skull, and fixed me with a piercing glare.

'Very well. You may attempt your *method*, as you call it, though I am not certain it deserves the name. In any event, it will take a little time for my frictional machine to arrive. Then you will surely be able to see that she is in need of more than you can offer and you will harden yourself to administer such treatments as will see her restored to her home and willing to do her duty.'

He was serious, then, about using electricity. My flash of triumph was overwhelmed by dismay, and a great and terrible responsibility settled upon my shoulders. I had not before con-sidered its weight. But she could not have such treatment. Mrs Harleston was no unconscious body to be laid out upon a table to be toyed with. She was not a skull to be weighed and measured. I thought of the look in her eyes when I had seen her last, their curious, unreadable depths, and the words she had spoken: *You were there, among the dead men.* That was surely only the effect of the opium; now the poppy dreams could dissipate and she would be herself again. She would make no more strange pronounce-ments. She would learn to trust and confide in me – for she *must*.

Doctor Chettle took up his skull again and I could no longer see his expression, only his extravagance of beard and moustache and whiskers. I wondered, somewhat uncharitably, why he went to such efforts to conceal his features if their form were truly the key to a man's character.

It came as no little relief to leave him and his obsession with the past and turn instead to the living patients below. Now we would see what common sense could do. My work could truly begin.

As I entered Mrs Harleston's room I almost collided with Miss Scholes, who was staring down with something like satisfaction at the towel she held. A pair of scissors rested upon it, along with clippings of lustrous brown hair. I nodded in response to her 'Good day,' fancying she relished her work a little too much, but fortunately, Mrs Harleston looked much as she had. Even Scholes, I supposed, would not risk Mr Harleston's wrath by ruining such a crowning glory as Mrs Harleston's. Her locks now framed her face in so natural a way I could not help thinking it was finer than any primping with perfumes and bandolines could achieve.

She raised her head rather languorously – perhaps Doctor Chettle's drug had not yet worn off? Although she said 'Good morning' in a civilised fashion and I recalled myself enough to return her greeting.

I sat in the chair facing hers and took from my pocket that which I had brought for her. It was a small volume, cloth-bound in a simple green, far less grand than her own beloved book, but she took it as delicately as if it were a bird. It was poetry by Robert Browning, one of a two-volume edition that had been published the previous year, entitled *Men and Women*.

She opened it at the flyleaf and read quietly, 'To Nathaniel, from your mother. Ardent affection and love always.'

I said, 'I thought you might like to peruse the poems in your quiet hours.'

'Browning.' She spoke softly, almost with reverence, although I did think I perceived her tone to be tempered with amusement.

I suddenly felt perhaps this was too intimate, that I had placed something of myself in her hands, and I added airily, 'It may be of some little interest to you.'

'It shall,' she said, and there we left it and moved to other matters.

I had decided that open honesty would be the way to gain her trust. The Quakers treated their patients with Reason, and I would do the same. 'I wish you to enjoy all the peace that Crakethorne can provide,' I said. 'Nothing shall trouble you or disturb you, and we may take this time to discuss what has done so in the past.'

Her expression did not change.

'Perhaps we could begin with the omnibus, and your impulse to flee your husband's side.'

She stirred.

'Pray, do not alarm yourself. There is no need. Remember: to be able to converse evenly and without excess of emotion is the very outward sign of sanity.'

'Do I not appear sane?'

I concurred that she did and expressed a hope that she would continue to do so. At that, she compressed her lips so tightly their rosiness paled.

'We could discuss your position as a wife, your duties and suchlike. Were there a great many calls upon your time as the presiding lady of Milford Lodge?'

I thought her gaze had become a little more distant. Would she continue evasive, moving ever further from me? But then she spoke, in a voice so sweet and clear I doubted my first impression.

'I will tell you something,' she said, 'that has preyed upon my mind of late. Perhaps you might see some reason in it where I cannot.'

'Please,' I said, leaning a little towards her in encouragement. 'Anything.'

'My father's ruling passion was botany. Like so many others, he was, in an amateur way, quite caught up with it. Our garden was long and rambling and when I was some fifteen years of age, he built a hothouse at its furthest extremity.'

I was a little disappointed, for how could this be relevant? But I had resolved to listen, to ensure my patients' voices were heard, and so I remained silent, and Mrs Harleston went on in her soft, musical voice, 'He filled it with beautiful things – or at least, he told me they were beautiful. His especial interest was vespertine plants: those that open only at dusk, and so his was a moonlight garden – and how terribly romantic I thought that sounded.

'He described the wonderful flora therein: night-blooming jasmine, which had, so he claimed, a most intoxicating scent in the evening; horn of plenty or devil's trumpet, which opens, said Papa, into an extravagant display; moonflowers, which he described as luminous in the half-light; four o'clocks; queen of the night and Nottingham catchfly, with fragrant petals that open three nights in a row before dying. He told me about them all, but I did not see them in their full beauty.'

I could not but help interject, 'Why ever not?'

'Oh, I could view them during the day. I saw them tight-furled, hiding their glories from the sun. I smelled the jasmine before it released its fragrance into the air and fancied I caught some hint of what that might be. I peered at the buds, closed like fists, and tried to make out the colours lying within. Papa did not think it seemly, you see, for a young lady to go into a garden after sunset, spoiling her skirts and tripping over stones. He said it was not proper. He liked me at home and silent, and should I protest such a prison, he would quiet me with laudanum.'

She paused. 'Can you imagine having within your care such fabulous blooms and never allowing them to be admired?'

'It is perhaps a little . . . *careful*,' I agreed. 'But surely you must have attended many evening engagements? And his was a fatherly concern, surely, out of love for you, was it not?'

'Oh, yes, he cared for me very greatly. He would not have me scratch so much as a finger upon a thorn. He would have me perfect whenever he chose to display me.'

Her gaze had gone distant again; she stroked my little book with her fingertips. Then she said, 'How much of a woman's life, do you think, is spent being buried alive?' She looked up at the bars laid over her window.

I attempted to draw her from such a painful subject, and such unwelcome memories, to more pertinent matters. 'Perhaps, if you are ready, we could discuss the incident of the omnibus? It is important, I think, to reach the heart of it.'

'I am tired.'

'We must try. I do not think that you conceive—'

'Why? Because my husband wishes to hear of it? I do not think he would like what he heard.'

'Oh? Why is that?'

She turned her face from mine and shook her head. Then she insisted she must rest and rose from her chair. How provoking it was! If only she would open herself to me fully . . . but I must find ways to draw her out, for she could not drift here indefinitely. I must push harder, although always with sensitivity. I must believe she had not passed too far into the mire of madness to be lost to me; that she remained within my reach.

Case notes: *Mrs Victoria (Vita) Adelina Harleston*

Patient continues calm and a trifle subdued. Will engage in rational conversation on many subjects other than her hysterical fit of August. Sleeps well and eats simple, plain food, as suggested. She has grown a little thin about the face, either through insufficient sustenance or concealed anxiety. Physical signs are normal. Inclination towards solitude is unlikely to be leavened by mixing with our current patients. A little light reading may improve her situation.

Chapter Nine

A little light reading may improve her situation. I set down the words, wondering what Doctor Chettle would make of them. And yet I could justify the Browning, I think; it must surely be better than spending so many hours in solitude, turning only inward. That poet's gentle words would not only help dispel her *ennui* but make her feel a little less lonely. For lonely I am certain she must be, being so often in her room, looking out of her window – or at the bars covering it.

In an attempt to alleviate the lack of society provided by her fellow sufferers and her attendants, I had decided to walk with her into the grounds, and so we set out, meandering between the slanting hawthorns. I surmised that the deformed and stunted growths were the source of the word 'thorn' in 'Crakethorne'; and Doctor Chettle had been a little precipitous in describing his rose garden, for it transpired that he had not yet planted any such blooms. It was an apt name nonetheless, and surrounded as we were by the rasping of crows, the impression was complete.

I intended to direct our steps towards the Crow Garden. It would be the first time Mrs Harleston had been there since her dousing in the pool and I wished to see her reaction.

Who were they who stood all about – who watched, yet had no faces?

I wanted to see if her wild words had been provoked by her rough treatment, or if there was some other cause. I hoped to glimpse what lay beneath her unruffled surface.

When I turned to her I found she was observing me quite closely, her expression half wry amusement and half concern. I returned my thoughts to the present. We had reached the edge of the graves and now all about us were the birds, gliding down as if falling to earth, their notched wings spread wide. One caught a nearby branch with strong, scaly claws. Its gaze did not dart around but was fixed and staring. Its eyes were deeply black and very bright, and it did not make a sound. I blinked and saw more of them, settling in the trees or upon the unmarked grey stones that were all that remained of the dead.

I could not think where they had come from so silently, and what she had said returned to me again – her words about *watchers*. Perhaps she had been affected by the uncanny impression of their gleaming eyes?

She turned to me, smiling brightly. 'Is this your Crow Garden?'

'I believe that is what the patients call it.'

'And yet *I* did not.' She paused. 'Did you know that the ancient Greeks thought crows dwelt in the underworld?'

'I did, indeed. It was the god Apollo who turned them black. Crows were once white, or so it is said. There are several tales: one says that he scorched them for telling a falsehood. Later, he discovered they had spoken true and in recompense, he made them sacred. Thus did they become the harbingers of death.'

'Or spirits of the dead. I believe that is what they think, in these parts.'

I looked at her, startled, but she went on, 'Apollo was also the god of medicine, you know. Of healing.'

I inclined my head. 'And of poetry.'

She reached up and ran her fingers through the shrivelled

brown leaves of an oak tree, soon to fall, and she recited the lines:

> *'And having thus created me,*
> *Thus rooted me, he bade me grow,*
> *Guiltless forever, like a tree*
> *That buds and blooms, nor seeks to know*
> *The law by which it prospers so.'*

'Browning,' I said, with warmth. I knew the lines; they were from my own little book, from a poem about Johannes Agricola. Then I remembered what followed:

> *But sure that thought and word and deed*
> *All go to swell his love for me*

At least she had stopped before those lines. And I was glad that she had gained some innocent pleasure from my book – it was a sign of trust too, perhaps even simple friendship, that she had committed them to heart. I wished to reciprocate somehow and I recollected my own recent nocturnal reading. I often clasped at night her little volume of Byron, and as I saw her standing there, cast into the dappled shade of the tree, I found myself saying:

> *'She walks in beauty, like the night*
> *Of cloudless climes and starry skies;*
> *And all that's best of dark and bright*
> *Meet in her aspect and her eyes.'*

Her expression returned me to myself. Whatever had I been thinking? Such a verse was surely not apposite. I cast about for another subject but there was nothing I could fix upon; we were quite alone, in a garden where no roses grew.

I thought of the Greek myths she had struck upon and recalled the story the crows had told Apollo: that the maiden he loved had been faithless, that she loved someone other than he to whom she was committed. He had trusted her, assumed it a lie and punished the crows unfairly. I did not think, as a subject, that it would do at all.

I waved my hand, encompassing the trees, the graves and, less fortunately, the flash of water in which she had been doused. 'The poets tell so wonderfully of nature, do they not?'

Mrs Harleston looked perplexed, as well she might. But she walked on and I moved with her, skirting the sad mounds in their rows until we reached the very edge of the water. I hoped it would not be too much for her, but she looked quietly at the opaque surface.

'We would not bring you to any harm,' I said.

She looked surprised. 'No,' she replied. 'I do not believe that to be *your* intention, Doctor Kerner.'

'That could never be our purpose – mine, or that of anyone else here. We wish to see you well and happy, as soon as—'

'As my husband wishes it?' She grimaced. 'Is that why they would quiet me with their medicines? Is that why they poured freezing water on my head, to make me do whatever they require of me?'

That was an unfortunate leap, particularly as it chimed so nearly with my own thoughts on that dreadful day.

Then she said, 'Did you know that Perry wished to put me in Bedlam?'

It took me a moment to realise that she spoke of Peregrine Harleston. 'I did not.'

'He chose it especially. It is known to be rather behind current practice, even as it stands in these establishments, is it not?'

I had to admit that she was correct. And I wondered for a moment if that was why Crakethorne had also been chosen, because it lingered behind the best in current practice; perhaps Doctor Chettle's proclivities were known to everyone except me. Was that why she had been torn from her gentle spa and sent to the rough north?

'He wished them to try everything,' she said. 'I heard him say so. And they do try everything there, don't they? Restraints, even. I have heard of women whose treatments are designed only to make them docile and dutiful before they are restored to the bosom of their families.'

'You cannot think that to be the case here,' I exclaimed. 'Crakethorne is not Bedlam. I dare say your husband is only anxious to—'

'Anxious? I stand accused of anxiety also, do I not? Is my husband *anxious* to the point of straining his nerves? Does it drive him to madness? You do not have to answer. Society would deem it otherwise, of that I am quite certain. But did you know that the Board of Governors at that veritable Institution would not admit me?'

'I did not.' I met her eye. Had she taken their refusal for proof of her sanity? 'But that Institution takes very few, I believe. There are always many more patients awaiting admittance at the public asylums than there are places. I imagine they thought your case more suited to a private establishment.'

We stood in silence with the sad graves at our backs. Perhaps I had made a mistake in bringing her here. She seemed to have forgotten her odd words after her treatment; it was I who was discomfited. I must endeavour to assert Reason once more.

'Perhaps we could turn to the cause of your being here,' I said. 'You may consider me your confidant. It may be a relief to your heart to lighten yourself of what burdens you, and I am happy—'

'Happy!' She turned to me; her eyes flashed.

'I did not mean—'

'Happy,' she said once more, looking at the dead leaves cast at her feet, her voice so mournful and so lost I almost could not bear it. But I was her physician; I *had* to bear it. An image rose before me: Doctor Chettle, leaning over her. She was lying on a table. She could not move for the straps that bound her; she could not speak for the wooden spoon gripped between her teeth. And her fine features – those delicately formed lips, the lovely curve of her cheek – were all transformed in a moment; she writhed, becoming something else, something *less*, as the electricity took her and she twitched and convulsed in its power.

I felt the soft touch of a hand on my cheek, then it was gone. I opened my eyes to see her standing close by, staring into my face. 'What is it?' she asked. 'What is it that you see?'

I could not move. I could not speak.

'Doctor Kerner.' She whispered my name, and there was so much in the way she spoke; but receiving no answer she whirled and walked away from me.

I watched her go, the weeping boughs of the trees making it appear that she was vanishing into a tunnel. And the crows departed at last, fleeing at her approach; all that remained was the beating of their wings, resounding about my ears with the mocking sound of hands clapping.

Chapter Ten

The next day, I found Mrs Harleston in her usual place and engaged in her usual occupation: reading the book I had given her. I asked which poem she had reached, and she glanced up and read to me:

'Round and round, like a dance of snow
In a dazzling drift, as its guardians, go
Floating the women faded for ages,
Sculptured in stone, on the poet's pages.
Then follow women fresh and gay,
Living and loving and loved to-day.'

'"Women and Roses",' I exclaimed. 'A lovely poem.' And it was a lovely sentiment for her to read, one that would perhaps put her in mind of her husband. I decided to recite something back to her – it could be a private game between us, strengthening our bond as physician and patient – but I hesitated over my choice, realising of a sudden that Browning could be a little more sensuous than I had heretofore supposed. *Drink but once and die!* – that would not do – nor would *Eyes in your eyes, lips on your lips!*

Then it came to me:

Roses will bloom nor want beholders,
Sprung from the dust where our flesh moulders.
What shall arrive with the cycle's change?
A novel grace and a beauty strange.
I will make an Eve, be the artist that began her,
Shaped her to his mind . . .

Ah, but that was altogether tactless! At least I had not recited
it aloud. That 'Shaped her to his mind' rather reminded me of
mesmerism and I recalled, uncomfortably, that my favourite poet
had penned verse about that too:

Have and hold, then and there,
Her, from head to foot . . .

I found I could remember almost word for word the content
of the letter I had received from Professor Lumner: *we shall provide
the relief of discussing their troubles in an entirely relaxed fashion* . . .

It was some years since 'mesmeric mania' had swept the nation.
There had been lectures and magnetic conversaziones, showmen
demonstrating their somnambules, gaudy displays in meeting
rooms and temperance halls, a tide of pamphlets and chapbooks
and of course, accusations of the worst kinds of mendacity and
deception.

And I recalled of a sudden that medical procedures had been
carried out under its influence: operations that had taken place
without chloroform or ether, and yet the patients had felt no pain.

I looked at Mrs Harleston. She met my gaze quite calmly and
I wondered what lay beneath her composed and lovely visage.

'I know you do not wish to discuss the source of your illness,'

I said, 'but there is perhaps another way, and I am beginning to wonder if it might be of help.'

She remained silent and I was encouraged by that silence; it was easier than her words had been. And I wondered then why the Professor had chosen to approach Crakethorne. Did he too wish to make progress for the benefit of humankind – had he tried everywhere else, and found their doors closed against him?

'I am in possession of a letter of introduction from a gentleman who thinks he can help you.'

'How so? Is this gentleman in possession of thumbscrews?'

'Of course not. It is by relaxation, only that. He is a therapeutic magnetiser.' I did not wish to use the word 'mesmerist', although in the next moment she said it herself, in tones of deepest disgust.

'This *mesmerist* – is he to make a marionette of me? Will he stick pins in my arm?'

I flinched at that. 'Please be assured he would do no such thing. It is nothing like the public demonstrations. It would all be quiet and dignified, like falling asleep.'

'And if I do not *wish* to fall asleep? Is my liberty to be curtailed in such a manner, from within as well as without? I beg you: I have no say in anything; I never did. I have no control even over my physical being. I . . . I left my father's house because of it, and now this – this *asylum* – must be enough! I cannot go where I will. You cannot seek to control my mind, also – my soul, even! It is all I have.'

'There is no question of interfering with your soul.' I had almost said 'mind', but could hardly do so, since that was in fact my very purpose. I smiled to show her what a silly notion it was, how inconsequential her fears. 'I simply wish to provide you with the release of unhindered conversation.'

I fancied I understood her reluctance better than anyone.

If anyone should understand the power of words to heal – or indeed, to harm – it was I.

She closed her eyes. When she opened them again, they were full not of anger, but fear. 'I shall tell you, if I must,' she said. 'I will tell you about the omnibus, about everything. Only, please, spare me that. I cannot enter a trance – I really cannot. I cannot lose control of my own self. I *will* not!'

I stared. Was it all to be within my grasp, after all? I could not read the answer in her eyes. She simply waited, as if for my assurance that I would not press it upon her, but I did not speak. Even now, she betrayed the turmoil within. Was it all to be so unexpectedly laid naked before me?

She looked away with a little cry. And then, gazing at something far distant, she began to speak.

'I was always a little afraid of my husband, though I do not know why. He never struck me. It is only that he has a way of exerting his dominance – you felt it, did you not? Even on so short a meeting you will have. He is forceful, and he was so very decided that I must be his wife, so insistent, that I felt myself shrinking before him from the beginning.

'He was married before; did you know that?'

I affirmed that she had mentioned it, but I offered no further comment. I did not wish to stem her flow.

'His first wife had a child. She too had been married before – I believe her husband had been something in the East India Company; at any rate, he died in Madras of a gastric fever that progressed to his brain. She was left widowed and wealthy and still a beauty by all accounts.'

By all accounts? But she had seen the lady herself, had she not? It felt a careless way of speaking of her.

'Perry married her some four years afterwards,' Mrs Harleston continued matter-of-factly; there was nothing of jealousy in her tone. 'She would not have him before that, for all he had pressed for it. She did not think it decent. He needed money, I believe, his estate being much encumbered. She made it a condition of the match that he adopt her son as his heir.

'He had been rather dictated to by women then, I suppose. He inherited Milford from an aunt who insisted he take her name, Russell, into his own. For all that was also a condition, he has already begun to drop it, as quietly as he may.

'So the lady died and Perry was left with a small boy – not his, motherless, but tied to him. Some would have called it a blessing, others a burden; either way it was not to last, for before long the child too was called to his Maker. He was buried in the same coffin as his mother. It was a terrible thing; all felt it – but they did not know all.'

I waited for her to continue, wondering where her tale would lead.

'I shall tell you of the day of which you are so curious – the day I left him. We were in town for the Season, which was a little trying for Perry, who had no use for parties and dinners, since he had acquired his new wife already. He was impatient for the grouse shooting to begin so that we could return to the country without being dull. But we set out that morning to visit the Burlington Arcade. He wished to obtain a stiff collar from Drew's, and I planned to call at a corsetière. It was quite ordinary. We alighted from our carriage on Piccadilly, near that casket of curiosities, the Egyptian Hall, and strolled to the arcade. It was summer, but the day was as dull as everything else – not cold, not warm. We turned in at the promenade, escaping the horse-traffic and dirt, and I said to Perry I would just look in at Hancock's the jewellers. I did not reach it, however, for I saw that one of the shops was filled with a display of oil paintings.

'I do not entirely remember going in; I simply found myself

among the portraits of people I did not know, and some whom I did: our Queen of course, and King William the Fourth, and the Duke of Wellington – and then I stopped, because from the corner of my eye, I saw quite plainly my grandmama.'

'Quite plainly?' I interposed. 'From the corner of your eye?'

'Yes,' she said. 'I may not have been looking at her directly but I knew it was my grandmama all the same, because as I passed, she turned and watched me go. When I turned to meet her, she had vanished.'

She paused as if expecting some further objection, but I made none. She already knew what I would say. That her crisis had been preceded by some visual hallucination surprised me not at all; it was in keeping with her diagnosis.

'But I knew she remained by my side. I heard her.'

An auditory hallucination also? It was a recurrence of what she had suffered in childhood; that was not promising. 'What did she say?'

'She told me to get out, at once and without hesitation. And I saw in my mind's eye, as if surrounded by mist, an omnibus pulled over to the side of the road. The conductor had seen a young man likely to board and I knew even at that moment that this was real. The omnibus would be by the entrance to the arcade, really engaged in touting for his business.

'I have told you before how I trusted my grandmother. At that moment, believing her to be in a realm that could admit no falsity, I did as she said. I hurried to the door, and I think I rushed along the walkway – yes, I am rather afraid I did. But there was the omnibus, just as I had seen it in my mind. The conductor wore a look of disgust; he had gained no fare after all, and the young man I had envisioned was walking away down the street.'

'The same man? But you did not see his face?'

She acknowledged that she had not, but continued as if it did not signify, 'The conductor was surprised, of course, when I hurried over. I am not in the habit of taking omnibuses, Doctor Kerner, and I felt all the impropriety of it, and yet this is what my grandmama had wished me to do, so I did it. I balked at taking a seat within, however; three rough men sat there, smoking their pipes, and the straw covering the boards was filthy. But I saw there was a secluded compartment, so I stepped in and pulled the door closed after me. It was so narrow it crushed my skirts. Much of the light was shut out and I was trapped inside, and I had no idea why I was there or what I was doing.'

'You must have been frightened.'

'Oddly, no, I was not afraid. But I was most uncomfortable. The compartment was like a coffin turned upright. It jolted as the horses started away and I heard the conductor's cry, though I could not make out his words. I was confined and alone, free from prying eyes and any contact at all, when I felt a presence in the compartment. Oh, I know you will say it was my imagination, but in the same way that walking into an empty room feels different to entering one that is occupied, I knew that someone was there. I heard no breathing and there came no whisper, but I *knew*.

'Then I felt my skirts pressed down, as if someone was patting at them. The sensation did not cease; instead it slowly moved its way upward until something touched my waist and found my arm; then something seized my hand.

'I was too frightened to draw away. It grasped for my fingers, gripping tighter, so tightly — and it was *cold*. There was a little hand in mine, a child's hand, and there was no life in its touch.'

She met my eyes. 'I might have shrieked. I am not sure what I did. But the certainty grew upon me, then and since, that I knew who the child was — confined to a coffin, just as he *had* been. I think he had taken me for his mother.'

I wished to assure her it was impossible, that she had suffered some hallucination conjured by her odd situation, but it did not seem enough.

She broke our gaze. 'It was him,' she said. 'Perry's son. I do not believe he was dead when he was buried. I think he awoke in the dark, crammed into his mother's coffin, and finding her there, he felt for her hand and found . . . Oh, what horror must he have found? What must his feelings have been? She so cold, and all he wanted to do was cling to her—'

'It is all right,' I began, but she flung out her arm in repudiation.

'It is *not* all right – do you not see? *He* had him placed there, rushing to inter the child in the arms of a corpse because he knew that her coffin had lain in the mortuary for two days already – those requisite two days to ensure that none would be buried alive while lost to consciousness through illness, or – or poison! He knew it would soon be committed to the ground and he could be rid for ever of a child not his.'

So here was her delusion. It was worse than I could have imagined.

'They stopped the omnibus, of course,' she went on. 'You will know the rest. My husband was called for and they returned me to him, his poor, ailing, hysterical wife. I accused him; he said I was mad. The weight of Society and authority was all on his side, and what proof could I offer?'

I did not know where to begin. I glanced around me, seeing the sane and rational world. There was Reality; and her story resembled it so very neatly, in everything but Truth. So delusions are built. At least, now, she had revealed it to me.

'I am certain we can resolve this,' I said. 'There is a reasonable explanation, I am sure. For now, a sedative draught and a little sleep will revive you, and then we may discuss this further. I hope that speaking of it has provided you with some relief.'

'Relief!' She laughed, and everything was in that laugh: her fear and horror of her husband, her desire never to return to him – and, yes, the tinge of madness. At least Doctor Chettle was not present, for his frictional machine might arrive at any moment and, seeing her, how would he resist? But Olive Scholes, his little informant, was standing by the wall, her arms crossed before her. In her eyes was the judgement of the world. I resolved I must protect Mrs Harleston from it as far as I possibly could.

Chapter Eleven

When Mrs Harleston had rested, I went to see her again. I found her quietly occupied in sewing in the day-room under the watchful eye of Miss Scholes. She looked calmer and more lovely than ever, the light caressing her hair and spilling across her work. I wished I could dismiss her attendant, not wanting her vulgar ears to hear our discourse, but of course, that would have been irregular. Instead I drew up a chair and turned my back upon the girl. Mrs Harleston raised her eyes to my own. Hers were in shadow, yet so lucent they could not be dimmed by mere shade. Again, she put me in mind of one of the poems she had placed into my hands:

> And on that cheek, and o'er that brow,
> So soft, so calm, yet eloquent,
> The smiles that win, the tints that glow,
> But tell of days in goodness spent

I could only hope that, with me at her side, the next part could also be achieved:

A mind at peace with all below,
A heart whose love is innocent!

I said, in a low tone, 'I wonder if you could allow me to discuss your earlier disclosures? I think I can place quite a different cast upon them.'

A bow of her head was enough, and so I continued, 'You had for some time, perhaps always, been disinclined to your husband's company. Perhaps you even harboured notions of being free of him, although your conscious mind would not have allowed that; your sense of duty would have quelled it. Yet your longings' – she raised her eyes, just for a moment – 'expressed themselves in a vision brought on by the occasion of having to appear in public by his side.'

I waited, but she did not look up again, though I very much would have liked to have seen her expression.

'And a vision in such a form – someone so trusted as your grandmama urging you to leave him, after having encouraged you to do the opposite – why, surely it would remove the dreadful dilemma in which you found yourself. You had to flee, whether or not it accorded with your own wishes. Your choice in the matter had been removed.

'You found yourself enclosed in a coffin-shaped compartment, chilled by the cool air rushing past, with the idea of a deceased wife and son in your mind. It is not surprising that so dreadful a scene presented itself to your imagination. And if your husband were a monster, well, you had to leave him. You could have your secret desire.'

She lifted her head and at last I saw the blaze of fury concentrated in her face. 'How dare you? How can you – or anyone – suggest I would do such a thing – that I would invent such an awful story, all because I was undutiful and fickle, that I was ruled by caprice?'

I wanted to comfort her, but the battleground was upon me; here was Lunacy raising its face to mine, controlling her lovely features. I forced myself to meet her anger with the quiet calm of Reason.

'Could you not admit that you might have been mistaken? Do you not realise that is the way to free yourself of this—'

'This what? This living *tomb* in which I find myself?' She inhaled deeply. 'Do you think I do not realise that all Society requires of me is to say that I was wrong – that it was a trying day and my nerves were agitated and the fit is now behind me? To look upon my husband and call a monster good? I believe in Truth, Doctor Kerner. Is that not more important than Falsehood? For any such declaration must be so. Is *that* not madness?'

'It is the way things are. It is reality. I beg you to accept it. Pray ask yourself, if your husband is so wicked, why would he send you here? Would he not shut you away so that your precipitate accusations could never reach the world's ears? But no – instead he conveyed you here to me – to *us*, and by his own hand at that. I do believe he wishes more than anything to see you cured, so that you may return to him.'

She looked up at the ceiling as if she might find there an answer. And yet, as was the way with delusions – they could have a fearsome inner logic – she did.

'Why should he wish to have a wife, only to keep her locked away? He keeps nothing that is not useful. He would shoot a dog he reared from birth if it no longer possessed teeth. How much more does he require of a wife? He wishes me to think myself insane; he *wishes* me to deny everything. It is not enough that he paints me mad and thus makes the world reject my notions utterly. No, he must also possess my mind.

'In one respect I believe you have the right of it: he hopes I *will* be cured – if by which you mean, broken utterly and made a stranger to my own thoughts. If I can forget what he has done, if I can forgive such a dreadful act, why, perhaps then his own conscience may forgive him! Perhaps he thinks that I will come to love him and be in his home again – in his bed – and he may beget another heir on me, one more to his liking!'

I flinched at her bluntness. She could not have intended to say such things; the words had surely escaped her in her passion. I took her hand and pressed it. It was perhaps not altogether proper, but I wanted her to know I would support her, that I might be trusted as her confidant and friend. If only it were a simple matter to refigure her mind – not physically, not by Doctor Chettle's electricity, but from within.

I found myself saying, 'The mesmerist would help you see all this more clearly. I will write to him.'

She drew away from me. 'But I told you all – I thought, if I did . . . I *cannot* see him, I *must* not.'

I took back my hand, emptied of the warmth of hers, and I opened my mouth to tell her I had made no such promise, but it would have seemed like weakness somehow, and I was her doctor. I said simply, 'It will all be all right again soon. That is all my desire for you, you know.'

Was it scorn or fury I saw on her face? I heard the attendant shifting her feet behind me and I felt myself flushing, though I knew not why.

'I shall be present continually,' I told her. 'I shall ensure that all is as it should be and that nothing is done to upset you.'

Of course, I had already upset her, and I could see no way to avert it, for truly, she could not decide for herself: her mind, her body, her very being were all in my care, and I must do something before Doctor Chettle or anyone else parted her from me.

I was decided: Professor Lumner might be able to help her; some might say he already had, for the mere mention of him had prompted her confidences. Now he could assist me in nurturing her mind — and I could prove my method. I would show that conversation and exploring together the formation of delusionary ideas was the way to cast them out, just like the demons of old. My talking cure might even become the subject of a book of my own; in future, doctors might refer to my methods and try to emulate my ways. Perhaps it could improve the treatment of all who were so afflicted — and restore the name of Kerner! I could make my father proud at last.

Unseen, her hand snaked out and grasped my arm. 'The voices,' she said. 'I am so afraid they will come back — please, do not allow it. I have so carefully constructed a door against them. Do not allow him to throw it wide.'

I was astonished. 'Voices?'

'Those from my childhood — I often fell into a kind of trance when it happened. My mother hated it; it frightened her. It frightened me too. I don't want to be like that again. I don't want to hear the things they tell me.'

'And yet,' I said gently, 'you said you knew the voices in your head to be nonsense. Your grandmama's too — they were merely an echo of the same malady, do you not see? Do you not believe them to be an illusion, a phantasm conjured by the brain?'

She bit her lip and turning away, picked up her sewing and stabbed frantically at the fabric with her needle. Crimson bloomed through the little circle where she had impaled the hand holding the frame; it spread, casting its ruin through the whole.

Miss Scholes stepped in at once, grasping the work and pulling it away from her. 'None o' that,' she said.

I opened my mouth to caution the girl, and yet Mrs Harleston was indeed overcome, for she let it go and covered her eyes.

'*Doctor*,' said the attendant, in a voice that made it plain I was required to act, and I dare say she was right. I ordered a sedative and left her under such tender care as Olive Scholes could offer, and I went to see about providing a treatment that I hoped would free her from her woes for ever.

Chapter Twelve

I found Doctor Chettle in his rooms and much as usual, although his inner sanctum had now crept into the outer. He was poring over an intricate diagram of the human skull, comparing it with the trepanned specimen I had seen before. I could have no comment to make when the letter grasped in my own hand must rival his affairs in eccentricity. His eyes dulled at my intrusion, but shone out again when I gave the reason. I held out Professor Lumner's letter, but he did not take it.

'Mesmerised!' he said. 'There would be as much efficacy in ducking her for a witch.' He laughed, and in that laugh I felt all the smallness of my position.

'I cannot countenance it. To begin, it is supposed to be impossible to hypnotise the insane, since their minds are too disordered. Then there is the reputation of such men! A libidinous crew – there was one in France, you know, who used his "art" to seduce a banker's daughter. And what kind of person would wish to possess such influence over a vulnerable female? It would be unconscionable.'

I scarcely knew how to reply to that – and to worry over any risk to the lady when he had so firmly stated it could not possibly work appeared to me to be muddle-headed. But of course I did not say so. That paled in comparison to the idea of having to retract my words to Mrs Harleston.

'The lady is already married,' was my response, 'so there could be no financial purpose in seduction. It is quite different.'

'Charles Dickens was a believer, you know,' Chettle said, as if he had not heard my words. 'Oh, yes; he once magnetised his wife into hysterics inside six minutes.'

'This gentleman is an experienced practitioner,' I said, 'neither showman nor dabbler. He is not an amateur. It would be quite calm and dignified.' An idea occurred to me and I pointed out one of his books: *Human Physiology*. 'That author, Doctor Elliotson, found his patients benefited from short courses of mesmerism, I believe.'

Doctor Chettle sighed and sat back in his chair. 'I was there, you know.'

'I beg your pardon?'

'When John Elliotson began his demonstrations at University College Hospital. It was, oh, 1838. You won't remember, I suppose. You would have been a child.'

He was correct: I *had* been a child. It was soon after that date when my father began his own experiments, with me as his subject.

'He used their lecture theatres,' Doctor Chettle went on, 'although no one had given permission. He demonstrated two charity girls there, the Okeys. Men of a decent class of Society arranged their limbs like puppets. They forced snuff up their noses to see if they would sneeze whilst being told they were smelling roses. The girls' personalities changed – they laughed and joked, became brazen and impertinent. It was quite convincing and very improper, and if that is the future of medicine—'

I flinched, wondering if Elliotson had also stuck pins in their arms, but Doctor Chettle had not finished; he went on, 'A short time afterwards, the girls were put to a test. They failed to pick out a glass of water that had been magnetised. Their arms were paralysed at the touch of a coin which had not been magnetised at all. It was all a pretence. And now you wish to bring this exploded theorem into my asylum?'

My mouth fell open at that, and I had to turn it into a deep breath before I began. 'Those girls were paupers, dazzled by the glare of attention they were never meant to receive. One example of play-acting does not negate the whole idea. I do not believe this fellow would treat his subjects in such a way.'

'Elliotson was dismissed, you know. He now spends his days indulging in hocus-pocus at his Mesmeric Infirmary – in *London*.'

He emphasised the word as if that city were of the worst repute; I had to take another deep breath before I put my own case. 'In truth, it is not something I would have thought of – but I am beginning to make good progress in my discussions with Mrs Harleston, and the idea of holding a full and frank conversation while she is entirely unguarded . . .'

I suddenly wondered if that was all of it. Was I merely seeking some short path to glory – some new discovery? Perhaps I should concentrate on the old ways; certainly I never had managed to fix her with my eye, as Pargeter had suggested. But surely a mesmerist could do that . . . ?

Doctor Chettle lifted the letter from my hands and I waited while he perused it. He read carefully, slowly, until he had almost reached the end, when suddenly his eyes fixed upon one particular line or two. He stared; then he looked up and said, 'Is the lady willing?'

I hesitated. Then I said, 'She will concur with my judgement.'

'Then write and tell him to come.' He handed the letter back. 'It may have some small effect, as you say, if she believes it will. And it can have so little true efficacy that it can do no harm. It might even satisfy her husband until my frictional machine arrives.'

He laughed as if making light of it all. 'Of course, there have been experiments into *phreno*-mesmerism that have, I believe, yielded some interesting results. A Doctor Buchanan stroked his somnambules' heads to enhance certain characteristics. He claimed to have discovered the organ or faculty of Sensibility, you know, which has been associated with the psychic senses. Some, they say, have played upon their subjects' heads as if on a pianoforte.'

His eyes narrowed, musing, and I had an awful image of being forced to stand by while Doctor Chettle ran his hands through Mrs Harleston's hair, feeling every curve of her skull while he stared into her blank eyes.

I shuddered and said, 'It is a rather mechanistic notion. Do you really think the human mind can be reduced to such?'

I knew my mistake as soon as the words were spoken.

He looked up sharply. 'Have a care, sir.'

'Excuse me – I really know very little of it.'

'You should, if it is your intention to become an alienist. Why, even our dear monarch sees the sense in it. She had her children's heads read some years since.'

'Of course.' I bowed. I did not dare mention the rumours rife in some circles: that Queen Victoria might be falling prey to the same mind-malady that claimed her grandfather, George III.

'It is obvious that cerebral diseases proceed from physical deformities in the brain. We are not French!' Doctor Chettle announced firmly. 'We shall not find Mania in the intestines or Melancholia in the lungs. No; phrenology is a most useful adjunct in trying to locate the source. And we *must* find the source: as physicians, it is incumbent upon us to find the physical cause for madness. All our reputation and authority depends upon it!'

I inclined my head in a gesture that could have meant anything.

'Even Franz Joseph Gall, the discoverer of phrenology, was the physician to an asylum in Vienna. It is entirely apt. And I am quite current, you see; I make use of the latest system of faculties from Combe. I have all the requisite instruments and most of the requisite subjects.'

I thought of the portraits hanging on his wall, but I did not quite like to admit that I had seen them. I covered my confusion by indicating the skull and saying, 'May I?'

'Of course.' He brightened at my interest and placed it into my hands. I saw at once that it was not the trepanned example I had seen before but another, entirely whole and boiled clean. I wondered what poor soul had found themselves subject to this indignity. Many believed that such a thing would prevent their bodies being resurrected on the Day of Judgement, and spent their lives in fear of what would happen to their bones after death. To me, it seemed only sad. The skull in my hand felt frail and I set it down and attempted a smile, for all the form my lips assumed did not feel quite right. It must have been enough, however, for Doctor Chettle nodded and returned to his book.

I left the room before he could change his mind, and as I closed the door behind me, I glanced once more at the letter – and I realised which of its lines must have so fixed the good doctor's attention: *there would be no charge for my services at this time.*

Was that what had changed his mind? Mrs Harleston's husband required new treatments, and here was something to pander to his demands. I need not imagine how Doctor Chettle would slant it in his reports. I wondered what Harleston would pay for such novel therapeutics. Was profit, rather than effectiveness, to be our watchword at Crakethorne Manor?

For the rest of the evening I dwelled upon certain uneasy questions, fixing upon nothing; but the one that returned to me time and again was: *Is the lady willing?*

I tried to tell myself that my answer had been not entirely untrue, for how could Mrs Harleston truly know what she wanted? Yet it was nonetheless with a sense of profound unease that I wrote my letter to Professor Lumner, carried out my ablutions and prepared for bed. I even had an intimation that, in a small and well-intentioned way, I had carried out some little betrayal of the lady's feelings.

Doctor Nathaniel Kerner's Journal

16th September

The arrival of Professor Lumner followed hard upon my invitation: he came today, earlier in the week than I had anticipated, and indeed, earlier in the day. He brought with him louring skies and squally showers, rain lashing about the grounds and blasting the windowpanes; it ran in torrents from the branches of trees and sprayed from overflowing gutters.

The place felt as if it was under siege, but all that arrived at its gates was a drenched cart with driver, passenger and pony alike all covered in oilcloths — I realised I had half-expected the man to arrive in a carriage. Steam rose from beneath the coverings; the pony snorted in disgust at it all.

I hurried to meet the Professor. I wished that duty to fall to me and no other, for many of the servants did not know of his coming (although perhaps I had not allowed for their gossip; I thought I heard a titter of laughter as I drew back the bolts, though when I looked around I saw no one, not even Peter Ambrose peeping through the bars).

I was oddly apprehensive about whom I might find on the step. I had built the mesmerist in the mould of a soldierly adventurer striding into the unknown: muscled, loud, self-important and a little overbearing, with singularly piercing eyes. Instead, I discovered a slightly built fellow with rain dripping from his hat brim.

I motioned him inside. He touched his hand to his sodden hat and flicked away the moisture. The droplets landed on my shoes, though he did not appear to notice.

I was surprised to see that he was not especially old, and of no greatly prepossessing appearance: his hair was a dull shade of light brown, his clothes a little shabby — but his letter had said he left Oxford just before I matriculated. Perhaps I looked for grizzled authority that it might have lent confidence at such a time.

The pony had already trotted miserably about the turning circle and was returning the way it had come. Beyond it, I could just make out the misty form of the porter and, at his heels, soaked and no doubt smelling worse than ever, his old brown dog.

The Professor removed his dripping waxed coat. I took it from him, then realised I had nowhere to hang it; I must perforce carry it to the room I had arranged for him.

On closer inspection, Professor Lumner is not quite so ordinary as I had first supposed. He is perfectly clean-shaven and his features are regular, if perhaps a little too sharp. I was mistaken too about his eyes, for although they are unremarkable in colour, there is an intensity in his gaze that makes him striking. I wonder if it is a natural attribute, or if his profession lends his orbs a force they would not otherwise possess. I found myself wondering if I disliked him — although perhaps I should not commit such an ungenerous notion to paper, even in my private journal.

I expected he would like to rest after his journey, but he assured me that he was not in the least fatigued, after which we walked in silence up the stairs. I thought of introducing him to Doctor Chettle, but swiftly reconsidered; I did not want our principal inviting himself to the proceedings.

When we reached his door, the Professor spoke at last. 'I am most interested to see my subject,' he said. (I wondered if his tones were perhaps a little rough. He seems to lapse now and then — though, I suppose, we all endeavour to better ourselves. I shall try to be more charitable.)

I wished very much to inform him that the lady was not his subject, but manners won out. Instead I explained that Mrs Harleston would soon be at luncheon and that I should first like to discuss how to proceed; then we could see her. He concurred in a tone that told me that was exactly as he expected it to be arranged.

I left him at the door, promising to have some refreshment sent up, after which I would return. A short time later I was taking my own repast of boiled mutton, boiled potatoes and boiled cabbage when I heard a tap on my door and found the man himself standing in the passage; he had eaten and was most anxious to begin, and perhaps we could do so at once?

I was somewhat surprised; I had not even heard his approaching step. The Professor had found his way about this establishment more quickly than I! He did not give his surroundings a glance as he took the chair I offered, fixing his gaze only upon me. He rarely blinked as we spoke, although he did not appear to find any discomfort in his staring.

I asked after his journey from London, which he assured me was tolerable, and his meal, which he declared to be likewise. I told him a little of the patient – I somehow did not call her my patient – and the crisis of which she was reluctant to speak. I hinted at the delusions about her husband that must be removed before she could be called quite well.

He answered with, 'Perfect – she is perfect! That is just the kind of thing I am looking for.'

I thought I would give some hint of my irritation and said, 'There will be no stage antics, nothing to which her husband could object?'

He replied immediately, 'There will be nothing of that kind; I abhor lurid displays. I am not interested in them. I have given up on the supernormal – what are termed the "higher phenomena".'

(I did not altogether like his use of the words 'given up', and was confirmed in my slight apprehension when he went on to admit he had pursued such studies for a time, but with little success.) He said, 'They are only one part of the mesmeric doctrine, but they bring the whole into disrepute. That is not my purpose here. This is something else entirely, I assure you.'

Well, I was glad to hear that, anyway, and he spoke softly, meeting my eyes with his own frank stare; I decided I could not doubt the honesty of his intentions.

'And the lady is irreproachable?' he asked. 'She is of a certain standing, so that none may question her integrity?'

I did not like the question and answered somewhat curtly, countering it with one of my own. 'Forgive me, but I must ask it – you will not touch her?'

He said stiffly, 'Naturally, I will not. There is nothing improper in it.' Then he went on, 'And she must concur – it is all hopeless, you know, if the lady does not on some level of her mind agree to be mesmerised.'

'Really?' I was somewhat dismayed.

'My art cannot be claimed equally effective for all,' he said, 'but let us hope she proves a good subject. If so, the results can be quite dramatic. I hope to set up in practice on that basis, and this will help immeasurably. It is a simpler matter with the weaker sex, of course, since mesmerism is about asserting dominance of will over the subject.'

I had decided: I did not like him.

'There is one thing I must ask of you,' he said, and I will endeavour to set down in a full approximation the warning which followed.

'It is no small matter to be in a trance: It means sinking into the depths of one's mind, even the very soul. The journey may be inward, but it is a great one nevertheless. Once begun, it cannot be interrupted. I cannot be interrupted. I must guide her through that *journey in careful steps, and I must be free to do it as I see fit. If her trance is interrupted in any way — if she is startled or shaken out of it — I cannot answer for the consequences. The dangers may be such that even I cannot foresee.'*

I affirmed that I would do no such thing, for all my misgivings are greater than ever. I wonder if Doctor Chettle should be present after all? But Mrs Harleston will scarcely succumb to a relaxed state with a crowd about her, and he would only interfere.

Professor Lumner has gone to his rooms to prepare. Once more, my journal provides its balm; I am quite rid of my irritation and am ready, I think, for the treatment to begin.

Chapter Thirteen

We found Mrs Harleston in her room, standing with her back to the door, looking out of the window so calmly she might have been a painting by Vermeer instead of a living, breathing woman. Without turning she said, 'I know why you have come.'

There was no reproach in her tone, but I felt it anyway. 'I have brought Professor Lumner, the mesmerist,' I said, and she turned and looked at him with no surprise or curiosity. There was something about the way she stood, however, about her slight form, that was fragile, even helpless; it reminded me of her words about being unable to go where she chose. I felt more than ever determined to help her, to protect her. An image rose before me, of myself as a boy stretched upon a table, rendered insensible. If I had only submitted to my father, everything would have been all right. She must do so now; this could release her from the shackles of her own mind.

The two of them stood motionless. 'I will place your chairs by the window,' I said, and arranged them a little distance apart. The Professor stepped in, pushing them closer until there was not a foot between them. Suddenly mindful of moving chess pieces about a board, and finding no third chair in the room, I sat upon the bed with my knees angled between where theirs would go.

'I will explain a little of the process,' he said.

'There is no need.' She sat in one of the facing chairs and arranged her skirts.

'You are concerned,' said Professor Lumner, and again I felt a stab of irritation. 'Do not be. I am merely to help you relax. The magnetic trance is quite safe.'

'Is it?'

He smiled and took the opposite seat, leaning forward, and she moved her knees aside. I shuffled a little closer, though neither party looked at me. He stared into her eyes, asserting his dominance of will, I supposed. Her gaze was as intent as his own; the light from the window fell upon her cheek, making her appear suddenly very young and hard and pale as alabaster.

'Be calm.' The Professor's voice was soothing. 'There is nothing to fear.'

He reached out with both hands and I opened my mouth to protest, but he did not touch her. He made a stroking motion, palms down, a few inches above her own hands, clasped in her lap. I had heard of such mesmeric passes. Now he elongated them, stroking the air from her elbows to her fingertips.

'Do you feel that?' he asked in a low voice.

'Of course not,' she replied – and then she caught her breath.

'Now?'

'I feel . . . something.' She looked puzzled. 'Like a tingling, and there is warmth, but—'

'Be calm,' he repeated, his voice smoother, more mellifluous. 'I wish you to stare into my left eye.'

A line appeared momentarily across her forehead as she leaned forward, her full lips slightly parted.

'You are drowsy.' He half rose, making his passes from her forehead around her temples and down to her shoulders. He did not blink or look away from her eyes, which were growing heavy, half closing – then she opened them wider than before.

He murmured words I could scarcely hear, something about peace and sleep, and I did not at first realise that it was me he was now addressing. 'It is well. She does not hear us. Outwardly she is the same, but see the way her pupils are dilated, as one recently dead.'

I did not like the notion, but I looked into her eyes. It was difficult to make anything out, her eyes were so beautifully dark; then I saw that the orbs were blank. She showed no sign of hearing him speak.

'She is entering the trance, but not deeply. Some insufflations may be required, if you have no objection. There will be no contact, as I have said.'

I did not reply, somehow feeling that, if I did, Mrs Harleston would surely hear *me*, and he took my silence for consent. He rose from his chair and circled hers. Still she did not move. He stood behind her, reaching for her massy, gleaming hair, stopping himself at my look and instead bending low to the nape of her neck and breathing upon it, just where that lovely hair was caught up in its ribbon. He made further passes along her shoulders, as if moulding the shape of her clavicle where it emerged from her dress; as he did so, her eyes slowly began to close.

He whispered, 'You are going deeper. There is a stair before you, leading down. Do you see it?'

'I see it.' Her voice was low and breathy, unlike her usual calm tones, and I did not altogether like it.

He breathed once more on her neck, his lips not quite touching her skin. 'You are descending the stairs. As you go it will become darker, but you are quite safe, for I am with you.'

She began to breathe more deeply. Her face was entirely quiescent.

'You see,' the Professor said softly, 'the hands are the magic wand of the mesmerist.' He faced her again, though he continued to make his stroking motions from her wrist to her fingers. 'My hands are the focus for my will. I thrust my potency into them and infuse her with it. See how I rid her of bad magnetism!' He moved more vigorously, shaking his hands once they were clear of her fingertips as if flicking water from his skin.

This was not what I had expected and I wondered if he were a believer in the odylic force, that mystical substance said to pass between mesmeriser and subject. Surely it was all nonsense. I shifted in my seat – but then I stilled, for she murmured, 'The crows are here.'

Her eyes darted to left and right, but did not open. The Professor frowned, leaning towards her as if he could peer through her translucent eyelids.

'I do not like the way they look at me. Their eyes . . . I do not think they are crows at all.'

'We are alone,' he said, his voice still soft, but firm now. 'There are no crows; no one else is near. You are safe—'

'I am not. I am not!'

'You are quite safe. I want you to cast your mind back a little in time, to your journey on an omnibus. You are going to take that journey again, this time in reverse, so that all your distress will turn to calm and you will end once more in the arms of your husband. For now, you are in that closed compartment. You are in the midst of a fantasy that a small hand is holding your own. I wish you to look deeply into your memory of that moment. Look about you. Touch the sides of the compartment and know it to be empty. Do you feel it?'

She gave a slight nod.

'Do you see?'

She shuddered. 'All is dark to me.'

'But you may touch the sides of the compartment with your hands. You will feel that no one could possibly be there.'

She began to move her hands through the air as if making her own mesmeric passes, far more graceful than his had been.

'Tell me. I wish you to say it: that you are alone, that you allowed your heightened nerves to alarm you, that you gave way to panic. You will not do so again. You feel yourself returning to calm . . . Calm.'

Her hands were still raised, and then her left continued to move while her right remained motionless. She caught her breath, as if she felt a sudden chill or had touched something unpleasant. I thought for an instant I saw vapour hanging before her lips, as on a winter's day; I blinked and it was gone.

She closed her fingers, shaping them as if they were held in another's hand. A tear brimmed at her eye.

'Remarkable,' the Professor breathed.

'Perhaps tell her again that the impression is false,' I whispered, but he gestured for me to be silent.

She turned as if to look at me, yet her eyes did not open. 'He says the painted eye does not always speak true.'

'What? Who?' The words burst from me before I could prevent them, though I did not need to ask; I could see the answer even before she shook her head.

'Is it the conductor?' Professor Lumner said. 'Do not pay him any heed.'

I knew he had not understood. How could he?

'Think only upon what you are doing there, of the empty compartment—'

'No.' She spoke with emphasis, though I gained the impression she was speaking to someone unseen, and she raised her hands once more, this time as if to ward someone away. She had no time to explain, however, because at that moment a thud sounded from the window and I looked up to see splayed feathers, tattered and black, batting at the glass, the flash of a heavy, sharp beak – then it was gone.

A shriek rang out from the direction of the day-room, followed by more thudding against glass, running footsteps and the crash of something overturning. A volley of barking – barking in a human voice – broke in, and a trill of high and intemperate laughter.

I turned towards the commotion and saw only the door, though it was ajar – had I left it so? Had Olive Scholes been spying upon us? But there was no one there now. I heard more hasty footsteps, and a pained cry.

I was rent in two: I must assist outside, and yet Mrs Harleston remained with her head thrown back, helpless, the length of her white throat exposed. Her lips were parted; she was insensible.

The Professor did not appear to have noticed anything amiss. He was leaning closely over her, staring into her face – and I had promised not to leave her.

I must wake her, then, and yet she was so deeply entranced I found that even without the Professor's warning, I would not have dared touch her.

Another thud followed by a shriek decided me and I caught Lumner's shoulder, gripping more tightly than I had intended, though he did not appear to feel it. 'I must see what is the matter. Do not continue. I shall return forthwith.'

With that, I rushed from her side and into chaos.

The day-room was the image of Bedlam. Ruth Roberts, one of the sturdier attendants, was sitting on Della Martin, who writhed and clawed at the cocoa matting. Olive Scholes struggled with Lillian Smith, whose sweet passivity had evaporated so that it was all Olive could do to press her down in her chair. Matron was trying to pacify another patient, one of Doctor Chettle's domestics, from a distance that put her out of reach of her fists. Peter

Ambrose barked at them all with a fury I had not known him to possess. And all the while, large black birds flew at the windows.

Nellie Briggs stood with her head lolling, her hair in straggles across her face. She must have overturned the card table, the only one in the room not nailed down, for its contents lay strewn about her. She sprang towards the fire-cage and in the next instant had caught up the poker – but in this she was frustrated, for it was attached to the grate by a chain which rattled furiously. She added to the cacophony with laughter entirely lacking in sense.

And then the chain broke.

I ran to intercept her, seizing her from behind, and she twisted in my grip, yellow teeth snapping at my cheek. I jerked my head away and she writhed again. Then she was taken from me and I saw James Farrar, one of the attendants from the male wards, lifting her into the air. He threw her to the ground and knelt on her breastbone.

Another attendant rushed in, bearing a strait-waistcoat, and I could not help but be grateful for it as he pinioned her, enveloping her in its straps.

I hurried to help Miss Roberts, whose hands ran with blood from her scratches. I caught Della's wrists and Roberts stood, leaving me to wrestle the beldam until another attendant rushed in. Soon there was only Lillian, and my heart contracted at the thought of laying hands on the old lady, but Olive Scholes had no such compunction. She reached back a hand and slapped her, hard, across the face.

Calm began to reassert itself, until there was only young Peter, running on all fours about everybody's ankles, giving out his din; one last thud of a crow against the window.

The crows are here, she had said.

I could not think on it, for I saw Farrar walking towards Peter Ambrose. I threw out a hand to stop him but it was too late;

he aimed a kick at his ribs, just as if he were truly an unwanted cur. The boy collapsed in a little heap.

And suddenly, all was silent.

Clenched fists eased; frozen features melted to their previous state of repose; the patients blinked as if they had all shared the strangest dream but had now awakened. I could still envision the untamed light in Lillian's eyes; there had been not the faintest grain of sanity in that look. She would have happily torn out our throats with her teeth.

Then I realised there was a distant sobbing – not in a woman's voice, but a man's, and I hurried from the room and found the men's day-room in a state of relative calm, save for the figure crouching in the centre. The farmhand, Jacob Thew, was cowering and casting fearful looks at the window through his hands.

'They're come,' he said, 'the sperrits. There's nowt'll keep 'em off, not now t' door's open.'

I uttered some hasty words of comfort, but there was no time. My prior duty, abandoned, asserted itself again in my thoughts, and I could think only of Mrs Harleston, whom I had left quite alone with the mesmerist.

I tore myself from Jacob, though not without a pang, for he called after me, 'Don't leave me – don't leave me here!' as he raised his head, his face aghast, his eyes like two silvery coins shining in his head.

I hurried away from it all, ignoring the looks the attendants gave me. I had to return to her. My heart, hitherto strangely calm, was racing at the idea of what she might be enduring at that moment.

I threw open the door of her rooms, but she continued in the same supine attitude as when I had left, her head thrown back, her arms hanging limply down – and Professor Lumner was clutching one of her hands.

He leaned over her, so close I almost thought his lips were pressed to that white throat – and then I saw he was whispering in her ear, his words a meaningless susurration. His attention was entirely hers, so fixed upon her that he had not yet noticed my presence.

I coughed and he turned at once – I expected him to start away from her, but he did not. I strode towards him, ready to throw him aside – yes, out of the asylum! – and vowing I would never allow such a man to touch her again, when he said without changing his tone, 'I cannot wake her.'

Everything within me stilled. It was not so much his words, which I had to reassemble in my mind for in truth I did not at first take them in; it was the realisation that he was afraid. His dull hair was darkened with sweat and his eyes were clouded, not with the mesmerist's art, but with dismay.

My gaze went to her for whom I cared more – and rightly, as was my duty. She was pale as a corpse; her breast scarcely rose with her breath. I wished I could see into her eyes; I was certain she would return to me, if only I could do so.

'Let go of her hand at once,' I said, 'I will chafe them. Go and bring water to bathe her temples.' I did not want water; I wanted only for him to leave us.

But he remained where he was, clinging to her hand, and I noticed he was holding it in a peculiar grip, the ball of her thumb pinched between his fingers. 'I *must* bring her back,' he said, 'or she is lost.'

His tone restrained me more than force ever could. 'The stair,' he said, and I realised he spoke to her now, 'is just behind you. You went down it so recently. It is all returning to you. You will go to it and calmly ascend, and as you do so the light will grow brighter. Your consciousness will rise as you surface.'

She shifted, murmuring something; a fearful expression flitted across her features and was gone. 'It is not there,' she said. 'I do not think I am any longer in a room. It is . . . I hear a sound, like whispers. So many—'

'There is no such sound, no voices. The stair is before you. Look about and you will see it.'

'Ah – there *is* a stair.'

'Good!' He could not keep the relief from his voice, though it was hardly soothing. 'Now all is plain before you. Step on to the first tread. Look up and you will see the glow of the light of the world above you.'

'No – no.' She shook her head. 'I see a stair, but it is wrong, all wrong – it is not the same one.'

'There is only one stair: the one by which you descended.'

'No, for that is gone. I do not see it any more. This one . . . Ah, I am afraid!'

'It is all one, Vita. You are quite relaxed, as you were moments ago. Go up the stair. As you do, count to ten. The light is growing brighter, do you see?'

Vita? He had dared to call her *Vita* . . .

'I do not like it. The others—'

'There are no others. There is only you and me. Listen to my voice. You are not afraid; there is nothing to be afraid of. Go up. Begin your count.'

'One.'

'Good.'

'Two.'

'Two, and you feel yourself awakening, as from the most refreshing sleep.'

'Three.'

'Three, and you feel the memories of what has passed leaving you as the night is dispersed by the dawn.'

'Four . . .' She twitched, glancing from side to side. '*He* is here.'

'No one is there. Five.'

'Five,' she repeated, her voice uncertain. 'Six. I see it! Though it is not the same light, I think.'

'It is God's own sunlight and you are returning to it. When you reach ten, that step is the last. You will open your eyes and awake.'

'Seven . . . Eight . . . Nine.'

'You feel wonderfully refreshed and calm. Your nerves will be restored to balance.' He spoke hastily, as if he had not opportunity enough to instil in her all the ideas he should – but what of that? I wanted only for her to be returned and him to be gone.

'Ten,' she said, opening her eyes just as he let go of her hand.

She looked about her, blinking, and her gaze lit upon me. She smiled, and I felt an inexpressible relief. Her expression was clear and candid; it was as if she looked upon me as a friend. Then she seemed to recall everything and she looked away, focusing instead upon the shadow of the bars cast from her window.

'How do you do?' I asked, suddenly formal, as if I were meeting her for the first time.

'Tolerably well,' she replied. Was there a hint of amusement in her tone?

'Are you relaxed?' the Professor put in, without invitation.

'Who are you?' She looked at him, then at me, giving a faltering smile. 'Oh – are we to begin?'

'No.' I could not help but smile back at her. Her own look was so guileless, as unknowing and innocent as a child's. 'Here is a visitor to see you, that is all. He will leave you now. You may rest a little, if you wish.'

I felt the Professor bristling, but I did not look at him. I was certain now that I did not care for *him*.

'I think I shall.' Her voice was quite steady.

I recollected that I should take her pulse, ask her to put out her tongue, perhaps see if her fingers were warm or cool to the touch, but she was so like a child ready to be tucked into bed, so close to the peaceful repose that must be God's finest restorative, that I could not bear to impose upon her.

I left with Professor Lumner. We had not yet passed through the iron gate leading to the hall when he reached out and grasped my arm. I endeavoured to compose my features, for there was something about the fellow I had come to quite detest. His too-sharp features, his cool look angered me more than I could say.

'This is not to be borne,' he began. 'She is my subject, and I must – I *need* – to consult with her as I will.'

'You will not, sir,' I returned, 'and you never shall again.'

'But – her character! – and her susceptibility! She is a magnificent subject; you must see that. I would even suggest that her like has not before been encountered – so easily put under, and once there . . . Why, I had never thought to discover . . . I had given it all up, but one could almost believe—'

'Believe what? That it was acceptable for you to touch her, to lay your hand upon hers, in the absence of her physician?'

'What? No, sir – I apologise for it. It was a necessity, for she fell so deeply into the trance that unusual measures were required to bring her out of it. You saw it for yourself.'

'I *did* see: with my own eyes, I saw it.'

'I apologise, sir, and again, if you insist; but there was nothing of impropriety, of that I assure you. I have discovered a fine subject, one whose consciousness may hold secrets that my chosen field has yet to dream of. Why, it was beholden upon me to go further. It was my duty.'

'Your *duty*?' I was all astonishment.

'Exactly! You must know that some claim mesmerism to be a doorway to supernormal powers, to higher phenomena. I did not believe it, I could not, and yet she . . . She seemed to see into another realm, did she not? She said she saw crows, and the crows came. I wonder, after all, if it is impossible for the trance to impart such powers, but possible instead to awaken them?'

His eyes looked inward, intent on his own ravings, and I wondered if he might be as mad as the rest – if we all were. His words were fit for nothing more than a drollery in Blackwood's. What else could I have expected from such a man? I should never have invited him.

When I returned my gaze, the Professor was peering at me as if to read my thoughts. Indeed, they must have been plainly written upon my features.

'You will not reconsider.'

I did not reply.

He straightened. 'Then I must leave you.'

'I bid you a swift and pleasant journey.' I matched his icy tone.

He answered with a stiff bow and stalked away, presumably to retrieve his belongings.

I felt no regret in watching him go. If Doctor Chettle made enquiry, I would report that the man had failed to induce anything but a deep sleep. He must be satisfied with that. And there would be much to distract us: casebooks to bring up to the present, reports upon the use of restraints made for the Commissioners in Lunacy, rooms to straighten, furniture and possibly limbs to mend.

And I needed to prepare Mrs Harleston for whatever treatment would follow, one that would no doubt be dictated by Doctor Chettle. I knew I must steel myself to see her eyes clouded by the tincture of laudanum or made glassy by electricity, to have her sheeted so she could not move an inch, to have her plunged into the dark of the seclusion chamber; to see our early bud of trust murdered by the frost before it could even begin to bloom.

Chapter Fourteen

Once I had parted from Professor Lumner, I returned to my room and tried to engage in quiet reflection, to ponder all that had passed. Quiet reflection! I would that my mind had stilled enough for such a thing. I stared into the mirror; I paced; I looked out of the window. My mind whirled with questions but found no answers. The only thing I could fix upon through the glass was the Crow Garden and the little flash of water beyond. From here, it appeared quite black – as dark and depthless as her eyes. What strange thoughts were concealed behind them!

I allowed myself to drift, thinking of those fathomless eyes, and from that attitude of light repose I must have sunk into the restful arms of sleep.

However, it was not to last. At some dead hour, I was roused from my dreams by someone shaking me by the shoulder. I woke suddenly and found – not the eyes which consumed me, but Olive Scholes' dull orbs staring into mine. I started away, half mortified, but she informed me in hesitant sentences that Lillian Smith had awakened and was in some distress.

Her lamp was placed on the floor somewhere behind her, casting her face into shadow. My own features must have been quite visible under its gleam and I endeavoured to straighten them.

'She'll not settle, sir. She 'ad a dream, only she says it were too vivid for a dream. She says 'er dead brother came and spoke to 'er.'

They're come. The sperrits. There's nowt'll keep 'em off, not now t' door's open.

I supposed her half asleep and did not enquire further what had happened; I doubted she could recount it in any way that made sense. I would see and judge for myself.

She added, 'You mun bring your keys.'

I caught them up, for all she had no need to ask, since carrying them was already such an ingrained habit that if I had not felt their weight in my pocket I would have sorely felt the lack. I followed her to my door, aping her endeavours to walk quietly. The whole place was silent – an odd, tangible, *present* sort of silence – and I did not like it.

I did not wait for Miss Scholes to open the gate leading to the female wards but did it myself. There was the empty, darkened day-room with its unoccupied chairs and cold hearth, quite forlorn in appearance. Everything remained so quiet and I wondered why, if Lillian was in distress. I felt misgivings I could not name and somehow found myself walking towards Mrs Harleston's door. I pictured her within, sleeping through another incarcerated night and preparing for another day of the same, her hair sweetly strewn across her pillow.

'Not there,' Olive whispered, though her tone only made me walk more quickly. Lowering the little shutter, I looked through the peephole. A dark shape had fallen to the floor by the bed.

'Nay,' Olive said, pushing her face up close to mine. 'It's Mrs Smith you need to see, only she's not in 'ere; she 'as to get *out*.'

I ignored her and unlocked Mrs Harleston's door. The fallen shape resolved itself into a heap of crumpled and discarded clothing. The room was otherwise empty.

'Where is she?' I turned to Olive.

'There,' she said, pointing towards the abandoned garments, empty of the slender form which had filled them.

'She is *not* there. Answer me at once – where is Mrs Harleston?'

Her face remained stolid and expressionless. In that moment, I hated it. I opened my mouth to protest her foolishness, but a slight metallic rattle sounded from the day-room and I rushed towards it.

The room was just as it had been. A trace of moonlight limned the backs of chairs and tables, filling all the spaces between with the deepest shadow. Yet as I glanced over it something must have snagged at my consciousness, because I returned my gaze to the iron gate and saw someone standing next to it, quite motionless.

'You there – halloa!' I called out softly, not wishing to rouse the whole place. The person made no reply, but twitched as if with discomfort. Tiredness pressed upon me as I went closer, my limbs becoming leaden. I longed only for sleep – indeed, I think something of my dreams had clung to me, for I almost felt that I were still lost within them – but I forced my eyes wide as I neared and saw to my consternation that the figure's features were concealed by a hooded cloak.

'Who is there?' I asked. 'And where is Mrs Harleston?'

I could make out only their eyes, staring darkly into mine. 'She is asleep,' a woman's voice said, 'quite asleep, in an empty chamber. Her own is in need of tidying and so she sleeps elsewhere . . . It is quite routine, I assure you . . . Quite ordinary.'

I realised, with relief, that it was Matron. And yet to see her here, now – there was surely more. 'What, may I ask, is the reason for your being here at this hour, and for my being awakened?'

'It is nothing at all,' she replied in the same soothing tone. 'Lillian Smith awoke suddenly, certain that someone was looking in at her window – someone she knew when she was young.

It was only a dream. I managed to quiet her with the promise that I should go and see for myself that there was no one outside, no one who could possibly have climbed the wall. She is watching for me now – I must hurry, and then all of us can return to bed.'

I thought it foolishness to entertain a patient's silly dream, but it seemed she must and would, and so I bowed and followed her as she left. I locked the gate behind us as she went to the front door, grasping for her keys beneath her cloak.

'Wait,' I said, thinking it fortunate that I had brought my own – for only those in authority and certain trusted servants had keys to the front door, rather than every attendant in the place. For that, at least, Miss Scholes need not be chided.

I unlocked it for her as she slid the bolts. 'I will wait here until you are finished.'

'There really is no need.'

'Of course I must. You will not be long, and I shall lock the door again.'

'Thank you, but I am perfectly capable of doing my duty. I am only going to be a moment – I will not go out of sight of the door – I can lock it myself.'

'Come, sir.' Miss Scholes tugged at my elbow. 'I shall bring a light and show you up t' stairs.'

I pulled free of her grasp. I dismissed her as Matron had dismissed me a moment ago and turned my back upon them both, making my way up to my room. It took no little time, for Scholes was right: the corridors were terribly dark.

I could not all at once go to sleep, but went to look out of the window. There were the gentle slopes of Crakethorne, barely discernible in the dim light. The trees were darker shapes still, ranked around us, appearing closer than ever. I thought I could make out shadows flitting and shifting across the sward as ragged clouds passed across the moon; or perhaps the nightbirds were flying. For a few moments I remained there, just watching, and then I retired again, and knew nothing more until the morning.

Chapter Fifteen

I awoke on the instant, roused by a thunder of footsteps passing my door. I sat up, half expecting someone to be leaning over me, shaking me by the shoulder, but there was no one. I straightened my collar as I hurried into the passage. It was empty, but Doctor Chettle's door stood wide and I could still hear hurried footsteps coming from below. I went down the stairs and found a gathering of staff in the entrance hall, everyone gesticulating and speaking at once. I could not catch their meaning but I somehow knew it boded ill, and indeed, as I reached them, James Farrar pointed at me and proclaimed, ''e's 'ere!'

They all fell silent and the little crowd parted to reveal Doctor Chettle at its centre. His moustache was uncombed, his half-hidden lips compressed to whiteness. His eyes, however, were as sharp as ever. 'What is the meaning of this?'

'I beg your pardon?' I felt like a child accused of a falsehood. 'Whatever has happened?'

'What has happened, dear sir, is that your charge, Mrs Harleston, is missing, and no one can account for her. None save Miss Scholes, who has been telling me some muddle about your going to visit that lady in the dead of the night.'

I was astonished. His imputation was shocking – it was not

to be borne. 'Sir,' I responded, my blood rising under the scald, 'I shall not be spoken of in such a fashion. I tried to attend a patient in the night because Miss Scholes sent for me, and furthermore, she was with me constantly. There has been nothing untoward. I discovered that all was well – in fact, it was not even Mrs Harleston I was called to see.'

Olive had the temerity to look puzzled, then she shot me a glare so ugly I longed to reprove her. But such was not my purlieu when our principal was present and I swallowed my indignation. I waited for Doctor Chettle's response but he was not yet permitted to speak, for the saucy wench piped up, 'He *was* with her, sir, and not for the first time, neither.'

My cheeks flamed. 'How dare you, madam? That is entirely false – a damned lie! I did not even see her.'

The doctor's face, if possible, went a shade paler. He appeared too mortified to speak.

Before he could, I said, 'Sir, I should tell you that I know of Mrs Harleston's whereabouts.' I realised I could be playing into Scholes' hands by revealing that I was privy to this information, but that did not matter now. 'She was moved some time yesterday by Matron, who will no doubt show you to the door of her new chamber. I do not know exactly which it is.'

Doctor Chettle shrank in on himself, and I noticed of a sudden he had failed to fasten one of his shirt buttons. 'I can assure you that every room has been looked into, and Mrs Harleston is in none of them. I have had them searched.'

He turned to one of the attendants. 'You. Go and bring Matron – I cannot think why she has not come down. Ask her to come to my rooms directly. Doctor Kerner, with me, please. Miss Scholes, you should also be on hand.'

And so I was marched once more up the stair, never having set foot in the day-room, where I was certain my patient would be waiting – somewhere – with her calm features and quiet smile. As I ascended, Doctor Chettle's words repeated themselves in my mind – the fact of her absence, of having been sought and nowhere found – and a cold dread nestled into my chest. I felt I had somehow done wrong, been negligent in my duties or some other thing, and beneath that was the icier thought that I might never see Mrs Harleston again. I would never converse with her. I would never look into the depths of her eyes and wonder what she was thinking.

I brushed the thought aside. It was painted with the colours of Olive Scholes' vile accusations. What could have possessed her to make them? And then it rushed upon me, with a flood of heat, that she had asked me for my keys.

I suddenly saw it all: Mrs Harleston must have fooled her somehow, waiting until Olive was occupied with supplying fresh towels or warm water or some such thing, and had taken her keys from her. Miss Scholes, realising the lack, had called me during the night to let her into the ward; she must have wanted to find them again. She had planned to search for them at a quiet hour, yet the dove must already have flown its cage – and at that very moment Matron had gone outside and against all regulations, left the front door open. The outer fence, imperfect as it was, would not stay the lady.

Heat suffused my cheeks, prickling under my shirt. It was by my hand that the door had been unlocked. Matron had wished me to do it, to be certain – but I *had* done it. I had seen the fence upon my arrival and done nothing to have it repaired. I had robbed myself of my most interesting patient. She had flown and I remained – and it was only now that I felt the cord that bound us, stretched so thin it might at any moment break.

Doctor Chettle led the way into his room, his back stiff, and moved to stand behind his desk as if deliberately distancing himself from my presence. 'I must ask you to account for your actions.'

'I shall, sir,' I said, 'and fully. But first I must ask if a search is being made for my patient?'

'*Your* patient, sir, is being hunted everywhere. Now perhaps you can tell me why she is in need of searching out?'

I took a deep breath. 'It began with my being awakened,' I said, and recounted, rapidly but in full, what had taken place during the night. I told him of the way Olive Scholes had shaken me to wakefulness, of the way she had asked for my keys, and of how we had entered Mrs Harleston's chamber but had not found her. I told him of what Matron had said and done. I did not tell him of my feelings. I did not tell him of how I had looked out into a night lit only by the silver moon, at the shadows flitting below; indeed, in my memory it seemed the night must have been half enchanted, to allow a woman to vanish into the air. I said nothing so fanciful, but presented him only with facts.

A grey hue overwrote the pallor of his cheeks as I spoke. Then a knock sounded and the door opened to admit Matron, her forehead furrowed with concern. She entered at Doctor Chettle's gesture and looked only at him, not at me.

'Agnes, I understand you were abroad last night, that you attended a patient – and at their behest actually went outside, and that for a time you left the door unlocked.'

Her expression changed from concern to the utmost puzzlement. She said, 'Sir, I do not know what you mean. I slept all night through – there was no disturbance. I was not there.'

Something within me turned cold. What could she possibly mean? What was she – and Olive Scholes perhaps, the two of them together – trying to do to me, to my reputation, my career? Were they attempting, for some black reason of their own, to ruin me?

Yet she turned and looked at me with an expression of honest puzzlement and saw the horror upon my face and looked the more bewildered.

'I am sorry,' she said, 'but whatever has happened? Mr Farrar told me that Mrs Harleston is missing, and now this—'

'And you truly know nothing of it?' Doctor Chettle asked. 'You had heard nothing of it until this morning? You say you did not wake in the night, that you did not go out—'

'Certainly not!' She was indignant; she actually looked angry. She must have been the most consummate actress outside the West End, for if I had not seen her in the middle of the night, I would have believed her myself. In that moment, I hated her; I hated them both. Nay, all three of them, and it struck me that of all the people in the place, it had been a madwoman with whom my sympathies – my feelings – vibrated the most exactly. And that person had gone.

Doctor Chettle turned to me. 'What do you say to this?'

I did not know how to reply, because – for how many years had he worked with Matron? *Agnes*, he had called her. I did not know how to fight that *Agnes*.

But perhaps Matron had been as much a dupe as I. Lillian Smith had been coerced into helping with Mrs Harleston's desperate escape. She had enlisted Scholes to help her, and they had *persuaded* Matron to go out of doors. Now Matron was ashamed, mortified – perhaps even afraid.

A loud sniff drew the physician's attention once more to Olive Scholes. I no longer knew whether to think of her as a ringleader, an apprentice or another dupe. How many had Mrs Harleston managed to fool? I remembered her quiet looks, her wry smiles, the way my poet's words had flowed from her lips. Had she ever meant any of it?

'Miss Scholes, kindly compose yourself,' Doctor Chettle said.

'I have heard nothing but drivel from you. Stop crying, straighten your shoulders and tell me clearly and simply what you did last night. Did you—?' But there he stopped himself, for fear, I think, of putting words into her mouth.

The girl's face was made even more unprepossessing with crying. She tried to speak and could not; she buried her face in her handkerchief.

'For heaven's sake!' the doctor cried.

She peeped at him over the plain-sewn edge, blemished with her tears. 'I 'ardly know, sir,' she said. 'Thing is, I don't remember.'

I had not expected that. I could barely keep from laughing in her face.

'You can,' the doctor said, 'and do. Go on.'

She looked around in despair, though I think she saw nothing, for her eyes welled with tears. 'Well, sir, it's like this: I know I was up in t' night, since I were dressed when I woke, and I remember putting me nightdress on when I went up. And I seemed to remember I were taken by t' hand and led downstairs, but I don't know why, sir, and it in't even possible, because—'

'Because?'

'Because it were me mother what come for me!' She sobbed freely once more.

The doctor threw up his hands. I was no less frustrated than he. What new foolishness, what malignity, was this? But I did not have long to wait before he demanded to know what she meant.

'I just remember this weird dream,' she gasped. 'Me mam, she couldn't see so good as she got on. She'd been a seamstress, an' even in t' dark they 'ad to keep on, just wi' candles. It did for 'er sight, so's I 'ad to lead 'er about. And that's what I did last night, sir. She called to me and told me she needed t' young doctor, and a lamp, and a key, and so—'

'You do not deny, then, that you asked Doctor Kerner for his keys? And why was that? Where are your own keys, Miss Scholes?'

She looked confused and reached for her belt. I held my breath, fully expecting to be vindicated: her keys would be missing; the whole story would come out. But she withdrew her hand, holding a bunch of keys.

Doctor Chettle looked at me. 'Doctor Kerner?'

'Why, I do not know how she has them – unless she found them again after Mrs Harleston had used them. Or unless the patient realised there was no key to the front door and returned them somehow to her accomplice.'

''er what?' Miss Scholes looked alarmed.

'I agree,' said Doctor Chettle, 'and I have heard enough. Miss Scholes, you are dismissed.'

'But I din't do owt – I'm sure on it! It were just a dream, that's all. It 'ad to be, see, because my poor dear mam – she's been dead these five year! And she were in it, an' him, an—' The girl turned to Matron as if to say 'you' and I bit my lip, waiting for the word, but Doctor Chettle was quicker.

'Matron, see that she gathers her baggage and leaves at once. I will not have such a person under my roof.'

'But sir!' Her pleading rose to a wail. 'Please! I 'an't got nowhere else to go—'

'At once.' His tone brooked no interruption.

'Sir, please.' This time her voice was no more than a whisper, and I felt guilty for judging her so harshly and disliking her so intensely, because the look upon her face held nothing but despair, and it was dreadful to see.

I did not have to look at it any longer, however, because Matron was already leading her away, both hands on her shoulders, never having admitted her part in it, never having been *asked* to admit it by the man who was not only her employer but her friend. Perhaps he was even more than a friend, but I could say nothing; the look in his eyes bade me to keep silent.

I did not know what would happen next. If I had not been complicit I had certainly been fooled, and either would be just cause for dismissal. A chasm gaped at my feet. To be cast out before I had established myself in my chosen field, without so much as my good character left to me, would be terrible indeed. I thought of my mother's face – my dear, proud mother, whose eyes had shone with approval the day I left, so full of hope at what the future held. And I thought of *her* eyes, the way I had imagined there was friendship between us, and felt it fallen and broken at my feet.

I waited for the axe to fall – and yet somehow it did not fall. A rap at the door announced another visitor and Ruth Roberts put her head around the gap and said, 'Sir, we're done searching the rooms again. We can't find her nowhere.'

The physician sank into his seat, as if his knees had suddenly failed him – and perhaps they had. His elbows struck the desk and he sat for a moment with his head in his hands. Then he lifted his face and said, 'It is the gardens you need to search, you fool!'

She withdrew, presumably to begin afresh. But had they not been throughout the grounds already? And the doctor said, sounding so tired, 'I need you to *think* – think of anywhere she might go. You spent the most time with her, did you not?'

I affirmed that I had, and he repeated, 'Then you *must* think. I cannot see a way to prevent her husband knowing of this – he, and others. This will harm us, I fear. Only please, think.' He let out a juddering sigh. 'The night coach passes close by, of course, in the darkest hours. It goes to London.'

He said nothing more; indeed, there was no more to be said.

He did not look up from his desk as I quietly left him. I do not think I had yet fully taken in that Mrs Harleston was gone; or indeed that I had not been dismissed.

Chapter Sixteen

Under the circumstances, I felt it apposite to delay my morning rounds and retreat to the relative peace of my room. I brought discord with me, however, and could settle to nothing. Uppermost among my thoughts was, *Where has she gone?* I could scarcely believe she *had* gone. I could not imagine her little whitewashed room with a different occupant. And *how* had she gone? Had Olive Scholes truly been complicit in her escape – and how could Matron have told such a blatant untruth without flinching?

A part of me wished to stride downstairs and have it out with her, but I remembered the task she had been given, to see the hapless Olive Scholes out of the building, and I stared at the door, wondering what wailing and imploring she must now be enduring. If the girl had been some kind of accomplice in all this, she was truly cast now to the Devil.

I could not think why either of them would speak the way they had. Lies had been told – terrible black lies. I thought of Mrs Harleston's lovely face and the thoughts that must have been hidden behind those calm features. I could not prevent myself from seeing her, all the time knowing that she had gone – and knowing that she had left me behind.

I paced and watched the clock and endured the torment of

my thoughts. At least, cloistered as I was, there was no need to look upon Olive Scholes' despair. But the time came when I could not doubt she was gone and I went to seek the one person remaining who could shed light on what had passed: Agnes Langhurst.

I found her clearing Mrs Harleston's room with the help of another attendant, who was drowned beneath an armful of sheets. In her hand, Matron held a cloth-bound book. She peered down at the flyleaf, her features arranged into an expression of disdain, and I recognised my own little volume of poetry.

When she looked up and saw me, she barked at the attendant to get to the laundry, and the girl fled.

The room was already bare. Any trace of its graceful occupant had either been taken with her or expunged; the story about the room being cleaned was now reality. There remained only a faint scent of carbolic, and the book, which appeared to have been abandoned. Matron set it down and looked at me, her eyebrows raised.

'I saw you, quite plainly.' My voice shook, although I spoke quietly. I did not wish our conversation to be overheard. 'I cannot imagine why you would deny being there. I must ask you again, in the fullest confidence if you will, to please tell me what you were doing last night. Did you have me open the door on purpose? Did you know—?'

The look she gave me, full of the most incandescent fury, made me take a step back.

'Doctor Kerner,' she said, 'I knew as soon as look at you that you would do no good here. You had no idea! You, full of your book learning and fine notions, and not the faintest clue what it is to care for a fellow human. You may as well attempt to fly to the moon as effect a cure for one of these poor souls. And now you are so far gone in your own madness – yes, *madness*,

I call it – to accuse me – *me*, who has served in this place ten years if it is a day . . .'

I had not expected such passion from her. I had expected secretive looks, even shame, some shift in her stance to betray her.

'I shall waste no more words upon you,' she said, 'other than to press upon you – and let this time stand for all, because I shall not speak of it again – what I said before: *I was not there.*'

She turned on her heel and stalked from the room, which seemed smaller than ever. Its whitewashed walls pressed in upon me; stray sunlight found its way between the bars and laid their stripes across the floor. I felt lost, and the mute and empty furniture had no comfort to give. The only thing within it that spoke of the solace of another human soul was the book thrown down upon the mattress.

I picked it up. *She* had read it – her fingers had leafed through these very pages. It was odd that she had not taken it with her to sell and pay her way. Had it been so very useless to her? Or had she left it behind for some other reason – perhaps even for me?

I leafed through it, looking to find some message scrawled in the margin or on a blank page, but there was only the small, regular print.

> But had you—oh, with the same perfect brow,
> And perfect eyes, and more than perfect mouth,
> And the low voice my soul hears, as a bird
> The fowler's pipe, and follows to the snare—
> Had you, with these the same, but brought a mind!

I closed my eyes. I stung under Matron's accusation; I dearly wished I could find anything within or without to prove her falsity. I found I was rubbing my fingers over the book as if it could answer and moved instead to set it down. Why should I require it more? To take it back meant that she was gone indeed; yet in the next moment, I had slipped it into my pocket.

I looked at the empty chairs. They were still drawn close together where she had sat with *him*. I pictured her lovely face – her eyes closed, the lids so fine, the lashes resting on her soft cheek – and I pictured his hands passing over it, his fingertips so close to her skin she must have felt their warmth.

And a dreadful idea raised its head, turning me to stone. I do not know how long I stood there, but no matter how I tried to dispel it, it would not be banished. My question was no longer what Matron had done, but what had *he* done? For I had not seen Professor Lumner after he declared his intention to leave Crakethorne. I had not seen him return to his room; he could have gone anywhere. He might have done anything.

Another picture rose before me: his face staring intently into another's, breathing upon their cheek, but it was no longer Mrs Harleston I saw; it was Matron, cast into the deepest trance whilst he poured his poisonous instructions in her ear.

I could not imagine why it had not occurred to me before. He must have persuaded her to try his 'treatment'. He would have asked her to close her eyes, to think of nothing, and could have planted his seed – to have her compel me to open the door, and then make her forget she had ever seen me, or him. Perhaps he had done it to Olive, too. That would explain why the girl could not remember . . .

I had given Professor Lumner a glimpse of a subject whose aptitude for his art appeared untrammelled, and then banished him from her presence. Of course he had wished to see her again. And a sudden lightness born of hope sprang up within me. Had he taken Mrs Harleston against her conscious will? Had she not chosen to leave me at all?

I closed my eyes. Was such a thing even possible? Yet it seemed more likely to be true than that a woman of Matron's standing would tell a barefaced lie.

An image came: myself as a small boy, looking into my father's face. *I felt it*, I had said. *I could feel it every moment.*

I pushed away the memory of my own dire lie and shook my head. I found myself picturing instead Olive Scholes, that unhappy, square-faced girl, distraught and dismissed. All of it was my doing: I had asked the man to come; I had allowed him to lay his hands on my patient, against Doctor Chettle's wishes and her own – against all common sense and my own better feelings.

Another thought struck me, one that brought a cold heaviness with it. I turned and found myself staring, unblinking, into the mirror. How did I know that the Professor had not mesmerised *me*?

My lip twitched. It had not happened – it surely could not have. I had observed him so carefully, apart from my one brief absence from the room. I had watched every movement, every gesture, with close avidity. What opportunity had he had to cause such mischief? He had not led me away, nor told me I was tired or anything of the kind. And yet, if he had, would I even know?

But I *must* know the truth. I tried to recall what I had heard of the art. Doctor Chettle had mentioned Charles Dickens – besides mesmerising his wife, he had once practised upon a lady called Madame de la Rue. When torn by necessity from her side he would concentrate on her at a set time each day and she would enter a trance though he was miles distant. How difficult would that have been? Could he have made her his puppet even when he was absent?

I had heard tell of another practitioner called George Barth; he claimed to have kept one particularly susceptible young lady in a trance for a month. Its strength was renewed whenever she sat in a chair he had mesmerised or when she used a magnetised handkerchief.

Was *I* susceptible? How could I know?

Barth had referred to such a state as a 'living death'. Was that what I had subjected Mrs Harleston to? Had she gone from the 'living tomb' of the asylum into something worse, held captive not by bars, but her own mind? Was she held there still?

I had to recollect everything I had done the previous night. I was roused by Olive Scholes, of that I was certain. I had not awakened myself; I had not commanded myself to bring my keys. I had felt her unwelcome touch on my shoulder and had seen Matron – or had I only imagined that I had done so?

I paused. Had I only been responding to some previous sugges-tion? Had that dreadful man convinced me that that was whom I *should* see? Had I in fact been looking at someone else, into their very eyes – someone I had thought always to recognise – and *not* recognised her?

Matron might be telling the truth. She might never have been there. The second person I had seen last night might not have been Agnes Langhurst but Mrs Harleston herself – and I had opened the door for her with my own hand!

It was a peculiar idea, as fantastical as any delusion, but I could not rid myself of it. And how convenient for Mrs Harleston if it were true. We had all played our parts to perfection, each believing what we wished, seeing what we wished, and even afterwards had been mired in confusion. We had not even searched for her in the right place.

I closed my eyes, thinking of what it meant. Mrs Harleston could have had me open the door for her, asking me to betray my employer, my work, myself – everything. Would she have used me so thoughtlessly, so carelessly, to her own ends, and then cast me away – to what? Complete ignominy?

I could not take in the idea, or encompass the oddly sharp sorrow it brought in its wake. And I think there remained a part of me still that could not believe it of her. She would never have chosen to gain her freedom at such a cost – would she? Or perhaps it was not so much a certainty as a hope.

Had she been so very desperate?

I turned to the window. Despite the bright rays I had seen earlier, the sky was grey and overcast and spiritless. I could not at all make out its character; thin, watery clouds were here and there broken to reveal patches of sky still innocently blue. Somewhere beneath that sky was Mrs Harleston – but where?

She needed to be found, and I realised it was I who must find her. I had to look into her eyes once more; I had to *know*.

Doctor Chettle might be even now mulling over my position here. How better to appease Mr Harleston than to dismiss me? I could not allow that to happen, not if any action within my power might prevent it. My place here, such as it was, had not been an easy matter to find and I owed it to my father's memory to keep it. If I could bring her back, all might yet be healed. Even Olive Scholes' position might be restored.

I could not continue here, carrying out my daily rounds amongst the patients, without knowing what had become of her. I sighed as I looked out at the vista before me. Of all the places to seek her in the world, I could have only one certainty: that she would not return to her husband. Other than that, she could be anywhere – and I had not the first idea where to find her.

Part Two

London

. . . the veil
Is rending, and the voices of the day
Are heard across the voices of the dark.

Alfred Lord Tennyson

Chapter One

And so I returned home, having narrowly escaped a condition of disgrace, and with a new sense of purpose: to find, from among the thousands upon thousands in our great metropolis, Mrs Victoria Adelina Harleston. I had not even any certain idea that such was her destination. Enquiries had been made at a house that stood by the coaching route and they said a noise had awakened them in the night; they'd looked out to see a cloaked figure, which after some negotiation boarded the coach; and so I had been given leave to seek her here.

Despite the turmoil occasioned by recent events, and notwithstanding all the long hours spent along the road, it was soothing to find myself standing upon the old step. It still bore traces of this morning's whiting, and the door's brass fittings were all agleam. My mother's residence was set into a row of similarly constructed houses, but this was the home of my childhood and could never be forgotten.

I found myself reaching for the doorknocker and paused: I was no guest. And yet my feelings upon arriving here were not unmixed. If I had had any trepidation in going to Crakethorne, it was in leaving my mother alone. It was some fifteen years since my father had left this earthly plane and I had not wished to abandon her to empty rooms and whatever company her caged canary could provide while I heedlessly pursued my future. Still, she had protested that she had her friends; it was she who had insisted that I should go.

I gave a brief knock to announce my arrival, pushed open the door and went inside, the street sounds giving way at once to the soft notes of the pianoforte.

There was no sign of Harriet, the maid. The sound of my ingress must have been masked by the music hanging in the air; after some little difficulty I recognised Schubert's *Fantasia in F Minor*, always a great favourite with my mother. It had taken me a moment because the piece was intended for a duet and she was playing only the higher part. Still, it sounded like home. The events in Yorkshire might have been on the other side of the globe.

I stepped across the gleaming parquet and placed my coat and hat on the stand by a polished walnut table holding only a daguerreotype, the silver frame partially hidden by a black lace curtain. I did not wish to look at it, and I found Mrs Harleston's words returning to me, so clearly she might have been standing at my shoulder: *The painted eye does not always speak true.*

I felt the picture's eyes on mine anyway, drawing my gaze. The daguerreotype showed my father, seated; my mother was standing behind him, one hand resting on his shoulder, and I was sitting at his feet. I was eight years old – I knew my age exactly. I never could forget it. We had stared out, unblinking and unsmiling, while the fellow in his black hood counted out the seconds until we could move again, until we could escape. And how I had longed to escape! It had seemed an age until the plate was exposed, transforming flesh and bone into that smooth, cold surface. I had run into the nursery and cried like an infant.

Afterwards, I never could make out my guilt in my face, for all I searched for it. The focus was a little soft; my mother and

I had necessarily made those small movements which spoke of life – but my father was present in the sharpest detail. His eyes were the clearest thing of all, raised slightly from the surface of the picture, for they had been painted over his own closed, dead orbs.

My mother had desired this *memento mori*. The daguerreotype was an infant invention then, and she must have been among the first to turn it to such a purpose, perhaps thinking it more affordable than a mourning portrait. I understood there had been other children, brothers and sisters I had never known, lost in their cradles; she had not been able to procure such a thing then. This was the first and only image we had of my father. It had not comforted me, when I learned more of the photographic process, that cyanide was instrumental in its creation.

I pictured him for a moment, shutting himself in his rooms, tilting his head back and swallowing the white powder – the despair he must have felt; the agony. He must have cried with the pain, thrashing about with it, his old nemesis victorious at last. I wondered if he had cursed me while he did so.

None of this, however, was visible in his painted eyes. Mrs Harleston had been right, however unwittingly.

The music became apparent to my ear once more, though I did not think it had ceased while I stood before the picture, experiencing all the old emotions it conjured. I adopted a happier countenance before I went up the stairs to the drawing-room door.

As I opened it, a curiously soft sound came from the other side, making me start back: my mother's voice crying out, 'Close it – close it!'

There were feathers, beating quickly and too bright, for I thought at once of crows. I pulled the door to, my heart constricting, then realised what it was. I opened it more circumspectly and slipped inside. The music had ceased and my mother stood with her back to me, waving her arms in the air. Her little golden canary had fled to the furthest corner, where it fluttered against the wainscoting. It was the second prisoner I had almost loosed in as many days.

The bird hopped and flapped its way up and on to the piano-forte, claws clicking against the polished rosewood. My mother must have been content with that for she turned to me, her expression changing instantly to one of delight. She spread her arms wide and threw them about me in an embrace that made me feel all the fineness of her bones hidden beneath the layers of black silk. Then she stood back and stared as if I was an apparition.

She had not said a word; neither of us had. I barely knew what to say, for I wished to explain my appearance without telling everything – that it was my hand which had turned the key, my mind that may have been the instrument of another.

Then she said, 'I was playing for Sholto. Did you hear me?'

I must have appeared quizzical – rather than enjoying listening to her canary's song, the situation had been reversed; she had been practising upon the pianoforte for the benefit of the bird. The idea was somewhat melancholic and I looked at her more minutely. Her hair, once lightly silvered, had turned almost white. Her cheeks were softer, the skin more fragile and now creased, though her look was as bright as ever. She still wore black, as was her way, though it was many years since the demands of respectful mourning had passed. Her only jewellery was a brooch bearing the design of an urn, woven from my father's hair; that same sentiment was echoed throughout the drawing room, each chair being draped with a black antimacassar. Immortelles, flowers of remembrance, dominated the mantelshelf; the artificial crimson roses and sprigs of rosemary were shielded from soot by a glass dome.

But my mother needed no garish colours, no flashy ornament; her appearance was dearer to me than if she had been decked in pearls and wearing a crown.

Just then, the bird flicked its tail, spattering the instrument.

'Why ever is the creature out of its cage, Mother?' I could not help saying, though they were the first words I had spoken. I had always thought it a pity she would not keep it in the parlour, away from our finest room; she always insisted it preferred the view offered by the higher windows.

She looked upon it fondly, as if it had not just befouled the shining surface. 'It is good for the air, my dear,' she said, 'to be stirred by its wings. It can be so stuffy in these enclosed rooms.'

The image of her so cloistered, with not even an open window to lighten the atmosphere, was as sad as that of her playing the piano for a bird. But of course this was London, and she could not simply throw the casements wide. Even closed, they could not entirely muffle the sound of iron-shod wheels on granite setts as the constant stream of carriages and drays and cabs passed by. The air outside reeked of coal-fires – we were fortunate that nothing more odoriferous was positioned by our street – but all the same, I had not remembered the air so very choking. Had I so quickly become used to the clean air of Yorkshire?

'Of course, I did not play *only* for the bird,' my mother said.

I frowned, for her tone suggested something hidden in her words, but I could not immediately decipher her meaning, and I was uncertain I quite wished so to do. I decided she must mean that she played for herself, to refine her skills, and for her own edification. It was only afterwards that I remembered: although she always claimed the *Fantasia* as her favourite, that was perhaps only because it had been dear to my father.

She let it drop, however, as did I, and the maid finally appeared and my mother ordered tea, bread and butter. Whatever she had meant was lost in the taking of refreshment, and then, of course, she enquired as to why I had returned home. I told her I had come to seek a patient, little more, and fortunately, she did not press me. She only reached over now and then to pat my hand, as if reassuring herself that I was indeed truly present.

After a time, I went to my rooms to restore my clothes to their accustomed shelves and pegs, feeling as if I had never left. In the bottom of my bag I found my book, together with Mrs Harleston's Byron; hers was the only object which had no place here, and after some consideration I placed both volumes together on the little table by my bed.

Soon, Doctor Chettle would write to me here. He was to visit Mr Harleston without delay – I did not envy him that interview – and request of him a list of possible friends or acquaintances to whom his wife might appeal for assistance. She had, as far as we could ascertain, no money and no means: she must go to someone for succour.

I wondered what locales would appear before me when the doctor sent his list. She might even now be on the next street. Perhaps she was concealed behind some curtain, peeking out, dreading every moment the appearance of a coach and attendants come to take her back – and here was I, the man who must clap her in chains.

I did not know what I felt about it, and I supposed it did not matter. The thought of curtailing the freedom of such a bird must always be painful, but it was surely necessary, and furthermore, it was my duty – to my employers, the sacred trust I held as a physician, and to her – yes, to her most of all.

I had not told anyone of the other line of enquiry I had resolved upon, but that could begin on the morrow. For now there was something I wished to see, and with that object I soon stood upon the old step again and hailed a hansom cab.

By turns lulled and half deafened by the rumble of wheels on macadam, I found myself wondering if this was the route *she* had taken. What must her thoughts have been? I remembered the curve of her lips as she opened herself to me, describing her husband, her grandmother, the words she had said: *I was certain to find deep and genuine love.*

I sighed. How many occupied asylums at this moment because the world had failed to give them that one simple thing? How easy it was to be thwarted. *The course of true love never did run smooth.* Was it not the Bard who had said those very words?

I did not know why I dwelled upon it, but the cab drew to a halt and the horse's steady trot turned to an idle stamp. I paid the driver and stepped down outside the Burlington Arcade. The day was much as she had described it then: not cold, not warm. There was the shaded walkway, the gaslights, and the gleaming windows glowing from within. I stepped under the arch, dazzled by all the brilliant displays and gilt signs, feeling as if I were following a ghost.

I passed the beadle in his livery and top hat and proceeded along the covered way, mercifully clean and quiet after the busy road. Here, a cornucopia of goods was laid out: a draper's window displayed waistcoats in a confusing variety of tartans; the next window had fur tippets from a menagerie of creatures; next was all the despondency of a mourning outfitters. Beyond them was the shop that had caught her eye, a selection of oil paintings divided and divided again by small panes of glass.

I scarcely remember going inside, but inside I found myself. The walls within were so densely covered that the frames touched. Faces and landscapes and horses, there were, faithful hounds, and ships tossed on storm-whipped seas. I paused before a picture of the Queen, perhaps the very one she had mentioned; indeed, Mrs Victoria Adelina Harleston might have stood in this precise spot, on another day, in another time. I was so close to her – and yet so immeasurably far away.

I glanced over scenes of tree-shaded dells and rolling lawns. I could not see the Duke; perhaps he had been sold. There were several faces I did not recognise, and I wondered which she might have taken for her grandmother. There was an elegant lady in a white collar, her hair grey, her eyes dark. I stared into them until all else blurred, her face softening so that it could have been anyone's. It might almost have been *hers*. I blinked and she was gone.

The rows of paintings flooded back, each available at a price, ready to give some merchant's new townhouse the semblance of ancestry. There was nothing more, and I retraced my steps to the street – where it surprised me not at all to see an omnibus waiting there, bright with advertising placards; a woman with a large basket over her arm was trying to alight through the narrow door. In a moment I had waved my arm and hailed the conductor, hurried across and pulled myself aboard.

There was a seat inside, possibly vacated by the same woman, and I took it. It was a pity there was no secluded compartment so that I could ape Mrs Harleston's movements more exactly, but even if there were, what gentleman would use one? They were meant to shield delicate females from indelicate stares.

With a jolt, we departed. I did not even know where we were going. The air, stirred by our passing, was not kept out and I felt chilled at once; I may as well have been seated on the open roof. I remembered the tale of a dead wife, a dead child, and the shadows seemed to deepen all about me. Once summoned, the idea of coffins and cold hands and presences was difficult to cast off.

But she would not have been thus; she had been alone, the light and sound all but shut out. Not caring what anyone thought, I closed my eyes to bring me nearer to her, and as if slipping into her story, I heard the echo of her words: *There was a little hand in mine, a child's hand, and there was no life in its touch.*

The hairs at the nape of my neck prickled as if there was something behind me, though I knew there was nothing. We must have entered an older, rougher street, for the seat rattled and shook, making me minutely conscious of my bones, my flesh – the temporality of my own form. Death felt so very close, to me and all my fellow creatures, and for a second I thought of Jacob Thew, attempting to wrap his arms about his skull. How very terrible the lot of man could be . . .

The melancholy was hard to dispel, and yet how much more difficult must it have been for a mind such as hers? So sensitive, her nerves strained by her relations with her husband, her mind weakened by her grandmama's notions. All of it could so easily be explained – if only she had listened to me; if only she were *here*.

Something brushed by my fingers, so slightly I scarcely felt it. I gasped and snatched back my hand, but my movement was restricted; I forced myself to keep my eyes closed. And then came a cold exhalation on my cheek . . .

I cried out, leaping from my seat, almost falling as the omnibus made a turn. I stumbled into a rough-looking fellow's lap and he remonstrated with me, but I did not heed his words. I tried to straighten but the world was unsteady, everything in motion; the conductor banged on the roof, the bus suddenly stopped and I staggered again. The door opened. Someone was trying to board.

I found myself looking into the conductor's face. He frowned, indicating for his fare to wait. Against the usual behaviour of such men, notorious for starting off before passengers could take their seats or climb the iron rungs to the roof, he called to the driver to 'hold up'.

My cheeks felt bloodless. I think he was waiting for me to speak, but I could not.

Then the world returned to me. We had stopped on an ordinary stretch of road. A butcher's boy had paused, a slab of meat balanced on his shoulder, trying to see what the matter was. Had I looked so antic? If he hoped for a display, it would not be forthcoming.

I uttered some explanation about being ill and stepped down, thrusting some coins into the conductor's palm – too much for a part-journey, but it did not matter. Mollified by their jingle, he stepped up on to his platform and seized his strap. The omnibus, now hateful to me, pulled away, turned a corner and was lost to sight.

I did not recognise the road, but that was not my first concern. There were eyes affixed on me. A woman in a stained apron had paused from washing a shopfront splashed with road dirt. Another stood in the window, hiding her smirk behind the copper kettle she was polishing. A costermonger, oddly silent, stared over the oranges piled high on his donkey cart. How dare they? But then, how white had been my face? What was it I had said to the conductor?

I turned and walked away. I told myself it was nothing, quite different from Mrs Harleston's case. She had failed to distinguish between reality and the impression of a moment. I had only *imagined* the touch of a hand – unless another passenger had rested a false hand upon their lap and, seeing my eyes closed, had reached for my pocketbook with the real one.

Thus was the substance of events easily banished. I walked more fluidly as I came to familiar streets, dismissing the idea of hailing a cab. I did not wish to board one. I resolved to walk, reflecting that although I had known of the powers of suggestion, I had not considered them so very great. The coldness still clung. What disturbed me more than that, however, was how easily I had been reduced to a madman in the eyes of the world.

By the time I reached home the day had turned to evening, and it came as a relief to leave the crowded foot-pavements behind me. All was familiar again, until Harriet mentioned, upon my entering the hall, that my mother had gone out.

This was not in character. My mother was accustomed to spend her days quietly at home, playing the piano or employing her needle in fancywork; she had always preferred such to calling on her few acquaintances. I did not like to ask the maid where she had gone, thus revealing my ignorance, and so I went to my chamber to read.

I found myself reaching for Mrs Harleston's book, running my fingertips over the little ridges along its spine. She had vanished so completely, leaving such a tenuous connection behind, and yet I could imagine her reading it as if she were in the room. I opened it and drank in the words. Byron had written so many odes to so many ladies, tender sentiments addressed to an Emma or a Caroline or an Anne. Despite the wildness, however, there was such straightforwardness, an honesty of tone, that I could almost forgive it all. Heat at last began to suffuse me again, warming me to the ends of my fingers, and I read:

> But when *awake*, your lips I seek,
> And clasp enraptur'd all your charms,
> So chill's the pressure of your cheek,
> I fold a statue in my arms.

I stared down at the words, returning to my earlier assessment of her poet. He could never have helped a mind so disturbed as hers.

My reverie was interrupted by the sound of the door and I smoothed down my clothes before going to greet my mother. I found her in the hall, emerging from the shadows as she removed a black wrapper and bonnet to reveal her spotless white collar. I kissed her cheek and enquired whether she had had a good afternoon, upon which she looked away before saying, 'My dear, I have attended a circle.'

She said this as if I should understand her meaning, but I was puzzled.

'A spirit circle,' she said with a wistful smile. 'You should know, Nate, I have been trying to contact your father.'

For an instant, my gaze went to the daguerreotype, half lost in shadow. Did she mean a *séance*? I had heard of the fad of tea and table-turning, of asking questions of the dead and listening to their rappings in answer. It was not something I ever thought to hear spoken of in my own home. This was surely an occupation more suited to those I had left behind.

Mrs Harleston had mentioned it too, of course: her *voices*, and the girls who began the new mania – the Fox sisters; indeed, this was nothing but a whimsy begot by children. Their messages, supposedly from beyond the veil, had startled America first and then these shores. They stood accused of creating their raps by clicking their toe joints, no doubt justly. But then, perhaps my mother did not view it seriously either.

'Have you been to some show, then – an entertainment?'

She looked horrified. 'Of course not! It is nothing low, nothing disreputable. It was a séance in the parlour of my friend, Mrs Grainger. She invited the medium herself and it was all quite proper. I have attended before.'

'I am astonished.'

'And it is – it *is* astonishing! I have heard such things. Your father has always been near me, Nate. At least,' she faltered, 'he was.'

I did not know how to reply. What manner of person would so deceive a widow? It was cruel – cruel to all concerned. I swallowed, thinking for a moment I tasted the sickly sweetness of chloroform at the back of my throat. I looked again at the black-mantled picture on the table. There we were, the three of us ghostly in the dim light, my father staring at nothing with his painted eyes.

'He loves you, my dear; don't you know that?' she went on. 'The medium said so.' There was an odd light in her face: zeal, I supposed. I had seen the like before, though not in anyone who could be judged sane.

'She could not reach him today, however. Madame Lodensia said he has left my side for a while, because he needed to be with another.'

I shivered, though the hall was not cold. When had this taken hold of her? She had never expressed any curiosity in that direction. Had it taken so short an absence to bring her to this? I should never have left her.

My mother walked away from me, entering the drawing room, and I followed. She stood by Sholto's cage, clicking at the canary with her tongue – a sound as meaningless as anything her 'medium' could provide.

Without turning, she said, 'It is not as you think.'

I sighed. 'I do not know what to think. Indeed, I do not like to think of it at all, Mother; really, I do not. Do they have you sit in the dark while they play their tricks? Do they hold your hands? Do you pay for the privilege of listening to their non-sense – *cruel* nonsense?'

'It is not nonsense! Madame Lodensia is a protégée of Maria Hayden herself – and she was a fine woman who came all the way from America with her husband. Mrs Hayden is a medium, he an adept of electro-biology – of mesmerism. They have offered many proofs of their insights. Or do you think his pursuits all jugglery too?'

My cheeks reddened. I wished to denounce the whole barrelful of them, along with their fairy tales and illusions, but thankfully she did not wait for my answer.

'If you heard the things she told me, Nate – why, there were things she could not possibly have known! You would have believed it too.'

I tossed my head. What person, ridden by desperation and grief, would not believe any bland pronouncement a stranger might make? And her parties were made up of her friends, though not perhaps of the finest sort; they would be privy to the intimate facts of her life.

I recalled that she had not answered my question about payment, just as she said, 'She demands no fee. She does not trade in her gift like a shopkeeper, as if it were so many blackcurrants. Why, that would bring the whole thing into disrepute. She would have to find messages for us if we paid for them, would she not, even if none came through? Such is not her way. She hears what she can and requests only a certain kindly consideration. We give what we will.'

'How much did you give? How much would anyone give, to be offered the chance to speak to their loved ones again?' My voice rose; I could not help it.

Her lips moved without sound, though I saw the words form. 'A guinea.'

'A guinea! Mother, even half as much – why, she is nothing but a scoundrel, and you – I would not have expected it of you.'

Her eyes flashed. 'I will not be spoken to in that way, Nate. You may not believe it, but your father is with *you*. He has seen your need and he walks at your side – where else could he be? He is watching over you now!'

'He is *gone*, Mother. He is dead!'

She stared at me, her eyes wide, and then she stalked from the room, the black silk of her skirts sweeping my feet.

I was overwhelmed with emotion. What could I say to her? I could not go after her, not then. It was all so distasteful, so bizarre, and I could think of nothing to mollify her.

I wondered what my father would have made of it. He would have banished any such outlandish notion at once. I wondered what he would think of me for failing to do so. I felt all the weight of his disapproval settling upon my shoulders. In a way, she was right: my father was in his grave, yet his judgement lingered still.

I did not see my mother again that evening. She did not come down and I sat at the mahogany dining table amidst the echoes of times gone by – not relayed by a medium, but hanging in the air and voiced by memories.

I was silent, which made it even more like the past. My father always insisted I did not speak at table when I was young. I supposed, if he had lived, things would be different; we could converse as men, discussing our work, all the progress we had made. I could almost see him at the head of the table, his back perfectly straight, his demeanour unsmiling.

In truth, I had no idea what we might have said to each other. Would I ever have admitted to him I had lied about his experiment? Years after, when other men's work had reaped the fruit of his labours, could I have told him that his chloroform had stolen the pain from what he did? I did not know. He could not bear the disappointment of thinking he had failed. Could he have stood the disappointment of knowing how *I* had?

The ticking clock always had seemed too loud. How many of its clicks and metallic pings and whirrs had I heard during my lifetime? I thought I had escaped them, going to Crakethorne. It had not been so very long before I was drawn back again.

The 18th day of September

Doctor Kerner,

I have spoken to Mr Harleston. A most unpleasant encounter. He has threatened my establishment and person with all that the law and his influence may command. He agreed to hold off only when I said we were assured of finding her.

She has no living relatives to whom she might make immediate appeal. Her mother, he is certain, would never admit her under such a circumstance, and his wife in turn would not deign to go to her parent.

Bring her back. If we do so he will no doubt remove her from us, but I hope he will be content with that and take it no further, particularly if his fees are refunded. He said he is himself bound for London; he may call upon you to see how you progress.

In haste,

Doctor A. Chettle

Chapter Two

Doctor Chettle's letter arrived early in the morning and I seized it and read it avidly, my hope fading to dismay. That Doctor Chettle must have given the husband my address was unfortunate indeed. And no relatives to whom she could go? How lonely, how lost she must be in the midst of this great city, if indeed here she was. But she *must* be here. Soon, I would see her again, of that I was certain; I would look into her eyes, and I would know – what?

I frowned, shaking the thought away. If I found her, I would do what we were all endeavouring to do: I would return her to her husband. And I could return to Crakethorne, to my new life, and begin again.

Now it all hung upon a single thread. I had but one lead to follow: Professor Lumner. If I were mistaken in that . . . I supposed I would, in a sense, be vindicated if her escape was unconnected with the mesmerist, but then I would lose her entirely; I might never see her again. It *had* to concern Lumner, and so it *had* to be my fault.

So be it. All that mattered was bringing her back to safety. She could not possibly remain as she was. Propriety, Society, her standing and temperament, all cried against it. And so I glanced at the clock, eager now to see its face, took up my cane and went out.

A lengthy cab ride took me to the address given in Professor Lumner's letter. Rothbury Gardens had sounded pleasant enough, and so I had not previously noticed that it lay in a somewhat equivocal neighbourhood on the wrong side of the Thames. My first impression was not improved by a fine drizzle, the droplets so light they hung in the air, casting everything into a grey haze and making all around dismal.

I alighted at the end of the street, where some low characters were standing about a shabby stall; the odour of stewed eel rising from it mingled unpleasantly with the emanations of the river, which were quite distinct with the breeze coming steadily from the northwest. I decided not to enquire of them after the property; it would surely be a simple matter to find it myself.

I walked along a row of terraced houses, interrupted at intervals by narrow alleyways and courts piled with refuse. The opposite side held more of the same, along with a public house with an indecipherable sign and an evil aspect. Even at this hour it was doing a brisk trade; raucous voices lifted momentarily in song before dissolving into laughter; the scent of gin pervaded the whole. The windows were obscured by steam, or rain, perhaps.

I kept on, swerving to avoid two ill-dressed boys with ill-mannered faces, who bowled their hoop straight at me and ran on, not bothering to smother their laughter. A lady stood at the corner, although from the way she lifted her skirts above her ankles, I was not certain 'lady' was the right salutation; in any case, I did not meet her eye. Where under God's Heaven had I found myself?

I emerged at the end of the road without having chanced upon the residence I sought, so walked back, again avoiding the gaudy unfortunate's eye. This time I espied, set back from the other houses, a smaller row of mean residences all leaning against one another. From the cards in the windows, I judged they were mainly given over to boarding houses. As I approached, I made out a card less curled than the others, hence more recent, announcing a vacant room. With a growing sense of dejection, I saw this was the address I sought.

I picked my way over discarded oyster shells, burnt lucifers, the mouthpiece of a clay pipe and piles of ashes to approach the door. Long years past, it must have been painted black. The brass knocker was tarnished and scabbed, in keeping with the shabby little domicile. I had no great hopes for its servants or their promptitude in answering, but I reached out and tapped the knocker with the head of my cane.

A clatter from within was followed by an ungenteel shout and the door was tugged open. A narrow face thrust into the gap, crowned by an indifferently white cap. I ascertained that it was a woman, though the arrangement of features she presented was unrelieved by a smile or any suggestion of feminine softness.

She jerked her head as if to say, 'Yes?'

'Might I speak to the lady of the house?'

She let out a spurt of laughter. 'Tha's me, then.' She looked me up and down. 'Need a room, do yer?'

'I do not,' I said, 'but I am looking for one of your residents, a Thaddeus Lumner. He is a professor of sorts.'

''e's gawn.'

'Gawn? I . . . He's gone?'

'Said so, din' I?'

'Perhaps he gave a forwarding address?'

She shrugged, then shook her head.

I had to press on, for I had nowhere else to look. 'Is there anyone who might know where he is now – some relative, per- haps? Do you know where he came from?'

'Somewhere up Vauxhall way,' she said. 'Said 'e liked it better 'n this, Lor' knows why, an' took 'isself off back again.' She leered. 'It was nearer, see, for when 'e 'ad 'is *hengagements* at the Hegyptian 'all.'

I blinked, trying to grasp her meaning, thinking that if there was anything worse than misplacing one's aitches it was muddling them as she did. *The Egyptian Hall?*

'Oh yes,' she said, running on with sudden alacrity, as if I had asked, or she were proud of the association, "e did 'em regular. 'ad 'em all quackin' like ducks an' waggin' their arms like chickens an' Lor' knows what.' She demonstrated with her skinny appendages, opening and closing her mouth, though thankfully no sound emerged.

'*Quacking?*' I repeated, my forlorn tone reflecting my bewilderment, though a dreadful suspicion was growing upon me. 'You mean he is a stage mesmerist, that he does such things for entertainment?'

'*Hentertainment.* Tha's it.'

I was aghast. I could not believe, after everything he had said in his letter, that I had engaged a common showman. And I had allowed him to see Mrs Harleston. I had left him alone with her—

'Anyhow, 't ain't long since 'e said 'e weren't doin' it no more, couldn't get the work nohow, an' time to try 'is 'and helsewhere. Said 'e was on to sumfink better, out to make a name for hisself. You know that, though, don'tcha? Professor Lumner bein' 'is stage name, hafter all. It ain't Lumner, though. It's *Lumière.*'

She pronounced it *Loomy-air*, but I knew what she meant and heard it with increasing dismay. I had not even known his real name. I did not like to admit it to her, but I had to and did.

She shrugged, as if it mattered not a whit to her, and said, "is proper name's Terry. Terry Lumb.'

It was as unprepossessing a moniker as any I had ever encountered, and I could not in any meaningful way connect it with the person I had met. I merely nodded, as if it were what I had expected.

"'ere, you ain't wiv the bailiffs, are you?' she said suddenly, her eyes narrowed in suspicion. "'e's not left nuffink, if that's what you're after.'

She had forgotten her extra aitches in her consternation, but I did not mention that; I told her that I was not, and being thus assured, she recovered her equanimity enough to slam the door in my face.

I lost no time in walking away. So my quarry had flown, gone to somewhere in Vauxhall, an area more degenerate even than this sad neighbourhood. It was no direction at all; it would be hopeless to seek him there with so little information.

The Egyptian Hall, then. It seemed fitting that my odd search would take me to one of the most curious places in London.

Chapter Three

The Egyptian Hall was at once a part of the street and a monument to another world entirely. If viewed without care, perhaps from the window of a carriage passing down Piccadilly, it would have presented nothing peculiar to the eye. It stood as tall as the rest of the mansions on the southern side of the thoroughfare, imposing and stolid. It was as wide as they; it was made of stone, as they were; the cornice, which bordered its first storey, was level with their own. Upon closer inspection, however, it had as little in common with them as a lord with the boy who shines his boots.

Casting the eyes upward from the pillars about its door one saw two gargantuan exotic figures more suited to a pyramid of northern Africa than to any structure in London. Three large pylons, sloping inward as they rose, further suggested some lost and forgotten tomb. A mist of fine rain hung about it, so that one could almost picture it lost in a desert haze. The Hall was famed – notorious, even – for its displays of the fantastical and outlandish and outré, and there was nothing like it in the whole of this great city, or indeed, beyond it.

Since its inception as Bullock's Museum of Natural History the Hall had displayed everything from Napoleon's coach, seized at Waterloo, to a family of Laplanders offering sleigh rides, to the euphonia, a machine which spoke like a human in response to the pressing of certain keys and levers. Tom Thumb, the American dwarf, had once been in residence, as well as a pretend mermaid and a man so thin he was known as the Living Skeleton.

I shouldn't wonder that a man such as the Professor, who had told me such barefaced lies, had performed in such a place.

It was not yet time for the evening entertainments to begin, but a sign announced a display of glass from Italy and the door opened at my touch. I stepped out of the smell of rain and into that of dust.

Lofty arches supported by huge pillars rose far above my head. The interior was said to be a replica of the avenue at the Temple of Karnak, and the cavernous space, redolent with echoing whispers and the footsteps of unseen people, the atmosphere of hushed awe, brought home the sense of entering a tomb.

The pharaonic arches were adorned in the Egyptian style, which was continued everywhere. There were winged globes, figures adorned with serpent headdresses, and incised lotus and leaf motifs. Stelae stood about the walls, the upright slabs each covered in hieroglyphics.

Away to one side, a corner was bright with advertisements for the various spectaculars and *hentertainments* on offer. A large playbill announced an exhibition of dioramic views; another, larger and gaudier still, the arrival of yet another medium from America.

I turned from it and looked about for the manager's office, already knowing that I had missed something. I slowly turned again, this time minutely examining the various notices.

I did not know what I had seen, only that something had snagged at my mind. I searched them for the name of Lumière, or Lumner, but it was not that; of him there was no sign. And then I saw among the rest a much plainer bill, rapidly got up perhaps, and simple in its design:

SHE WALKS IN BEAUTY, LIKE THE NIGHT

Witness magnificent feats of the human mind, hitherto thought impossible!

Pierce the secrets of the veil — see the wonders of the magnetic trance!!

Discover what lies in the realm beyond the shadows!!!!

Nightly at seven o'clock: commencing Saturday the 20th of September.

Stalls: numbered and reserved, 2s (it is respectfully intimated that no bonnets may be worn).

Children: 1s, &c. &c.

And above it all, in vermilion letters larger than the rest:

MADAME VESPERTINE

Chapter Four

I had wasted little time in purchasing my ticket for the mysterious Madame Vespertine's performance. I had not been in the habit of visiting the theatre or any such show, even as a medical student, and yet now I found myself eager, my hands shaking as I donned a new white collar and freshly brushed frock coat.

I wondered what I should find. It might not be her; it couldn't be her. It had to be her. And what should I do, if I were to see her? I could scarcely bundle her out of the Hall and into a hansom cab. I did not suppose their management would allow it, or their audience, or their ushers. Even constables were not known for their willingness to curtail citizens' liberties at the behest of a mad-doctor. And I had no female attendant. It would all be most improper. I had given no consideration to anything beyond finding her, and yet I could not quite drown the hope that she might be persuaded to accompany me.

I left without informing my mother where I was going. I could not bear to see the triumph in her eyes if she realised it was little better than one of her 'circles'. I had no desire to pierce the mysteries of the veil. I fancied I could see them already in the dead and painted eyes in my father's daguerreotype, and there was nothing there I sought. I wanted only to see *her*, so fervently I was almost dismayed by the intensity of my longing.

I found myself once more at the Egyptian Hall, this time not even pausing to peruse the edifice. Now that I was here, it seemed grossly unlikely that such a lady would degrade herself by standing upon a stage. I imagined the place to be dark and smoky, its gaslights shrouded in coloured film, turning the faces of all those within lurid and devilish. She was a delicate woman, refined in her sensibilities and vulnerable of mind – she could have no business in such surroundings. She needed my *protection*.

And yet . . . she was mad, wasn't she?

I stepped under the vast, indifferent promenade of arches, my heart thudding. I was ushered not towards the capacious stair but towards the side of the building into a smaller hall in part tricked out as a theatre, but there were no tiers of galleries, no proscenium arch, no orchestra pit. Instead, rows of gilded chairs faced a raised circular stage with a central dais, adorned with celestial signs and sigils, raised higher still. I wondered if it had been painted especially for this evening. The back of the stage was hidden by extravagantly swagged and tasselled curtains, and the whole was lit by great globes hanging overhead.

I had paid two shillings for a reserved seat and found it in the centre of the second row. The room was growing crowded, the aisles filling with rustling skirts and muted conversation. I felt light-headed – I had not thought I should be so close to the platform. The idea that she might soon be here, standing just in front of me . . . I found myself shaping her face in my mind, the clear forehead and gentle curve of her cheek, the dark eyes, the long lashes – her soft lips.

She walks in beauty . . .

The globe lights went out and a sombre note sounded from behind the curtain, deep in timbre and dirge-like. There was no flare or eruption of fireworks or blare of trumpets, no announcer with gleaming top hat and waxed moustaches. Instead, a lone figure walked out on to the stage, her step sure and her back very straight.

It was not her. That was my first impression. This woman was commanding of expression and, I was certain, taller than Mrs Victoria Adelina Harleston. Her hair was massier still, and gleaming, caught up into a sweep. She wore a rich gown – how could Mrs Harleston have come by such a gown? It was of a velvet so deeply green it appeared almost black. It threw back the light from the gas-jets surrounding the stage in iridescent sparks, like a beetle's wings. And her eyes – they were rimmed with black, so dark they could almost appear painted—

'Welcome,' she said, and I jumped in my seat because it was *her* voice, so dear to my memory; and yet it could not be.

I peered at her, longing and dreading that she should see my face among the rest. At least mine was cast into shadow. Could our situations be so changed as to make her the queenly possessor of a stage and I her willing audience?

'You are not here to witness a great display of showmanship.' Her voice was not loud, but it was like crystal, and singularly composed. I was certain that all within the room could hear every word, and when she paused, the silence lay deep and heavy as all about me held their breath.

'And I am no showman. I do not possess the slightest ambition in that direction. Yet I have recently, against my will, been plunged into a world of twilight, into the hinterland that lies between the living and the dead.'

Had her gaze became accusing? But perhaps she said such words only to intrigue the audience. And they *were* intrigued. Men and women alike leaned forward in their seats, and I realised I was already doing so.

'I shall do my utmost to speak to the shades in answer to your need. Perhaps I shall enter a trance, immersing myself in the hidden world. I may cast you into a trance also, if you possess a little of the gift; then you may see and experience those lands for yourself.'

Could she truly cast anyone into a trance?

I found myself focusing on her lips – those lovely, darkened lips. They had looked just that way in my dreams.

'We have all lost souls who are dear to us. My own grandmama dwells in the borderlands. Now she has come to be my guide. Look!' She held out an exquisitely formed hand, indicating the space at her side. It reminded me of when she was mesmerised, how she felt for the sides of an omnibus. I stared, but there was nothing to see, no trickery, not even an ambiguous shadow to gull the audience. Yet I could feel a presence, could almost see it in the thickening air, in the certainty that emanated from Mrs Harleston – for I was certain now that it was she who stood before me. It was within my power to claim her; to clasp that hand in mine.

Madame Vespertine. She had become a creature of the evening indeed. I wondered how it pleased her, or if she regretted anything – or anyone – she had left behind.

She pointed to a woman in the audience, who sank into her seat as if to escape notice. 'Your mother is recently departed,' she said. 'She still wears the widow's cap you bought for her, the one with the little tear-shaped beads. They were in black enamel, not jet, but she never minded that.'

The audience gave a collective sigh, but I told myself this was nothing peculiar: she could have surmised the woman's situation from her slightly frayed half-mourning. And there was nothing dramatic, no show of limelight or phosphorescence, no rappings coming from under chairs. But then, she had no need of such.

I realised I had not once thought of Professor Lumner – though I must stop thinking of him by that name. Perhaps he was watching from behind the curtain. Yet seeing her now – not Mrs Victoria Adelina Harleston, but Madame Vespertine – I somehow knew that she had no need of a man to put her into a trance: she could command the stage alone.

'Your mother says to look in the little chiffonier in the empty room,' she went on. 'You shall find there a letter, scented with the rose petals she loved so much. She wrote it for you, but when the time came to put it into your hand her courage failed her. She thought she had a slow consumption. She had not thought her heart would fail.'

The woman gasped and put her hand to her mouth. There was nothing more, no declaration that it was true, and yet no one could doubt her belief.

Still, there was nothing supernormal in it. What woman disliked rose petals? What dying parent would not pen a letter to her child? Would the lady now hurry home, rushing to her chiffonier – a common enough article – and find it empty? Or perhaps discover some dusty old household receipts, bearing no trace of a message for her?

What must Mrs Harleston be thinking? And yet what desperation had led her to this? She was lost – not only in the city, but within the labyrinthine corridors of an unsettled mind. She had not meant to leave me. She had not meant to parade herself in such a way. It could only be her delusion, returned with doubled strength now that she was outside my reach. Of course she was not cruel, not a charlatan, not wicked! She only needed my help.

I raised my head to look at her, wishing I could comfort her, and saw those bright, dark eyes fixed upon mine.

'You are wearing the mask,' she said.

I started.

'You still wear the mask he set upon your face.'

I put my hand to my cheek, fearing to find it cold and inflexible, but it was not; it was living skin. I felt eyes, eyes turning to look at me. I was a child again. I had awakened in confusion, a dark shape leaning over me. It was my father, and his eyes had depths I had never imagined; they were fathomless.

I blinked and it became her own sweet face again. I did not know what it was I saw there. I was no longer certain this was the woman I knew. She did not look lost. She did not look confused – not so much as I felt. I was no longer rooted in reality. I might have been anywhere. My hands crept out, unbidden, and clutched at the edges of my seat.

'He is by your side,' Madame Vespertine proclaimed. 'See him – look!'

I did look. I could not help it. I turned to see a man with a short grey beard, shot with threads of white. I saw his whiskered cheeks, his lined forehead. I did not see his eyes, however, for his were paint; they did not blink and they did not look away from mine. They would never change, those eyes. They would not forgive what I had done.

I had lied. I lied to him and I could never take it back. I shook my head as if to rid myself of the sight. What had she done to me? Had she mesmerised me? Was this some kind of revenge for imposing the Professor upon her? But I was caught by it, like a specimen pinned to a card: a vespertine moth perhaps, exposed to a blinding and deadly light.

She raised her voice. 'The messages from the other side are not always kind. I have heard it said that spirits find wisdom beyond the veil, that their land does not allow falsehood or calumny or resentment, or any dark thing. But sometimes it *is* dark. I have been there and I see it still.'

I opened my eyes. Beside me was not my father but a small,

neat lady with auburn ringlets. I longed to flee, but was frozen in my seat. I could not even uncurl my fingers from their grip.

'You had only to tell the truth,' she said, her voice so soft I wondered if I had really heard it, if anyone had. Her words seemed to be only between us. I was not certain she still spoke of my father or if it was about her, somehow – something I should have said or done. Did she think I could have called her sane, set her free?

But she was looking into me again with those depthless eyes. I did not think she was sane – or perhaps it was I who had run mad, for I wished I could cross the room and banish the space between us, sweep away all the doubts and obligations and clutch her to me.

'The gentleman, there, with the green waistcoat,' she said. 'Your third son is here. He wants you to know he is very happy . . .'

The golden thread that hung between us had been severed. I felt it part, turning dull and lifeless until only the ghost of it remained, a connection to her I felt like an ache in my chest. I could not stand by and listen as she spoke to others. Ignoring the murmurs of protest, I forced my way along the row, brushing past voluminous skirts and canes and damp umbrellas until I reached the empty space beyond. There, I turned. I did not know if I hoped she would be looking back at me, but she was not. A woman in the front seats was leaning forward, her arms around Madame Vespertine's waist, sobbing.

I turned and left, not seeing the grand hall or anything about me until I stood once more in the street. The door closed behind me and I was quite alone.

I could not do as I wished and leave, casting aside everything I had seen. I must meet with her on rather different terms, the moment her display ended.

You are wearing the mask.

What a dreadful thing to say. I wondered how she had come by those words. The image of my father had surely been summoned from my own brain, called up by suggestion. I had placed myself at a disadvantage before her and suffered some momentary weakness; it did not mean she possessed any genuine insight. The great practitioners of my art — Pargeter, Reverend Willis, Haslam, Conolly, all the rest — would be arrayed in disappointment.

Unless she truly had mesmerised me a little — *had* some species of magnetic force passed from the Professor to her during his experiment? Or had she merely learned from him, learned quickly and well? He might, after all, have awakened something within her. And her eyes . . . They had been so lovely, yet so very dark.

Unbidden, a line returned to me from Byron: 'We must admire, but still despair'.

I shook away my confusion. If my sane mind was thus affected by such thoughts, how much worse must it be for her? I must persuade her to return with me, to accompany me far from such dangerous dreams.

I reminded myself that I was a physician, a man of science, and straightened my bearing, a gentleman once again. I stepped on to the pavement. The performance would not end for a while yet, and then there would be whatever bows and accolades any such tawdry show could expect. I would walk and clear my head before speaking with her again.

I set off northward, thinking to turn at the Circus and follow Regent Street, to walk past the shop windows with their gas-lit displays. The streets were busy, men and women alike thronging towards Leicester Square, some for its Monster Globe and less salubrious delights, and ladies and gentlemen in their finery bound for Her Majesty's Theatre. The night was redolent with the usual London sounds at such an hour. A grinning fellow, muffled to the chin, squealed on a penny whistle, while a child — his son, perhaps – raised his voice in some popular ballad. The cry of a girl selling violets was all but drowned by the endless noise of iron wheels, hooves and traces; gruff laughter emerged from a public house, alongside squealing giggles from painted ladies. Beneath it all there was soft laughter that could have been coming from everywhere and nowhere at all.

The air was growing unpleasant; mist was creeping up from the direction of the river, or perhaps from the lake in St James's Park a little to the south. It was not our usual yellowish London fog, more an exhalation of the damp evening, glowing here and there with diffused gaslight. Shadows moved within it, indistinct and distant, anyone or no one. It was strange that the street was suddenly so empty, and as another pale drift passed before me, like layers of gauze hanging across a stage, I realised it would be easy to become lost. The mist was turning to fog, thickening as I watched, unusually dense at this time of year. Even sound was softened; no voice was raised in song; I could not now hear the clopping of a horse or the rumble of wheels, and I wondered if I had already wandered from the straight way. There was only the dim recollection of laughter, there and then gone, and somewhere behind me, the hollow echo of footsteps.

I reminded myself that Piccadilly ran quite straight, that this could only be a pause in the evening's traffic and nothing more. My fingers outstretched, I went on. And I stopped, putting my hand to my mouth as a smell reached me – not of the lake or coal fires or a hostelry but something worse, at once sweet and terrible—

I choked, tasting the memory of chloroform, but this was something different. It was the odour of a graveyard and I pictured an open pit, the bodies piled by, waiting until there were enough to fill it; or perhaps it was the pestilential contents of some brimming burial ground already too full to admit more, and yet more there would always be, more and more of them—

Someone was approaching. I heard it with distinctness, a steady and unremitting tread, and for some reason my mother's words returned to me:

She could not reach him today . . . Madame Lodensia said he has left my side for a while, because he needed to be with another.

I think I whispered beneath my breath, 'Oh, God—' I willed the footsteps to halt, but they did not. I knew that the source of that loathsome smell was approaching. The thing walking towards me was not alive, but dead; it was my father, returned from the place of which Madame Vespertine had spoken . . .

Another sound: the harsh, scraping rattle of a crow.

I pressed back against a damp wall, watching as the mist created illusions before my eyes. I told myself I had wandered into one of the squalid alleys behind the main thoroughfare – that was the source of the smell, the reason for the street being so empty, for the quiet. It could be so easily explained. I pushed myself away from the damp bricks. I could no longer hear anything. And I turned back the way I had come, thinking to take a little brandy before my return to the Egyptian Hall, and I saw my father standing before me.

It was he: I knew his face so well, every wrinkle in his cheek, the lines furrowing his brow, the pained twist of his lip. All was just as it had been, save his eyes, which were not unforgiving and blank; they were not painted.

I tried to speak, and could not. I tried to step towards him, and could not. I shrank instead against the wall, the now hated wall through which I could not pass.

My father gave an awful smile, the like of which I had never seen before upon his features. Then he turned, and the vision was gone.

There were no footsteps. I stared after him, my mind awhirl, empty as the mist.

He was not there. I told myself that as I hurried away, although I do not think I listened for I repeated it to myself over and over and yet the vision still hung before me. It was all because of *her* words, I decided – the fraught evening, the emotions running through my mind. Had the impression she had made been so very difficult to dispel? And yet, I had been unsettled but now Reason was restored: that was, after all, the mark of a rational mind.

I attempted to collect myself as I walked towards the Egyptian Hall. The mist obscured everything and still I heard no one, not even a carriage passing by, and I could not help wondering what had happened to the crowds thronging Piccadilly.

Just as I dispelled the fantastical notions that had come upon me, it struck me that perhaps, like Mrs Harleston, I had ventured down some unnatural stair, only to miss my way. Perhaps I never would find my way back to the world again, but could only wander some twilit and dreadful land between the living and the dead.

'Halloa?' My voice emerged thin and weak. How lost it sounded! I wished I had not permitted myself to call out. I rubbed my eyes, but it made no difference. All was white, and I put out my hands to feel the wall at my side and found nothing – nothing I could touch.

When a face loomed out of the fog, I almost cried out. It was a woman, huddled into a shawl, her face pinched and pale – then she was gone. Was she some fellow wanderer, or one of the dead? And then a man wearing a top hat and a bewildered expression was before me. He jumped as if I had startled him, then continued on his way with rapid steps.

I put my hand to my chest and I could not help but laugh. At least, it was intended for a laugh, for all it sounded very little like.

The Egyptian Hall was in front of me. The mist was thinning and behind it was all its stone solidity, just as it had always been. Light gleamed from the open door – how had I not seen it? Sense at last returned and I banished all else from my mind: the curious illusions, my father's face, the strange deadening of sound, my own odd cry.

Two ladies stepping from the door gave me a look of alarm before gathering in their skirts. What must I look like? I imagined my face white with shock. Then I saw a diminutive woman with auburn ringlets leaving the Hall and I realised the performance was over. Madame Vespertine might have already left.

I pressed forward into what became a tide, muttering apologies. An usher in a scarlet cap put out his arm, but I said I had mislaid my umbrella and he let me go. As I went, I examined the passage for any narrow door that might lead from the public areas to the private, but there were none. I thought of going outside and searching the back of the building through that awful mist, but I could not bear to make the attempt. Instead, I stepped once more into the theatre.

The gaslights were all ablaze, the seats no longer aligned but pushed into disarray. Only the stage was dark. I stared at the place where she had stood, remembering her calm silence, contrasting it unflatteringly with my own conduct. I could not think what had happened.

But I had a duty to perform. I could think of no better way to find her than to follow where she had gone, so I walked to the front of the hall and climbed up on to the stage. I swept the swags aside and stepped behind the curtain.

It was more cramped and less gilded than I had expected. A pile of boxes and a broken chair narrowed the already small space, which was dark and smelled of turpentine. An unexpected eagerness, a sense almost of greed, rose within me: soon I would see her again.

I remembered her little room at Crakethorne, and the Crow Garden – the way she had looked when we walked there together. She had spoken of the asylum as if it were a prison, but we could be together there. I knew I could help her. Such a cage must be better than freedom such as this. And with her hand in mine, she would soon be truly free again.

I pressed through a narrow gap into another passage, not papered or hung with paintings or incised with hieroglyphs but plainly whitewashed. I started along it towards a corner, only stopping when I heard raised voices. For a moment I thought one of them sounded familiar, but it was smothered by an angry interjection; it was not the voice I had longed to hear. This was a woman's, but uncouth, redolent of the gutter, not Society drawing rooms. I thought I must have missed my way.

Then lower, icier tones cut through and I knew that I had not.

I hurried to the corner to see Mrs Harleston standing opposite her husband. A young woman in a servant's dress stood to one side; she was brandishing a knife. As I watched, she thrust it towards Mr Harleston – a warning only; her movements were too well-practised to have missed by accident. The other man present was a footman, cowering behind his master. I saw at once he would be of no use.

Mrs Harleston did not look afraid. She did not look lost; she did not look at me. She stared, unblinking, at her husband.

'Peg,' she said, 'there is no necessity for that. Pray, let Mr Harleston leave – he *will* leave us now.'

''e'll leave 'is dog-ugly face behind 'im if 'e don't.' The girl's face twisted into an ugly sneer. She was young, younger than Mrs Harleston, though her eyes spoke of hard experience.

'You will return with me now,' Mr Harleston said. I did

not look at him, but I could easily imagine his expression: the beetling brows of thwarted authority and cheated ownership. I wondered if I could prevent her from going with him. She was still under her Lunacy Certificate. She was in my care. Though for how long, with her husband so angered, I could not guess.

She looked up and caught my eye. There was no surprise written on her features. It was as if she had known I was there, feeling my presence across the space that divided us. She fixed me with her gaze.

'I will not see you now,' she said. 'I will see none of you now. Peg, you are quite right. You have my permission to do as you will.'

'Me chivy's 'ungry,' the girl said with glee, waving her knife again. 'I'll slit all yer froats!'

'This will not do.' Mr Harleston took one step back but retreated no further. His tone was low and dangerous. 'You know it will not. I have the right to take you home. This will be over soon. I shall see you again, *Mrs* Harleston.'

The lady bowed, the merest tilt of her head, as he backed away. He kept the girl in view as he did so – I did not doubt she would gladly sink her sharp little blade into his neck. She betrayed no sense of horror or shame at her actions.

The footman blundered into me, momentarily blocking Mrs Harleston from view, forcing me back to the corner, and then Mr Harleston turned. Like his wife, he betrayed no surprise at seeing me. His eyes merely narrowed as if to say, 'Ah, there you are.'

He pulled his coat straight and drew himself taller, recovering his lost pride, perhaps, and barked at his servant to follow. The fellow scurried after him and they were gone. Along the corridor, a plain door closed and a bolt slid home.

I approached, listening, raising my hand to knock before lowering it and trying the handle. It would not turn. I placed my ear against the panelling and started away when the thud of a knife slammed into the other side. Then, more distantly, another door opened and closed. Was there another way out?

I will see none of you now, she had said. I did not doubt that she had spoken true. She would already be hurrying away, down passages I did not know and could not reach. I thought of raising the alarm, but by the time I was in a position to seize her they would be gone, and I did not know where she lodged. Any hue and cry would ensure she would not return. She could be lost in all the teeming life of London, and I would not see her again.

But if I let her go this time, allowing her to feel secure in her ability to elude me and her husband, perhaps she would come back. Her engagements were nightly; she had responsibilities – she had an audience. I must hope she would not abandon them as lightly as she had abandoned me.

It was not until I was in a hansom cab and hurrying away from the whole ugly business that I thought to wonder how her husband had found her. I could not put it together at all: he had never heard of Professor Lumner; he surely had no reason to connect his wife with the stage. It had been her first performance – none of his acquaintance could have happened upon her and reported it to him.

I remembered the way he looked when he saw me standing in the corridor, his perfect lack of surprise. And I remembered Doctor Chettle's letter: *He said he is bound for London; he may call upon you to see how you progress.*

I wondered if he *had* called upon me – he had certainly not approached me as he should. How many servants had he brought with him from Hertfordshire? Had he instructed one of them to follow me?

No, that was impossible; Mr Harleston was a gentleman. But what a ruffianly kind of gentleman! I knew him to be brash and ill-mannered, and like to do anything to recover her. With a flush of shame, I wondered if he might have been at my heels all evening, observing each strange expression crossing my face in the mist.

For a moment I pictured him as a murderer with a child in his arms – then I pushed the image away. It was only spite for a man I disliked, one whom it was surely not possible to like. Why ever had she married him?

I determined to think on him no more, other than to allow myself the brief satisfaction of knowing that if he had indeed followed me, it was only because he considered me the more likely to find his wife. But if he *had* followed me, and if I had led him directly to her, the need to do so had passed; he too knew where to seek her again.

Chapter Five

I was circumspect when I stepped from the door the following day. I had no wish to encounter Mr Harleston again. He might have the moral right to reclaim his wife, but I had the right of law, and I did not like the idea of his regaining her first. Neither did I enjoy the thought of his man trailing after me, and I looked about as I walked, although seeing no one suspicious amid the coffee stands and orange-sellers, the boys bound on errands and the bonneted ladies.

I had decided that I would be as direct as I could in approaching Mrs Harleston when I made my way to the Egyptian Hall, and I made enquiry of the ticket-seller. She rang a bell and a boy came rushing; she asked him to see if 'that spooky one' was at liberty to see a caller. I wondered what they must think of her, for her to have earned such an appellation in such a place in so short a time.

She asked my name and I hesitated before reminding myself of my intent, and gave it. Then I waited, without hope of success. Madame Vespertine was of the evening; there had been no matinee performances listed on her bills. I had no reason to believe she would be here so early — yet the boy appeared again and said that yes, 'Modom' was in her room, and that she would see me now.

What consternation I felt at those words! It was at that instant I realised I had not even thought to send a telegram informing Doctor Chettle I had located his fugitive. I might by now have had a closed coach and attendants at my disposal, but here I stood, alone – *why?*

I had not time to dwell on it. I followed the boy along a passage to a door unmarked by any sign. When he knocked, I thought it could not be so simple; I could not be about to see her.

Unseen hands pulled the door wide and the vicious girl I had seen previously appeared in the gap. The urchin was neatly attired as a maid and she smiled as demurely as if I had never seen her brandishing a knife. She stepped back, leaving me to follow her inside.

Mrs Harleston was there, seated as I had so often seen her, with her back towards me, though here there was no window to light her cheek. She did not rise when I entered. Her dress was pale blue, like the morning sky. I walked towards her and she did not turn until I stood at her side.

I did not know what I had expected, but she tilted her head and smiled a smile so sweet it stopped my breath. It was not the look of a patient for her mad–doctor come to take her back. Rather, it was as if we were old and dear friends.

I roused myself and said, 'Good morning, Mrs Harleston.'

'Good morning. Is that why you have come, to bid me good morning?'

She gave an arch smile and I found myself smiling back. 'It is not.'

The door closed with a *snick*, drawing our attention to the street girl – her maid? I could not imagine where she had found her.

Mrs Harleston said, 'Kindly leave us a while, Peg.'

I did not know whether to be pleased we should have our privacy or insulted that she felt she needed no protection from me when, like her husband, I had come to return her to her past and all the obligations she had fled.

'I like it when you smile that way,' she said. 'It is better so. Or are you expected to glare and posture – to fix me with your eye?'

I started. Was I so transparent? But I recalled that I had never managed to do any such thing. Her gentle mockery made me feel less a physician than ever and I shifted with discomfort.

Mrs Harleston remained quite still, perfectly composed, and I did not know what to say. Inwardly, I cursed Crakethorne and all the obligations it placed upon me. An image flitted across my mind: Mrs Harleston standing in a pond, sodden and shivering, her hair hanging like rags. I flushed with shame.

'Please, do be seated. We are civilised creatures, are we not?' She put out a hand and I reached to touch her fingers, yet let my own fall at the last moment. A low ottoman occupied one corner and I sank on to it. I was forced to look up at her as if I were a child.

'Better,' she said. 'I suppose you are very surprised to find me here.'

'One might say that, Mrs Harleston. How you came to depart Crakethorne so precipitately, and came here of all places, is somewhat—'

'It is unexpected, I shall admit. But when one is lost and friendless, one does what one must. I must earn my bread if I am to live, Doctor Kerner, and this provided a particularly easy way of going about it.'

'But how *did* you go about it? Who helped you, Mrs Harleston? Was it the Professor?'

She arranged her skirts more closely about her feet. 'I have need of no one.'

'I do not doubt it.' Indeed, in that moment, I could not. I was almost overwhelmed with relief. She was so self-possessed, so entirely calm, and I was filled with – what? Almost a kind of joy at the thought that she was not with *him*. And I was certain she did not lie. She was free of the 'Professor'. Of course a man such as he could have no power over her! But how had she come to be here?

I waited for more, but she met my gaze in silence. I opened my mouth to ask how she had done it – evaded her keepers, opened the locks, boarded a coach – how she could have simply walked away. And I saw her again as she had been on the stage: proud, composed – free. Speaking of the dead. Speaking of things that could not be.

I took a deep breath. 'Mrs Harleston, you must know that you have need of all that the asylum can provide, of all that I can do. Pray, permit me to conduct you thence. I will see that you are given the utmost care. All that consideration can do shall be done. The very fact that you are here, endeavouring to contact spirits – it can be nothing but a delusion, and a dangerous one.'

'Can it?' She met my eyes searchingly and after a moment I looked away, haunted by the memory of my father's eyes. But that was not real, and at least I knew it. I must help her to see it too.

'We can help you. I said once that I would, and I intend to do so, Mrs Harleston. You have no idea—'

'"In vain our fate in sighs deplore",' she said softly. She quoted her poet, reminding me of the handsome book still in my possession, and she smiled so wistfully, so tenderly, that it stopped my words. She appeared so calm, so beautiful – so *sane*.

I replied with words that were not mine, but Browning's: '"So free we seem, so fettered fast we are!"'

She straightened at once. 'It was very good of you to come.' She spoke as if I had been paying her a morning call. 'I will call for Peg.'

I looked at the door. I could not be so dismissed. 'Peg? But—'

'She has been of the utmost service to me.'

Did she mean as a maid, or with her 'chivy'? I could not tell what lay behind her words. 'This cannot be countenanced. You must return. It is imperative for your health − for your life. Nothing is as it should be. Order must be restored.'

'Must it?' She paused. 'Is there no difference, *Mr* Kerner, between what you know to be right and what you *feel* to be right?'

I stared at her.

'Is this what you truly meant? Is there nothing else you would say to me, nothing different? Have you no other feeling to express?'

After a pause in which I did not answer, she held out her hand again. Was I to take it in farewell, to press it to my lips? Was this her way of dismissing me?

Then she said:

'We can't command it; fire and life
Are all, dead matter's nothing, we agree.'

What did she mean? Her eyes flashed as if expressing all the fire and life that could possibly be in her words, and I realised she had quoted not Byron, but Browning − though such a Browning I scarcely recognised, not when his words were on her lips.

I hardly knew what happened then. One moment I was looking into her eyes, so deep and so lovely, and she shook her head as if dismissing all the world, and only her smile remained − her lips. And the next moment I was stepping towards her. I do not know what I did. I knew only that her eyes were depthless and that I must reach her, and then I found those lips and everything else stopped as I kissed her: the world, Crakethorne, all its demands upon us vanished. And I murmured his lines again, but changed, so changed:

'We penetrate our life with such a glow
As fire lends wood and iron . . .'

I held her close against me. I did not know what had taken possession of me. I could not even think. There was only her slender form, so dear, held to mine, and her eyes, and those lips. I did not curse myself for a fool; I did not pause to wonder if this was some lascivious turn taken by her hysteria. Indeed, in those precious seconds I believed in nothing and no one at all; there was only her. We were a man and a woman, warm and living, and there was nothing to divide us.

I raised my hand and slipped my fingertips beneath her dress. I touched the smooth whiteness of her shoulder. Her lips parted under my own and I felt the touch of her little tongue.

It was only when I stepped away from her that I felt the loss of everything: Crakethorne, my livelihood, the approval of my remaining parent, perhaps also the one who was dead; it all returned at once, only to fall from me.

Then I remembered my responsibility to *her*, and that brought horror with it. She was my patient. She did not know what she did. This was terrible, a sin — we risked not only the world, but our very *souls*. And yet it did not feel so — indeed, in that moment when I kissed her, I felt rather that I had found my soul; that I had found everything.

Mrs Harleston — for so I must think of her — stood back. She must have seen something of my feelings in my face but she took my hand and smiled, as if this were not a dreadful thing, an unholy thing. She smiled as if it were simple. Then the door opened behind us and her husband walked into the room.

I stepped back, my cheeks draining of blood. Had she arranged it so? Did she wish us to fight over her, so that she could escape us both?

There was another man with Harleston, taller and sturdier than the footman of yesterday. By his demeanour I knew he would not be so easily dismissed.

I felt Mr Harleston's stare. I could not look at him directly.

'What does he do here?' He addressed his wife.

'Why,' she said, her tone casual, 'he was pleading with me to return to *you*, Husband.'

I knew from her voice that she was not afraid of him and I wondered how that could be. Did she not believe him a brute and a murderer? The other man started, slowly and deliberately, to roll up his sleeves. He did not look at me, but I felt I was the subject of his attention.

Mr Harleston gestured towards him. The man took up his cane, an object so sturdy it might have been a club, and he smashed it down upon a shelf. The crash was startling. Wood shattered and splinters flew; face paints and powders and rouge disintegrated.

Peg rushed into the room, ducked beneath Mr Harleston's arm and stood before her mistress, drawing her knife from some unseen pocket in her skirts.

No one moved but I. Raising my own more slightly built cane I stepped forward, knowing there was nothing I could do but have my brains dashed out of my head.

I had heard tales of people entering a madhouse and being unable to ascertain who was the lunatic, who the keeper. If anyone had entered the room at that moment they would not have known whom to accuse. The only thing of which they could have been certain was that they had wandered into Bedlam.

Mrs Harleston appeared saner than anyone. She stepped forward, ignoring the thug with his cane, and coldly eyed her husband. That illusion of sanity was shaken when she threw back her head and let out a trill of immoderate laughter.

'I have friends now, you see,' she said. 'More than you realise, perhaps. But you also see that although I welcome them, I do not need them.' She raised her hand; in it, she held a pistol. She pointed it towards her husband.

The world itself had turned lunatic. One moment she was a woman, soft and warm under my touch, and now this? Her pistol bewitched us all. I stared at its softly gleaming barrel. However had she come by it?

Her husband gestured to his man, who let his cane drop. It rattled to the bare boards. The strange, wild urge to laugh came over me and I fought it down.

'I want only to love you.' Mr Harleston's words surprised me – it was not only their intent, but the way he spoke, soft and earnest. 'Do you not understand? You are my wife, my comfort – everything! Come home with me and we shall forget all that has passed.'

She did not answer; her expression did not change. She was like marble.

'I could compel you,' he went on. 'I could bring physicians.' Was I not present?

'Every one of them,' he went on, 'would restore you to me, but I refuse to force you. You will be subject to no asylum; there will be no bounds upon your freedom. Only come home to me of your own will, and take up the position that belongs to you.' He held out his hand, palm upward. I did not know if he wished her to take hold of it or give him her pistol. In spite of myself, I willed her to do neither.

'We are leaving now.' She was quite unaffected. 'And tonight – he will come to you, my dear.'

Mr Harleston faltered. 'Wh—?'

'Oh, do not ask whom I mean. Do not pretend. He will come to you while you sleep – *if* you sleep. He will place his cold hand in yours. Perhaps then *you* will be the one to shriek. You might be carried out screaming, and the servants will have to bind you. They will throw you to physicians worse than mine.' She smiled. 'Perhaps they will bleed you until you are so weak you must crawl. They will purge the vileness from inside you until there is nothing left.'

He looked at her, blinking in confusion.

She nodded as if to say, 'Yes, you understand it now.' As if he accepted her words. Then she looked at me.

'We are leaving,' she said.

I opened my mouth to point out that I was the physician and she my patient, but she cut in.

'Come with us.'

My heart leaped. She had seen sense after all – or would soon be brought to do so. I made to follow her as she secreted her pistol within a beaded reticule.

'Thank you, Peg,' she said. 'We shall not return to my lodgings this evening. We are leaving with Mr Kerner.'

Doctor, I thought, but it did not matter; nor did the little confusion over who was leaving with whom.

Soon the three of us stood outside the Egyptian Hall. We paused only for Mrs Harleston to call inside, to inform the ticket-seller that there could be no performance that evening. Then she took my arm. 'We had better take a four-wheeler,' she said, gesturing at Peg. It appeared that the girl was going with us, so a hansom could not convey us all. She spoke normally, and as if all that had passed was normal too.

I found myself enquiring of a crossing sweeper after a suitable conveyance and on being informed where a 'growler could be got', capitulated to his request to 'tip us a brown', and led the way to the indicated corner. There I found a driver in a prone position across the seat of a clarence. I roused him and engaged him for the journey, but when he asked our destination, I looked blankly at Mrs Harleston.

She nudged me with her elbow. 'Why, home, of course,' she said. 'Where else would you wish to take your wife?'

I was lost in astonishment, able only to gather my wits enough to give the fellow my address. I was suddenly painfully conscious of her hand still tucked into my arm.

Chapter Six

I barely spoke to my companion all the way to my mother's house, though I was constantly aware of her skirts brushing against my leg. I remained painfully aware of her servant also, and felt all the insolence of her stares. Indeed, our situation was hardly conducive to conversation – of what could we speak?

I had no time to think of my mother and what she might make of her unexpected guests before our clarence arrived at the door. I led the way inside, at a loss as to how I should introduce Mrs Harleston and only hoping she would not refer to herself as my wife.

If I had harboured any hopes of respite, they were dashed at once. As the door closed behind us my mother came to meet me, drawing back in surprise when she saw the finely dressed lady and her maid standing in the hall.

What should I say? That she was a madwoman, connected to me only through my employment? That I had brought a lunatic to her door? That her servant concealed a knife within her skirts, one I had not contrived to take from her, and that the lady of suspect sanity concealed a pistol in her reticule?

I drew a deep breath, when Mrs Harleston stepped forward and said, 'Pray forgive the intrusion. Your son has been most generous and has been of assistance to me in a trying situation. You will be very proud of him, I am certain, and justly so. I am Miss Milford. He has offered me shelter.'

'Shelter?' my mother asked, coming forward to take Mrs Harleston's proffered hand. 'Forgive me, but from what?'

'I have had some difficulty from persons unkindly disposed towards my means of making a living,' Mrs Harleston said.

My mother's expression passed from surprise to confusion to wariness at a lady's admission that she possessed any means of making a living, and melted when Mrs Harleston followed her remarkable statements with a disarming smile.

'And how—?'

'Ah, I am a clairvoyant, Mrs Kerner. It is most irregular, I know, but a facility for speaking to those who have crossed into another realm was rather forced upon me, and I cannot now refuse it.'

My mother narrowed her eyes, then her expression became avid. 'You can speak to the dead, truly? Why, I have myself attended circles . . .'

My heart sank. I had not thought of this, although I surely should have.

My mother went on, 'And how do you know my son?'

Mrs Harleston stepped forward and took her arm. My mother gathered herself and led her guest first towards the parlour, then instead up the stairs to the drawing room, reserved for callers of quality.

I caught Mrs Harleston's words over her shoulder. 'I became acquainted with your son through his experiments in mesmerism.'

'His experiments in . . . ?' my mother echoed her as she led the way – or was led, rather – into the room.

I was left standing in the hall with Peg. We exchanged a stare before I said, 'You may go into the kitchen. Harriet will give you some tea whilst you wait.' There was a truckle-bed there, intended for an under-servant we did not at that time have, but I hoped it would not come to that.

Peg smirked as if she knew better than I what would happen, but she left through the door I indicated and descended to the kitchen without contradiction. I looked up the stairs, lost in disbelief. Had Mrs Harleston so quickly mastered my mother? Was she so brazen? But she did everything with such quiet reserve I could not apply that word to her.

My gaze went to my father's daguerreotype, sitting in shadow, but his painted eyes caught the light and for a moment they were all I could see. When I could bring myself to turn my back on it, nothing remained but to follow the ladies into the drawing room.

I found them standing by Sholto's cage, their elbows touching, like old friends. They admired the little creature as it flittered from perch to floor to perch again. They did not speak of the bird, however, or I did not think so. Odd phrases reached me as I approached.

'Yes, I see. He was a little stern, was he not?'

'—missed him for a time—'

'Yes, but he has returned. He is here now, where he belongs.'

A chill oppressed me and I wondered if the room was a little cold. I called to my mother, 'Shall I ring for tea?'

She informed me that it was already in hand and returned to her new companion. There was little to do but watch Mrs Harleston as she stood there, so strange to me and so strikingly beautiful. I do not think, until I saw her in my own home, I had realised how singularly handsome she was. That such a woman should be made unhappy! She was a jewel. To have her as a wife – ah, that would be something indeed.

Tea was brought and they talked of circles, endless circles, the conversation itself turning in loops as they meandered about the theme. For a time they skirted their true object, Mother casting little glances in my direction as if asking whether she could, but I did not meet her eye. Then I heard them speaking of my father, of his death as well as his life; my mother opened it all to her. And I longed to ask if my father really was present, where he was seated at that moment? By the window? In his chair by the hearth? And yet as I looked about for a likely place I felt as if the air in the room thickened with an unseen presence.

I shifted in my seat, reflecting on what folly it was to entertain such thoughts. It was an invitation to the mind to play tricks upon itself. Such a thing could have no place in any well-regulated disposition.

Yet Mrs Harleston answered all my mother's questions with a quiet countenance – I felt as if they were by now almost like family. When my mother asked if the use of a room would be of service in Miss Milford's present difficulty, and she accepted, it surprised me not at all.

Chapter Seven

My mother and Mrs Harleston remained awake long after dinner, their heads close together and voices lowered, in the attitude of those who have secrets to impart. I thought I could guess at what those secrets might be and I wanted no share in them. I sat a little apart, musing, watching the way the lamplight played across Mrs Harleston's form.

I still had not taken the opportunity of sending a telegram to Doctor Chettle and my neglected duty preyed on my mind. I told myself I could not bear to see my mother's face if this little illusion of domesticity were to be thrown over so soon. I could almost see my father's accusatory stare from the corner; I could not now think of looking upon hers.

Still, the choices open to me circled like crows waiting for a death. The clock counted the seconds during which I failed to act. I was conscious every moment that her husband knew where I lived – but still he did not come; I was the only person standing between her and the asylum, when I should have been the means of returning her to it.

The shadows grew deeper and the room took on a rather sombre aspect. I stood and said that I would retire to bed. I made the briefest answer to their calls of 'Goodnight' and went to my chamber, whereupon I stared at Mrs Harleston's book on my nightstand. I should have returned it to her, but I had made no move to do so.

I sat on my bed for what felt a long time, listening to the creaks upon the stair that spoke of others retiring for the night. The light from their candles spilled briefly under my door before the night returned and all was silent.

Then I heard another sound: a soft step. The lightest metallic rattle told of the doorknob moving in its housing. I rose and went towards it and as I did, it opened on to darkness. The shades of the night took on a new form, that of a figure, and I quailed, for I saw again my father: just as he had been, except his eyes, which were nothing but emptiness. He carried no lamp. I supposed he did not need one, for the dark was his home now. Perhaps it would soon be my home too.

Then I blinked and I saw instead Mrs Victoria Adelina Harleston. Her hair was loosely pinned, half tumbled about her face, and the line returned to me: 'She walks in beauty, like the night'.

Although this was a living, breathing, lovely woman standing before me, I shivered. Her appearance was hardly less strange than that of a spectre. I could not think how she had come to be in such a place and at such an hour. It was more than improper – my mother would be scandalised. All spoke against it: my profession, my honour and, more than that, my concern for her.

Then she wrapped her arms about herself and whispered in a voice scarcely her own, 'Forgive me. I am so very cold.'

She sounded so lost that I stepped towards her. Her skin was pale, her lips almost blue. I touched her shoulders, her form so slight beneath her nightdress – so vulnerable.

'What is it?' I said. 'Are you in need of anything? An extra blanket, perhaps . . . ?'

My voice tailed away, for she looked up through her eyelashes and for a moment I saw her as she had been, standing in a freezing pool in the Crow Garden – the *death* garden, and it felt almost as if death were clinging to her.

It was all my fault. *I have recently, against my will, been plunged into a world of twilight*, she had said upon the stage, and it was I who had forced it upon her. I realised that my hand had closed more tightly on her shoulder. She stepped further into my arms and leaned against me.

I closed my eyes. She was so lovely, so *present*, and yet distressed, and I must offer such comfort as I could. I stepped back from her and she looked up, bewildered, and I turned and saw her little volume at my bedside.

I placed it in her hands. 'Here,' I said, smiling gently. 'Perhaps this will comfort you.'

'Warm me?'

That was not what I had meant. She reached out and pressed a finger to my lips, though I could not speak. She looked at me for a long moment. Then she sat down upon my bed.

This could not be – she must not be here. I half turned away, hoping she would rise again, but she did not. She opened the book and began to read. She did not say the words aloud, but I knew the matter lying within. I wondered where she had opened it; I think I blushed.

At last she said:

'When I dream that you love me, you'll surely forgive;
Extend not your anger to sleep;
For in visions alone your affections can live—
I rise, and it leaves me to weep.'

It was all wrong. I reached out to help her up and she took my hand and instead drew me to her side. She turned towards me and I felt an odd sensation of falling; I sat beside her. I still could not have said what expression was in her eyes. She was no longer cold, however – indeed, warmth radiated from her to me, and in that moment, with the memory of my father so recently upon me, I was the one who felt comforted.

She said, '*Your* poet, then.'

We could not stay here together to discuss poetry or any other thing, and I began to push myself away from her. Oh, to turn such a creature over to her husband! If I could only cast him from my mind – to send that, and the man himself, to the very depths of hell! The idea rose before me that perhaps she was right: she was sane and he a murderer who would hang, and then she would be free. But it was not his sin but my own that haunted me, setting my skin shivering, my bones crying out.

She began to speak, in a soft voice.

> 'And so, you, looking and loving best,
> Conscious grew, your passion drew
> Cloud, sunset, moonrise, star-shine too,
> Down on you, near and yet more near,
> Till flesh must fade for heaven was here!'

She was reciting from Browning. It was a noble, good poem from a good, noble man, but it raised feelings within me I had never suspected of him. And yet it was so apt, and she in the right, for it was a poem about an impossible love, one that could never be: the tale of a man and a woman who were to be parted, and accepted that parting.

> 'Thus leant she and linger'd—joy and fear!
> Thus lay she a moment on my breast.'

Oh, God – she leaned in towards me, and I did not push her away. It was only that. A woman and a man taking comfort from each other, and I was a *doctor* – if I could not give her comfort, what use was I?

She did not say the next words; I closed my eyes and heard them anyway. I knew each line of the poem. But as so often before, they were different when I was with her. Had my poet always been such, and I had simply not seen? Was this always lingering underneath, apparent to all and yet escaping my notice so utterly?

I think I whispered:

> 'Then we began to ride. My soul
> Smooth'd itself out, a long-cramp'd scroll
> Freshening and fluttering in the wind . . .'

We kissed. I could not help myself; I was drowning. I touched her – oh, that form – I had seen it first beneath a nightdress clinging to her in the cold water and I ran my hands over it, touching her delicately curving back, her waist. I slipped her gown from her small white shoulder and kissed her skin. I could not let her go. Had I longed for her so deeply? I had barely known it, but in this new language of fingertips and lips and tongue and skin, I knew I *had*.

I caressed her lovely face. I think I truly saw her at last, limned only in moonlight, her skin pale and perfect. Her pulse beat rapidly in her slender throat. Afterwards, I could not have said who first reached for the other. I only knew that she was mine.

I did not awake to my sin until light crept through the window and I found her gone. For a time, until sleep shook off its mantle, I was there still – she was with me, and beautiful – and in that half-dreaming moment I could almost believe that nothing else existed. We were the only creatures under the moon and it was simple, so simple. I could still feel the lovely weight of her head against my chest as I held her.

Then it all returned: my mother's house, Crakethorne Manor, the whole world beyond it. And our sin – *my* sin. I sat up straight, my heart quickening. She was not Miss Milford. She was not *Vita*, as I had called her in the night. She was Mrs Harleston, my patient, a lunatic – and a wife. I had dishonoured her – no, I had dishonoured us both.

Thoughts spun about my mind. Had anyone heard us? I did not know what sounds we had uttered. Doctor Chettle must even now be impatient for my telegram. I should take her back to him, to her husband. And yet fragments remained: her warm lips, her legs wrapped about me – dear God! Was she even capable of making such a choice? She was hysterical – was her will not warped and twisted? So many medical texts warned of its effects upon the weaker frame, the way it could overwhelm the fragile sex, leading to uncontrolled, unreasoning debauchery – was that all it had been? And she had taken my arm outside the Egyptian Hall and called herself my *wife*. Had she truly imagined herself such? Was this merely her delusion, transformed into another dreadful shape?

I was in the position of the most delicate trust. I had known her situation. I had read so much . . .

I covered my eyes. My only answer was the image of my father's face, his eyes painted and blank, but behind them – what awful judgement would be written there? But I could not fall into that delusion myself. The dead did not visit us – did they?

Perhaps she was right about them. If she was, that made her sane, didn't it? As sane as I. Was there not some sliver of daylight in that? And she *seemed* so sane. She had navigated London's dark waters. She could manage her own affairs – indeed, at times she possessed a degree of composure that would credit a countess.

She had paraded herself upon a stage.

I sighed. Soon the lights would come up; the theatre would be abandoned and obligations would take the place of dreams.

I wished Mr Peregrine Harleston to the Devil with all the intensity of my being. Her grandmother had said that if she married him she was certain to find deep and genuine love – and she had, but not with him. It had led her to me, to Nathaniel Kerner. We should have been together – there would have been nothing, then, to disturb her, to mar her lovely mind. Perhaps it had been fated, after all – she had taken the path meant to lead her, not to that swine of a man, but to *me*.

I tried to delude myself, because to be deluded could be so sweet. Truly it has been said, many times, how easily a man in love may run mad.

Chapter Eight

It took a long time for me to steel myself to go downstairs. Each sound I heard from below reddened my cheeks. Had anyone heard Mrs Harleston opening my door? Did the servants gossip of it even now? Was my father's spirit – if such a thing existed – mortified that I had surely by now destroyed not just one man's career, but two? But most of all I desired to know what *she* thought, in the cold light of a new day. Was she mortified, shamed, driven deeper into madness?

And yet I heard footsteps below, elastic and light, and something within me strained towards her. The anticipation of seeing her again sent a thrill through me and I found I could move at last. I hurried to wash and dress, just as the first notes sounded from the pianoforte.

I entered the drawing room to find my mother seated at the instrument and Vita standing by her, filling the room with song. I had not known her voice was so beautiful – as beautiful as her person! She sang only for us, or perhaps for me, but it was worthy of the Swedish Nightingale, her voice so pure I hardly dared look at her. I must have surely betrayed every feeling in my eyes. If only she truly lived here, as my own – if only I could pretend for just a little longer.

And then I recognised it, and everything crashed down. The song was from Bellini's opera, *La Sonnambula*. It was the tale of an innocent, pure woman, who went to a man's chamber whilst sleepwalking and was later blamed as a harlot. Had she chosen it – had she meant it?

My gaze went to Sholto, hopelessly outdone and quite forgotten. He hopped from perch to floor and stayed there, staring with his tiny, brilliant eyes. I felt as useless as he.

She tilted her head, sending me a piercingly warm look, and lifted her voice to even greater heights of loveliness: '*You cannot know how those dear eyes gently touch my heart.*'

She had not meant it. How could she? Or perhaps only in some arch way: a method of speaking from her heart to my own so that none other could hear, though imperfectly – not as we had been last night, entwined in each other so that nothing could fit between us. And she was sweetness itself, her voice vibrant with emotion. How I might have felt if I had come across her thus, and she had been unencumbered!

She fell silent and the room, the very air, was left flat and bereft and empty: the perfect image of what life would be without Vita, and I knew that such a thing was impossible.

With a feeling a little like vertigo I went to them as they smiled and held out their hands and drew me to the pianoforte. There could be no shame in it. There could be no blushes. I felt as I had before – as if instead of losing my soul, I had found it, and all was perfectly natural and good and whole. And I remembered, suddenly and completely, a dream I had had the previous night – a dream I must have had with Vita in my arms.

We had left London far behind us and were standing by the sea. My eyes were closed, but I knew we were there, for I was holding her hand and I could smell the brine of it, feel the faint gentle touch of spray on my cheek. Instead of narrow grey streets there was all the wide blue dazzle before me. I knew we need never return; we need not cram ourselves into a narrow train carriage, one I could almost see, its hard benches bringing no comfort, its door slamming and enclosing us, unable to escape the wooden panels hemming us in . . .

I pushed even the idea of it far away. We sat together at breakfast and helped each other to boiled eggs and bread and fried kidneys, and we conversed of ordinary things. I do not recall what we said; I only remember that Vita sent me little glances that were far more eloquent than words could be.

And so for a while longer we lived our little dream. It was the perfect counterfeit of marriage, and I would have been happy, if only I could have allowed myself to be so. I stopped dreading the sound of a knock at the door, her husband, come to find us out. Still, something gnawed at me – and most of all when I looked at her lovely, serene face with nothing troubling it at all.

That afternoon, we sat together in the drawing room. We smiled and laughed and nothing could spoil the illusion we spun together; it hung in the air like crystal, with naught to shatter it until Vita announced her intention to perform that evening at the Egyptian Hall.

I think my mouth fell open. Everything cried out against it – decorum, sense, safety; everything! Yet in the face of her implacable expression I realised I could not gainsay her, and the knowledge rebounded upon me that I was not her husband.

My mother looked up from her embroidery, all eagerness.

'Surely it is not wise?' was all I could say.

'Peg shall go with me. I will be quite safe.' She looked at me as if to remind me what Peg was capable of, but I did not wish to be reminded. I could not bear the idea of my sweet Vita exposing herself before strangers, donning that strange green dress. How could she wish to do so? Why should she seek out the environs of death when we had found such life?

My mother cut in, 'Why, surely Nate shall accompany you.'

The shock of it stopped my words. Even with all her 'circles', she could not suppose that Vita belonged on a common stage for every man to gawp at.

'Oh, I shall be quite all right,' Mrs Harleston replied. 'Perhaps *you* might like to attend, Mrs Kerner? There are not likely any tickets remaining so late, but I am certain I can arrange it.'

I half stood. 'No!'

They both turned to stare at me. I wanted to say more, but I could not explain that Mr Harleston might be waiting for her – that Mr Harleston even existed. There might be a struggle; she could be bundled into a carriage and I would be cast off from the asylum and would never see her more.

I had not telegraphed Doctor Chettle. I had sent no word to the asylum that its fugitive had been discovered.

I closed my eyes. I had done none of those things. Why not?

An awful idea, a gorgon of a creature, flitted across my mind: lovely Mrs Harleston, standing in the day-room, putting me under some spell to help her escape, her face inches from mine, staring into my eyes. Mrs Harleston, to whom I had clung – had she clung to me only in order to bewilder me, to ensure she remained free, that I went on helping her? Had *she* been the one to reach for *me*? Was this all part of some terrible scheme?

I felt a hand on my arm. It was Vita. I had barely been conscious of her crossing the space between us. Now she smiled sweetly up at me. I could still taste her skin. I wanted to touch it now; I wanted to kiss her and never let her leave these rooms.

'But of course we shall go,' she said. 'I do hope you will be there, Nate.'

It took me a while to answer. I felt the weight of their gaze on me, of their expectations: my mother, anxious to seek whatever it was she so badly needed; Vita, slipping her hand into my arm, so trusting, so innocent. How could I have ever thought her scheming? I was the one at fault. I knew that because I could feel another gaze, one that was weightier still: that of my father, somewhere impossibly distant and yet never far enough, waiting for me to resume my life, to distinguish myself – to redeem what I had stolen from him.

We stepped out into the murk and formlessness of mist – not a true London fog, yet it draped everything in a shroud, robbing our surroundings of life and colour and casting a peculiar silence over all it touched. It was as if the strange vision I had encountered previously had spread itself across the city. We might have been anywhere in the world, or without – even in the borderlands that Vita was to try to penetrate.

We took a four-wheeler towards Piccadilly, with the girl, Peg, accompanying us. I was unsure if it was my imagination or if her glances had changed from snide to downright wicked; I tried my utmost not to notice her. The journey passed in a mist of its own with only fragments emerging: the rocking of the carriage; my mother's smiles; Vita's lovely glances; the maid's leers. I felt a long way from the reality of stone and street and so was disorientated when we were set down a short distance away from the Egyptian Hall.

We stood by iron railings gleaming with damp. The driver named some outrageous fare, no doubt inflated because of the mist. I paid him, having no wish to argue, and tried to get my bearings. I realised why he had set us down here – shapes milled through the mist and I made out a cluster of cabs by the Hall's entrance, all trying to set down at once. Sounds emerged also, snatches of voices speaking as if across an immeasurable divide, or from nowhere at all. I found myself glancing at my mother's face to see if she heard them too.

'—said she is magnificent—'

'—quite real! You would not believe—'

'—nothing false in it at all—'

Vita had borrowed my mother's most copious travelling cloak, an unflattering garment but useful now. She bowed her head into it and we moved through the throng unnoticed. I scanned the crowd for any sign of her husband, but I recognised no one; there was only a succession of unfamiliar, eager, even greedy faces.

Immediately we were inside Vita left us, taking her servant with her, returning only briefly to press tickets into our hands. It was less busy within, save for a horrid commotion about the ticket booth, where arms waved and voices remonstrated. We turned our backs upon it and stood beneath the great pillars. I felt we were small and insignificant in such a space.

Soon it was time to lead my mother into the theatre. We had seats in almost the same position I had been before – it felt a thousand years ago that I had discovered her here, and yet everything was just as strange and unknowable as it had been.

My mother remarked upon the gilded fittings and crimson curtains. She squeezed my arm as if to prompt a reply, but I could not speak; my gaze was fixed upon the stage, for that was where she would appear: not Vita or Mrs Harleston, but Madame Vespertine.

In that period of waiting, I felt a little afraid of her. I had seen my father standing in a London mist. *Had* it been he? I was overwrought. I should know, better than anyone, what that could do to human perceptions.

The sudden deep note of an unseen instrument stilled the audience. All shifting and whispering ceased and the lamps went out. I thought I heard a quiet step, though I could not be certain

– but yes, a form was becoming visible amidst the shadows. It was her, Madame Vespertine, her face cold and set, her magnificent gown shining like the wings of tiny, beautiful, dead creatures.

She spread her arms, sending darts of light flashing from that dress into my eyes, and thanked all the gentlemen and ladies for attending. Then she said, 'Before I commence, suffer me to tell you a little of the mesmeric trance.'

I did not know where to look.

'It is a peculiar circumstance,' she went on, 'that men – and women – may be compelled to do any variety of outrageous thing whilst in that condition. And yet it is said that such a trance cannot make any man act against his inclination.'

Her eyes, darkened to black in the gloom, stared at me. My throat dried and I wished I could shrink from it all. A chill had taken hold of me and it spread, slowly, along every nerve and vein, numbing my hands, rendering me motionless. And I smelled it again: the sick, sweet scent of chloroform, but it did not make me giddy as it once had; it made me want to weep. It was terrible, and it was everywhere, and I could not escape it.

Her eyes bored into mine. They were all that existed in the world. Her lips moved and I heard the sweet tones of her voice, but I did not know what she said. Gradually, a new sensation crept over me: that of little fingers feeling their way across my coat, along my arm, finding my wrist.

I knew what it was: it was a child's hand, and it was dead.

I turned. My mother no longer sat beside me; my father was there, and he too was dead, as we all would some day be. He looked at me, knowing everything: the lie I had told, my failure, my betrayal. His eyes were bright and would not give me the mercy of looking away. He had come for me, and I had no explanation to make.

'It cannot be healed,' Madame Vespertine said. 'Once in the

borderland, you are lost; that is why I shall accompany you there this evening, and I shall not let you go. I would not leave you for anything.'

'I tried to see what lay behind her eyes. Was there some particular message meant for me? But they told me nothing; I could not read them.

She crossed the stage, that mesmeric gown sweeping the floor, and looked away. The spell that hung between us was broken and I could move again. I looked down at my hand, half expecting to see little fingers entwined in my own, but there was nothing there. The cold had not dispelled, however, and I suddenly wanted – *needed* – to be out of that room. The walls were too close; I was hemmed in. I muttered some apology to my mother and stood, pushing my way out once more, never minding the disturbance. I did not look back at Madame Vespertine.

I did not know what she must think of me; I just wished, more than anything, that I had never permitted Professor Lumner to try his damnable experiments upon her. I could almost believe he *had* awakened something terrible in her, something that wanted revenge for what I had done – and then I remembered that he was called Lumb and was nobody, nothing but a trickster and a scoundrel. He could have no special abilities. I should simply have been more careful of her delicate state. She had been in my power, not I in hers, and I had failed her.

Yet now it was I who acted like a madman – and not for the first time. I heard again all the sounds of irritation as I made my escape. This time, my mother had witnessed it all.

I took deep breaths, gathering myself, and realised a little group standing by the entrance had noticed my behaviour. Their heads bobbed like birds over a titbit as they tutted and laughed. I could not look at them. How had I come to act in so unfortunate a manner? There was only one place I could go. I stepped outside into the night air; I would regain my equilibrium before I met her again – as a gentleman and a man of Reason.

I walked directly into the path of a couple walking along the street and they skirted me with barely muted sounds of irritation. I turned in the opposite direction from theirs, forcing a regular pace. The mist had lifted a little but its acrid humidity was still in my nostrils.

Just out of sight but from every direction came indications of the noise and busyness of Piccadilly. A snatch of song burst from the doorway of a public house as it opened and closed, spilling intoxicated patrons on to the street. I turned from them without design and turned again. I continued along the footway. Shrill laughter bled through the mist ahead of me; another turn and I found myself in a narrow lane, little more than an alley, reeking of refuse and dead cat. I halted in confusion. Before I could leave, a shadow detached itself from the wall and stepped towards me.

I thought at once of garrotters and cutpurses, but the fellow's voice, when it came, froze me at once: it was not rough and uncouth but the well modulated voice of an educated man – and furthermore, I recognised it, though I could not welcome it.

'Hold, sir! Hold there a moment!'

Mr Harleston had lost none of his peremptoriness. I was inclined to hurry away from him anyway. I did not wish to see him, to face him – least of all here, in such a lonely passage. I envied him. I hated him.

Then he added, 'Please,' and the unexpected politeness did what his commands could not. I waited for what would come next, but he did not speak and I was suddenly profoundly shocked. The man was struggling to speak, not because he was trying to restrain his tone, but because of his distress.

I took a step closer to see his eyes were wide, like a child's, and rimmed with red; they looked as if at any moment tears might spill from them. He drew a deep breath into his lungs. What was he doing here? Had he been waiting for me, huddled against the rot-blackened wall like a vagabond? But how had he known I would come to so dismal a place?

'She is with you,' he said at last. 'Isn't she?'

I was taken aback, but took care to compose my answer. 'She is within, giving her performance.'

He could not know she had been living in my home – that she had been in my bed. And yet my words were almost as wild as his. To tell this man to his face that his wife was at that moment standing upon a stage, acting a part, and that her physician was merely waiting for her . . . He did not protest, however. He only looked more cast-down.

'Do not bandy with me,' he said. 'I *know*.'

My chest seized.

'She loved me once. I know she did.'

My alarm gave way to contempt. Were all about me deluded?

'You are not the fellow I would have expected.' He met my eyes. His were shadowed, and I could not make them out.

'I—'

'I could demand satisfaction.'

His words seemed strangely ordinary. Some part of me knew that such things were no longer done, that this was a relic of a more barbaric age. And yet I could almost see us standing on some lonely field at dawn, the mist rising all about us, hiding our deeds from the world. The sudden fresh breeze of hope stirred. I might be able to best him – I could be rid of him for ever and she would be mine. There need be no more nonsense about the dead; there need be no asylum. She could stay at home with me, spending each night in my arms, with nothing and no one to part us.

I opened my mouth to say that yes, I would meet him – indeed, a part of me longed to do so, and as soon as I could. It was as if that was why I had come here, for that very purpose. In my mind's eye, for an instant, Vita's dark eyes flashed, as if she was waiting for me to act.

He drew another deep breath and made as if to speak, but I did not want to hear him. Everything would be snatched away; he would retract – he would negate his words with sighing and despair. I did what I must. I stepped forward, pulling the glove from my hand, ready to dash it in his face in challenge, when the thought entered my mind, as if someone had whispered it in my ear – why not do it now? Why not be rid of him at once?

I dropped the glove and clenched my hands into fists. I stepped towards him. This was nothing he did not deserve. He was a murderer. He had killed a child, and had no right to live, and someone must deliver justice. I could be that man. I could be free of him!

In a daze, I stepped towards him, my fists raised. As his brooding look gave way to surprise and then to anger, I said, 'How did you do it? What drug did you give the boy?' I could almost see the child, stretched supine upon a scarred table. I saw colourless liquid dripping on to a sponge, smelled its cloying odour, the sickly-sweet stench of a living death.

He shook his head in confusion. 'What the deuce do you mean?'

'Your son – or rather, your first wife's son – you drugged him, did you not? You drugged him and had him placed in her coffin. Chloroform, or laudanum—'

'Damn it to the Devil, man – whatever do you say? Drugs? – what is this of drugs?'

Had the boy been insensible when the lid was nailed down upon him, as it stole away the light, his breath, everything? I could not answer.

'Is that what my wife said?' Harleston was incredulous, and I could not think why. He knew all of this already. He himself had told me of Vita's 'strange notions'. Why should he ask me what she said?

'Do not act as if you do not know,' I replied. 'You stand accused of killing the boy. Face up to it, man.'

'I . . . what, sir? Are you as mad as she? She accused me of burying him before he was dead – accidentally. Of course she would never say I murdered him. She is not so lost as that. He was my *son*.'

'You adopted him – you made him your heir – he was the son of your first wife and she forced you to do so, or she would not have you. You did it, unwilling as you were, and then you wanted only to be rid of a boy who was never your blood.'

He stared stupidly, and I pictured myself beating that expression from his face until everything turned red. I swung back my arm to do it and he raised his. It would all begin – but he only blocked me.

'Not my son? Is that what she told you? Are you *insane*?'

I shook my head; I could not reconcile his words with the image that had been spun in my mind. He was a killer; he was ruthless and cruel and wicked. *And yet . . .*

I blinked. I had never really believed all that, had I? So why was I standing here, my hands raised, repeating the accusations of a lunatic?

I rubbed my eyes. He pushed me back and I stumbled, putting out a hand and catching myself against the damp-slimed wall. My fingers came away dark and I stared at them, knowing it could so easily have been blood. I could not imagine what I had been thinking. What had I almost done?

Mr Harleston muttered something about little George, his son, his boy, and his voice broke over the words. I could not listen to them and I turned and stumbled away.

'My George – my son – is dead,' he called after me. '*Dead!*'

I did not want to hear. I could not see clearly through the filthy web of delusion. I rushed from him and he did not follow. There was only relief as I spilled out on to the street, pedestrians moving away from me as from something distasteful. I must have looked as he had called me: insane. An image flashed before me: not Vita, nor even Mrs Harleston, but Madame Vespertine, her face set and cold and beautiful.

I wandered the streets about Piccadilly and saw all and none of it. A youth of fourteen or so retched in a gutter; a woman curtseyed in grotesque fashion from a doorway, her cheeks rouged, her words lewd; costermongers and scullery maids spilled from a penny gaff, laughing over the show, shouting the words of a bawdy song.

I did not know how long it was until I stood once more outside the Egyptian Hall and found that it had closed. The patrons were all gone. Only three figures remained outside, at once familiar and strange to me. A hand slipped into mine and gripped tightly. I thought it was my mother's hand, but when I looked it was Vespertine – no, *Vita* once more, and she smiled sweetly, her eyes all concern.

'A cab, Peg,' she snapped. 'Quickly!'

She took charge of everything and soon we were bowling along, Vita wondering over the loss of my glove and chafing my hands. I assured her I was quite well. My mother looked relieved. Peg glowered from her corner. And thus ended the evening which might have seen me kill a man.

We said our goodnights and I retired to bed the moment we arrived at home. I lay awake, staring up at the curtains of my bed until I heard a familiar step. I was at the door in a trice and

I opened it and she smiled at me. I took her hands in mine and drew her inside.

I kissed her. I drew her nightdress over her head and clutched at her, grasping her thin shoulders, her slender form, and pushed her to my bed. She lay beneath me and I smothered my wondering in the scent of her skin and the touch of it beneath my lips. I did not allow myself to think. I would not believe her wicked; how could I, when she held such sweetness? I refused to believe it. Indeed, I should have challenged her husband – I should have been rid of him. She could so nearly have been mine. She should be mine, and now she was.

I whispered words to her and I knew not if they were from Byron or Browning, for they were all one, all made of the same hallowed or unhallowed fire. I loved her, and I said that I loved her, and she answered. It was—

Oh, I could not say what it was – only that it was an inexpressible delight and a wonder, and poetry, and joy.

I satiated my longings and lay there quiescent, wrapping my arms ever more tightly about her – trying so very hard to hold on to her.

Chapter Nine

We broke our fast the next morning as if everything continued perfectly ordinarily. I could not help being taciturn, but no one appeared to notice. Vita made little commonplace observations on the fineness of the day and my mother made similar pleasantries, smiling as if she envisioned a world where the three of us lived together always. But then, she thought that Mrs Victoria Adelina Harleston was a Miss Milford; little wonder if she entertained hopes that could only be painful to me when I could not resist doing so myself.

'It is a lovely day for the season,' she said. 'Why don't the two of you go for an excursion to Hyde Park and walk by the Serpentine? It would be delightfully cooling, and there might be music.'

Vita exclaimed over what a splendid idea it was and pressed my mother to join us, as if that was all that needed to be decided. My mother said she was too weary and I was opening my mouth to join my protestations to hers when the maid entered, carrying a telegram upon a tray.

She stopped before me. I reached out and took it, already guessing at its contents, though horribly anxious about what they might be, and I looked up to see it was not our own maid but

Peg, wearing a similar costume. The little vixen winked before making her retreat and I could do nothing but glare.

'Is it anything important, Nate?' my mother asked.

'I have not yet read it,' I snapped, though I had not intended to, and I smiled, to soften my words. I examined it. It was, as I had suspected, from Doctor Chettle, and as terse a communication as I had come to expect, even considering its form:

IS SHE FOUND TELL ME AT ONCE STOP WHEN DO YOU RETURN STOP DR A CHETTLE

I told my mother it was of no consequence and slipped it into my pocket. I could not think about Doctor Chettle now. I supposed he had received no news from Mr Harleston or his despatch would have taken on a tone of even greater brevity – and indignation.

A little later we alighted from our cab by the magnificent gates at Hyde Park Corner and entered through one of the arches set aside for pedestrians. Vita took my arm, and it struck me then that my mother had likely expected Peg to chaperone her mistress, but we had not paused to consider it. We had perhaps been blinded to impropriety by the forbidden intimacies we had already shared.

We walked away from the carriage drive and Rotten Row, which looked a little forlorn now that all the brilliancy of the season had faded. Only the hardiest equestrian swells and bucks remained, cantering along with their heads held high; a few elegant figures yet watched, trying to make out those who passed.

As if by unspoken agreement we put our backs to it all, and likewise the Serpentine, where a few hardy anglers shivered and little groups of nursery maids pushed baby carriages by the water.

Instead, we turned towards the more shady bowers where we might find solitude.

We kept silence until we reached a place where all about us was evergreen verdure. Soon there was not another person to be seen and Vita pulled away from me, her eyes bright, her cheeks pink with emotion.

'Nathaniel – Nate! You cannot toy with me further.'

I blinked.

Suddenly she stepped into my arms and pressed her head against my shoulder. 'Will we not be together, dearest? Oh – do not move away from me! Nate, we *should* be together. Do you not see that? The strictures of Society can have no hold over us. We can be bound only if we permit it – and we should not permit it.'

'Mrs—'

'Oh, do not call me by that name! It was a mistake – I was a *girl*. Must I always be punished for it? Must I submit to being the chattel – the belonging – of such a man? I am a *woman*, and I must and will live free, though all the world cries against it.'

I glanced around, a part of me expecting half the world to be ranked about us, censure darkening their eyes, but there were only the few remaining leaves, silvering and flickering as a soft breeze turned them. 'Victoria – Vita – I do not know—'

'You *do* know!' She actually stamped her foot. 'You allowed me to . . .' At last, she lowered her voice. 'Nate, you have taken me for your wife already. Can we not live decently – happily – at liberty?'

I was astonished. I had not expected this – although perhaps that was because I was a fool. 'What can we do, Vita? We are not married, nor can we have any such expectation. This is . . .' But I suddenly did not know what it was; it was no more than an asylum, a little oasis of peace, not somewhere we could stay. Soon we would have to leave it and all such dreams behind us.

'But we can leave, Nate.' She spoke fiercely. 'We can go to the Continent.'

I stared. This I had not foreseen. Was it what she had intended from the start?

'To Italy, perhaps – not the fashionable places, where someone might know us; we will go to the quiet places, Nate. Somewhere by the sea. And I will not go as your wife – your belonging – or your patient. I will go as your equal. We will find somewhere we can be as we are, married only to each other, and *happy*.'

I had a sudden image of the sea of my dreams, blue and endless. The susurration of leaves was that of waves meeting the shore. I could smell the brine. I felt the spray against my skin. Perhaps I had foreseen this after all. I had thought it a meaningless image, but had I received some prescient insight?

Happy, she had said, and I frowned. Was I happy, even in this little interlude? I was much beset by concerns and worries and doubts; there was too much pressing around us, too much of sin for true happiness. But there was such a sense of freedom in that image of the sea, and I could taste it. It was dizzying. The idea struck me for the first time that perhaps I *could* cast everything off: my past, the future that was laid out before me. I could seize upon happiness as I had clutched her to me in the night.

She stood silently by, awaiting my answer. And then I thought of my mother, her face stricken in the knowledge of our elopement; of Doctor Chettle, his once welcoming expression replaced by disgust; and my father – him, too – glaring at me from a daguerreotype with his painted eyes.

'We cannot.' I drew away from her.

I heard her sharp intake of breath. Her hand went to her skirts, as if mindful of the way I had undressed her so short a time before, and guilt twisted in my stomach.

'I must . . . I must go on, you see,' I said. 'I have to distinguish myself, to achieve—'

'*Nate*,' she said, and her voice was small. I had not heard it so before.

Another image rose before me: Vita sitting at a piano, but not in my mother's house. She was seated by Mr Harleston, playing a duet with him while his wife watched. What manner of woman would have done that? Had she been so very desperate to escape her father's house – only, in turn, to dream of escaping her husband's?

I closed my eyes, and as if in contrast, I saw before me Madame Vespertine. She was ready to summon the dead; her eyes were cold. And I thought of Mr Harleston, his face so strangely changed – not belligerent but despairing, his voice breaking over the words *my son*.

I had not yet asked her of that. Suddenly everything seemed to hang upon it. Had she lied, or spoken the truth? Had she really felt the lifeless hand of a child in her own and been forced to flee?

'Was it really his true child that was buried, Vita?' I asked. 'Was it his blood?'

She threw back her head, startled.

'Your husband assures me that the boy who died was his own son. He said he was bereft over the child. I do not believe him an actor.'

'An actor?' Her eyes flashed.

'Did you tell me he was not his blood because you *needed* to? Because you wanted a way to—'

She spun away from me – I thought it was because she could not look into my eyes, but she did not pause; she began to walk away across the grass. She said only one thing more as she left, and it was not what I had expected, and it stole my breath.

'I love you,' she said.

I love you.

And she was gone.

I stared after her. I could only think, *The child was called George.*
I had never once heard her refer to him by his name.

Chapter Ten

The rest of that day dragged interminably on, failing to break our silence. We returned separately to the house and my mother did not speak of it, but I saw her disappointment. She fluttered from the pianoforte to her fancywork to Sholto's cage until she reminded me of a canary herself, hopping from perch to floor and back again.

Eventually Vita stood with a sigh, setting aside the book she was reading, and announced that she must depart for the Egyptian Hall.

I did not know what to say. A variety of emotions passed through my mind, along with a series of images: her face up close to mine, kissing me; the brilliance of her eyes as she implored me to flee the country with her; the disappointment in her face as she walked away, hurling those last words at me: *I love you.*

I wished to ask her to stay here with me. We should be together; it felt natural even if it was not. But I had no right to press her. I could ask her to do nothing unless it was as her physician, but I had scarcely been that, and it was the last thing I wished to remind her of now.

It was my mother who exclaimed, though I do not recall her words. Vita quietly stated again the necessity of earning her bread, just as if she were alone and friendless in the world, and again I could say nothing. My mother subsided before her insistence and turned to me, her eyes full of reproach, and said, 'Nathaniel will accompany you.'

Vita proved recalcitrant, saying that she would be quite all right with Peg. I knew my mother was waiting for me to speak, but I did not – indeed, how could I? Twice I had been to her performance and twice I had had to rush hastily away. As ridiculous as it was, her demonstration had had some strange effect upon me and I did not wish to experience it again. Nor did I wish to see her that way, so cold upon the stage, so distant from me.

She left the room to prepare herself and my mother lapsed into silence, only glancing at me now and then with a look now musing, now disappointed. I almost reconsidered, but I told myself I needed a little space in which to reflect. I had to think about Doctor Chettle's telegram and consider what I must do; it would be better if I could do that alone, without Vita's figure ever in the corner of my eye.

After she left I sat a while before going to the window. It must have been later than it felt, for it was quite dark without. The drab street could not have been more distant from the brilliant seas of my dream. I imagined Mrs Harleston at this moment in a glittering gown, throwing her arms wide to the rapt audience. Did any of them know her real name? Did they think her mad? And yet they flocked to her and listened to her. If they presented a picture of Society, it was Mrs Harleston who was at the heart of it, accepted by all. If a physician arrived with his attendants and closed coach, would they stand by while she was snatched from them? With so many to take her part, could she even be considered mad?

I thought of Doctor Chettle in his asylum. In my mind's eye he was gloating over his skulls, running his long fingers into all their prominences and declivities, taking them for proof of the genius or otherwise that had lain within. And yet Vita's lovely head was without fault; I had held it in my hands. I had run my own fingertips along it as I called her my dearest.

An irritated sound drew my attention from my thoughts. A pale face appeared next to mine in the glass and I started, but it was only my mother. She set her hand upon the sill and leaned closer. 'What a dank night,' she said. 'So fearful, for such a girl to wander abroad with only a maid for company. And returning so late! I do hope . . .'

She did not say what she hoped, although I knew. And the awful thought came to me that Vita's husband might have decided it was not quite hopeless; he might try again. He could go to her and seize her by violence – this time he would be prepared for Peg. He might already have found another asylum. Or perhaps he would take her home and keep her a prisoner in some musty attic from whence she would never escape.

She could not live in shadow, unable to feel sunlight on her face! I do not know what I said to my mother, only that I must meet Miss Milford after all, and see her home – *home*, that was the word I used – and I gathered myself and went out into the evening. I would take back my refusal. She need never go to the Egyptian Hall again, or degrade herself in such a manner, and she would stay with me somehow – she must.

I soon stood before the Hall's entrance. Its strangeness had evaporated and it appeared almost to have grown where it stood, its barbaric outlines softened by shadows and the moisture dripping from its statuary. There were no crowds, not now; all must have left already. Hoping I was not too late I hurried inside, turning not towards the public rooms or the ticket booth but to the less obvious passage which led to Mrs Harleston's dressing room.

There was no one in the passage, no sound coming from

behind its doors; soon I would look into her face and all would become simple – as simple as she would have it. I would know exactly what to do.

I turned the corner, dreading for an instant that I might see Mr Harleston and his roughs standing there – I did not, but the sound of voices reached me and I realised they were coming from her room. I did not wait to knock; if her husband was there, unbidden and unwanted, I would take charge of everything. I was her physician, after all.

There were two people standing in the room. I blinked; the other was not Mr Harleston. I saw, with sickening dismay, that she was deep in conversation with Professor Lumner.

Vita was still wearing the green dress from her performance. She stepped hastily back – she looked alarmed and I saw at once that she could be under no trance; she had chosen to be here, with *him*.

Lumner betrayed no sign of embarrassment nor discomfort, nor did he move to shake my hand. He stood there silently, as if waiting for Mrs Harleston to speak for him. His black coat was turned rusty brown at the seams; his hair was unkempt and it was easy to see that he was plain Terry Lumb, not the grand professor I had once believed him to be.

She was motionless, only her gaze moving between us. Peg was not there. They had been alone together.

'Nate,' she said, and how much meaning was wrapped in that little word! I could not look at her. I had no wish to look at him.

Lumner stirred as if waking, his eyes blank with confusion. He made a shallow bow and said, 'Tomorrow, then.' He did not speak to me. As he went to leave, I reached out and grabbed his arm.

'No,' I said, my voice low. 'You will never attempt to see her again.'

He met my eyes. His were not piercing. They were empty,

as befitted his low character – how had I not seen it before? He was nothing but a common trickster, and I should have known it the instant I saw him. Perhaps I *had* known it. He glanced at Vita, then shook off my hand and left, banging the door closed behind him.

I still could not look at her. Had she been meeting him all along? *Had* she left the asylum with him? But of course she must have. I was a fool – *her* fool, for I knew I would never have dismissed the idea of the man so easily if a part of me had not so very badly wished to do so. Now everything I had put from my mind was before me again. He had travelled the long road from Yorkshire at her side, just as if she were with him – as if she were his wife. He had settled her in London, provided the dress she wore, her position here – he had arranged everything. How could I have doubted it, when it was his trail that led me to her?

When I looked into her eyes at last, I knew. I had not seen the truth because I had chosen not to.

The lunatic, the lover and the poet are of imagination all compact.

Still she had not spoken. She was looking at me so quietly, so earnestly – could I really doubt her? Perhaps she had never chosen to go with such a man.

It was I who had left her alone with him – what had he whispered in her ear during that time? What dreadful instructions might he have given her? She might never have been in control of her own actions, her words, at all.

But that meant the things she had whispered to me in the night were not real. Everything she had done, each tender touch of her hand . . . Had she ever truly awakened from her trance?

I love you, she had said. *We can leave . . . go to the Continent . . . to the quiet places, Nate. Somewhere by the sea.*

How I longed to do so, even if it meant having nothing in the world but her – and now I realised none of it might be real;

it might even have been a trap. Had he planned to lie in wait at some railway station as we fled, ready to steal everything I possessed – even *her* – and take my place?

She stepped forward and attempted to throw her arms about my neck, but I prevented her.

'Nate, you came.' Her voice was hurt, as if that was all there was to it, as if the sight of him could be so simply forgotten. But it was not simple. It never had been. The waters had never felt so black.

'Things are not as I expected to find them,' I said.

'Mr Lumner helped me.' She straightened, speaking with quiet dignity. 'He found me lodgings when I came to London, and my engagement here at the Egyptian Hall. I did not want to turn to him, but what could I do? I had no one else.'

'You told me you did not need him.'

'And I did not – not any longer.'

I did not reply. Had she used him, then cast him aside? What did that mean? An image of her husband's face flashed across my mind, imploring, his eyes reddened.

She loved me once. I know she did.

And something else returned to me, this time spoken by her: *Is my liberty to be curtailed in such a manner . . . ? I have no control even over my physical being. I . . . I left my father's house because of it . . .*

I could not think what it suggested of her, but she went on, 'Professor Lumner insisted he had discovered a remarkable facility within me – even after I told him to leave me alone, he kept coming here. He reminded me of his assistance and asked for coin. He claimed to be down on his luck. I told him to come back tomorrow. I have not yet received my disbursement for these past few evenings.'

If she had any shame, it did not display itself. Her words did not falter; her cheek did not blush.

'He helped you escape,' I said. 'Did you go away with him, that night?'

Her lip trembled, and I realised that despite her composure she was close to tears, but I could not take back the words.

'You do not answer, but I see it all. I must ask you to come with me, Mrs Harleston.'

She looked up, her eyes sharp. 'For what?'

'You know why.' I softened my tone. 'You know what has to be. You must get better. I should not have—'

'No,' she said, 'you should not.'

She looked at me as if her heart would break. I forced myself to think of what Doctor Chettle had once said to me: that I should have a care lest I become infected by the disease I endeavoured to treat. It was a mistake I would not make again.

'I do not know what I did,' she whispered, 'the night I left Crakethorne. I only remember seeing your face, Nate. I looked at you and that was all it took, I think. Our souls must have spoken to each other, yours and mine, and you led me to the door and opened it for me. For a moment you seemed to take me for someone else, but I knew that beneath it all you saw me then, really saw me, to my very heart. I walked through the Crow Garden after we parted. I knew how rotten the fence was beyond it, although I am not certain I fully intended to walk away, not then. But when I stood there, among the graves – the remnants of people who remained trapped in that place for ever – I remembered the words you spoke to me. "She walks in beauty, like the night" – that was what you said, and it was all right; I felt as if I was safe, as if it was all meant to be.

'I had a pendant my grandmother gave me. It was a single pearl on a very fine chain – so fine, the keepers never thought it could cause mischief. It was a comfort to me, so I was permitted to keep it on my person. I always had remained so calm, you see.

I could have taken your book too, Nate, but I remembered the inscription and found I could not remove it from you – do you see? I wanted you to have it. Instead I put Grandmama's jewel into the coachman's hand in return for passage to London, and received a few coins from him to pay my way. I discovered Mr Lumner already on board.

'I do not remember much. That part of things is dark to me, hidden in a mist, or as if I was lost at the bottom of a dark stair and unable to find it again. Did you hear him say something of that sort, Nate? You were there, were you not? You would not have left me alone with such a man.'

Dismay crept over me. I had left them alone – but how to tell her? But her words gave me hope, of a kind. She might really have been half cast into a trance. She might not have fully intended to leave me. All might have been the result of his power over her, and yet she had thrown it off; he could not hold her. She remained the sweet Vita I had always imagined her.

But I had remembered my obligations at last, and I could not now forget them. It was incumbent upon me to give her the opportunity to become well. Even as I opened my mouth to speak, something deadened within me at the thought of it.

I did not like that I could not reside where I chose, do as I chose or go whither I chose. I did not like wearing the things they gave me. I did not like being subject to their constant watching.

She stepped forward and into my arms. I felt her smooth hair against my lips – such lovely hair. I closed my eyes, not knowing how I could ever be parted from her. And somehow, I did not move to do so.

I stole away with her to my mother's house. It felt as if I was reclaiming her – from Lumner, from her husband, from all the unforgiving world.

I did not look at my father's daguerreotype as we walked

into the hall. I did not see Peg's stares as she locked the door behind us. We went into the drawing room, since my mother had waited for us; Vita and I soon lapsed into silence, but the air was redolent with all we shared.

My mother, perhaps feeling herself separate, rose and turned to her canary. She occupied herself in allowing it to peck a little seed from her fingers, which it was accustomed to do, without ever once causing her pain.

Chapter Eleven

My father's study remained much as he had left it. I knew not why I had felt drawn here, of all places. I had wished only for a little solitude in which to sit and think, and try to understand what I should do. I had brought Doctor Chettle's telegram with me, though what further meaning I could possibly find between its meagre lines, I did not know.

Ranked around me were my father's books, his phials, jars and bottles of esoteric substances; his chemical apparatus, flasks and tubes, syringes and pipettes, scales and balances. His inkpot still stood upon the desk. The drawers remained full of his papers. There was the table where I had lain insensible while he stuck me with pins. And on a shelf was something I had almost forgotten: the reproduction of a sculpture from classical antiquity, *Apollo of the Belvedere*.

It must have stood behind me all the time he had dosed me with chloroform, his god of healing. There the hero stood, the image of physical beauty, having fired an arrow from his bow. The stories could not agree for whom it had been intended; perhaps it had never found its mark.

The sight of all this no longer filled me with dread, only a lingering sadness as I pictured my father, labouring so hard and so long, only to have the passion of his life destroyed by my lie. I did not know how I ever could have done it. He should have scorched me, as Apollo did his white crow.

I had left London so full of determination to set things right, to restore the good name of Kerner, and had returned with nothing but questions. In this room, if my father was truly present, I should surely be able to sense the answers he would give, but there was nothing — only an absence in his shape. I heard no spectral voice. No rappings sounded from the furniture. So short a time ago I thought I had seen him glaring at me from a seat in a theatre — it was surely a vision conjured by my own guilt. He was not here. He had gone somewhere I could not reach, slain by his own hand and striving for something he never found, and he was *gone*. He lived in my thoughts but never in reality. There was only the quietness of a room where he had been, and there would never be anything else.

The handle turned and the door softly creaked as it opened.

It was my mother. She came towards me, tilting her head as if to see how I fitted my father's desk. I hid my shame in staring down at its surface.

'Forgive me,' she said. 'I did not mean to interrupt. I rarely entered this room, you know, when it was your father's. But I need to enter it now.'

I could not lift my head.

'I must speak, though it is not my place. Though in a way it *is* my place, Nathaniel, because your father commands me to do it. You know I have been trying to reach him, my dear.'

I started. Her words were so close to my thoughts, and yet did she really imagine she could speak with him? It was nothing but empty comfort: a lie.

'I find there may be a little of the spiritualist in me,' she said. 'I always felt so close to him, you see, in this house. I do not think

I could converse with any other spirit, but I hear him, Nate. I know what he wishes me to say and I must say it.'

I closed my eyes. Was this madness so contagious?

'He is ashamed. He would not have you live this way. You know in your heart that he would not. I cannot countenance it, the two of you – I cannot support it. You must marry her. What do you do, carrying on in this fashion? Did we teach you to ruin another, to be indecent?'

I wished to deny her words as false, and yet I knew that she spoke true. Still, I had no answer to give. If my father truly spoke, would he not know that I could not marry her, no matter how I would wish it?

She stared at me and waited, until finally she whirled about and left the room. Her steps diminished along the passage; she could not rid herself of the sight of me quickly enough.

I rose from my father's seat, left his desk and went to the table where he had carried out his experiments. I had not asked for them then, but I wished for them now. I would have done anything if only he would return, his eyes restored to human warmth. I leaned on the table, making out my father's history in the indelible stains written there, the marks from his knife, the ghosts of old wounds. I ran my fingers over them. They told me nothing.

I found Vita in her room. I went to her and wrapped my arms around her waist. I could almost fancy that her hair smelled of ozone; in her whispers, I heard the endless susurration of the sea.

Chapter Twelve

The two of us sat uncomfortably together that afternoon. Vita leaned over her book while I stared at Sholto's purposeless hopping from place to place. My mother did not come down. Once she walked to the door and paused a moment before continuing down the stair, but she did not enter and her absence did nothing to relieve our awkwardness. At times the clock's tick was the only sound and it doled out the minutes without cheer, proving them to flow even more slowly than I could imagine.

Eventually, Vita set down her book. I knew she was watching me. The intensity of her gaze burned my skin. I looked up as she glanced at the clock and I realised it was time for her to prepare herself for the Egyptian Hall. The idea was anathema to me. Would Lumner be waiting there? Would she entertain him in her room?

I looked at her and she knew at once, from my expression, what I meant by it.

'Nate,' she said, 'do not ask it. I must go.'

My frown turned to a scowl and she paled and looked away.

When she spoke again, her voice shook. 'Oh – very well! I shall send word that I am ill. But you must listen to my wishes also. I will not go this evening or any evening, but we *must* leave.

I feel it – there is some danger approaching. I know my own mind, Nate, and I know what I must do. We must go tomorrow, or never.'

I stirred. 'Would you have us both run from our responsibilities, from those about us – like Byron, perhaps – and flee to Italy?'

Her gaze hardened. 'You and your – *superiority*! Do you think Browning any better? He married a woman forbidden to him, did he not? Her father would not approve; he disinherited her and cast her off. Your poet also fled to Italy, did he not? – and he *lived* there, and he was *happy*.'

I caught my breath. I did not know what to say. Browning married his wife to the benefit of the lady; he took her to Italy because she was ill, and that was the remedy she needed. He had known how to do the right thing. And he *had* married her. He had made her his own.

I looked at the window. The world was growing hazy through a fine layer of soot accruing against the glass. I could wish the city a hundred miles away, and all the people in it. Still the thought of stepping out and leaving it behind, of breaking with everything, was intolerable.

Yet my own mother had said she would not support our actions. This little oasis, the asylum her roof provided, was illusory. It must and would fail. My profession would be gone. All that I had learned would be cast away. All my father's hopes would be lost and would remain so for ever.

My head ached dreadfully. I could not think.

I came around as Vita took my hands in hers and pulled them from my face. I think I had been murmuring something, though I did not know what. I was not certain I had been myself.

'What is it?' she asked. 'What about him?'

'I . . . my father. He would never approve,' I said. 'That is all. He looks down and he scowls – see! He is so very disappointed.

And he would not help us, you know. Nor would my mother. My profession would be gone. There would be no money.'

She started back. 'Is that all? I can earn our bread, if we need it. I can sit for people who ask me. It will be easy, dearest. Do not think of it at all.'

I blinked. What was she saying?

'We go as equals, do we not?' She smiled. 'I know what you will say: that as a man, you must make your way in the world. I thought I needed such once – one does what one must – oh, but you must not mind all that. Such things cannot matter between us.'

I endeavoured to straighten my expression. I suddenly wanted to hear what she would say next. When she began, her tone was soothing. I recognised that voice. It was the one she had used on the stage.

'He is watching over you.' She nodded eagerly. 'Oh, yes, he is! Do you not feel him near to you? Your father loves you. Of course he does not disapprove. He wants only for you to be happy – I see him now, and he is smiling. He is at your shoulder, Nate, he sees all, and he is proud, so proud!'

I stared at her. I did not know what was happening. I did not know what I should think. I thought I felt a presence, but I had imagined that before, hadn't I? And why had I done so – because she had told me I would?

She clutched my hands in her own. Her eyes were bright; there was joy in them. 'Your father is all happiness, my dear,' she said, 'and so should we be. Nothing matters except the love between us. Forget all your cares. Your mother – I must tell her what your father says. Shall I go to her now?'

'No,' I said. I think the coldness of my tone, more than the word, stopped her. 'I must go and lie down. We cannot speak more this evening.'

I left the room and closed the door behind me.

I heard her, later. She did not come to my door. She paced the floor above my head, the sound constant, so that I could not straighten my thoughts. I lay upon the bed and waited for sleep. I felt as if my mind were filling with the deadening weight of chloroform.

Chapter Thirteen

I awoke with Vita's words echoing around my mind. One moment she was my sweet love, the next a monstrous creature with thoughts and intentions I could scarcely even imagine – I, who had made it my profession to probe the depths of the human mind. I had believed I *had* known her, but I was no longer certain of anything, except that I must be the captain of my own thoughts.

I wondered why she had not simply bewitched me with her powers and forced me to go with her. Perhaps she was not so very lost to me as that? Or perhaps something within me prevented it.

If she could not compel me with her 'powers', she would not persuade me with a falsehood.

I went to find her, and did not have to look long. As I descended the stair I discovered her standing at its foot, looking up at me. Her face was pale and I longed to go to her, to forget everything that divided us, but I knew I could not. I must have the truth.

I went to stand before her. 'Why did you lie to me?' I asked quietly.

A sharp glance was all my answer.

'You did not know my father, but if you had, you would have known him to be unbending, unforgiving; a man of the strictest principles. I failed in his estimation. Wherever he is, if he is able to see all and understand all, he would not be happy for me. He could never approve. So why? How could you do it?'

She stared up at me through her eyelashes. 'Can you never accept that things are not always as you see them?'

I opened my mouth to reply but she cut in, 'Why do we wait? Nate, you keep us here, knowing the only way we may be together is far away. You linger and you do not act. You cling to the past, to a dream. Staying here will end only in our destruction. We could have *life*.'

'Life?' I echoed.

'Yes – that! I wished only to free you from the shackles you place upon your own wrists. Of course your father wants your happiness. If he did not, he would not be worthy of the name. And still you allow him to stand between us. Do you not care? Do you not love me? Would you lock me in a tiny room, like a canary, to sing at your command?'

I stared. Was that what she thought of my work? I had tried to *help* her. And she had *needed* my help. I had been blinded by her, perhaps. *She walks in beauty*, I had said – such a stupid thing for a doctor to say, so inappropriate. Had that, and only that, been behind all of my decisions? I was a man of science, and I had to live as my father's son. Should I turn my back on the whole of Society and place myself outside it? Was not that the very definition of madness?

'When you were placed in a trance, you found yourself in just such a position,' I said, 'at the bottom of a stair. Look! You thought it a place beyond death, but I think it was only a creation of your own unconscious mind. Do you know why you should be so afraid of it – why it was so dark?'

She frowned.

'You do not speak to the dead. You have no special insight.

How could you? You have no concept of what my father would think. You see your own fears and dark imaginings, or perhaps those of the people around you, and that is all. You lied to me, Vita. You lied to the audiences who came to see you. Perhaps you mesmerised them a little. You conjured spectres from the signs they gave you and perhaps even believed your own falsehoods. They believed them because they wished to – that does not make them real. It does not make them sane.'

She shook her head vehemently. 'How can you say that, when you have seen it yourself? I know you have, Nate. You walk half in death. You have crossed the boundary—'

'No.'

'I *know* you have! I saw it. You must trust in me.'

'Trust?' I did not know how to answer her, for the word struck strangely on my ear. Had there ever been trust between us?

She let out an exasperated cry. 'You will not believe in me,' she said, 'and yet I believed in you, many times, even when you betrayed me!'

'*Betrayed* you?'

'You had the attendants watch me all of the time. You forced me to speak about things I did not wish to speak of. You pushed me into the hands of that awful man, Lumner, when I begged you not to. And you are content to live with me as if I was your *wife*.'

I stepped back, all my certainty giving way to dismay.

'And now you accuse me of a falsehood, like – like Apollo's white crow!'

I did not know how to answer. Something shifted in the shadows behind her. My mother? I could not look.

'If I *had* lied, Nate, should you not have forgiven me as I forgave you, over and over? Or will you punish me still?'

I raised my eyes at last. The hall was empty. There was only a darkening, as if the shadows had coalesced into a form a little like a figure. It stood quietly against the wall. It was not there. It was not my father. That was lunacy. It was a pit gaping before my feet.

I blinked and there was only the daguerreotype, two brighter points gleaming from the dimness. They were his eyes – only paint, but still they told me all that I needed to know.

Someone tapped my shoulder and I almost cried out. My mother was standing there, her expression all bewilderment. She held something out: a telegram. I took it. She waited, no doubt for some explanation of our behaviour, but I had none to give. I opened the sheet and read what was written there. My eyes widened.

'Mr Harleston,' I whispered.

'What was that?' my mother asked. 'Who is Mr Harleston?'

I shook my head, trying to restore my senses. 'It does not matter now,' I said. 'Excuse me.' I walked away. I could see neither of them further. It was the girl I had to find; I needed to speak to Peg.

Chapter Fourteen

I suppose Mrs Harleston would say that I betrayed her again. She would say I broke trust with her, though I do not think I did either of those things. And yet . . . and yet.

I must believe I did the right thing. I *must*.

The carriage came a few hours later. Mrs Harleston had returned to her room, although she had not eaten. I suggested my mother take up some cold meats and bread and butter on a tray, but the lady made no reply to her knock and I would not allow my mother to press her. Mrs Harleston remained closeted behind a closed door, and there was some advantage in that.

I did not look at the telegram again. Mr Harleston had not persisted in the pursuit of his wife – all the time I had dreaded a knock at the door, he had not even been in London. He had returned to Hertfordshire, and there he had attempted to take his own life.

Doctor Chettle had sent the intelligence to me. The man had retired to his study with a pistol and sent a bullet into his skull – and yet he lived still, in spite of himself, by whatever grace he could find.

I thought of bone cracked and shattered and the life that nevertheless still throbbed within. I wondered what Doctor Chettle thought of it; if he still imagined he could trace all the sorrow and despair and dread of man in the shape of his skull.

I did not wish to think of Peregrine Harleston, but I had been able to do little else. In my mind he was no longer a bullying brute; he was crouching by a filthy wall, his eyes red-rimmed, his face full of despair at the thought of all he had lost. And that he had tried to take his life by his own hand, as my father did? – I could hardly bear the comparison. Was death to be so desired, and life so wretched?

Mr Harleston might yet die. He lay at Milford Lodge as nearly a corpse as it was possible to be. I supposed a more cynical man might see it as an opportunity: it could provide us a little respite in which to make our escape; the lady might be mine after all. But how could anyone bear to profit from such a thing? I would not even try to convince myself now that he was so unnatural a father as to poison a child – his own child. He had been broken utterly, because of *her*.

Mrs Harleston did not come down when they arrived at the door. I had sent Harriet away and opened it myself. I had already taken Peg aside and paid handsomely for her assistance; I told her she would better serve her mistress by listening to me, and the girl had done as I said: she brought the knife and the pistol and allowed me to relieve her of them. She listened to my words, although I think it was my coins that spoke loudest, judging by their reflected gleam in her eyes.

Two broad men and a female attendant had been lent to us by a moderately sized asylum a short distance away – one which, I now remembered, had once refused me employment. I had telegraphed Doctor Chettle and suggested he request it of them, for suitable reimbursements.

It was the woman who came in first. With little preamble she cast about the hall for the patient. Her gaze fell upon my mother, who had appeared at the parlour door, but I shook my head and indicated the stairs.

'I will bring her myself,' I said. 'It is better that way.'

When I passed the spot where I thought I had seen a shadow taking form, an involuntary shiver came over me. Regardless of the attendants' eyes on my back, I climbed slowly. Would my father be proud at last? I was doing the right thing, the thing he would have expected me to do, and yet everything within me was sinking.

Here was the passage to my room where she must have stood, waiting to come in. Here were the steps that led to her door. All above me was silent. Only my footsteps were loud, as if announcing my intentions.

I knocked at her door and turned the handle and went in. She was standing as usual, her back to me, facing the window, and she did not move. I did not know what she gazed upon so intently, when outside, all was lost in the gloom of another London day that would never grow bright. I wondered if she was thinking of what lay beyond the serried ranks of buildings: the sea, perhaps, and ships waiting there for passengers who would never come, and the waves ceaselessly breaking on the shore.

But only she was leaving now, and she knew it. She turned, and for a moment, all I could see were her beautiful eyes. She was more than ever possessed of that outward calm that had so moved me when she had arrived at Crakethorne. She did not acknowledge Peg, who stood so quietly in the corner. She met my eyes, and I could have lost myself in her own dark depths . . . I almost had.

I heard the attendant's rough tones, floating up the staircase as from another world, 'Make no trouble about it.'

Mrs Harleston made no remark on the woman's coarseness. She looked at me silently, her expression giving away nothing of her feelings, and then she stirred and walked ahead of me, without even a glance over her shoulder to see if I would follow. Her tread retreated down the stairs, trailed by Peg, and voices rose to meet her from the hall.

My mother must have realised at last that something was the matter. I heard her wail of distress and indignation.

It was too late. The door closed, and Mrs Victoria Adelina Harleston was gone.

Chapter Fifteen

My mother sat in her black dress, her eyes cast down, the image of a woman in mourning. I knew it was no longer my father she was thinking of – or perhaps it was them both. I had been forced to explain to her the imposture that had been carried out in her home: that Miss Milford was a Mrs Harleston, and a runaway, and mad. She had not recovered from her confusion and dismay; indeed, it would be some time before she did.

I wished I could have lied to her. Now she knew all my failings, save one.

I went to her and knelt before her. Her hand in mine was cold and I pressed it to my lips. 'I am sorry,' I whispered.

Her fingers brushed my hair, finding their way beneath the strands; I felt them against my scalp. Unmanly tears rose to my eyes and I laid my head on her lap, not wanting her to see. I knew I could no longer continue as I had. She must know all, and if she cast me off, it would be her choice, based upon honesty, and I would accept it.

'That is not everything,' I said. 'Mother, you must know: it was I who killed my father.'

Her hand stilled in my hair.

My voice broke over the words, but I had started, and I would reveal the whole. I told her of my trance, how I had been lost to the chloroform, of the silver pins – and of the falsehood that had robbed my father of his achievement, his life, his good name.

Her fingers tightened, pulling my hair, but it did not matter.

'Is that what you thought?' she said. 'Is that what you imagined, all these years?'

Her voice was desiccated, like something heard from beyond a veil – and yet there was life in it too. I lifted my head: I could not think what she meant, but my mother's eyes were the same as they had always been and, as ever, they looked kindly upon me. Was she trying to spare me?

She put a hand to my chin and lifted my face. 'He did not take his life because of you,' she said.

I pulled away. 'Mother, I must face it: I know what I did.'

She smiled – she truly smiled on me, and it was wistful, and there was sorrow in it. 'He knew that he had failed,' she said.

'He did – but he should not have thought it!' I exclaimed. 'Father did not fail. His method worked, only—'

'He killed you, Nate.'

Everything stopped. There was no sound in the room. I could not even hear the ticking of the clock.

'He gave you too much of the drug,' she said. 'He could hardly bring himself to tell me – he barely managed to revive you.'

'What are you saying?' I whispered.

'Chloroform is dangerous.' Her expression was so soft I could not bear to look at it. 'You know that, don't you? You are a doctor.'

'I knew that someone had died,' I stammered. 'I heard of it, but that was years later, Mother, when its use was established. A girl, I believe, seventeen years old, but that was because they gave her too much . . .'

She nodded agreement. 'If your father would regret anything, it is that he failed to tell the world of the risks.'

'But I . . . the pins—'

'There were no pins,' she said softly, 'and should never have been. He had intended to use them on you, Nate – although if I had known of it, I would never have allowed it. He should not have used you as a . . . a *subject*. You were his *son*. But he never marked your flesh, my dear: he rendered you unconscious, and he would have done his experiments, but you stopped breathing. He almost lost you.'

She stroked my cheek, but I could only stare. Was this some story she was spinning to save my feelings? But no, there was too much of reality in it for that.

'He brought you back,' she said. 'If he had not, it would have broken my heart. It broke his anyway – oh, but that was not your fault, Nate. You were a child. You were not accountable, do you see? If you lied to him, I think he had forgotten it. He would not have blamed you. He was only glad you were *alive*.'

I buried my face once more and wept; we both did. And then I quieted as Vita's words came back to me.

You walk half in death. You have crossed the boundary . . . And you returned, but different.

Vita had told me the truth – and I had accused her of a falsehood. I had cast her out, cursed her, like Apollo had his white crow. How she could have seen the truth was a mystery to me. Had she truly glimpsed my soul, seen into some land of the dead? I pictured her as she had stood upon the stage, with her darkly rimmed eyes – her *painted* eyes – and I did not know.

The painted eye does not always speak true.

I pushed myself to my feet and rushed from my mother's side. I went to the hall, where my father's picture stood. I snatched it from the table, fumbling with the frame, pulling the daguerreotype free. I ran my finger across it. The paint felt dry and slightly raised from the surface. I set it down on the table and scratched at it with my fingernails.

The paint crumbled and fell away. There, beneath it, were my father's eyes. They were closed, of course; I would never see into them again. But somehow, his expression seemed different. I had taken his look for disdain. I had taken it for hatred. Now I saw written there only sorrow.

He was only glad you were alive.

My mother's words haunted me, for I was not alive, was I? I did not feel so. Indeed, I doubted I would ever feel truly alive again.

PART THREE

Crakethorne

And who are you? said he.
Don't puzzle me, said I.

Laurence Sterne

Doctor Nathaniel Kerner's Journal

13th October

*Several weeks have gone by since I last took up my journal. It is
not that I have been unable to do so, or that the time has been
uneventful; rather, I have lacked the will to write. Still, much has
happened, and there has been some progress, so the horizon is tinged
with the promise of a new day.*

*I have been fortunate to escape the censure of Doctor Chettle and
the world, for the quiet return of our patient to Crakethorne did much
to alleviate the scandal of her leaving it. Furthermore, although Mr
Harleston continues ill, his payments are kept up by his steward,
which has cheered Doctor Chettle immeasurably. Doubly so, I think,
since there can be no thought presently of removing his wife from our
care.*

*I have, however, made a removal on my own part. Rather than
continue in my old rooms at the asylum, I have taken one of the
small cottages in the grounds. This was partly for my comfort, since I
wished for something that more resembled a home, but it also seemed
important that I bring my mother to Yorkshire with me. It was
time to close the book of the past. I could not leave her among the
memories and the dust, and I wished, too, to remove her from the
influence of her 'circles'. The spiritualist mania gathers apace, but I
cannot bear the idea of her being caught in its tide, only to be cast on
to some strange shore with no means or comfort remaining to her, and
friendless after all.*

Perhaps it will one day be proved that spirits can leave their graves and speak, but for now there is nothing conclusive, nothing certain, and I do not wish to be mired in it further. But even without such things, my mother's house was haunted: filled with my father's presence. He was there in his study, his possessions all around him; there in the hall; there in my mother's eyes.

My mother acquiesced to the notion more readily than I had anticipated, even considering our destination. She had never thought to remove to Yorkshire, nor to live within the environs of an insane asylum, but she made no objection. She has passed no comment upon the uncouth accents of its occupants or the lack of variety of our society. She frowns only when she hears the crows calling, which is a pity, for we are now situated within their close vicinity.

They are not the only source of birdsong, however, for my mother insisted that Sholto should accompany her, and so that bright little fellow journeyed also to Yorkshire. I hear his trilling now, the sound of life overlying that of death. There is no need for his wings to stir the air of these rooms, however, since the windows of our domicile may be thrown open as we wish it. They admit only sweet breezes, albeit rather more chill than when I left, with no taint of London smoke.

For myself, I was strangely relieved to return to Crakethorne. I was pleased to be greeted by Peter Ambrose's wagging behind, by Samuel Brewer's proclamation that he is made Emperor of the Northern Wastes, even by Della Martin's scowls and hisses. There has been one sad change, however: Jacob Thew succumbed to the crows at last. He never did bring to memory the rhyme to see them away, and when he died, he was buried in their garden, amidst the other souls whose families did not care to claim them. Now the crows may perch upon the stone that marks his grave and he shall not fear them or cower before them. I wish I could have been there, for I cannot efface the memory of his last cry to me: Don't leave me here!

But I shall not dwell on melancholy matters. Despite the lack of

*picturesque views, of sunshine, of civilisation, I find myself glad to see
even the old slanting hawthorns, for all they are so often lashed with
rain. And the crows' rough song of death is well suited to their home.
As bleak as it may be in this unforgiving season, however, it feels less
wild than the metropolis had sometimes been.*

*The view from our window, thankfully, is all of life, despite the
leafless trees and the black birds with their morbid associations. It is
true that there are no formal avenues or gently undulating lawns or
gravel walks, but there is a certain grandeur in the natural landscapes
that finds echo within the soul.*

*Sometimes little groups of patients pass by, huddled into their plain
winter apparel and herded by their keepers. They skirt the Crow
Garden of course, and stay well away from the porter, who continues
a surly fellow. Indeed, he is worse than before, for he makes complaint
to all who will listen that his old dog, Brown, is these days very often
absent from his side. Its lack has become his chief cavil, though I dare
say it is the ruling comfort for all who pass by the lodge.*

*At least the fence around the grounds has undergone repair, though
I do not know if he has done it to prevent the escape of a patient or
his dog. I do not suppose it matters.*

*It is a pity my mother does not always relish the views — she does
not care to see the patients taking their daily exercise, and at those
times she draws the curtain across the window. She says nothing, and
I do not complain of it, for it is her choice. She always makes one
exception.*

*My work continues apace. Doctor Chettle has softened toward
me somewhat; he even endeavours to draw me into his world of dry
bones and empty skulls, but I continue to be more interested in the
animating spark contained therein.*

*I try to engage with all of the patients, however difficult. Samuel
Brewer submits to no sensible conversation, but wishes me to read his
journal. Peter merely barks. Constance Glover, a new admittance,*

turns and walks away when asked how she does. Lillian Smith is all gentle smiles, but she looks more wasted than ever and I have but recently discovered that the amendment to her diet which I previously prescribed has not been carried out. Her case notes, updated in my absence by Doctor Chettle, give no clue as to the reason, instead being full of phrenological foolery about her organ of adhesiveness and attachment to the society of her fellow humans and the need to more closely examine the posterior edge of her parietal bone. I have again stressed the necessity for a good, wholesome diet. Some of the patients really are on very simple fare.

Despite all my hindrances, I remain convinced by the idea of a cure by conversation. I am certain it would have been of immeasurable relief in the case of my father; perhaps a greater understanding between us might have turned his hand from his fatal action.

Doctor Chettle scarcely feels my 'method' to be worthy of the name, however, and it is my greatest source of frustration that he has felt it best to take Mrs Harleston into his own care. I can barely make objection after all that has passed. At least with her husband incapacitated and the doctor distracted, she may pass her days in relative peace. And so I do not see her now, not as a patient – only as a friend, when she visits us here.

Such a thing would not be possible at all, of course, were she not permitted some degree of latitude not afforded the other patients. Indeed, her progress has been such – although she is troubled still, in some respects – that she has been put on a special kind of probation system, whereby she resides in the asylum but is permitted to wander the grounds at will and without her keeper. Her maid, Peg, continued with her for a time, I suppose in some belated remorse for her treachery, and she sometimes accompanied her mistress on her perambulations, until she departed. Soon Mrs Harleston must walk into the world alone; here she is provided with some little trial of her ability to do so.

And so we see her often. She wanders to the door with little preamble and I open it before she knocks and let her in. I settle her in the most comfortable place by the fire and I sit at her feet and talk to her. I might even say that her improvement is as much to do with these visits as Doctor Chettle's contrivances, and I try not to feel jealous at the ease of access which he enjoys.

I realise now that my jealousy and, I will admit it, my feelings for her have lurked behind many of my ill-considered choices. Now I endeavour to guard against anything indelicate happening again, and all is propriety. As one of the poets said — how strange that I do not remember if it was Browning or Byron? —

Whene'er I view those lips of thine,
Their hue invites my fervent kiss;
Yet, I forego that bliss divine,
Alas! it were — unhallow'd bliss.

Yet Mrs Harleston loves me still, I think, and despite my position and her own, I know now that I love her, or could freely do so, were it permitted. I dwell sometimes on what might have been if her husband had succeeded in his bid for death. We might have fled; we might be together on some distant shore, bathed in warmth and joined in mutual bliss. And yet, we would not be accepted, for in the eyes of Society we would not be proper, not respectable. Such a thing is only the province of hope and of dreams, but I shall write no more of such here. Truly my journal is become my confessor as well as a comfort!

As things stand, we find a little happiness in our restricted circle. Mrs Harleston spends many an hour enjoying the aspect of the room and gazing at me with her liquid brown eyes, and as I look into hers, the love we have for one another permeates the air. It must be enough. Perhaps, when she is discharged, we may yet find a way to be together. And though we share little confidences in the touch of a hand, the straightening of her hair, of course we are chaste; I would have no one say that I take advantage of her vulnerability — although I am not her physician, not at all, I remain a physician, and I would have us do right, if only in our own hearts. I cannot give way to that particular madness again.

I mentioned that my mother sees one patient — and she does see Mrs Harleston, but it is, sadly, without the easy friendship she offered heretofore. I suppose the discovery that she is a patient must have come as a profound shock, but she remains silent on the matter and will not be drawn.

I am afraid that, even though Mrs Harleston's visits here are not improper, my mother thinks it scandalous for her to be in my company.

Chapter One

I have received another visit and all my worst surmises are confirmed. I wonder if my mother has not fully relinquished her
'circles'; that she should prefer me to associate only with the dead
and forego the living. But I must swallow my feelings, if only to
preserve the peace of the household.

Vita came again today. I sat with her in the parlour, feeling
peace penetrate my very bones. I was enjoying the quiet sense
that here, in the midst of the asylum, we had truly found a haven,
when my mother went past the door and let out an irritated sigh.

Vita looked at me, and I at her, upon which my mother passed
the door again with another noisy exhalation.

Something must be done. I covered her inconsideration towards
our guest with the offer of bread and butter, but Vita had no time
to answer; she was cut off this time by a loud tutting.

Vita was magnanimous; she rose and, saying more to me
with her eyes than words ever could, we made to leave – or so I
thought. Instead, finding the passage empty of my disapproving
parent, she led the way along it and into my room.

I began to protest, but she sat on the bed. I bent to raise her,
whereupon she rested her head on my shoulder and I realised it was
nothing more than that. For a time we stayed there, communing

in the silent language we had perfected between us, and I knew that if any would accuse us it would be to their shame, not ours.

Still, it is fortunate that Doctor Chettle appears to be unaware of these visits, as is Mr Harleston, of course, who is still recovering from his injury; and so it is only my mother who fails to understand.

Indeed, I know her understanding to be deficient, for after Vita had taken her leave, she broke her silence on the matter – it could not have been easy for her to do so. She could barely form the words as she fought to repress her emotion; then she began and it all poured from her.

'I must speak to you,' she said, 'of this unnatural relationship.'

Unnatural! That is what she called it. She could not see its purity, its simple innocence. She could not acknowledge that love and all its associations was the most natural thing of all.

Tears sprang to her eyes. 'You are mad,' she declared, 'madder than any of them!' And she rushed headlong from the room.

I did not follow her – indeed, I took some time to gather myself. Unnatural? Mad? She was so lacking in insight, and yet I knew that if it were not for her presence in the house I would not be able to receive Vita at all.

I would surely die if I could not see her, if only as a dear acquaintance. Only the glow of her presence kept me from morbid thoughts. Even now, I was itching to see her again.

Chapter Two

The following morning, I applied myself to my duties, first making a tour of the male ward, where I found Adam Sykes as usual, Walter Eastcott playing a solitary hand at cards and Samuel Brewer noting down the bounteous sums due to him in the pages of his journal. It is a pity he will not turn its use to quiet reflection, rather than such wild scribblings.

I spoke to them pleasantly, patted Peter Ambrose on the head and made my entries of 'no change' in their casebooks. From thence I went to the female ward, where the attendants were organising a 'swarry' around the pianoforte, since it was a Saturday. They were guiding Lillian Smith into a seat and trying to persuade Della Martin to remain in hers.

I assumed they meant 'soirée' and nodded with approval, although they took little notice of my presence. I do not think the attendants have ever truly recovered from the escape of one of the patients and what my part in it might have been. I do not know if they think of Olive Scholes and her plain, sorrowful features, and blame me for her dismissal.

I did make mention of her upon my return, broaching the matter first with Matron. I was informed that the girl was soon to be married and would require no position thenceforward other

than that of a wife. I intended to speak of her possible innocence
to Doctor Chettle, but it availed nothing; I was unable to convince
him, and it was without purpose since she was gone beyond us
all, and no doubt the happier for it.

Whatever their feelings on the matter, I returned their dubious
expressions with good cheer. Then I realised that, despite being
our most personable patient, Mrs Harleston was not present.

I asked after her. They exchanged sly glances and said that she
was in the treatment room with Doctor Chettle, and that he had
asked most particularly not to be disturbed.

My cheerful demeanour was all stripped away. I hurried from
them, through the barred gate and towards the stairs, taking them
two at a time. I was surprised at this turn, for although the doctor
had insisted on taking charge of her care, he was still not so very
assiduous in his duties to be often called from his own rooms,
and her husband was unable to press for anything to be done.

I heard her screams as I ascended.

I began to run. Curse the man! Why did he fix so upon all
the novelty that science might invent, rather than the simple
and straightforward and human? I would not have it – I could
not allow it.

I reached the door, breathing heavily, and forced myself to
stop and collect myself. It would not help my cause to engage
him in so lunatic a fashion. I took several deep breaths before I
tried the handle and found it locked.

Another shriek came from within, and then—

'Damn you to hell, you whelp!'

My mouth fell open. What must he be doing for her to speak
so wildly? And she had done so well – when she first returned to
Crakethorne, she had been so wonderfully quiescent. It flashed
before me that I had suggested she try to cooperate with whatever Doctor Chettle wished of her. I had stressed the importance

of keeping him in good humour. Perhaps she was in some way trying to do so now, in playing the part he expected of her?

I had scarcely thought she would do so with such alacrity. I stood there aghast as she cried, 'Get your damned idiot paws off me!'

For such foul language to emerge from such sweet lips – I could not bear it. He must have dosed her with one of his medicaments. She was surely not herself, uttering vileness that was not of her own mind, her own will – and what was he doing? His intemperate treatments were driving her mad at last.

Wild thrashing came from within, followed by more exclamations better suited to the gutter than a gentlewoman. Had she spent too long with Peg? Another dreadful thought came to me. She was on a probationary system to see if she was prepared for life outside the asylum. Was she saying such things now to *prevent* herself being sent home and parted from me? But if she overplayed her hand, she would only be confined more closely and we would be parted anyway.

I stood there, frozen, trying to push aside the thought that lay deeper still – that perhaps she intended every word because her mind was truly unseated. Was she more disturbed than I had ever suspected? Had I had so blind? Could I have so misjudged her? If only I were able to take charge of her myself – then I would surely know.

She cried out again. I had to look. I could not bear to see what Doctor Chettle did, and yet I could not bear *not* knowing. I unhooked the little cover of the peephole and looked in.

I had thought to see him with a Leyden jar, sending shocks into her finely formed skull, but he was not. Doctor Chettle was making a study of her. Standing by him on a table was a selection of his books, engravings and charts; he held in his hands a pair of callipers. Mrs Harleston was immobilised in a chair. Leather cuffs secured her hands; her fingers clenched and clawed. An iron band passed about her forehead kept her still. She looked very alone – as indeed she was; there was no attendant in the room. Perhaps Doctor Chettle did not feel his actions would withstand scrutiny.

He ran his fingers over the back of her scalp, loosening her hair, and my own hands curled into fists, but I saw at once that he did not know the riches beneath his fingers; he did not see that innate beauty. He only wished to better feel each protuberance and declivity of her skull.

He frowned, referred to a book and returned to her forehead. From what little I knew of his subject, I imagined he was examining her intellectual faculties. He took up his callipers and tried to gain a measurement of the depth of that smooth forehead, but he was hindered by the band that secured her – that, and the fact of her spitting full in his face.

I flinched as if the spittle had dampened my own cheek. It was too much. This was not the action of a lady. I knew what vexed her so, of course: she wished only to be free.

I did not like that I could not reside where I chose, do as I chose or go whither I chose. I did not like wearing the things they gave me. I did not like being subject to their constant watching.

I shrank from the sight. It was hard to see her deprived of her liberty, but Doctor Chettle used neither leech nor lancet. He was not spinning her until blood gushed from her eyes and lips. He was not disfiguring her tender skin with caustic substances. He did not employ a frictional machine. It would all be over soon, and would prove as ineffectual as the rest of his quackery. There was no need to bang on the door, no need to break it down.

She let out another piercing scream and I winced. I must warn her of a propensity to play-act. Perhaps she had become a little too attached to the delights of the stage? It was not becoming in a woman, and standing accused of hysteria as she was, she must particularly guard against such shabby excitements. She must not breach the fragile walls of her personality by a surfeit of pretence, no matter how pure her aims.

Doctor Chettle wrapped a tape measure around the circumference of her skull, just above the delicate curl of her ear. Mrs Harleston endeavoured to throw herself aside, but her exertions were useless. She glared horribly – there was venom in her eyes and it was fearsome to look upon, but Doctor Chettle was untroubled; he continued calmly recording his numbers in his book.

Did he think he could take the measure of such a woman in such a fashion? Who would not be angered by such unfeeling behaviour? Little wonder her words were not just outrageously chosen, but lent vehemence by her predicament. It minded me of the lines from the mad poet, James Carkesse:

> Says He, who more wit than the Doctor had,
> Oppression will make a wise man Mad.

What a pity Doctor Chettle would not see sense. She was so nearly sane that any study of her physiognomy must be without purpose. The only right method was to treat her as sane, to spend time with her, to speak to her – to engage with the matters that lay within, providing a mental release rather than the bodily kinds to which so many physicians remained attached.

Doctor Chettle, in his own way, was too lost to his obsession. One might almost call him a monomaniac – and yet he presided over us all, so one must let it pass, as must the lady herself.

I turned my back upon the room, unable to listen further. I too had to bear with my discomfort. My little informal sessions with her were more vital than ever. Doctor Chettle must never become so concerned by the lady's lapses that he stopped her leaving the manor unaccompanied. That would be the end of everything.

I could only pray that we were safe in the hope of her freedoms continuing. I had never heard anybody else, the attendants or Matron, question the sense of it – only my mother. And if they did not mention it, I resolved most decidedly that I would say nothing of the matter.

Vita came to me afterwards, nursing her pride and her head. I sat by her and she leaned against me, and I comforted her as best I could. I found myself stroking her forehead and her temple, feeling each modulation of bone beneath the skin and knowing it all to be perfectly formed. Then I forgot myself and turned to her and set my lips to the little tender place behind her ear.

I froze in the act of doing so. My mother stood in the doorway. Her eyes were fixed on us, her face crumpled in disgust, no doubt forming the most ugly and mistaken of suppositions.

She turned and passed out of sight. I pressed my face close to Vita's, feeling the warmth of her rapid breaths. This must not end; it *could* not.

Chapter Three

It was with great consternation that I awoke and found myself sleeping on a blanket at the foot of the bed, rather cold and stiff. At first I did not know where I was, and then I heard from behind the bed-curtains the deep, regular breathing of Mrs Harleston.

I must have known she slumbered there; I must have known she had stayed. I had after all arranged a nest for myself to allow her to continue in peace, but I had little memory of it, or indeed of what I could have been thinking. I could only imagine that faced with the idea of losing what I held so dear, I had longed to cling to it the more tightly.

I leaped up. Despite the panic that hammered within my chest I could not draw back the bed-curtain; instead I rushed to the window and for a moment saw what I expected to see: a crowd of angry attendants, Doctor Chettle at their head, brandishing a strait-waistcoat for her and a pitchfork for me . . .

But no . . . I saw only Crakethorne Manor, its old grey stone brightened by an unaccustomed burst of sunshine. The verdure around it remained in darkness and there was no trace of anyone, not even a face pressed against the barred windows.

I turned to see Vita yawning, revealing the pink inside of her mouth. She stretched and smiled at me, quite unconcerned. It appeared to be the most natural thing in the world to her, to open her eyes and see me waiting there. It was a lovely thing indeed, and I wished I could smile back. I wished all that prevented me were at the bottom of the ocean.

I resolved to relish these few moments with her. For an instant we might have been in my mother's house in London, Vita having named herself my wife. And what moments those had been! I went to her; I could not help myself. I kissed her and pressed my hand to her heart, feeling her pulse beating against my fingers.

I knew it must end. I stood again and urged her from the house, but at first she did not go. She expressed a desire to eat breakfast and she did so, managing a surprisingly hearty repast. I could eat nothing, but she needed to sustain herself against whatever rigours the day might bring. Only then did she take her leave, smiling back at me over her shoulder like a woman glimpsed in a dream.

When I returned to the parlour my mother was waiting for me, her arms crossed over her chest, her brow drawn down like thunder.

'How could you?' she demanded. 'How can you permit that . . . that *creature* in the house?'

I stared. I wished to disabuse her of any filthy notion she may have entertained, but before I could speak she exclaimed, 'It is monstrous. Monstrous!'

That was too much. I said, 'How can you say so? You, who took her in and harboured her as if she was a daughter?'

She looked puzzled, then threw up her hands. 'I will not have it, Nate – I cannot! Tell me this will not happen any more.'

I drew a deep breath. 'I promise you that nothing untoward, nothing immoral, nothing impure will happen under this roof, whilst I remain its proprietor.'

She stared at me for a long moment as if trying to make out

the meaning behind my words, then she nodded curtly and left the room. I let out the breath I was holding and glanced towards the window. Mrs Harleston had almost reached the manor. The sun was low and her shadow stretched long behind her. She looked alone and friendless and vulnerable. I did not know what Doctor Chettle would think. I did not know if my mother would complain to him. My own heart thudded against my ribs, as rapid and light as hers had felt, pulsing so closely beneath my fingers.

Chapter Four

I attended to my duties more assiduously than ever, first sitting through a Sunday service held by a visiting parson – although I absorbed not a single word he said – before calling on Doctor Chettle. If some dreadful fate awaited me, I thought it would be best to face it at once. He merely bade me good day and invited me to view a new skull he had obtained, as clean and dry as a bird's egg.

'See what an interesting subject this was,' he said, turning it in the light, demonstrating its planes and curves. 'You see? The head is exceptionally broad in its lateral, upper and hind parts. And yet the faculty of cautiousness is so very well developed; it has been named that, you know, but we are essentially speaking of fear. And the base of the brain – it suggests a love of life, you know, to the extent that death carries the utmost terrors.'

I nodded and admired as I was meant to do, having no need to make pretence of pleasure at the sight. I *was* pleased. A new skull might draw his interest for a time from his living patients. And he was so engrossed, so untroubled, that he could not have discovered Vita's absence. Indeed, it struck me that after the dismissal of Olive Scholes, her keepers would scarcely wish their negligence in watching her to be known. Perhaps we were safe after all.

I had an image of my mother marching across the grounds, her lips pressed thin, gesticulating like a harridan, and my look of interest wavered.

Still, I went about my rounds, burying my concern in duty and observation. Peter rushed up on all fours; Adam Sykes drooled into his own lap; Samuel Brewer declared himself the King of Norway. Then, whilst going about the female wards, I thought I would just call in upon Mrs Harleston.

I found the lady pale and silent, sitting in her accustomed place by the window. I gave her a meaningful smile and asked if she had slept well.

She scowled at me and turned away, saying in rough tones that if I had quite finished she would prefer me gone.

I froze. Whatever could be the matter? But I heard a light step behind me and found an attendant standing there.

'I'd take no notice, Doctor Kerner,' the girl said. 'She's allus like that these days.'

How easily I might have betrayed us if Mrs Harleston had not heard her step! Thankfully, I had said nothing of last night and the girl showed no suspicion. Perhaps she thought her charge had left her chamber early, to walk amid the dew – not a recommended action, to be certain, but the idea might avert a worse disaster.

I gave Vita a knowing look before I left her, one of gratitude and affection. It would not do to linger, though I longed to do little else.

My ability to maintain my composure was rattled, however, when I met Matron and Ruth Roberts outside the door. Matron informed me that Doctor Chettle was to resume Mrs Harleston's cold-water treatments that very hour.

She must have seen the horror in my eyes, though I tried to cover it. I had no authority to countermand such a thing, although I did protest over the inclemency of the season.

It was the girl who replied. "'appen that 'un needs a bit o' coolin' down.'

I opened my mouth and closed it again. Doctor Chettle would have his way. I could already see his expression if I interfered – and just as he was beginning to accept me a little more. If our *entente* continued I could have more influence. At least it was not some infernal electrical machine, and I could comfort her later. I could not risk being banished from her, or her from me; if I were too obstructive, I might even be dismissed.

And it would be over soon enough. Even he would not risk freezing the lady to death.

I went to my old rooms, which had not yet been repurposed, so that I might look out over the grounds towards the little flash of dark water without being disturbed. It was fortunate that no one was there to witness my reaction.

Mrs Harleston and her attendants appeared on the damp lawn below. This time there were three of them as well as the doctor. Vita was bent double in her efforts to pull away, and I knew that she was shrieking because I heard it quite plainly through the thin glass. Her hair was loose and flying, her face positively contorted with rage. They dragged her and she pulled against them and they hauled her onward again.

I heard, faintly but quite clear, 'Gor blind me if I don't put yer on your back seam! I'll shut yer snaky bloody sauce-box for you!'

I closed my eyes. I had not yet had any opportunity to speak with Vita on the subject of her play-acting and here was the sad result. She did not wish to be declared sane. She had no hope that we might find a life together outside this place. She wished only to continue here always, so that she could remain close to me.

It was inexpressibly painful to me that she could sully herself and her reputation in such a way for my sake. The risk she took was too great. She would find herself the subject of constant vigilance, of restraint, of doors that were always locked – even of the padded room. I shuddered as much at that awful thought as at hearing her next words.

'Fink I'm yer bloody patient, do yer? Sound like I'm from the hupper suckles, do I?'

A pause, whilst they dragged her along.

'Don'tcha like me chant? This is me wiv a fevver in my mouf! You've 'eard nuffink!'

Her words were distorted by the glass, her tones coarsened. I leaned closer to it as she faded into incoherence. I was just in time to see her turn and bite the hand of one of the attendants.

I gasped. Whatever was she thinking? To see her so feral when in my company she had been more lovely than I had ever known her, so much at peace, so beautiful in her womanly gentleness – it was not to be borne.

Now she was a tigress, struggling as they seized tighter hold and pulled her all the way to the water's edge. I could no longer make out her words, only indecipherable sounds of protest as they grasped her legs as well as her arms. Her underlinens, all she stood up in, were in disarray; I saw a flash of her shapely white thigh and pressed my eyes closed. When I opened them she was in the air: they had thrown her, and she flew and landed in the water with a prodigious splash. She went under and came up choking.

I could bear to look no more. This was our place, the Crow Garden, where we had walked together. She had run her fingertips through the dying leaves of an oak tree. Now they had driven her into hysteric fits. They had made everything worse. Under Doctor Chettle's treatment she would surely be entirely mad within the month, if he did not kill her first.

I turned and slid down the wall to the floor. I could not bear to see her treated in such a manner, and to know that it was my fault, when I could have prevented it with some well-placed words in her delicate ear. And I could do nothing else, now; words must suffice, for I could not risk alienating my principal. What a dreadful thing it was to be subject to his whims and fancies, and yet I could see no way out of it.

If I thought to find respite from the day's events on my return to the cottage I was disappointed, for my mother was waiting for me. She sat in the parlour, her back very straight, her arms folded before her. She waved a hand at the chair opposite her own, as if I were an unfavoured guest.

'I must speak to you,' she said, 'upon the matter of that creature in the house.'

I glanced up at the bird's cage, wondering if Sholto had got loose, but no, he was there, a little flash of gold, just as always.

'Not him,' she said. 'Nate, you know exactly what I mean.'

But I did not wish to think about what she meant. Had she witnessed Mrs Harleston's unseemly behaviour, for her to be so insulting about her, and to my face? It could not be countenanced. She had once seen her in the position of a daughter; indeed, a part of me clung to the hope that such a thing might still come to pass.

'It could not be helped,' I began. 'She was most upset. She had her reasons.'

She looked puzzled, waving my words away. 'I refer to the animal,' she said. 'I smell it all over the house. It is malodorous – it is all around us now.' She wrinkled her nose as if to demonstrate, but all I could smell was the suggestion of canary.

'And the hair,' she went on. 'Our maid is upset – she threatens to leave us. She says it is all over your room.'

'I do not know to what you refer.' A sudden fear rose in my breast. What was this that had taken hold of her? Doctor Chettle's words returned to me: *There are inherent menaces in spending your*

*days surrounded by brain-sickness . . . guard your mind — or you may
discover one day it is entirely lost, and you may not find it again!*

She hid her face in her hands. 'Nate, are you so far gone in
madness? Have you succumbed to what is all about you?'

Her words were so close to my own thoughts, and yet so
distant. I should have remained calm but I blurted, 'And you?
You are deluded!'

When she looked up, I realised her face was wet with tears
and I could not look upon her. I was a physician, an alienist —
my father's son. I should never have spoken in such a fashion.
I wished to apologise, and yet did not know how; I could not
retract what I had said.

I had not considered such a thing before. My mother was
elderly. Was this the start of some senile decay? Was her brain
softening? I peered at her. There had been no history of it, not a
trace of reduced mental capacity in her family, and while I did not
subscribe to the notion that such things were always hereditary,
that must be a good sign. Her parents had died young, however.
Had it not had time to develop? Did I too have the taint of
such a disease in my blood — and in my position? The idea was
dreadful. I drew in a breath. Now I could smell nothing at all.

An idea occurred to me — not one of dread, but of relief. If
my mother did tell anyone of Mrs Harleston's visits, and it was
found she had a kind of dementia — who would believe her? But
that was a despicable notion, quite unworthy, and I pushed the
thought away. She was my mother. Yes, she had been prey to
some ill-considered advice, to unhealthy influences, but that was
a temporary aberration. My idea of moving her here, under my
eye, had been wholesome and would prove to be for the best.

I would watch over her and ensure that she came to no
harm. Who better to care for her than her son, and in her own
home? I must endeavour to do my duty as well as I knew how.

No matter how odd her statements, my mother would never be half drowned in Doctor Chettle's pond. For now I would keep silence on the matter and observe and guide her myself towards the bright light of sanity.

My mother pushed herself up from her chair, pausing for a moment to stare at Sholto's cage. She did not give the impression of seeing what lay before her eyes. Was she thinking of the bird, or something else? She shook her head as she approached the bars; now she did look at it, staring intently between them. She stared as if she did not know what it was any longer, or why she should care for it as she did.

Doctor Nathaniel Kerner's Journal

20th October

*It is before dawn, and the house is silent. I shall not sleep again —
my mind is full of concern about my mother and with ideas about
the nature of delusion, and I will try to settle it by writing down my
thoughts.*

*It is said that a well-constructed delusion is an almost impenetrable
fortress. A delusionary concept is built brick by brick, in a fashion
entirely in keeping with its own logical system. It forms a smooth
edifice, near impossible to scale or find any weakness. Its structure
forms the perfect semblance of sanity until one loose stone is
discovered — the single fancy or distorted fact that is the foundation
of the whole — the removal of which leads to its collapse. That is the
task of the alienist.*

*Identifying such might take the closest observation and the greatest
care, but find it I must and will. I cannot allow my mother to
succumb. I made the choice to be surrounded by lunacy, but she did
not. I must ensure she does not fall into its clutches. Perhaps she is
still affected by the shock of my deception over the matter of 'Miss
Milford', or perhaps her mind was weakened by her 'circles'. They
must surely have left her subject to a misassociation of ideas, which
must not harden into anything even resembling the truth. Delusion is
pernicious; it is clever. And nothing could be more disfiguring to her
respectable and dignified old age.*

It is fortunate that Vita did not visit me yesterday. Probably her own distress had tired her. I do not know the reason, but it is well that further strain was not placed upon my mother's constitution. Vita could hardly have been more considerate if she had planned it all.

I only hope, when I look out of the window and towards the manor, standing palely in the unfledged light, that she can sense how fondly I think of her.

Chapter Five

I broke off my writing, rattled by the sudden realisation of what I was setting down. I had done it without thinking but now I saw, as clear as sunlight, the look on my mother's face if she was to come across it and read these pages – my contempt for her 'circles', my fears for her mind. Of course she would never seek to betray my privacy and go prying, but in her current state I could not be certain of what she might do.

I looked about for somewhere to conceal it and went to slip the journal under my mattress. I stooped to push it in further with my fingertips so the maid would not find it, and I noticed something rather odd about my bed. It *was* covered in hairs. I could not think where they might have come from. I plucked one from the white sheets. They were short and brown and strewn everywhere. Once I had seen them, I could not think how they had escaped my notice before.

Whatever could it mean? And I realised there was a scent too, though it was not so unpleasant. It was no perfume to be sure, but it was not *malodorous*, as my mother had said. It must simply be the smell of the asylum, brought in on my clothes or ingrained in imperfect laundering. And then I saw the answer plain before me; I almost laughed with relief.

They must have cut Mrs Harleston's hair again. The attendants were unskilled and clumsy and not fit to touch her, but they must have hacked away at her poor head and not even troubled to brush away the clippings. Now here they were, her sweet hairs scattered like a gift to me. I smiled and ran my hand across the sheets, so lost in the image of her that it only then struck me that here perhaps was one of the 'bricks' my mother had used to build her delusion.

She must not see this, now or ever again. I resolved to have the maid clean my room more thoroughly in future.

I carried out my ablutions and went downstairs, still full of my resolve to be vigilant and prevent any harm from falling to me and mine, determined to stand guard at the portal of my mother's mind as well as Vita's. I went straight to the parlour, thinking to find her there, but I found only an empty room, and furthermore, one that was rather chilly, since the window was thrown wide. Cold air stirred the curtains before letting them sag against the casement.

I started towards the window, thinking to close it, when I noticed Sholto's cage was empty. The gilded door was pinned back on its hook and the little bird was nowhere to be seen.

How could such a thing have happened? How distressed my mother would be! I started to search, looking under the table, between the chairs, even behind the bookcase, but I could not find the canary in any corner of the room. Then I looked everywhere again, not wanting to believe it gone. At least my mother had not come in, though that was odd in itself; she was not usually so tardy.

I turned back to the window and stared out at the rough slopes and at Crakethorne, its stone darkened under a sky heavy with the promise of rain. There was nothing to be seen, nothing living, not even a crow; and a dreadful feeling of being lost crept over me. I felt as if my mother as well as her little bird had already passed beyond my reach.

A sound behind me made me whirl, but it was only the maid, who started away when she saw my expression. I called her back and enquired after my mother. I must have been in a state of some anxiety for I waved towards the cage as I did, as if that lady would appear within it.

Jane did not notice anything strange in my conduct, for she merely said, 'She din't think animals should be kept in t' 'ouse no more, sir. Din't think it were right. So she let it out.' Her lips were pursed in disapproval, though I could scarcely follow her meaning.

'She let it out?' I repeated in dismay. My mother would never do such a thing if she were in her right mind.

Jane nodded. Her next words froze my blood: 'Then she went to see that Doctor Chettle.'

I forced myself to nod, not wanting her to see how the very idea distressed me; she took that as a dismissal and slipped out of the door. What was my mother thinking? Her dementia must be progressing at a prodigious pace — it must have seized hold of her at once and entirely.

I hurried outside and started towards the manor, ignoring the cold that crept beneath my shirtsleeves. I had neglected to put on my coat. I was nearing the entrance, my heart thudding more quickly than ever, when I was hailed by an uncouth voice.

I ignored it, but the man shouted again louder in a brusque 'Halloa!' and I could no longer pretend I had not heard. I could not place the tones, however, not until I espied the porter half hidden behind the shrubbery that ran about the corner of the manor. He beckoned me over and I smothered my annoyance at the interruption and the manner.

As he watched me approach I tried to make out any sign in his features that would give me a clue as to the disturbance, but he gave none, remaining entirely blank until I stood in front of him. Then he jerked his head towards a nearby hydrangea.

The shrub was not prepossessing, with its dead flower-heads yet untrimmed and the leaves tending to mildew. I raised my eyebrows, he twitched again and we continued in this pantomime until he gestured with his stick and said, 'Thee-er.'

At last I saw what he meant and my infuriation gave way to dismay. There, beneath the lowest leaves, was a little crumpled heap of gold. Feathers lay about it, damp and soiled. Its tiny, perfectly formed beak was open as if ready to sing, as it had used to do.

There was no sign of the cause of its death upon it. Perhaps it had spied the bars crossing some window above and thinking itself home, had endeavoured to fly through them, and broken itself against the glass. Perhaps some fox or cat had tormented it until its heart burst. Perhaps the crows, finding a bright flash of life intruding into their black world, had destroyed it between them.

I sighed. It might have been simply that the prospect of unaccustomed freedom had so terrified it that the creature had been paralysed by fear.

Whatever the cause, it was dead. I stood over the tiny body and sorrowed for its loss, and for my mother's. What had she been thinking? Had she so quickly lost dominion over her mind? Now Doctor Chettle would see it in her and she too might soon be gone from me.

The porter said, 'Hard that, when they're gone. It's the same wi' my Brown.' He fixed his eye upon me and glared with such an intensity of hatred that I took a step back. Had the whole world run mad?

I had no time to indulge the man further. I nodded and turned to leave, but his arm snaked out and he grasped my elbow. His filthy fingers soiled my white shirt and I stared at them, but he did not loosen his grip.

Could events grow any more strange? 'I want 'er back,' he said; his voice shook with emotion and his eyes shone, though not with rage, and I was entirely at a loss as to how to account for it. 'See?'

I realised how alone we were. The windows were above my head, so that no one within could see us. And if they did mark us – well, they were as mad as those without and could offer no help. I did not know what to say, so I only nodded and attempted to back away.

'You'll 'ave to bury it.'

I blinked and opened my mouth to remonstrate, but something in his eye stopped me and we stayed like that, staring at each other, until I had gathered myself enough to protest at his effrontery. Then he turned quite deliberately on his heel and walked away from me. I roused myself. The whole exchange was quite fantastical.

I looked down at the little bundle of remains and knew I could not leave them as they were.

I bent and scraped a cold, muddy hollow beneath the bush with my hands, pushed the corpse into it and covered it again. I did not suppose it deep enough, but it was something, at least. If my mother asked, and if I considered it best to tell her the truth of what had become of it, I could at least say I had shown it that decency.

I stood back. It was sufficient, at least for the moment. There was not a feather to be seen upon the earth. The sun speared down from behind a cloud and I realised how I must appear. My shirt was stained where the ruffianly fellow had laid hold of it. My cuffs were streaked with earth, and my hands were blackened, each nail marked by a crescent of grime. What would Doctor Chettle think?

I stood back and looked up at the windows. Somewhere behind those blank surfaces was my mother. She would have found him by now. Would it help my cause to charge in amongst them, raving? Or should I approach him afterwards, having gathered myself and brushed my clothes, and endeavoured to look like a gentleman?

I allowed myself a glance over my shoulder as I walked back towards the cottage. I wished to stand tall, but I had the most dreadful presentiment of what was being said at that moment and found myself almost scurrying in my haste.

I let myself in at the door; everything was too quiet within. Why did it all feel so portentous – as if the emptiness of the hall was a sign of things to come, my mother already gone? And yet Jane was there, entering the hall with her duster, raising her head to stare at me.

I was conscious again of the condition of my clothes, but reminded myself of my standing. It would not do to excuse myself to her. I drew myself up and for want of anything else, I said, 'You must take better care in cleaning my room, Jane. Kindly make sure to brush away any hairs that you find there.'

It came upon me as I said the words that it might make her think more of Mrs Harleston than anyone had already, which was not what I had intended, but she looked sulky and said, 'Ma'am says I don't 'ave ter go in there no more. Not wi' there bein' an animal, like.'

'An animal! Why then, you shall no doubt be happy it has flown away!' I replied, wondering that she seemed to imagine birds to be in possession of hair and not feathers.

I left it at that, giving another frown before I went up the stairs to change my clothes and to think, and find solace in noting down all that had passed, while I waited to discover what the end of it would be.

Doctor Nathaniel Kerner's Journal

27th October

I have found neither the time nor the inclination to write for some days past. I once considered that lunatics are happier than those whose vocation it is to look after them, and I have found the sentiment returning to me often.

In fulfilment of my fears, Doctor Chettle, so eager to probe into my affairs, has seen fit to take the charge of my mother into his own care. I suppose it is kindly, in a sense, that he has been so assiduous towards her, but I cannot help wishing that his sudden meticulousness had not taken this particular turn.

Indeed, since he has our most interesting case and, albeit thus far unofficially, my parent under his eye, he has asked me to take especial care of the male patients whilst he takes entire charge of the female. Despite his increased duties, he has also visited the male side more often than heretofore. I could almost wish he had not taken so sudden an interest in my work, for he is somewhat disobliging, even refusing me access to case notes when the whim takes him.

I, however, have been careful to concentrate on the work before me and have seen little of my mother since the day she went to speak to Doctor Chettle. Despite my so rapidly ascertaining the cause of her troubled mind, I fear I was too late: she has progressed so far in her delusion that she has not been able to look at me since without some horror coming over her.

She is happier indeed than I. It is exquisitely painful to see the look that enters her eyes upon seeing me. I do not even wish to think of it. And so it is probably for the best that we do not see each other, though I cannot help feeling I have failed her in some way, as I feel constantly that I have failed Mrs Harleston.

I am more certain than ever that I could help that lady, if I could only speak to her — if I could impress upon her the importance of restraining her semblance of raving, I could calm her in a trice. And yet now I cannot see her. I have no reason to enter the female wards and it would be passing strange, if not decidedly suspicious, for me to do so. Piled upon such obstacles is the further difficulty that I am no longer in possession of a key, since I no longer need one in the course of my duties.

But I do not know what accusations my mother might have made against us, and so it is better to bide our time until her malady is in some wise addressed. I feel within me that there remains love between Vita and me, no matter what divides us. We will find a way to be together because God surely wishes it to be so. Indeed, I am certain that fate shall somehow arrange what man presently cannot. Our love cannot be without purpose.

My mother's illness has had another consequence, which is unfortunate, but again, cannot be helped, although it is an additional barrier to divide me from Vita. With her current strange aversion we could not well go on living in such proximity, and I had no wish to see her properly committed to the asylum, so I have moved once more into the manor while she continues in the cottage under Doctor Chettle's observance. I have not resumed my previous room but have resolved to bury myself more intensely in my work and thus am more closely situated to the male patients. My room was not purposed as a residence and bears residual signs of its previous usage — there is even an old peephole in the door, though of course that is sealed. In short, it is small and blank and joyless, and feels all the more fitting for that.

The idea of ceasing Vita's visits was inexpressibly painful to me, yet how could we indulge ourselves at such cost? We could not enjoy our small moments of happiness if they added to the distress of another. No — we had to do the right thing, although it was all so much worse because I had no way to tell her of the turn events had taken. I knew she would have agreed with me, but the idea of her seeking in vain to find me at the cottage, and of being unable to explain to her, is dreadful indeed.

I try not to dwell upon it, although it is hard. I must think of the time when we might find a way to marry, and that, I am certain, will heal my mother's wounds also.

I dream of it sometimes. I see us on our wedding journey. I am promenading by the sea with Vita at my side, her face half hidden by the shade of a parasol. The waves around us are rushing, ever rushing, towards the shore. I wake with the smell of the ocean in my nostrils.

I must stop indulging these fancies, particularly in my journal. At least the process of writing cools my blood a little. I really should suggest its calming effects to the patients — it could represent an extension of my cure by conversation, since its pages offer as much sense, at times, as the most regarded doctor. But if any saw these words they would think me as lunatic as Samuel Brewer — I should strike them out. For now, I shall go and face the reality about me. It is time to begin my rounds.

Chapter Six

This morning, to my dismay, Doctor Chettle emerged from his seclusion and came to see me, with a strange and outrageous request – and as if to add further insult, he did it with my mother at his side.

He came early, before I was fully dressed, though he wore a greatcoat and my mother a cloak. He opened the door without knocking, unfortunately with an attendant close by to witness his rudeness; James Farrar was at that moment engaged in distributing fresh towels, for I glimpsed him behind them, carrying several over his arm.

'Ah, Kerner,' Doctor Chettle said, not even gracing his words with the appellation of 'Doctor', though my mother stood by, silent and apprehensive. 'How do you feel?'

I was rather rattled by his appearance at my door and informed him I did somewhat ill.

His expression became more sombre. 'Ah – I knew it,' he said, as if he had been party to my mood from the isolation of his rooms. 'I have decided that a cooling balm this morning could work wonders – do you not think so? I am of a mind that we shall take the cold water.'

I did not reply but stared, wide-eyed, and they stared back

– and I realised that Farrar was staring too, for he still stood by, the towels over his arm.

'It works wonders for the constitution.' Doctor Chettle smiled and nodded as if I were supposed to concur with his crack-brained scheme. I opened my mouth to protest, feeling my heart constricting with rage, as he turned to my mother and said, 'It can be most efficacious in shocking the mind from a delusional state.'

She pinched her lips into a straight line, without nodding or showing any other sign that she had heard – and suddenly I saw it all. Of course, it was my mother he wished to shock from delusion; he was merely taking his lead from Doctor Pargeter, for sometimes a physician must cajole, sometimes comfort, sometimes compel. Sometimes he must be an actor, creating a false situation to support the patient's recovery, and such must be his aim here, though it was clumsily done. He should have warned me of his plan – ah, but how could he, for that might have ruined its efficacy. Even now, I could see it working upon her. Her cheek had paled: she *was* shocked, I think, even though nothing had yet been done. It was actually rather ingenious, though I begrudged crediting him with it.

It was she who needed the cold water, but he knew it would be too much for her: she could never stand the insult to her dignity or her person. It was a kindness of a sort, and I could not stand in the way of it. Seeing her son undergoing such a procedure could potentially administer as much of a jolt as if she had suffered it herself, and all without risking her own dear health.

For a second I wished to grasp his hand and shake it, but despite my sense concurring with his actions, a part of me could not forgive the manner of it.

I said merely, 'Of course I will,' and stepped forward, ignoring the look of surprise on Farrar's unprepossessing features, followed closely by his sneer of disdain.

I did the only thing any man of sense could do: I took no further notice of the man. I strode out with vivacity as they unlocked the doors and locked them again after us, and stepped out on to the sward, trying not to think of what must follow. It struck me then that it would be more unpleasant than I had previously considered: the air was not just chill but cold; it had already penetrated my thin night clothing and I had started to shiver. Farrar threw a towel about my shoulders, but it did not help and I would not look at him; that only served to underline what would happen. And stepping out into the day, in this state of undress – it was an indignity hardly to be borne. But then, *she* had done it, and if she could bear it, so would I.

I turned to say something reassuring to my mother, but Doctor Chettle took her arm, as if to ensure his patient stayed close by him. 'Walk on with him,' he said, gesturing at Farrar and me alike and the man had the temerity to smirk, as if it were *he* who was accompanying *me*.

But I must accept this indignity, as awful as it might be, for I would not upset my mother, who followed behind, looking very unhappy. I remembered Mrs Harleston's protests and her wild cries with a little more understanding than before and determined I would not succumb like that. I would set the example of sanity to my mother, demonstrating my quiet acceptance – especially as Doctor Chettle clearly did not intend to inflict anything too onerous upon her.

And so I found myself once more the subject of an experiment – this time of treatment by proxy – and it reminded me so strongly of being a child, eight years old again, that it suddenly made me *feel* like a child. I wanted to shout and shake my fists; I wanted to be free of them; I wanted to cry.

Naturally I did none of these things, nor could I have the relief of saying what I thought. Instead, I walked quietly through the Crow Garden, past the patients' graves to the water's edge, and once there I stared down into it, as if in search of answers I couldn't find. For a moment, no one spoke. Even the crows were silent, though I glimpsed them through the trees – the liquid movement of their bodies, the slower beating of wings – and then all was still. I felt terribly alone.

'You must step into it.'

Yes, I must. I had come here of my own accord and it would be better for my mother if she saw me comply; it would put too great a strain upon her nerves to see me struggle.

I shook off my shoes, feeling the earth damp and cold beneath my feet. I had thought once to walk like this on warm sands by the sea, but this grey place could not be further from it. I stepped forwards, feeling my skin slide against the mud, putting out my hands for balance. I was a civilised man. I had walked the streets of the city in a frock coat, holding a cane. I could not imagine what had brought me to this place.

'Further.'

There was no sympathy in Doctor Chettle's voice. Whatever else I thought of the man, he played his part well.

'Help him, Farrar.' Despite the lack of a 'Mr', I realised that at least he did Farrar the courtesy of calling him by his name. I scowled as the man followed me into the water, splashing with his tall boots, the cold droplets troubling him not at all while they splashed me to the waist. I shook with the cold, though I tried not to let it show. The chill was inside me now; there was no preventing it. I could not go whither I would; I could not even speak.

'Shall I scoop it over 'is 'ed, sir?' Farrar grunted, and I realised he carried no ewer.

'No,' Doctor Chettle said, 'submerge him fully.'

I cried out in outrage, all thought of compliance forgotten, striking at Farrar; but he was stronger. His boots rooted like a tree, he caught hold of my shoulders and pushed, and my feet slid. In the next moment I was under, clawing at nothing, gasping for breath, all sounds so distorted I knew not what they were. My eyes, ears and mouth were full of filthy water. My feet slipped on ground that could not be trusted and then a fist clumped my nightshirt between my shoulder blades and I found myself standing, gasping for breath, heaving cold water from my lungs.

I shook my head, seeing only misshapen figures on the banking: Doctor Chettle, I supposed, and my mother, and *another*—

Farrar kicked my legs from under me and I was down once more, looking up through slimy water at the dark, ill-formed shapes ranged around the pool, more and more of them, now: surely too many. One, more complete than the rest, leaned out over the water, eyes staring down into mine, and I glimpsed a grey beard tinged with white. His lips opened and closed, but his words were lost.

I shook my head again as Farrar pulled me clear of the water and there were only the trees, dark branches entwined all about, and crows – crows watching with their baleful eyes. I thought of Jacob Thew. I almost felt, if only I could think of the right words, I could ward them away – that I could ward everything away.

Then I focused upon Doctor Chettle and saw the dismissive little wave of his hand that told James Farrar to stop, and all I could think of to say was, 'It's you they've come for.'

Doctor Chettle looked upon me mildly, tilting his head as if he were gazing at a specimen in a jar.

I waved my hand, encompassing the graves, the trees, the crows sitting amongst it all. 'Jacob knew it. He saw them for what they are: spirits, restless spirits, unhappy with how you buried their bones.'

Doctor Chettle spoke sharply, though not to me. 'Bring him out.'

Farrar grasped my arm. I had no choice; I could not go where I would. If I spoke, they would not hear me. It was hopeless, and a wave of despair washed over me. I let him draw me on until I stood once more on the bank. I could not think how I had come to this, or what I had said to them, or what my mother was doing here, seeing me like this.

Doctor Chettle stepped in front of me. He leaned in, peering into my face. 'Interesting,' he said. 'It appears he cannot differentiate reality from delusion.'

I did not care what he said; none of it mattered, not now. And I heard my mother's voice, tremulous with emotion. 'No. Most assuredly, he cannot.'

They meant to speak of her, of course – had his foolishness gone so far he had forgotten his intention? But the thought left me because my mother had covered her face and a dry, painful sob escaped her. She stood there, her hands over her eyes, her shoulders shaking with emotion. I shuddered too; I thought I would never be warm again. But perhaps it was working somehow – perhaps she was feeling what I felt.

She said, 'I lost his father to despair. Must I also lose my son?'

I stepped towards her, but Farrar's grip tightened. I had heard tell he was a military man, a discharged soldier, and now I did not doubt it.

Doctor Chettle turned his back and began comforting my mother, but I could not bear to see it. I tried to pull away from Farrar, but he caught my wrist, pulling my arm up my back, and further, until pain stopped my words. *How dare he?* This was too much – he had gone too far, but Doctor Chettle could not see it; he was not looking at me.

My mother turned, revealing her face at last, and she said, 'He committed *felo de se*. He took his life with . . .'

She could speak no more, and everything fell silent. Even

Farrar was listening. He relaxed his grip a little, but I no longer cared for the pain, or anything about me. She must not – *could not* – tell of my father. They would say he was mad.

Then, quite distinctly, I heard Doctor Chettle say, 'With cyanide. I know it. But I am glad you told me.'

It was my turn to freeze. I watched as he placed his hand on my mother's shoulder. Then he bade her return to the asylum and she walked away from me, slowly and alone. I shouted after her, but she did not hear my call.

Doctor Chettle stood before me once more. 'Oh, yes, I know of it,' he repeated. His brows were drawn, but there was only quiet musing in his voice. 'You committed a deception upon me. It is really most fascinating.'

I opened my mouth to protest – how had I deceived him? My father's suicide was none of his concern, and could mean nothing – the world might call my father mad, but he was *not*. And if he had been, it was caused by circumstance and was not at all hereditary. And how could Doctor Chettle have known?

All of it rushed in upon me, everything that had happened: his filthy pond, the cold, the dreadfulness of it all, the way he had said, without hesitation, *Submerge him fully*.

I could not speak. All I heard was the *crake, crake* of a crow and I closed my mouth once more. It was anyway too late, for he was walking away; he had caught up with his patient, my mother, and was taking her arm.

I was left to James Farrar, who chuckled as he gave me a little push towards the asylum. I stalked away from him, still shuddering with cold. No help was offered; no towel was thrown about my shoulders. I straightened despite my shivers, determined not to show my horror at all that had passed. What stung far more than any of Doctor Chettle's words, more than the cold, than the indignity, was the look in my mother's eyes; and the fact that, after everything I had done for her, all I had lost, it was through her that I was cast so low, however unwittingly she had done it.

Chapter Seven

Once I returned to my room, I paced. There was no further sign of Doctor Chettle, and I was glad of it, for I do not think I could have stood to see him. If he had come, I might even have given way; I could not rid my mind of the way he had treated me, and indeed, I felt as close to madness as I ever had.

I told myself it had all been for the good of my mother, but I was still so cold and so discomposed I could barely reason with myself. She had in some way responded to seeing my immersion, at least: she had confided in the doctor, however unfortunate the tenor of her thoughts. Perhaps that might calm her, help her focus on reality rather than the inventions of the mind. But then, it must also have encouraged her to think me mad, which could not help her at all.

I would that I could pack my bags and walk away from Crakethorne for ever. But how could I? My mother would remain in Doctor Chettle's care, as would Vita, and I might never see either of them again. That would be unbearable. I felt that if only Vita could come to see me on one of her walks, and speak to me a little – if I could only feel the cooling touch of her hand – it would be of immeasurable comfort to us both.

A short time later another of the attendants came to visit me, presumably to see if I had survived Doctor Chettle's ministrations. At least he had not sent James Farrar, but this was another large, ill-favoured fellow with unprepossessing features, pallid skin and undistinguished sandy whiskers.

I should have known better than to confide in him – I did know, but I was so ruffled that I betrayed my better judgement. I remarked that, for the sake of all the patients in this half of the asylum, it was a pity that Mrs Harleston could not spread a little of her cooling feminine charms about the wards when she was privileged to make her perambulations around the grounds. She could demonstrate in her person the hope of sweet recovery to them all.

He must have been a little slow, for his face spread into a grin, though he did not immediately reply. In the next moment, he laughed in my face.

I already thought him ignorant; all the attendants here were ill-qualified and ill-suited to their occupations. They rarely stayed long. They included among their number not only discharged soldiers, but sailors, footmen, domestics worked too hard and relentlessly to appreciate any finer sensibilities. Now this man clearly wished to prove himself an oaf.

He was not stemmed by my look. He said, 'She's as like to fly away as 'ave any privileges whatsoe'er, sin' she goes on as she does.'

I answered his temerity with a stare. 'I shall not,' I informed him, 'tolerate such impertinence from a man such as yourself.'

'A free one?' he jeered.

I swallowed down my anger. He must know the purpose of this morning's outrage, if not the intricacies of the alienist's art which lay behind it. And I did not have to explain. I chose instead to conclude he was speaking of the patient.

'Mrs Harleston may not have her liberty, but she is a lady. She deserves your respect, not your censure. It is little wonder that her nerves are strained, as refined and sensitive as they are, with such people around her. And she is as close to freedom as any may be, which is proved by the liberties she is afforded.'

I did not specify whether the 'people around her' meant the other patients or his own mean tribe, and he did not ask, though I imagined he could guess.

He leaned in closer towards me, so that I could smell the sourness of his breath. And he said that Mrs Harleston had no such privileges. He told me that she never had. He insisted that I had never seen her, as I claimed, and would not; that she was kept under the tightest security and furthermore, since she had taken to raving like a commoner, she would be treated like one too.

This was intolerable. I glared upon him so fiercely I dare say I had become a basilisk at last. But I would not allow myself to be unsettled by so base a fellow, and I left him to his coarseness and his ignorance. I must accept such company as an evil of living on the premises; there is too much familiarity in being at such close quarters with the staff. He could not see what lay before his eyes; but as our esteemed principal had once said, they are of a class very prone to madness. I should not have expected sense from him.

I remembered the sweet rooms of home in London, of a sudden so very far distant. With my mother fallen into Doctor Chettle's hands, however, the situation could not be helped. And since she remained under his care, I could scarcely hope that her recovery would be swift.

Chapter Eight

Despite my growing aversion, it was not long before I saw Doctor Chettle again. He came to my room the next morning, James Farrar trailing after him like a dog. I did not greet them but cast only the coldest glance in their direction.

Doctor Chettle would not be deterred. Motioning to Farrar to leave, he entered my room without invitation. His only concession to civility was to ask how I did.

I replied, 'How does my mother do?'

He shifted his feet, as well he might. He told me she had spent a tolerable night, and despite her understandable emotion – that was what he called it – she was 'comfortable'. And then he said, 'Your treatment has had some beneficial effect, then – you think of her more calmly?'

'I dare say she *is* more calm,' I said, 'though the means were scarcely proportional, do you not think?'

He looked puzzled, then adopted a more sympathetic tone. 'What appears harsh at first may be best for us in the end.'

I hesitated, thinking of my mother's face, the way she had at least turned to another for comfort, even if it was to such a source. 'It was a novel attempt, at any rate. But that is the most I shall say for it, and I would not recommend such a thing myself.'

'I dare say.' He leaned in, unblinking. 'You do fancy yourself an alienist, then, after everything?'

I must have shown my surprise. Had he supposed I would leave, abandoning my mother?

'Well,' he said, brightening, 'perhaps, in that case, you will be happy to help me upon another matter.'

I must have looked eager. I was already deeply involved with the male patients' care; that he was asking could mean only one other matter: that of Mrs Harleston, for there was no other on the female side with whom he might need my help. I think my breathing must have quickened and I endeavoured to steady it.

He peered at me intently, although he did not appear to notice anything amiss. Indeed, I realised he was looking at my forehead – at my hair, or perhaps what lay beneath, for he said, 'You, sir, have a very interesting skull. I should very much like to take its measure.'

My mouth fell open. He could not imagine for one moment that I would agree.

'Sir,' I said, 'I would remind you that I am a *doctor*.'

'Yes, yes.' He waved a hand before his face. 'And I know that you would wish to extend the limits of our knowledge.'

'I shall be the subject of no more experiments.'

'Ah, of course. I understand you refused that before, did you not, when you were a child? A pity, for I believe it set you upon a path of falsity, did it not?' His words were accompanied by a sly little smile.

How dare he? For he must have been speaking to my mother of me. This was unconscionable. How could he intrude upon me in such a fashion? Was he so misled that he truly thought *me* mad? But of course, that was impossible. Even if it were not, he should surely have called for the Commissioners in Lunacy, for independent doctors to certify me.

'Perhaps we may discuss your mother further, whilst we work,' he said.

Again, I could only stare. I felt suddenly very tired. I remembered my father's eager pursuit of his studies and the way I had rebuffed him – misunderstood him; thwarted him. That may not have been the reason for his death, but if I had done more, drawn closer to him . . . And after all, what could it matter? It would avail me nothing to fight with Doctor Chettle. He might even cast me off, keeping my mother here – was that why he had mentioned her? Was some threat implied?

I told myself that if I could perform some small service, even this one, I should not refuse. Indeed, it might help heal the rift that had opened between us, which was of no benefit to us or our patients or anybody.

I tried to swallow my disgust and found myself acquiescing. It could not matter, after all. This was no public dousing in cold water; how could it possibly be any worse? And again I considered that *she* had done it, and so would I.

I yielded, and he called James Farrar, who had clearly been lurking all the time outside my room. That was too much – but Doctor Chettle said he would not be required and dismissed the man, as well he should. I went with him, not speaking, and took my place in his chair. I submitted to the iron band being placed about my skull so that any small involuntary movement I might make would not interrupt his work. The more quickly it was done, the better I should like it.

His books were already spread upon the table. There were his charts and diagrams, his callipers and measures. I half expected in the foolishness of it all to see a tray full of shining pins, but of course there was none.

He gave out more blather as he prepared, speaking of the importance of his method. He patted his own cranium saying,

'Intellect, you see.' Then he ran his fingers through his beard as if musing and added, 'The propensity to self-destruction is most interesting.'

I stiffened, not wishing to discuss my father, but he moved on, becoming engrossed. First, he measured the circumference of my skull. Then he took down the distance between my temples and likewise that of my eyes, his little grunts and exclamations presumably announcing that it was just as he suspected all along. I felt his fingers in my hair and I tried not to grimace. I had thought nothing could rival the cold-water treatment, but this, in some indefinable way, was worse. It was at once horribly intimate and indifferent. Disgust crept like ice through my veins.

He said, 'We should find an undeveloped faculty of hope, of course, with cautiousness and destructiveness rather large. I see, I see . . . The latter indicating a person somewhat in harmony with death.'

It came to me that he still imagined my father's actions were the outward sign of some hereditary impulse. And I asked, almost before I had known I would, 'How did you know what happened to my father? Was it before I even wrote to you?'

He started back, the movement of his whiskers betraying the surprised twitch of his lips. 'Of course not – I would never have admitted you, had I known. No – it was the girl, Peg.'

'Peg?' I was astonished.

'You knew her, did you not? The young lady who accompanied Mrs Harleston upon her return from London.'

'Young lady?' Could he truly describe that low girl in such a way? And how could she have known of it? My mother had spoken of my father to *Vita*. I could not imagine that sweet lady discussing such a thing with her maid, no matter how circumstances had forced them together. It was impossible that she would have made it the subject of low gossip, even of laughter.

The vicious creature must have been listening – snooping at the door.

'Yes, the young lady,' Chettle went on. 'Tall, dark, remarkable eyes. She did well to disclose it to me. I decided to observe you more carefully from that moment.'

I bit back the retort that naturally rose to my lips. *Observe* me? What right did he have? And yet he was my principal, and that of this whole mad place.

Then he said, 'Ah, secretiveness – yes, yes.' He resumed his prodding and measuring.

What could I say in the face of such gibberish?

'Ideality,' he said. 'I see.'

'*What* do you see?' I could not disguise my tone. Ideality – that included the poetic sensibilities, did it not? What could he know of those? I wished to ask, but bit back the question. He had hit upon nothing. It remained the most absurd flummery.

'Hm,' he said under his breath, as if unconscious of doing so. 'Amativeness. Yes, yes.'

I froze. *Amativeness* – sexual love? Whatever could he be imagining? I tried to shift on the hard wooden seat and was prevented by the iron band drawn tight about my forehead, cold against my skin.

But he had moved on, making some note before standing in front of me and staring into my face. No – not my face, for I do not think he saw me, not really. He stared at the lower part of my forehead, just above the nose, without meeting my eyes. It was intensely uncomfortable. Whyever had I submitted to be bound?

'Hmm,' he said. 'I wonder.'

'What do you wonder, man?' I expostulated, but he did not notice my tone. He returned to his book, then took up a smaller set of callipers.

'Individuality,' he muttered, 'defining the skill of observation.

The ability to take cognisance of objects about one, and of exist-
ence, and of facts apparent to anyone.'

My blood rose. What did he mean to imply? Was he calling
me delusional again?

'It is time to return to the wards,' I pointed out, wishing to
restore some sense. 'Our patients are in need of us, do you not
agree?'

He straightened, gazing not at my features but somewhere
beyond me – into me. 'I always did suspect the orientation of
the frontal bone.'

'I must return to my patients.' I struggled a little, as if to
demonstrate. It was undignified, but then all of it was; I should
never have agreed to it. 'My patients – yours – Mrs Harleston.
They are not helped by such matters.'

He blinked, as if seeing me for the first time. Then he said,
'Peter Ambrose.'

'What of him?'

'It will be pleasant for you, when he returns to the male wards.'

It was my turn to blink.

'A comfort perhaps, to be able to pat his head, to walk him
about?'

'I would never,' I said, with the greatest dignity I could muster,
'deign to encourage a patient in their false perceptions of the
world about them, or of their own being, no matter how harmless
you may think it.'

'But you do like him.'

I stared at him. I could not imagine what had made him ask
such a thing. Peter was nothing but a child, albeit an unfortunate
one in imagining himself a dog, a form of life so reduced from
his own. It was absurd to think a man such as I could somehow
benefit from his company, rather than the opposite.

Doctor Chettle must have seen his folly, for he turned to hide his embarrassment by writing in his notebook. That he should have so much authority and so little sense! Crakethorne truly was a madhouse. The affliction had broken its bounds; it was rampant.

Then he murmured, 'If I took measure of the anterior lobe . . . It would not be of any especial length, I suppose. Then I could be certain.'

I stared. It was the most outrageous twaddle, and yet I thought I sensed some meaning in his words. At first I could not think why, and then I realised what had struck so strangely upon me. The orbit of the eye, the width of the scalp, the hollow at the temple – all could be measured with whatever accuracy such a 'science' could provide. The bones could be examined – but the anterior lobe? There was no possibility of measuring the brain.

A memory: Doctor Chettle holding out an object, a skull, white and freshly clean. *See what an interesting subject this was . . . The base of the brain – it suggests a love of life, you know, to the extent that death carries the utmost terrors.*

I felt as if I were falling, no matter that I was strapped to a chair. If I hadn't been so dismissive, if I had seen, truly *seen—*

. . . the faculty of cautiousness is so very well developed; it has been named that, you know, but we are essentially speaking of fear.

And I thought of the farmhand, crouching on the floor with his hands about his head. Jacob Thew, lost to his terror, trying in vain to protect himself from the crows, from the thing that was coming for him.

I glanced up and saw Doctor Chettle looking back at me, his gaze one of simple curiosity, nothing more.

'Jacob,' I said. 'Our man of fear . . . of cautiousness . . . the love of life. You buried him in the Crow Garden, did you not?'

He tilted his head. 'Is that what you call it now?'

'Did you bury *all* of him, as he would have wished?'

Doctor Chettle did not answer.

'He gave you his permission, then?'

I felt the shock of it like a rush of cold water. The world seemed to go dim, as if seen through filthy layers, and I remembered the forms I had glimpsed from the pool: shadowy forms, indistinct yet distorted, wrong, incomplete . . .

Who were they who stood all about – who watched, yet had no faces?

Dear God. Vita had seen them too, and I had not heeded her.

Some say the crows are restless spirits, unhappy with how their bones are buried . . . They tell such lunatic tales.

I could say no more. And the doctor replied to my words with naught more than a look, one that said everything: that he had no one's permission, and would not ask, and that it did not signify, because the man was mad. And he had other things in his eyes, other messages, though it made me quail to see them – yet I could not look away because I was unable to move an inch.

Chapter Nine

Although free of the treatment room, I could still feel the grip of the iron band about my skull. My head ached intolerably and I tried to be calm, but could not stem the thoughts that crowded upon me. I could still see Doctor Chettle's look as he peered at me so closely, yet without seeing me at all. I saw my mother's face, tears standing in her eyes. Farrar's contempt. And Peg – her too. I could not bear that such a low character had betrayed me to Doctor Chettle, that she had managed him so easily. He even idealised her. I could still see her features stretched into wickedness, waving her 'chivy'; I certainly had not pictured her so tall, or her eyes so very dark. He could see nothing as it was.

The face that returned to me most of all, however, was that of Jacob Thew. He had *known*. He had asked me for my help and I had not given it; I had not even been here to comfort him at the end. He was gone, even his body taken from him. The only thing he had been able to cling to was his fear.

I recollected, as if from an impossible distance, an infamous case, not from Yorkshire, but Bedlam: that of Edward Wright, its apothecary. He was a phrenologist too, though he wisely kept it a secret. For years, whenever one of the incarcerated souls died, he placed their head in a pan and let it rot. He kept the skulls, spending hours in the dead room, until the scandal of his ghoulish occupations broke and he was dismissed.

He was not the only one. John Haslam had also been from Bedlam, although he was a surgeon. He had thought to find the physical source of madness by dabbling in dead lunatics' brains, hidden away in the asylum's dank cellars. He never did find the root of the maladies that surely haunted him as he worked; the cries of the incurables must have echoed around him in the gloom.

There was no one here to dismiss Doctor Chettle. There was no one to stop him. I could still feel the touch of his fingers in my hair. At least if he focused on measuring the heads of the living, he could not be hoping for the skulls of the dead. I comforted myself with that, and I had to, for there was nothing else.

I shivered. The season was drawing onward and it was bitterly cold, almost as cold as the Crow Garden had been. Soon it would be winter. What would Crakethorne be like then? I remembered the day-room as I had first seen it, the impressions I had buried under promises of hope and cures. It had been a joyless, lonely place. There never had been a fire in the grate. I supposed Doctor Chettle would not bear the expense.

I felt as if something that had been covering my eyes – paint, perhaps – was crumbling away, or as if a mask had been removed. All was now plain before me. I looked about my tiny room with its small bed, blank ceiling and close walls. This place was mouldering: I could see it in the damp plaster, smell it in the stale air. Rot was creeping through the manor, pervading everything. There was no hope in it and there never would be. I had been blinded by my aspirations.

Numb to it all, I tried to sleep. I was interrupted when an attendant – I did not notice who – brought me a thin gruel. It could not warm me; it could not fill me. I could not think why they were giving me a madman's diet, designed to cool the blood. And I thought of Lillian, and hoped she at least was receiving better fare.

I narrowed my eyes. I had ordered that before I left this place for London in search of Mrs Harleston, but the attendants had not carried out my instructions. Doctor Chettle had counter-manded me. I had looked in her case notes and found only more phrenological foolery.

Plenty goes in. Not so many comes out.

Could he not *wait* for her skull to fall into his hands?

I should have been concerned only for her physical condition, not that of her mind. How arrogant, how foolish I had been! It was all so different to what I had imagined. I had thought of achieving recognition, of finding cures. A picture rose before my eyes: Doctor Chettle clapping me on the shoulder, gazing admiringly at my intellectual faculties; my father standing behind him, his eyes no longer painted but clear, beaming his approval upon me.

I tried to clear my mind, seeking only the soothing oblivion of sleep. I know not if I succeeded or if I remained half-awake, but images circled like crows: madmen peered from their por-traits on the walls and laughed. Doctor Chettle stroked a skull, saying, *Most of the requisite subjects*. Edward Wright played in the dead room of Bedlam, peeling flesh from bones. John Haslam delved in gore to his elbows. Jacob Thew, unable to rest, searched endlessly for his skull. And I saw the Crow Garden, each of its mounds hiding some poor unfortunate, each with a black crow perched at its head: a *murder* of crows.

And Vita. I saw her eyes, her beautiful eyes, and the rest faded until only she remained. I clung to the thought of her, the idea of her. I longed to see her again. And despite everything, the despair of it, something within me changed. I had a new deter-mination: I must find a way to speak to her again.

Chapter Ten

As soon as I had eaten my sorry breakfast and entered the day-room I wandered to the gate that let on to the hall. I had no key but I could not let that prevent me, and so I paced, passing and repassing the gate, wishing for some glimpse of Vita. She surely still took her walks about the grounds and so at every moment I hoped she would appear in her little out-of-doors bonnet.

I did not suppose we would have long – perhaps only a few precious stolen seconds. An unwanted attendant might interfere, calling the lady away. Doctor Chettle could descend the stair. As if to prove my surmise, James Farrar passed at that moment and asked if I was watching for the dog, Peter. When I did not respond, he informed me that I might not pet him, not today, because Matron had taken him for his walk.

I ignored his impertinence. Despite all the differences that had arisen between us, I resolved to speak of him to Doctor Chettle. I hoped he would have sense enough to cast the fellow out, without pausing to seek his minuscule organ of benevolence or attempting to measure his thick skull.

I sauntered about the entrance, then returned to the bars. I saw Peter, in the women's ward, peeking through those opposite. He panted at me, his pink tongue dripping. I considered telling him to 'fetch' in the hope that he might bring Mrs Harleston, but I quickly dismissed the notion as irresponsible. I would not use the boy for my own ends, no matter how hopeless he continued. I imagined him sitting at Vita's feet and envied him. I pictured her sitting by her window, her expression so clear and calm, the light of a new day limning her cheek and brightening her lovely eyes; and then, as if I had conjured her, I heard her voice.

'Want an argol-bargol wiv me, do yer?'

I started. I went closer to the bars, pushing my face up against them so that their coldness chilled my cheek.

'I'll not take it – I'll not 'ave anyfink! Stuff it up your arse, you filfy slop-pot, or I'll show yer a back-answer. I'll 'ave yer all over red! If I 'ad me chivy—'

I froze in horror. Her unregulated tone, the coarseness of her shrieks, the decided unloveliness of her words – it was abominable. Was this the result of her acquaintance with that dreadful maid? Was her mind so overthrown?

I caught hold of the bars, rattling them – it was no use, of course, but I could not think of that. Rational thought was swallowed by her plight. To be able to hear her and be unable to go to her, to hold her, to restore her to herself, was unutterably painful.

I must have begun to shout, without thought of the consequence or who might hear me, for I heard running footsteps. I glimpsed Matron through the bars and I think I called her by her name. 'Agnes, come to me.' I shouted that I needed her, that she must come at once or all would be at an end.

It was some little time before I came to myself. All was quiet. I closed my eyes and lay back on my pillow, allowing myself to imagine Vita, herself again, all peaceful glances and calm silence. That poor lady. If her attendants at all resembled those in the male wards, how could she be expected to bear their company?

I had to find a way to reach her, and yet the keepers continued more insufferable than ever. As I lay in my room, thinking dreadful thoughts, I heard their voices outside the door.

'Scribble, scribble, scribble,' one called out, and I recognised the tones of James Farrar. How dare he? But it was Doctor Chettle's fault, allowing the man to accompany us to the pool. He had taken false arrogance from his position. I would not rise to it, would not even dignify him with a glance. I stared up at the cracked, mould-spotted ceiling as his words echoed about the blank walls, and a sudden thought struck me: *what if he had read my journal?* It would be the most dreadful imposition.

I leaped from my bed and found that document. I did not know whether to tear it into pieces or rend it with my teeth – but all my work could not be in vain. I looked about the room. There was nowhere to conceal it. I do not know how long I stood there; in the end, I could only thrust it beneath my pillow.

I could still hear footsteps outside. I hoped none had looked in whilst I was lost in indecision. And they whispered all the time, passing comments upon me, mocking my notions of curing the afflicted. They even called *me* mad. Their attitude was the greatest source of shame to them, or should have been. Relieving the mad ought to have been chief among their own wishes, but so long as their charges remained fed and clothed and were not troublesome, the attendants seemed to think nothing else was required.

They had to be made to think otherwise. This situation could not continue. And they needed to be forced to consider Mrs Harleston's position. It did not signify if she was driven to speak coarsely on occasion, or if she justly raged against her plight. She was a lady and they must remember it – even on those occasions when she herself did not.

Chapter Eleven

I have been somewhat incapacitated in recent days, but in spite of
it, I believe I have taken a great stride in discovering the source
of Mrs Harleston's mania. As I thought, it is not from within
that lady that such corruption springs; it is the fault of those who
surround her. If only I could offer her the release of conversation
and genial company, and the benefit of my sanity, I am certain
she would be cured in a trice.

 I have taken to creeping about the asylum in an attempt to hear
the attendants' conversations. It is only right that someone should
watch over them with the object of improving their habits, and
Doctor Chettle surely will not do it, so I must. And so I heard
two slatternly females, engaged in removing dirty linen from
the female ward. I could not enter their domain of course, but
had secreted myself by the gate and kept peering into the hall.
Thus I heard their tongues wagging, and it was at once sad and
enlightening. Such is the power of human speech, for good or
ill, when given in free and frank exchange.

First, they spoke of Lillian Smith. One said that she had shrunk
nearly to nothing and I almost called out to them, to see if my
instructions for her diet were now being carried out – but then
the other said it was a shame their easiest patient was gone. I

thought at first she was discharged – and then I heard them say that she was dead.

Poor Lillian, with her sweet smiles. I remembered the way she had squeezed my fingers. I hoped her family would claim her bones; I could not bear for her to be abandoned to the Crow Garden. But then they mentioned Mrs Harleston, and I pressed myself closer to the wall. What they said was this:

'Mad bitch. Got curly wi' me – bit my arm, she did – so I clocked 'er one. Don't act like no lady, does she?'

'She don't.'

'She's that much of a cat. If I were a lady, I'd know what to do wi' it. You wun't catch me in 'ere for nowt.'

A pause. And the other said, with some hesitation, 'You've 'eard 'er say she in't no lady, then? She said to me she in't no Missus Victoria Adelina 'Arleston, and don't want to be neither, and she's no patient on ours.'

The other spluttered with laughter. 'Like I says: mad bitch.'

'Yes, but—'

'What?'

'It's just, she don't rightly look like 'ersen neither, does she? When she come back from Lunnon, I mean.'

'Well, that's madness for you. That Della Martin don't look like 'ersen neither – not after she slapped me an' I busted 'er lip for 'er.'

'Mm,' the other said. 'I asked 'er maid about it, but she said there were nowt wrong and . . . Well, it's all fuzzy now, like, but she seemed so sure, an' the way she looked at me – I decided she must know best. It's just, when Mrs 'Arleston left 'ere afore, I could've sworn 'er eyes was a right dark brown.'

I frowned. What new foolishness was this? It was as if everything was upside down: the sane behind bars, the lunatics walking free. I did not now care if they noticed me skulking by, for here was madness indeed. How could Mrs Harleston possibly be restored when her keepers insisted on confusing her? What kind of females were they, to think she might not indeed be Mrs Harleston? Did they imagine Doctor Chettle to be so very taken up with the insides of her head that he would not notice if the outside were replaced? And it came to me then that *this* was the loose stone, the one faulty perception that Mrs Harleston's delusion was built upon.

The attendants had set her upon a dark road and she merely continued upon it. And for them to concur with her wild utterances – here, then, was the source of her wild behaviour. She had caught further infection from those about her; no doubt they had also schooled her in uncouth manners. They must be dealt with most severely.

I was vindicated. So soon after I arrived at this place, I had impressed upon the staff the danger of supporting patients in their delusionary states. This is what came of patting Peter Ambrose on the head or of calling Samuel Brewer 'Your Highness'. If they fed a boy from a bowl set upon the floor, there was little wonder he should think himself a dog.

No! They must treat my Vita in the manner to which she had, until now at least, been accustomed. They must address her with respect, and wrap her in silk, and cosset her – then she would remember herself, and only then, when she could once more converse with those she had known in happier times.

Knowing her to have only these rough companions was painful in the extreme. Still, it was progress, of a kind. I had found the danger; I must warn them of it.

Chapter Twelve

I have been ill and have made little progress, but that cannot be helped. I am starting to mend, I think. Cook has been sending me only the most meagre of rations, I suppose because it is simplest on my stomach with my constitution so weakened. I find it does not make me feel very much recovered, however, or not yet. I am somewhat listless and light-headed. I have no fire here as I had in the cottage and it continues very cold. My dreams are terrible.

At night, Jacob Thew comes to me. I know he is lost to his terror, although I cannot see his face; there is only a mask, impossible to read. I hear him, though: sharp little cries giving way to longer screeches and screams, and he taps at my window with a sound like skeletal fingers. He is looking for his skull. He will not rest until he finds it. And then I fancy I awake, and look at the window and realise the sound is real, for a crow is there, standing on the sill. Its eyes are small and black and evil. It taps against the glass and I truly awake, a cry upon my lips. Last night I think I called out, 'Restless spirits!' And I opened my eyes to see an attendant, roused by the noise, standing in the open doorway.

I suppose I cannot complain at his looking in when I have been so afflicted, but it was unfortunate. I can only trust to Providence that I shall be restored soon. But it is so difficult to *think* when I hear them all about me still – for I do hear the crows' rough voices, calling from beyond the walls of the manor, and almost there are words in the sound – like they are calling me home.

The attendants' rudeness has not been softened by my condition. Indeed, if anything, they have worsened. I hear them gossiping about me – sometimes they even open the peephole in the door and look in; clearly it was not properly sealed and may only be opened from the outside. I fix them with my eyes, but it avails nothing. Perhaps they have still not forgiven me my part in Vita's escape. But it is all they are fit to do, I suppose: talk, talk, talk, and ever of the base and ignoble. If only they could be persuaded towards some improving conversation – but that is beyond them.

At least they say that I am now a mad-doctor indeed. I tell them they mean an alienist, but they laugh all the more loudly until my head aches with their jeering. Indeed, I was prostrate with it when Doctor Chettle finally deigned to visit, to see how I did. I made complaint to him about them, but of course he would not listen. I tried to explain to him that it was everywhere, this madness, that it had broken its bounds and that it was not a matter of who has the sense, but who has the appearance of it – not who possesses sanity, but who has the key.

He made to leave. I pushed myself up and remonstrated with him, but he refused to engage with any of my arguments. I tried to stall him, shouting about his wicked practices, of starvation and crows, his skulls, his excess of whiskers. He informed me that I must be overwhelmed with a surfeit of rich food and should do with less, and that heretofore he would focus his studies on the faculties of imagination and invention. Then he left. It was worse than useless.

After he had gone I took up my journal once more and continued my work. I wrote of my approaches to mania in all its forms, the importance of gentle management and informed conversation. The attendants paused by my door to laugh at my 'mad scrawling'. But I must persevere, do what I must. For my father was at my shoulder again, always watching, sorrowing at my failure, grieving all that he had lost. And I knew I must surpass them all if I was to silence them, so I took a little of my precious ink and painted an eye – my father's eye, and Society's, and the world's – on the wall at my back.

It watches me always. I feel it even when I cannot see it directly. Even if rude hands wipe it away, it will drive me onward.

It is fortunate that I am a steady and well-regulated character, for the pressures of my work and the torments to which I am subjected make me feel at times as if my mind is splintering. In those moments, strange images appear to me. Vita is there, but not as I have known her. Her face is distorted and strange. She appears amidst a host of oil paintings, portrait after portrait, and I know I must find her from among them, and I try, but no matter how I peer into them, I cannot do it. There are only eyes, and all of them are hers, as deep and knowing as the abyss. Are *all* of them Vita? And yet, in that moment, I do not even know what name to call her. She is Madame Vespertine, cold and magnificent. She is Mrs Harleston, placing her hand in another man's. She is Vita Milford, looking up at me in the dark.

It is perhaps because I dwell so often and so strongly upon her that when I received a visitor to my quarters, at first I thought it was her. I was thoroughly engrossed in my work, my head sunk on my chest while I pondered the application of my ideas, and I looked up to see a female form before me.

She was dressed in black, and an ungenerous hope leaped within me, that perhaps her husband was at last dead – and then

I saw it was my own dear mother standing there, an anxious expression on her face.

'Mother!' I jumped to my feet and she stepped back; I had startled her. 'Forgive me. I am so happy to see you. So happy you have seen sense, at last.'

Her terse look became a frown.

'But let us not speak of that. How do you do at the cottage? Did the cold water help? Are you much improved?' I supposed she must be, to visit me here. I wished to ask about the bird, about why she had let it go, but dared not raise the matter. She was content to see me, and that was progress. She did not look confused, or hopeless, or lost. The sight of her own dear eyes gave me hope that despite Doctor Chettle's attention, or perhaps because of his more beneficial neglect, all might soon be well. I could move back into the cottage. I would see Vita again!

But my mother did not speak. Instead she held something out to me with a shaking hand. I blinked. It was a letter.

'This was directed to me,' she said. 'It is distasteful to me, Nathaniel, but the covering note begged that I should see it put into your hand. I did not know what else to do. Doctor Chettle would not approve, I think. But you need to finish this, Nathaniel, in your own mind, and I trust that this might help. I hope I do not do wrong.'

I frowned. How could she do wrong in giving me a simple letter? As I took it I assured her that she should not worry, that I would take care of all. She should heap no further anxieties upon her nerves, but only relax herself. I mentioned that she looked a little pale and suggested she be sure to regularly take the air.

I stumbled over this last, for as I said it I thought of her precious canary taking to wing, only to perish in a world that was suddenly too big; but she only looked penetratingly at me.

'I am sorry,' she said at last. 'What your father did to himself

'– I fear he had some taint in his blood that has passed on to you. If I had married a different man, perhaps . . . but I loved him.'

'Of course you did! Mother, do not think of it. I am quite well, you see. And soon you will be well, and Vita, and all of us.' But my words died away, for how could I suggest that we would be together? That might never happen. But I could hope, could I not? That would not be so very wrong.

I returned to the subject of her health. I had a sudden terror of her opening her lips and voicing hideous obscenities – it was a baseless fear, of course, but having heard such awful things spoken in Vita's sweet tones, I almost felt I could not now trust anything.

I remembered the comfort she had found in Doctor Chettle – as unlikely a source as he was – and I caught her hand. 'Mother, do not hesitate to do as Doctor Chettle wishes. Make no objection. He would not do anything wicked to *you*.'

I did not know why I said the words, only that she needed someone who would watch over her, and her condition, if distressing, was so commonplace he could have no reason to desire her skull. Even if he did, he could never have it. I would see to that.

My mother pulled free, her expression changing to one of strangeness, and then she just looked unhappy. She turned and glanced at the wall, and seeing there the painted eye, she started.

Without meeting my gaze again she clasped my arm, whispering, 'Very well. I shall,' and she turned and was gone. I thought to follow her, but perhaps it was enough for now. Indeed, I did not wish to push her, and in any case, I could think of nothing else to say.

I found myself gazing down at the letter I held, at the address made out in a hand entirely unfamiliar to me, wondering what on earth it was. I opened it and found within a most peculiar missive.

Dearest Nate,

I suppose I am writing to say goodbye, and yet I scarcely know how to begin. There are things unsaid between us. You may have no wish to hear from me, and yet I find I must say them.

You did not trust me and yet I did not expect you to, so perhaps I failed as badly as you did. I wished to say I forgive you, although it may anger you to hear it. I cannot help that. It is my letter after all, and I shall say what I will.

I told you once that I would live free, and I do, Nate. I have cast off all the constraints of the past: first my father, then Perry, the asylum, everyone and everything that enclosed me. You may not have expected that I could, but it is all around me now, that freedom. I write this from a little chair placed on a terrace over-looking the sea. It is so wide and so beautiful, and I could not give it up for the world, nor for any man or notion of respectability. And I cannot for another reason, one I am writing most particularly to tell you of. There is a life growing inside me, Nate. I feel it gaining in strength daily, and my excitement grows with it. I feel certain it will be a boy, don't you?

I still have the strange prescience that has been awakened within me. Indeed, I support myself by it. I appear to have found myself in the vanguard of a new movement; all that you would strive to achieve in another sphere, I have stumbled upon in mine. Many are eager to attend my circles. I suppose you would not approve, but I find myself respected, and valued, and well paid, and so I cannot complain of it.

I also have visions which repeat themselves to me so often I do not know if they are the product of my longings or of something I cannot truly understand. Still, I cannot help believing they will come to be. I see a small boy running along the sand, his light brown hair all disarranged by the wind. And he is laughing, always laughing. It will happen, Nate. I shall walk along the beach with my son and I shall know us to be free. His cheeks will grow ruddy in the healthful air. He will look out at the waves and hear the sound they make. He will catch at the sand with his little fingers and fail to hold it, and he will laugh at the failure. I shall not teach him to be great. I shall teach him how to live.

There is something else I need you to know. Whatever you suspect of me – and you did suspect me, I think – I used my mesmeric suggestion on you only out of absolute necessity. I could have compelled you to come away with me, I suppose, but what use would that have been? I stopped short of it, although I scarcely know why. Perhaps I really did it out of love for you; or perhaps it was my pride that was wounded. In the end, though, I find I have no great desire to control another's mind, not as an end in itself. I do not suppose you mad-doctors would understand.

However, if I had not done it, I would now be spending my days within the living tomb of Crakethorne. I can truthfully say I went only a little further than was needed to gain my liberty, and that, I hope, was for your own good.

I was told once that I would find deep and genuine love. It has been an inexpressible relief to me in the last days to believe my grandmama's words were true. I did find it, albeit for too short a time. It was too short for both of us, I think; it is the greatest pity that even true love cannot always be steadfast.

But I did not wish either of us to waste whatever remains on useless regrets. And so I was a little naughty, Nate, and did something of which I know you would not approve. When you came to fetch me from my room in your mother's house and I cast you into a trance, I suggested that you would find love again – that you would find someone who would be faithful and unquestioning, and who would always love you in return. Someone, in short, who would suit you better than I.

Indeed, I suggested that you would recognise true love when it appeared, and be able to return that love just as if your feelings were bestowed upon me. I said you might even think she resembles me in some way, so that what we shared would not be entirely lost.

I realised that, since you chose Crakethorne over me, it was quite possible that the first to happen along might be a patient: raving, senile, even an imbecile. Residents of an asylum are capable of all kinds of inappropriate attachment, after all, and you were rather likely to fall for the first to show you any affection. Who knows what manner of creature your new love may be? I confess, such a possibility did not stay my hand. I decided to leave it to Fate.

Whatever has come of my suggestion, I supposed you might learn a little of what I felt. You betrayed me, after all. I do not forget that.

That was all, Nate, save for the little mischief whilst I spent time at Crakethorne, preparing the way for Peg. I had to stay for a time, using my special skills among the attendants to ensure they accepted her in my stead, and if I made mention of your father and his death at his own hand — well, I can only plead that my days were otherwise really rather dull. I do hope you will forgive me for it. All else was your own dear feelings. It is a pity, I think, that you did not always recognise them, or understand them as you should, or indeed what was all about you. A mad-doctor, after all, should know himself first, not as he wishes Society to see him, but as he is. That part is left to you.

And now to end. I shall do so in the words of your poet, Nate, though forgive me if I change them a little to suit us better.

Round the cape of a sudden came the sea,
And the sun looked over the mountain's rim:
And straight was a path of gold for her,
And the heed of a world of men for him.

*We made our choices, and believe me when I say I wish you joy
in all you do, for we deserve what comes of them. And now I shall
only express myself,*

Your fondest friend,
V.

PS: *I make no apology to Peg. She would have sold me, after all,
and deserved the lesson. I am certain you will have discovered it
all by now. I was somewhat afraid of returning to Crakethorne
with her, but doctors and attendants alike had to be made ready to
welcome her, and I was quite safe; it had become clear to me that
you observers of the mind see so very little. It is a pity it must wear
off eventually, for her temper is much improved by being under my
influence. Mr Lumner thought me in possession of powers beyond
any he had seen, but I doubt even my suggestions could endure
this long. Though for your sake if no other, Nate, I hope they may
have some lasting effect.*
PPS: *I have been discovering the verse penned by Robert Browning's
wife. Do you not think her much superior to her husband and
Byron alike?*

I frowned over the odd phrases. When I reached the end, I read
the letter again. It did not help. Whatever did it mean – what
could it mean? The *V* suggested Vita, as did some of the refer-
ences, and the mention of Peg, but I could make no sense of
it at all. It was madness. Vita was not away by the sea; that was
a dream. She was here, divided from me by a few all-too-solid
walls. I could feel her presence. I heard her sometimes, through
the bars of her cage.

There could be no question of our saying goodbye, of me
loving another. And Peg – what had become of Peg? I had

not thought of it before, but I did so now. I remembered her decision to accompany her mistress to Crakethorne, to see her settled – out of guilt, probably. She *had* done so, had she not? I thought she had passed some days here, but it was a time I had strangely forgotten. I assumed she had then returned to London and continued there, probably much as she had before.

And this matter of a child – what child? I did not know, and yet the mention of it wrenched at me in some indefinable way, like little fingers reaching for mine. It was possible, after all, that Mrs Harleston might have been carrying my son; but there could be no child. It would have become quite apparent before now, and it would have been remarked upon. She could not have hidden it from her keepers. They would never keep silent on such a thing. I would have been cast off – and how they would have leered then!

No: such a thing could never be the case. I could only conclude this to be the result of some strange error. I might never know what this letter meant, or the identity of the mysterious writer. Possibly, they were raving. There was trickery in it, to be certain, or wickedness, or simply some foul jest. I thought of Professor Lumner – though that was never his name, was it? Perhaps this was some new scheme involving him? He could be spinning a wild tale in order to extort money from me, not knowing that Mrs Harleston was here, within these very walls.

The letter might not even have come from the Continent or any place by the sea, although when I held the paper up before my eyes, I gained the sense of its having travelled a long distance. The paper had turned brittle about the creases. The ink was smudged and faded, almost illegible here and there. It gave the impression of being passed on by many hands, and there was a faint smell about it: the sooty air of a train perhaps, and beneath that, something else – salt?

An awful idea struck me: that one of the attendants might have written it. They might be laughing at me even now. Farrar might have asked some low acquaintance to send it from a distant town, trying to goad me or trap me into some admission. That, I most certainly would not make!

I began, carefully at first and then rapidly, to tear the letter into strips. I tore those into little pieces until they resembled nothing but ash. I mourned the words even as I did it. It was the image it conjured, I think, of Vita sitting peacefully by the sea, as I had so often yearned to see her – but it was too late. The letter was already a part of the past, and only fragments remained; they flew about the room and were gone.

Chapter Thirteen

Today I have been beset by violent headaches and storms of the mind. I think it must be the medicine that Doctor Chettle has had me try. I did not want it, but as I swallowed I thought of my father, trying to discover something that had never before existed, and the way I had prevented him from doing so. I imagined his dreadful eye looking on.

I blinked. It was not my father but Doctor Chettle leaning over me. He stroked my head. I knew that he was feeling my skull beneath the skin and I did not like it. I asked him to cease, but I think he did not hear. His eyes gleamed. He was so taken up with his obsession, so avid, and I had a sudden image of gleaming skulls hidden away within a cupboard, and my own among them, sitting in a pan while the flesh rotted away.

I shuddered. But he was observing my every expression, tilting his head, still with that rapt look, greedy, almost proprietorial. I had a dreadful thought, something to do with my mother, something I had told her about doing everything he said, and her answer: a rapid clasp of my arm and the words, *Very well. I shall.*

I calmed myself. I reminded myself that Doctor Chettle, in spite of all, has done much to help my family. I have to trust that he will continue to do so. I cannot leave and I cannot be rid of him, so I must endeavour to keep him on my side.

I have been working without cease, though sometimes it feels as if my head must burst, or perhaps my heart. I am beset by fears that I shall never discover anything or make any progress at all. I will become my father, failing while others take up the mantle of my work. Others will develop my ideas for a conversational cure, and the name of Kerner shall be lost for always.

I continue to be prevented from seeing my especial patient or moving on from this place. It is difficult to imagine that my father would be watching with approval. It is hard to imagine myself forgiven. Perhaps after all I am being treated justly, and wherever he is, my father feels only satisfaction at my plight.

Still, it is hard to be so derided, not only for my desire to restore his name, but for my object of finding a cure for madness – and that, by the very people who should most hope for it! By whom I mean of course the attendants rather than the mad themselves, who appear quite content to remain as they are, and for the most part oblivious to the busy and indifferent world around them.

This afternoon I received a visit that impressed upon me more strongly than ever the futility of hoping for some kindly impulse within the attendants. At first, it was only James Farrar. He spent some time at my door pulling imbecilic faces at me as I worked, as if in imitation of my efforts. I decided his ignorance should be his own punishment and purposely ignored him, which only inflamed him further. Then for a while he vanished, and I continued peaceful until his surly visage appeared once more.

'Got a visitor for you.' Although his words were pleasant his tone warned me that no goodness was intended, nor should I expect any, and so I turned a blank expression upon him.

'It's your Vicky,' he said. Then, enunciating each syllable to exaggerated effect: 'Vic-tor-ee-ah!'

My mouth fell open. I dropped my pen and scraped back my chair. I had pushed myself to my feet and half turned towards the door when I saw, appearing in the gap, nothing but the porter, who smiled evilly upon me. And then he walked in without a by-your-leave, and I blinked. For a moment I was not sure what I saw; my vision blurred and shifted, and then I realised he was leading his old dog, Brown, by a leather cord.

In the next instant the rank, filthy smell of it reached my nostrils: the degraded creature with whom he kept company. I glared at him in fury and pointedly waved the stink away, though I doubted it could ever be effaced from my chamber.

The disgusting creature wagged its tail at me, wafting more of that odour about the room, and I think it would have walked right up to me, save that its master prevented it. His countenance fell and he hauled on its tether; the cord tightened about its neck and it let out a high-pitched wheeze, not even a whine.

'How dare you enter here?' I demanded. 'By what authority do you presume?'

'Why, it's your visitor, i'nt it!' the porter replied. 'Did tha miss 'er? Missed thee, she did.' At this he aimed a kick at the unfortunate animal, which yelped. He leaned towards me and I caught the foulness of his breath over the stench of dog as he said with venom, 'Got 'er back now though, 'aven't I!'

I started away from his words. He was clearly mad. I had seen signs of it in him before and here it was again: his strange intensity, his hostility where none was warranted, his odd possessiveness over such a foul creature.

Farrar had not yet had his fill of amusement from the scene. He came in behind the porter, almost dancing a jig in his glee. ''ow'd you like 'er?' he said. 'Does tha want to give it your bed an' sleep on t' floor? Tha's what 'is mother said 'e did afore.'

I opened my mouth to make some riposte, but it was useless

– useless! What could I say before such men? They should be dismissed at once!

I stared as the porter bent and patted the dog's head, his eyes fixed on me while he did, his look sly and insinuating. 'Now, don't be jealous,' he said. 'I'm just keepin' 'er warm for you, see? Or don't you like 'er no more? Cast 'er off, 'ave you?'

I was mute.

'See, she 'asn't flown away,' said Farrar. 'Told your maid she 'ad, din't you! Thowt she'd left you, did you? Will she fly now, do you think? Go on, Brown – fly!'

The porter shuffled his feet. 'Give 'er a kiss, then. Owd times' sake.'

I looked from one of them to the other. I knew not how to be rid of them. I did not know what to say to their madness.

A deep coldness took hold of me. I felt it creeping inward towards my heart. A cure by conversation? It seemed so meaningless now. What could I cure by conversing with such fellows? How could I reason with lunacy that bore such faces?

Farrar leaned over my books, picking over them as if he had every right to do so. He suddenly snorted – as if he could have any understanding! And he said, 'Byron, he's got! Din't yon feller demand to be buried with 'is *dog*?'

They hooted with laughter and I put my hand to my head; it was too much. A man could not be expected to work in such surroundings. He could never achieve the greatness to which I aspired and which the memory of my father demanded of me. I despaired of all of it.

But they must at last have realised, I think, that they had passed their bounds. Even the dumb beast must have felt it, for it jerked forwards, pulling the tether from its master's hand, and leaped at me, foul breath huffing, its filthy legs pawing at me in some debased semblance of affection. I yelped and fell against my chair.

Farrar caught the thing and passed the cord back to its master. The porter looked disgruntled, unhappy, even jealous, although surely no sane man could be possessive of the attachment of such a creature.

James Farrar muttered something and laughed. The porter looked subdued and together they dragged the beast away, closing the door behind them. So suddenly that it was almost shocking, I found myself alone – alone with the scent of dog and my own confused thoughts.

My head spun with images that whirled all about me and would not stand still. I saw Vita's gentle eyes, my mother's, full of doubt, and I saw my father's, staring at me from a daguerreotype, but his were only paint. And the smell – that most vivid prompt to the memory – it made me think of the first day I had come here, so full of hope and every positive emotion, so much younger then, it felt to me. But somehow it had all become mixed up with the dog, and the rooms in the little cottage in the grounds, and short brown hairs strewn across my pillow; and my head ached worse than ever.

I also suggested that you would find love again – that you would find someone who would be faithful and unquestioning, and always love you in return . . . you might even think she resembles me in some way, so that what we shared would not be entirely lost.

Who knows what manner of creature your new love may be?

I wiped my fingers against the rough shirt I wore. It was besmirched with the grease of the animal's coat where it had pawed at me. It was filthy. It was *malodorous*. Now the fools had gone it infuriated me more than anything, and I tore at the fabric with my nails. At last it ripped and I ceased; I sat and buried my hands in my hair. I rocked myself, and that gave me a little comfort; it soothed my aching head.

At last I was calm again. I looked down at the mess I had made of my clothes. My shirt was torn from the collar to the chest. I must change it and be respectable again. I ran my fingertips over it, half expecting to find feathers there, I was so confused and angry; but there was nothing – only brown hairs, so achingly different from the ones belonging to Mrs Harleston I had found in my room, and yet so oddly and exactly the same.

Chapter Fourteen

The worst times are when they make me look in a mirror.

I do not know why they do it. I protest, but they insist. I cannot conceal my distress. I have become haggard under the privations of my work and worse under my increasing despair. Of course I have; it is not easy, but then, I did not choose an easy road.

The most fearful thing is when they hold my face so that I must eventually lift my gaze, and I do, and I see my father's eyes looking back at me. He is not there, I know he is not, but I see him anyway, for his eyes are set into my own head. And I know then that I am truly haunted.

My father despaired because of me – if not because of my lie, it was still because I failed him. Now my work too has failed and it is difficult not to give way before it. Indeed, sometimes I barely know myself. I am set adrift in a boat without oar or chart and could be anywhere, or anyone; almost, it is as if the whole world is not as I imagined it to be.

But – ah, the sea! As my horrors subside I take some peace from the notion that I am there, and I simply float, closing my eyes and thinking of nothing but the constant rocking. It is as if I were an innocent again, lulled to sleep in a cradle, with everything before me and nothing yet spoiled.

In happier moments I close my eyes and live for a time within other treasured images of the ocean. I hear gulls calling like a child. The breeze lifts my hair and I smell the brine of it, the freedom. Cool water laps at my feet and best of all I hear the laughter of a young boy, trilling over the endless whispers of its motion. It seems to me then that I am home. In my mind, I am somewhere that, if I had not missed some half-remembered turning in the dark, I could really now have been.

In a sense it makes everything worse, but while the vision persists, it feels better. I would never leave that realm if something did not occur to drag me back. But there are clothes to change, or gruel to sip at, or someone wishing to shave me or cut my hair. The strangest part is that even when I am forced back to blank walls and cold stares, the image of that child stays with me. I do not know why it should be so. I do not even know who he is. But he has lodged within some faculty of my mind until the idea of him is all-encompassing, as vast and full of awe as the ocean.

I brighten then, for I feel a little hope for the future, all wrapped up in a child's laughter. He is there somewhere, a sturdy boy, stubby fingers clenched tight upon grains of sand he cannot hold on to, and puzzled exceedingly by the loss of it.

At night, the images that come to me are less pleasant. I try to tell myself the boy is happy, and *alive*. I try to shut out the thought of another child, closed in by a wooden lid while he slept so very deeply; and of Vita, longing to escape her father's house, clutching a bottle of laudanum. But that could not be, could never have been. For the unnaturalness of it would have driven her mad . . .

I think my dreams are tainted by Doctor Chettle's nostrums. I do not know what is in them and he will not tell me. He asks me to lie back and I do, and he drops them on to my tongue and there is a harsh scent and a worse taste, and I grimace like a child and feel cold numbness spreading over me.

Sometimes I think I cannot move. I do not know if it is only in my mind or a memory, for I am once again supine upon my father's table, waiting for my senses to be stolen from me. I picture the shining pins laid out and ready, waiting to be put to use. But he leans over me and it is Doctor Chettle, and it is no pin he holds but a dissecting knife.

At those times, I close my eyes and go into the dark. I am on a stairway, and at first I do not know if it is the right one; then I realise I am in the old house in London, and Vita is waiting for me. I start to go up the stairs, but it is not right somehow. Someone is following me, someone who does not care for her, who is come to take her from me. It is that day again – when I went to fetch the carriage, to hand her back to the asylum.

I enter the room and she is waiting. She looks into my eyes again, the way she did then. Hers are so deep, so fathomless, I could descend into them for ever. But there is something wrong – a third person is standing there with us, a shadow at our shoulder. My father? I turn and see that it is Peg. Her eyes are blank. I do not know why I should think of her thus. Had she not fled by then? Or had she truly been present – oddly still and quiescent? It is all confused in my not-quite dream.

Sometimes the third is Peg but sometimes it is Matron, holding a key just out of reach, though I cannot imagine what she would be doing there. I mistook her once for someone else, didn't I? But then all else dissolves and there is only *her*, my dearest Vita, but her eyes – they are Madame Vespertine's.

She stares at me and I hear her whispering, and I do not know what she says, though it does not matter. I do not need to find the stair again. I do not wish to. Soon I will feel her cool hand creep into mine and we will be together, and it will be enough.

I acknowledge now that she must have been a very powerful mesmerist. Indeed, her power was something greater than mesmerism, or different – greater than anything I had seen or heard of in my life. But then, I was susceptible: perhaps I wanted nothing more than to be in her power. I opened my mind to her in that room, and I do so again – it is as if my mind and hers may still meet somehow, and form a place where we can live, together, unbounded by anything about us.

It does not last. I think I awake and find myself standing in the Crow Garden. The japes, taunts, jeers, and all the dread cacophony of the afflicted sound from the trees – and then I see them. It is the crows. They are crying in human voices, gathering amid the thorns, their shadows mingling with the tangled and disordered branches. They are settling on the graves. Their wings gleam, seeming to turn from black to white and back again in an instant. I do not know who they are, only that they are restless spirits and that they have come for me. I do not know the charm that would send them away, and it does not matter, for *she* is not among them, and that is the worst thing of all.

Then a new voice calls me from this dream – or vision; do we not call them visions, here? – and hope rises fast within me, for it is her. It is real, for I hear her; Vita is raving again.

I push myself up and stumble as far as the door, then towards the bars which let on to the hall. I do not need to go further and cannot; I am too weak. I hear her screaming. There are words in it and I wish I could stop my ears and shut them out. It is a tirade, all the filthy insults she can find, and I do not know how she ever heard such words. Is this what her attendants have taught her?

I am grabbed by the arm and led away. It is James Farrar. He laughs; he says she's having the sparks and that she'll be silent soon enough. He says there will be no words left in her. I am reduced to begging him to allow me to see her once more, and he says I have *not* seen her, and never shall. It fills my head with mist – it is as if all the London fogs have followed me here to Yorkshire. And I wish myself there again, in our little moment of bliss, our haven – our asylum.

Now, of us all, only Peg remains in the city. I wonder what happened to her. It preys on my mind. I can see everything, all the little moments, though they are broken into fragments and without connection so that their meaning is lost. I stand across a thoroughfare from the Egyptian Hall, hoping to find in that strange edifice someone I know better than myself. I wait in a theatre, surrounded by faces I do not know – closed faces, their voices forming a rough and indecipherable sound like that of crows.

Then all falls silent. She walks on to the stage, but I do not know if it is Vita, or Mrs Harleston, or Madame Vespertine. And there is Peg. Vita is using her as a puppet. She is glassy-eyed and blank, and her skin is like alabaster but flexing as a face might, her lips moving in response to some hidden mechanism. And yet no words come out, only laughter, immoderate and endless, filling the rooms about me, the hall – the whole world.

I am tired. I realise I have been writing all this time in my journal, though I cannot think what I might have set down. My pen wavers in my hand; my words are difficult to read. My vision blurs. Yet I hear the attendants in the passage, talking, always talking, rough and empty sentiments pouring from them like a miasma into the air.

I hear the word 'Harleston', and I stop to listen. And then there is news that cuts through everything, that chills my blood.

Her husband is recovered, or almost so. I realise now that I had believed he would die, and it is like some last tie to my old self snapping. I am loose; I am unmoored. I imagine him sailing in, the air billowing with the force of him as he comes to claim his own.

I steel myself to listen and I hear my worst imaginings made real. He is on his way here; he is coming to see his wife. He has sent a letter, demanding of Doctor Chettle why she has not yet been returned to him, why she has not attended him in his sickness. He is looking forward to the day she will be restored, and indeed, he expects it imminently; the day we finally succeed in opening her eyes.

THE END

Acknowledgements

Huge and heartfelt thanks to my wonder-editor, Jo Fletcher, not only for working her editing magic on this book, but for the advice and rallying cries when things got tricky. I'm grateful to the whole team at Jo Fletcher Books and Quercus – I am a very lucky author indeed – with particular mentions to publicist extraordinaire Olivia Mead, Sam Bradbury, and to Patrick Carpenter, Leo Nickolls and Fiona Carpenter for the mouth-watering cover design.

Much appreciation too goes to my agent, Oli Munson at A. M. Heath, for editorial feedback and support.

Now to the lovey-dovey stuff . . . First of all, love and thanks always to my better half, Fergus Beadle. I'm not sure how we managed to clock up twenty-five years of being together (far too young, obviously), but here's to the next twenty-five . . .

Thanks to my parents, Ann and Trevor, for support, understanding, good times and curries. Oh, and for the fairy tales (look what you started!).

Thanks to my brother Ian, sister-in-law Amanda and nephew Callum, and to Liz Burton for sending essential writers' supplies (i.e. chocolate).

A big shout of appreciation to my fabulous, funny and talented writing friends, who make the genre such a pleasure to be a part of: particularly Cate Gardner and Simon Bestwick, Priya Sharma, Gary McMahon, Gary Fry and Mark West. And thank you to Joshua Rex for pointing me towards some very strange Victoriana.

A round of applause goes once again to Wayne McManus, for working his web wonderment.

A definite doff of the hat to all the researchers and historians who have delved into the era and produced such a wonderful body of resources. It has been an adventure following the sometimes peculiar, sometimes enchanting and sometimes horrifying paths you have opened. Any errors that remain are, naturally, mine alone.

Oh, and my apologies to Yorkshire for making you out to be rather grim. You know I love you really.

Finally, it probably isn't the done thing, but I can't resist mentioning my lovely Dalmatians: the handsome Dexter (kennel name Perry Bingle) and my cheeky little madam, Vesper. It seems entirely appropriate, in this particular book, that two of the characters were named after my dogs.

Poetry and Other Sources

I have quoted extensively from Browning's poetry collection, *Men and Women*. As Nathaniel says, it was published in two volumes, although I have not troubled overmuch about which he gives to Mrs Harleston, or which poems were included in each volume; I just felt it would be rather clunky for him to put both into her hands.

Mrs Harleston's copy of Byron is not based on a specific collection, since his work had been widely published and circulated by 1856. The poems quoted are 'To Caroline', 'To M.', 'To M. S. G.' and 'She Walks in Beauty'. Where Nathaniel becomes confused about which writer produced the quoted poem, the lines are from 'To M. S. G.'

The lines from Browning are from 'Johannes Agricola in Meditation', 'Women and Roses', 'Mesmerism', 'Andrea del Sarto', 'Bishop Blougram's Apology' and 'The Last Ride Together'. The poem quoted in Mrs Harleston's letter to Nathaniel is 'Parting at Morning' (since she is free of the asylum at this point, I have allowed her to expand her knowledge of the poet beyond *Men and Women*). The lines she alters are the last two, which should read:

And straight was a path of gold for him,
And the need of a world of men for me.

'Mad, bad and dangerous to know' was Lady Caroline Lamb's description of Byron.

Both quotes from Shakespeare are from *A Midsummer Night's Dream*.

The quote from James Carkesse is from *Lucida Intervalla*, a collection of poems written while he was committed to Finsbury and Bedlam, published in 1679.

Mental Health and Terminology

Sadly, the history of treatment for mental health problems would all too often leave us shocked nowadays. I have endeavoured to use contemporaneous terminology for mental health categories and treatments in this book, my intention not being to cause offence, but to give a flavour of the time.

Sources

Here are some of the books and websites I found useful during my research:

Daily Life in Victorian London: An Extraordinary Anthology, Lee Jackson, 2011

The Victorian House: Domestic Life from Childbirth to Deathbed, Judith Flanders, 2013

The Victorian House Explained, Trevor Yorke, 2005

How to be a Victorian, Ruth Goodman, 2013

Victorian London: The Life of a City 1840–1870, Liza Picard, 2013

The Victorian Dictionary of Slang & Phrase, J. Redding Ware, 1909

Servants of the Supernatural: The Night Side of the Victorian Mind, Antonio Melechi, 2009

The Table-Rappers: the Victorians and the Occult, Ronald Pearsall, 1972

The Darkened Room, Alex Owen, 2004

Medical Meddlers, Mediums and Magicians: The Victorian Age of Credulity, Dr Keith Souter, 2012

Bedlam: London's Hospital for the Mad, Paul Chambers, 2013

Bedlam: London and its Mad, Catharine Arnold, 2008

Mind-Forg'd Manacles, Roy Porter, 1987

Life in the Victorian Asylum: The World of Nineteenth Century Mental Health Care, Mark Stevens, 2014

Inconvenient People: Lunacy, Liberty and the Mad-Doctors in Victorian England, Sarah Wise, 2012

Voices from the Asylum: West Riding Pauper Lunatic Asylum, Mark Davis, 2013

My Experiences in a Lunatic Asylum, Herman Charles Merivale, 1879

Hidden Depths: The Story of Hypnosis, Robin Waterfield, 2011

Facts in Mesmerism, with Reasons for a Dispassionate Inquiry into it, Chauncy Hare Townshend, 1840

The Mesmerist's Manual of Phenomena and Practice, George H. Barth, 1851

Illustrations of Phrenology, George Henry Calvert, 1832

The Oxford Book of English Verse, ed. Christopher Ricks, 1999

The Works of Lord Byron, George Gordon Byron, 1831

Men and Women, Robert Browning, 1855

Robert Browning, G. K. Chesterton, 1903

Life and Letters of Robert Browning, Mrs Sutherland Orr, 1891

https://en.wikipedia.org
https://en.wikisource.org
www.gutenberg.org

www.bartleby.com

www.poemhunter.com

www.poetryfoundation.org

www.atlasobscura.com

http://www.victorianlondon.org

www.victorianweb.org

http://darkvictoria.livejournal.com

http://virtualvictorian.blogspot.co.uk

http://georgianlondon.com/post/55869874064/
lost-london-the-egyptian-hall

http://www.arthurlloyd.co.uk/EgyptianHallPiccadilly.htm

http://englishhistoryauthors.blogspot.co.uk/2012/01/madness-
in-their-method-water-therapy_31.html

http://www.bbk.ac.uk/deviance/madness/intro.htm

http://www.vam.ac.uk/content/articles/h/
health-and-medicine-in-the-19th-century

www.historyofphrenology.org.uk

http://www.histansoc.org.uk/timeline.html

http://homeguides.sfgate.com/pink-white-nightblooming-
plants-60955.html

www.rspb.org.uk

THE
HIDDEN PEOPLE

ALISON LITTLEWOOD

IN HALFOAK, TRAGEDY IS ONLY
HALF-A-STEP AWAY . . .

Pretty Lizzie Higgs is gone, burned to dead on her own hearth - but was she really a changeling, as her husband insists? Albie Mirralls met his cousin only once, in 1851, within the grand glass arches of the Crystal Palace, but unable to countenance the rumours that surround her murder, he leaves his young wife in London and travels to Halfoak, a village steeped in superstition.

Albie begins to look into Lizzie's death, but in this place where the old tales hold sway and the 'Hidden People' supposedly roam, answers are slippery and further tragedy is just a step away . . .

Jo Fletcher
BOOKS

A Cold Season

ALISON LITTLEWOOD

Cass is building a new life for herself and her young son Ben after the death of her soldier husband Pete, in the village she lived as a child. But their idyllic new home is not what she expected: the other flats are empty, there's strange graffiti on the walls, and the villagers are odd.

But Ben is changing, he's surly and aggressive and Cass's only confidant is the smooth, charming Theodore Remick, the stand-in headmaster. It soon becomes obvious he's not all he appears to be either. If she is to protect her beloved son, Cass is going to have to fight back.

Cass realises this is not the first time her family have been targeted by Theodore Remick. But this time, the stakes are immeasurably higher . . .

Jo Fletcher
BOOKS

PATH OF NEEDLES

ALISON LITTLEWOOD

Some fairy tales are born of dreams . . . and some are born of nightmares.

A murderer is on the loose, but the gruesome way in which the bodies are being posed has the police at a loss until Alice Hyland, an expert in fairy tales is called in and she finds the connection between the body of Chrissie Farrell and an obscure Italian version of Snow White.

But, when a second body is found, Alice is dragged deeper into the investigation - and finds herself a suspect.

And now Alice must fight, not just to prove her innocence, but to protect herself: because it's looking like she might well be next.

Jo Fletcher
BOOKS